The Birth Challenge

WHEN YOUR LIGHT SHINES, ANYONE CAN FIND YOU

LIFE FORCE SAGA

BOOK ONE

ASHLEY PITZER

PRACTICING LIFE LLC

Practicing Life LLC, 223 Salt Lick Rd, Num 57, Saint Peters, MO 63376
First Published in the United States of America in May 2023 by Practicing Life LLC.
Copyright © 2022 by Ashley Pitzer

The characters and events portrayed in this book are fictitious. Any similarity to real persons, living or dead, is coincidental and not intended by the author.

Summary: Sabina faces a rite of passage into adulthood where she discovers who she was always meant to be but was never permitted to become. Her father, Brom, desperately tries to keep her safe from Selectors, small groups of bandits looking for the prophesied one to possess all supernatural powers, and the Dark One. Brom will take any measure to keep his daughter safe, including asking her to marry.

ISBN 978-1-960260-00-0 (Paperback) | ISBN 978-1-960260-01-7 (E-Book)

Subject: Coming of Age - Fiction | self-actualization - Psychology| Supernatural - Fiction | magic - fiction | Silvedome & world - fiction

Library of Congress Control Number: 2023901545

To my childhood friend, Michelle. To my inner child who dreamed of being an author.

Content Warnings

Please beware that this book contains themes below that may be mentioned, suggested, implied, witnessed, conducted, considered, experienced, perceived, or threatened. Depending on your personal experience, these themes may be considered a trigger.

- Violence, including but not limited to war and acts of violence in war
- Magic
- Spiritualism
- LGBTQ
- Kidnapping
- Strangulation
- Death: people and animals
- Misogyny
- Blood
- Classism
- Slavery
- Prejudice
- Sexual Content/Nudity
- Sexual Assault
- Parental Neglect/Abandonment

- Mental health issues, including but not limited to panic attacks, controlling parents, trauma, nightmares, etc.
- Disabilities: curing disabilities, seizures, and neurodiversity
- Forced marriage

Acknowledgments

My husband, Brent Pitzer, for all your support in this process and for helping me to make this dream a reality. To my sister, Mickiala, for believing in me and helping me to flush out the story. To my mom, Shay, for leading by example with all your amazing storytelling. To my coach, Padma Ali, for helping me do all the inner child and energy work to share this with the world. Lastly, to Jim Fortin and the Fortin team in TCP (transformation coaching program) for helping me to see my heart's desire and giving me the tools to be able to go after it.

Contents

MOOWIN CHART

This chart is meant to give the reader framework of the Moowins and is not intended to be a complete list of skills or levels of abilities. Also, these are the charkas based on this post-apocalyptic world. The scale symbolizes the number of people possessing each type of Moowin. Mild Moowins are the most common. Super Rare means you may never meet someone with that ability.

SCALE	TYPE	CHARKA	SKILL
▄▄▄▄	Protector	Root	Survival/ Security

MILD: ENHANCED SPEED, STRENGTH, VISION, FLEXIBILITY, STAMINA AND AGILITY
RARE: NIGHT VISION, SLEEP SUPPRESSION, MATTER INGESTION, SHORT BURST OF FLIGHTS, SUPER SENSES, AND SONIC SPEEDS
SUPER RARE: INDESTRUCTIBLE BODY, ABSORB LIGHT/DARKNESS, INTANGIBILITY

SCALE	TYPE	CHARKA	SKILL
▄▄▄	Performer	Sacral	Creativity

MILD: SPECIALIZING IN ONE TO THREE ART FORMS (DANCING, ACTING, SINGING, PLAYING AN INSTRUMENT, PAINTING, DESIGNING)
RARE: MORE THAN THREE ART FORMS, ENHANCED INVENTIONS, MANIPULATION OF ART, ABILITY TO MESMERIZE
SUPER RARE: CAUSE ART TO COME ALIVE

SCALE	TYPE	CHARKA	SKILL
▄▄	Influencer	Solar Plexus	Emotions

MILD: CAUSE OTHERS TO FEEL SIMPLE EMOTIONS THROUGH TOUCH
RARE: CAUSE OTHERS TO FEEL COMPLEX EMOTIONS WITHOUT TOUCH BUT WITHIN PROXIMITY
SUPER RARE: CAUSES OTHERS TO FEEL COMPLEX EMOTIONS NO MATTER THE DISTANCE OR WHILE MULTITASKING

SCALE	TYPE	CHARKA	SKILL
▄▄	Healer	Heart	Heal

MILD: SCAN BODY AND IDENTIFY WHAT IS WRONG, SIMPLE BODY HEALING, HEAL ANIMALS, PLANT GROWH, CLEAN WATER
RARE: HEAL LIFE THREATENING WOUNDS AND ILLNESS, REGROW BODY PARTS, REMOVE POISONS FROM BLOOD
SUPER RARE: TRANSFER LIFE FORCE

SCALE	TYPE	CHARKA	SKILL
▄	Messenger	Throat	Communication

MILD: TELEPATHIC COMMUNICATION OF SHORT SENTENCE IN CLOSE RANGE
RARE: TELEPATHIC COMMUNICATION WITH LARGES AMOUNTS OF INFORMATION OVER ANY DISTANCE
SUPER RARE: TELEPATHIC COMMUNICATION WITH SOMONE WHO IS NOT A MESSENGER

SCALE	TYPE	CHARKA	SKILL
▪	Seer	Third Eye	Intuition

MILD: ENHANCED INSTINCTS, FORESIGHT INTO IMMEDIATE FUTURE OF RELATIVES, FLASHES OF VISIONS
RARE: CLEAR VISIONS OF PAST AND FUTURE, LONGER VISIONS, TALK WITH SPIRITS, TY PEOPLE'S ENERGY TOGETHER, DIMENSIONAL AWARENESS
SUPER RARE: CREATE PORTALS, TIME TRAVEL/ASTRAL TRAVEL

SCALE	TYPE	CHARKA	SKILL
▪	Persuader	Mind	Intellect

MILD: SCHOLAR, PHOTOGRAPHIC MEMORY, ENHANCED MEMORY, ACCELERATED LEARNER, MULTI-TASKER
RARE: PUT THOUGHTS INTO ONE'S MIND WITHOUT TOUCH, PROJECT IMAGES INTO ANOTHER'S MIND
SUPER RARE: READ PEOPLE'S MIND, MOVE OBJECTS WITH MIND

SCALE	TYPE	CHARKA	SKILL
·	Shielder	Aura	Illusions

MILD: PROTECT AGAINST A SINGULAR PHYSICAL OBJECT, MINOR ILLUSIONS TO APPEARANCES FOR SHORT PERIODS OF TIME
RARE: ENERGETIC FIELDS TO PROTECT AGAINST MULTIPLE OBJECTS, PROTECT MULTIPLE PEOPLE WITH SPECIFIC OBJECTS, CAMOUFLAGE
SUPER RARE: MAKING SOMEONE INVISIBLE, SHIELDING MULTIPLE PEOPLE SIMULTANEOUSLY AGAINST MULTIPLE OBJECTS

After a nuclear war destroyed most of the earth, leaving few survivors behind, the world would have ceased to exist if not for the phenomena of a few select individuals developing supernatural abilities called Moowins. Because of these individuals, the survivors were able to rebuild kingdoms, communities, and villages, setting their own rules and governing bodies.

Over time, the world slowly repopulated. As the world healed and flourished, fewer and fewer people were born with supernatural abilities. These special people who had once saved the world from extinction were becoming extinct. As the number of those with Moowins decreased, many societies treated them as a resource to be exploited. Some individuals with Moowins were forced into slavery as the threat to survive was eliminated. People began to believe these individuals were meant to be subservient. Why else would these powerful people with remarkable gifts have one limitation—that their gifts could be used only for the collective good of all?

Everyone was subject to a hierarchy of some order regardless of an individual's Moowin status. Where you were born and what family you were born into determined if the person's life would be hard or easy. But not all individuals with Moowins were destined to be slaves. Those with money and influence kept their liberties. Also, communities existed where people with Moowins were treated as equals and their talents were respected and appreciated.

Then came the prophecy of the Agni: that one said to be born with all eight Moowins of rare status. Despite hundreds of years passing since the nuclear war, the desire to own more land and be the most powerful individual pushed many to find this Chosen One. A common thought prevailed. If one had control over the Agni, then they had control over the world. It no longer mattered if a person was born into a wealthy or influential home.

The Agni had untold powers. If that power could be captured, harnessed, or even destroyed, the course of history would be changed forever. Groups of bandits known as Selectors were formed and took it upon themselves to find the Chosen One. Potential candidates with multiple Moowins were scouted for all over the world, regardless of their status. Those captured in hopes of being the prophesied Agni were sold into slavery or killed, but the search continued.

Small fights, battles, and wars broke out around the world at the injustice caused by the merciless Selectors. Yet, most felt powerless to stop them. Selectors were known to kill an entire family to capture one individual with multiple Moowins. The hunger to find and own the Agni led to a state of imbalance in the world once again.

In the year 2375, the frenzy to find the Agni was at its pinnacle. It was thought this would be the year the Chosen One was finally revealed. The Selectors were busier than ever as more people were born with multiple Moowins, yet they were rarely at full strength or rare in status. When the year 2375 came and went without anyone having found the Agni, a mad hunt for the Chosen One began. No individual with a Moowin was safe.

However, long before this scramble began, one village became a haven for those with Moowins. Silvedome. The village welcomed anyone with a Moowin as long as they agreed to live under their peaceful terms. Individuals with Moowins were welcomed, regardless of how many they possessed or the strength of those Moowins. It was in the far north, along a river that split off to give villagers fresh water on both sides.

Silvedome was a village of ancient traditions, and they operated differently from other places. Their motto was what one did for another, they did for themselves. They prided themselves on service to others, peace, equality, and community. Everyone was expected to work, and everyone was paid equally. They minimized ownership of material items and treated as many things as possible as belonging to the community. The village had a system whereby the higher value and service an individual brought to Silvedome, the nicer or closer one would live to the village square.

Silvedome was unlike any village, and not only for its way of life that encouraged self-expression and discovery. It was home to more individuals with Moowins than any other territory. Using the combined energy of several residential rare Shielders, Silvedome created a seemingly impenetrable dome wall around the village to protect the community. Unless permission to enter was granted by the Ori—the council of Silvedome—no one could enter. There was one exception to this rule. An individual with a Moowin whose life was in danger could have immediate access into the village. This exception was so old and unused that it was forgotten about, much like Silvedome was forgotten about by the world.

Because outsiders could neither see in nor enter the village, they considered Silvedomeies to be outdated, foolish people. Yet the Selectors knew Silvedome housed powerful Moowin individuals and many started to suspect that the Agni was hidden behind those walls. Selectors did everything in their power to break the shield and to prevent more individuals with Moowins from entering the village, which caused constant minor conflicts outside the walls.

Though most Selectors were small-time bandits, there was

one large group led by Borax. He held the most territories and was known to capture children before their Moowins developed. His bandits were often found at birthing rituals, or raiding homes in the middle of the night to take children from their families, but he was never at Silvedome's walls. Though Borax was feared and notorious throughout the world, Silvedome was free from worrying about such threats. The only credible threat that loomed in the back of Silvedomeies' minds was that of Dras. The Dark One. He possessed the ability to shapeshift and disappear into magical portals, which meant he couldn't be found. He turned people into animals that died within days. It was even said he lived before the nuclear war as a sorcerer. Dras was the reason magical portals were forbidden in Silvedome and the Shielders actively prevented them. The risk was small as few sorcerers and witches existed, but their magic was slowly being rekindled. Elemental magic was back and the Forddin race with their bright green skin existed again.

Brom Rockdin was a Scouter for Silvedome and was responsible for bringing in individuals with Moowins before the Selectors got to them. He brought in children whose gifts had come in early, or those who'd completed their Birth Challenge and had discovered through the ritual that they possessed Moowins. The Birth Challenge was a rite of passage held on an individual's sixteenth birthday. Villages all over the world performed a ritual of some sort. This was a dangerous day. Selectors watched, waited, and anticipated their attack and capture of anyone discovered with Moowins. But, despite the threat, it was still one of the most important days of an individual's life.

Brom knew the Selectors' ways better than Silvedome's warriors. The warrior's experience with Selectors was limited. The only time the warriors dealt with Selectors was when they would leave the safety of the dome wall to dismantle larger attacks on the village. These attacks could potentially thin the shield wall and could create holes if too much force was applied. The warriors also fought Selectors as they helped Scouters safely bring rescued individuals with Moowins into the village. As a Scouter, Brom encountered the Selectors on each mission he undertook and was used to their behaviors. Despite not being born as a Protector, Brom had been trained by the best warriors all over the land. Most would assume he was a strong Protector by his ability to predict movements and escape hits. Brom believed he had a better weapon than the Protector Moowin. He was a rare Influencer. His Moowin was as powerful as they came. His talent for influencing people's emotions was flawless in combat. He made his opponent feel weak, tired, sad, and if necessary, fearful, anxious, and uncertain. He was able to use his Moowin in this way because he believed he was benefiting the wider world. No matter how powerful one's Moowin was, there was no getting around the fact it could only be exercised for the greater good.

Brom had lost much in his life. He had seen the hurt caused by Selectors and Dras and he could not lose his daughter. If that meant taking risks to keep her protected, so be it. He was prepared for Sabina's Birth Challenge and he knew the dangers of it coincided near the year prophesied to reveal the Agni. If anyone threatened Sabina's life, he would do everything in his power to weaken them, or stop them.

Left Behind

A sadness rested like an ocean on Sabina's chest. Big, vast, and full of tidal waves that crashed and beat against her heart as if it was insignificant in its power. This sadness was . . . once again . . . brought on by her father's impending departure, which always elicited a set of stacked questions. Questions Sabina didn't want to acknowledge, but constantly teased her mind. Questions she couldn't bear to know the answers to because she feared what they would mean, and questions that also had the potential to give her the validation she so desperately needed. Hugging herself tighter as her soul wept, Sabina looked out over the still pond on another perfect day. It was not lost to her that her soul was as invisible to her as her presence was to the world. Even in nature, with serenity all around her, Sabina was unable to remove the pinched eyebrows, the stiffness in her crossed arms, or the roundness of her spine as she burrowed into herself, protecting her fragile heart from the brutality of the crashing waves.

She hated it when her father left for his work excursions. She especially hated the feeling of abandonment and isolation it brought her. Nonetheless, the countdown to her father's leaving had started. She could feel it in her body as the waves of sadness inside her chest crested higher and higher. Soon, Sabina would be physically, emotionally, and mentally alone as her father recruited a new prospect, Messenger from Aliward, for their village.

Painful questions popped up every time she thought of her father leaving. This was the inescapable cycle of her life. A cycle of always running away from the pain of those questions. Sabina couldn't outrun her own self-betraying thoughts. *Tullom*, Sabina thought. Those habitual torturous questions showed up no matter how often she silenced them or buried them deep within her. Tonight was no different. Those annoying, unwelcomed questions whispered incessantly as she stood alone, feeling like her world was dark in this bright, perfect place. *Will I ever be loved? Will I ever be enough? When will I be worthy? STOP IT! Be grateful for what you have.*

She forced air into her lungs despite them being weighed down. Closing her eyes and lifting her face to the warm sun, she attempted to soothe the ocean of feelings inside of her while a few tears gathered behind her closed eyes. Dark, brooding thoughts about the unfairness of it all made it difficult for Sabina to soothe her wounds. From the announcement of her father's trip, to the awareness of her teacher's mounting dissatisfaction with her poor performance, Sabina's wound festered.

It was unfair that the village cared more about gaining another resource than about her desire to have her father by her side for her Birth Challenge. The Birth Challenge was a defining moment. More important than any other moment in life, except for the rare cases where a devoted couple bound their energy together for eternity. Couples who were so devoted that they tyed.

~

The Birth Challenge was a rite of passage where a child transitioned into adulthood. It consisted of a ceremony where a child was recognized as an adult by choosing their name and their vocational path. The ceremony had two parts for residents of

Silvedome—named so for the faint silver dome encapsulating the village that kept the people safe. The first part was a spiritual ritual where the newly acclaimed adult fully opened their chakra centers to receive their Moowin talents, if they had any. Moowins were supernatural talents inherited randomly. Across the eight Moowins, there were variations in strengths and levels. The second part determined the vocation of the adult, and it required being tested in three different vocation options. After this, the adult was qualified and it was decided how they would serve the village.

Silvedome was a magical place that was unique, resourceful, primitive, and peaceful. It honored traditions and service to others. It was a village where people were mostly equal. Where people could be who and what they were. Inclusivity was the social norm. As rare as it was to have a place of inclusivity, it was not what Silvedome was known for, even if many came to Silvedome for that reason. It was mainly known for collecting individuals who possessed Moowins. Outside the dome wall, if someone had a Moowin, they fought for survival. Powerful people desired to enslave anyone with a Moowin, and small raiding groups—Selectors—killed or kidnapped individuals with Moowins. Silvedome was a safe haven, but it wasn't a place for everyone. Some viewed Silvedome's traditions as endorsing a type of slavery where no one could get ahead in life. As if it was a dull existence where competition or proving oneself was disregarded. Sabina didn't mind any of that. She only longed to be seen, understood, and included.

Sabina opened her eyes and festered over how unfair it was to have a father constantly traveling. He was the one person with whom she could be truly unguarded and herself. Although she didn't need to prove herself in the sense of accolades, she still needed to feel like she belonged. Sadly, she didn't belong, not in a way that gave her fulfillment. When her father, Brom, left for work, she lost the only person who showed her love, and she lost her main connection to the village. Despite his vital role in her life and her attachment to him, Sabina didn't feel like she knew her father. She didn't have a normal relationship with her parents like others did. Brom was always gone, and when he was home, his mind was elsewhere, like solving problems or consulting with people. If he wasn't doing those things, he welcomed another Moowin rescue into the community and housed them until they were acclimatized in the village. He was passionate about saving people with Moowins from Selectors, which was why he was a Silvedome Scouter—this was his vocation. He was responsible for finding and saving threatened Moowin individuals who would strengthen the collective of Silvedome. Brom was skilled at convincing them to become a resident of the humble village and he was the most successful Scouter.

Sabina thought his passion was more like an obsession, but she was proud of him all the same. He was known as a man who could do it all. He could work alongside different professions as if he had done their vocation all his life. He was recognized as intelligent, efficient, strategic, resourceful, and diligent. Plus, he was known as the traveler who brought back useful information to the village. No one would dispute that he was knowledgeable or that he had keen insights. People always sought his counsel, but to Sabina, he was a man who loved her even if he was obsessed with her safety.

She loved that he had a ready smile on his face that felt like it was just for her. Being around him felt like being in the sun. A feeling of loving warmth radiated from him, but then again, he was an Influencer. Brom was the only person who gave Sabina a nickname, Biny, and when he called her by that nickname, it made her feel like she was on top of a mountain above all the mundane things in her life. It didn't matter to Sabina that they spent most of their quality time training in various forms of martial arts. He made time for her, and that was enough. Sabina loved him for all those traits, but she resented that she had to sacrifice her time with him for the greater good of the village. Why was there so little time for her?

Shifting her focus, Sabina thought to herself: *Three days until my Birth Challenge.* She hugged herself a little tighter. To do this challenge without her father's presence left her with even less self-confidence. She was already a disgrace to her teachers. How was she to withstand the scrutiny of her every decision? How was she supposed to pick three studies to pursue when she was failing them all? And why couldn't the village let her postpone her testing until her father returned from his trip? Who cared if it broke tradition? She didn't understand why it had to be done on her birthday anyway. Her father only returned yesterday. One day with him came and went so quickly. It was all unfair.

She stared fixedly into the sun, refusing to blink. Letting her eyes burn and her vision blur as she tried to block out her emotions and mentally prepare to ask her father to stay long enough to see her Birth Challenge. Brom had influence with the council, but that was not because he was an Influencer who could make people feel emotions. The villagers respected him. Surely, they would arrange his schedule so he could attend her Birth Challenge? This should be a reasonable request. He had a right to be there. It was unheard of for parents not to attend their child's Birth Challenge.

Strands of hair tickled Sabina's face as a light breeze swept across the open land. No one was out in the fields at this time, and the emptiness soothed her. This was a place where Sabina could hide. A place where she could gather her thoughts and get her emotions under control. She knew Brom wouldn't tolerate self-pity, and he would use his emotional gift to make her feel the emotions he wanted her to feel, even if he regretted doing it. As she thought this, she heard the snort of his horse in the distance. She took a big breath, letting her chest expand as far as it would let her.

"You didn't eat dinner with us tonight," Brom commented as he rode lazily up on his rich brown quarter horse mare and looked out over the pond, avoiding eye contact.

Sabina felt the empty calm she worked so hard to achieve leave her as anxiety took its place. Bile rose in her throat, thinking about Brom leaving. Her feelings intensified as she thought of what she would select for her vocations. What if she chose the wrong study and it wasn't a good fit for her? *Stay FOCUSED, Sabina! You don't have time to be weak. It's now or never. You can do this. You can ask him to stay. Ignore the trembling. You are okay.*

She had come to the vacant pond to plan what she would say to convince Brom to stay for her Birth Challenge, but now she regretted her decision to skip dinner. She felt responsible for the disappointment thick in his voice. *Why was I so selfish? Ugh. That was so childish of me. I had only one day with him. I should have spent the last few minutes with him at dinner before he left. What was I thinking? I could have handled everyone's attention on me for not eating if it meant I could spend more time with him.*

Sabina now felt like she had wasted precious time with her father, and for what? She would not ask him to stay, no matter how badly she wanted to. While Sabina scolded herself, she looked down at the ground and started toeing a rock with her boot. Wishing she could stomp it into the ground with attitude and look into her father's eyes with the boldness she longed to have. She wanted to demand that he stay, but she knew he would go. The blanket of abandonment settled more heavily on her shoulders. He would go because he had to. It didn't matter what she was facing, Sabina thought bitterly.

"That's alright." Brom's voice was gentle now.

He is probably worried about me now. Great!

Brom swung his leg off the horse and stepped down onto the ground, gathering the reins into his wide, calloused hands. He was still looking out at the pond, but Sabina felt his discerning stare as soon as it fell upon her. Her head hung low with the weight of shame at missing dinner. She could feel her chin resting on her chest. She felt sweat appearing on her forehead and she could see it on her hands as she continued to look fixedly down. Sabina counted in her head. A trick she often did when she felt people staring at her.

"Are you going to tell me what's on your mind, or am I to guess?"

Sabina turned her head slightly to see Brom's one eyebrow raised higher than the other as he stood with a relaxed stance. She quickly looked back down, grabbed her tunic dress, and twisted it in her fist. Sabina bit down on the left of her lower lip and contemplated what to say. Only moments ago, she thought she was brave enough to ask him to stay, but not now that he stood patiently before her, waiting for her to respond. Her nerves fired, and her stomach cramped up. Then Sabina heard him sigh. She continued to look down, biting her lip.

"Sabina." Brom placed one hand on her shoulder. "Sabina, you will be fine without me."

Sabina felt his calm energy travel from his hand down to her toes. The warm energy was a gentle wave spreading through her body, and she felt the tensions she had been holding slowly release. Her shoulders lowered, and her head slowly lifted until their eyes met.

"I love you more than life itself, and I will be proud of any study you select," Brom stated. "You have nothing to fear and no one's expectation to live up to, except yours . . . perhaps."

He waited a moment, giving Sabina time to hear his words and for her to speak her truths. But she remained silent in the haze of his calm energy. She felt grounded, and in her carefree state, she struggled to be present in this moment. Sabina desperately rehearsed the words she had spoken in her mind. She tried to hold on to his words before they felt weightless, like everything else. She wanted to hug his words into herself. *I am loved. He is proud of me. He loves me more than anyone else.*

"It's time for me to go. I'll be back in twelve to fifteen days, and I want to hear all about your Birth Challenge. Are you wearing your grandmother's necklace?" He spoke all of this in a matter-of-fact tone, and seemed keen not to waste any time. The sun would set soon, and she knew he needed to be at a certain point for his lodging. Sabina always thought it was strange he liked to travel in the dark. *Wouldn't it be faster to travel in daylight?*

Pushing her thoughts away, she allowed the familiarity to settle in at her father's goodbye routine. This was their tradition, and Sabina's delicate fingers did not hesitate to pull the waist-length necklace from under her khaki tunic dress. She handed it over for him to hold. She stood motionless and calm before her father as his thumb rubbed against the dark crystal amulet. She looked at him as he looked at the amulet. He said, "May my journey be swift but successful. May you keep us both from harm's way and guide me safely home to the daughter I treasure." He looked up and gave his charismatic smile plus a quick wink before looking back down. Sabina loved this gift of departing words and felt her rare smile bloom across her face. "May you show favor to Sabina and keep her spirit strong." Breaking the traditional prayer, Brom added, "Bless Sabina's Birth Challenge and guide her to select the studies best suited for her. By the words we speak into existence, may our words return into action, now and forever more!"

"By faith," they both said in unison.

Brom gently let go of the amulet and rubbed his thumb across Sabina's chin as he searched her eyes. She didn't know what he was looking for, but it seemed like there was more he wanted to say. She still felt the heaviness of his calm energy, and it made her tongue thick with relaxation. Sabina broke eye contact first, looking over to the pond. The sun was setting in an orange hue and the water was still. It was a picturesque evening, and Sabina felt no worries.

"You will be home in twelve to fifteen days?" she murmured as she forced her tongue to form the words. Sabina knew the answer, but she wanted the affirmation all the same. She heard the squeak of the stiff leather rubbing as he saddled his horse. He looked down at her.

"Maybe sooner if the Spirit wills it," Brom confirmed, giving her a bright, reassuring smile. His face became serious once more, and he continued. "You have a right to be upset with me for missing a big day in your life, Sabina. It's difficult to understand what I am doing without going into an explanation, but I am bringing a Messenger named Flann Alf home to help you. This is **not** a work assignment. I had planned on discussing this with you at dinner . . . Mother will fill you in on the details."

Sabina cringed on the inside. She had missed a vital dinner conversation, and now she did not know what was happening. He had no more time to give her, and it was her fault that she was clueless. Sabina's shame at missing dinner caused her to cast her eyes over the water again, wishing she could avoid this topic. Sabina didn't realize she was missing another opportunity to ask questions. Instead, they whirred in her mind and she had no time to ask them. Why was this Messenger for her? If it was for her, why couldn't it wait another three days?

"If you hurry back, dinner may still be there. You know your mother likes to dispose of the food as quickly as it comes." It seemed to Sabina that her father was encouraging her to move on as his way of saying goodbye.

With that statement, he wasted no more time. He gathered the horse's reins into one hand and pulled his mare toward his course. As he turned away from her, Sabina's gaze lifted from the water to watch him ride into the tree line. Her arms dropped with regret by her side, and a burning sensation in her eyes started. *Why do I lack courage? Why can't I ask the questions on my mind? Why am I so embarrassed? Am I defective?* Sabina wrapped her arms around herself, watching her long, silky, dark auburn hair blow forward. Her mind was racing as her father left. The calmness he'd forced on her from his Moowin was already driven away by fear. Emotional despair surfaced as her mind circled on the notion that it would be twelve to fifteen days before she saw her father again. She was alone. Sure, she had her beloved and obnoxiously happy sister, her no-nonsense mother, and her only trustworthy friend, Crystal, who was weirder than she was. But nobody understood her like her father. He was the one person who could see behind her veil, with no explanation needed on what she felt or why.

Sabina sighed, resigned. This was her life, and there was no hope of changing that. She was invisible when she wanted to shine. She was the focus of everyone's attention when she wished to be invisible—every time she was that clumsy, stuttering, pitiful young girl. She was too tall, too meek, and too unaccomplished. She was nothing. Just the village's well-respected Scouter's daughter. She clenched her dress in her hands and felt revulsion spiral through her. Part of her wanted to collapse in a heap in the tall grass, but the more sensible side of her wanted to see her father for as long as possible. She stood and watched him go. A small act of defense toward the weaker side of herself.

As she watched, Brom's back suddenly became rigid. His mare stopped trotting toward the tree lines and was motionless for a long, drawn-out moment. Brom turned abruptly in his saddle to look back at Sabina and then looked pointedly into the trees over his left shoulder. He was far enough away that Sabina could not make out his facial features. She looked at him questioningly. She was not sure why he hadn't ridden off yet, but she quickly wiped at the wealth of tears on her face. Was he changing his mind about leaving? *Did he feel guilty for leaving me to face my Birth Challenge alone? Could I be saved from embarrassing myself? Maybe I could go with him.* Hope started to lift Sabina's spirits as she watched Brom return in her direction.

Brom shifted about-face quickly, and his horse sprinted toward Sabina with blurring legs. She watched Brom rise out of his saddle, leaning into the mare's neck so he could gain faster speed. Sabina's eyes narrowed, looking to see his expression. What she saw on his face made her swallow hard, and her stomach dropped. The urgency was plain on his face, and she had no idea what had changed. He was talking to her before he reached her, and despite appearing panicked, he spoke with controlled calm. "You will not want to hear this, Sabina," Brom called in a firm but resigned voice loud enough for Sabina to hear over the pounding hooves, "but there is no time for discussion. I have set up some union interviews for you."

Sabina's breath caught in a too-fast inhale, and she felt like she was falling forward. Her mouth fell open, and her hands opened wide. She stood frozen like prey before a large predator, except this was a predator she was not willing to fight. Brom stopped his mare mere feet before Sabina, which caused his mare to high step and turn in a circle.

"Biny, it's only a possibility," Brom pleaded, begging her to listen. "You don't have to agree with anything you don't want to, but it's time to consider this option. You are turning sixteen in three days and . . . and . . ." Brom rubbed the back of his buzzed head, dropping his chin as if unsure what else to say. Sabina strained her senses to hear what he wasn't saying, despite the ringing in her ears. She was breathing quickly, like she was looking down from a cliff, contemplating jumping into the depths of the cold, dark water below. *He. Wants. Me. To be mated??? Why? Who would even consider being in a union with me? What do I have to offer?*

He snapped his head up and turned in his saddle, looking over his right shoulder back into the woods. *What was he looking at?* Not understanding what held his attention, Sabina followed his gaze but didn't see or hear anything in the trees. *Was he hearing a Messenger?* Sabina could feel a slight energy shift, and she noticed Brom was acting like he could hear or see something she could not. He was still staring into the woods with complete focus, as if he was having a conversation and was not present with her. Without realizing it, she unintentionally moved forward, getting closer to the mare. Closer than she felt comfortable doing. She realized what she had done and stumbled back at once.

Balanced and a safe distance from the mare once more, Sabina looked at her father. The pleading had dropped from his voice when he spoke again. Instead, Brom's voice carried an intensity to it that made Sabina want to withdraw into herself. Something angered him. He stared directly into her eyes with a face that communicated his sincerity. "No father . . ." he forced out, "wants-to-tell-his-child. . . they **can't** reach for the stars, but I am telling you," he finished, in a softer but nevertheless firm tone, "it's best if you don't."

She tried to soak in the information. *Is he angry with me? Have I failed him?* She whispered "why" too softly for anyone but herself to hear.

It seemed Brom tried to speak gentler, but he spoke quickly, never taking his eyes from Sabina. "This isn't going to make sense, and it is hurtful to hear. It is a tough conversation to have, but I need you to trust me, Biny. I don't want to hurt you, and I don't want you to get hurt. Tying to one of the men from your union interviews will be the safest option for you."

"Fa-ther," Sabina croaked out with a dry throat as she tried to slow her breathing down. Immediately, her mind came up with plenty of examples as to why she deserved such low expectations from her father. *Does he think I am not good enough to do anything except tying? What have I done to deserve such low expectations from him?* Sabina felt like she should have been sad at those thoughts, but they were thoughts she often had about herself.

"Sabina, I thought we had more time. I wanted to wait until you were further in your studies, but . . ." Brom pushed on with firmness. "You need to meet these men. It is important. I ask you to consider each one of them and pick one for your future." Brom rushed on before Sabina could object. "I want the world for you, Biny, but what I want most is to know that you are safe. These men are good men despite whatever first impression you have of them. I trust them to take good care of you, but more importantly, I trust them with you." He paused briefly and went on. "Can that be enough for you to at least keep an open mind about a union interview with each of them regardless of whether it ends up in a tying?" Slowing down his speech, he gently asked, "Will you grant your father peace of mind, knowing you are safe?"

Sabina faltered in telling her father what she really felt. She wasn't ready for a union interview or to be in a union, let alone a life-altering decision like tying. She hadn't even had a friendly, flirty conversation with anyone. How was she supposed to adapt to the thought of considering a life mate?

This was an unspoken topic between them, yet it was clear to her that he had a plan all worked out. It was something Sabina had not contemplated, but her father obviously had. She felt unprepared for this conversation and didn't see a way out of answering him. Sabina fisted her tunic dress in her discomfort. She berated herself for not predicting that he would have devised a plan for her future. She knew how obsessed he was with her safety. Sabina allowed her annoyance with Brom to register in her mind. He could have at least discussed this topic with her while strategically putting her future into place. Instead, he decided to spring this on her with no time to discuss it. She felt cornered and pressured into accepting his plan.

As Sabina talked to herself, she paced back and forth in a tight loop. She lifted her arms up and let them fall as she discussed this with herself. Eventually, the initial shock wore off, and her annoyance simmered. She tried to think quickly. He was asking for her permission. No, he was really asking for her cooperation. Sabina did not delude herself into thinking she had a choice in this matter. When it came to her safety, Brom did not budge.

She didn't understand why her future partner fell into the spectrum of her safety. She shook her head. Only Brom knew the answer to that thought. Taking a moment to repeat to herself what her father wanted, Sabina reworded Brom's request in her head. What she understood was that her father needed her to consider these "trustworthy" men he had picked out for her as a potential partner, and the result of her agreeing to be in a union with one of these men would bring him peace of mind. He implied his ultimate goal of tying, but he was asking for something less permanent to start. As she weeded through what he was saying, she felt pressure, knowing that he rarely asked her to do anything except things he considered pertained to her safety.

A quick thought rushed into her mind. *What if I don't want a partner?* Sabina dismissed that thought with a huff. Who was she kidding? Her independence stemmed from no one wanting to spend time with her. It was a force of nature that she seemed to repel people. She was by herself most, if not all the time. Admittedly, she dreamed of being included, especially among her classmates. She longed to be asked to go fishing on a Friday night date, but since she was old enough to go fishing, the invitation never came. Instead, she sat at home waiting to hear her classmates' conversations as they returned from fishing. Sabina would listen to their conversations as they passed by her window. Their stores were reminders of what Sabina couldn't have.

The truth was that Sabina had given up on the idea of catching the attention of one of the many crushes she had. Despite not being asked out by any of the boys, she still secretly wished for an attractive mate with thick, wavy, long hair and a well-trimmed but stubbly beard. A man admired for his many talents who treated Sabina respectfully with light touches to her lower back as he escorted her to the village's weekly performances. Okay, okay, okay! Sabina had desires like any other young adult, but if she was honest with herself, she avoided thinking about the topic of romance because it hurt too much. Plus, she dreaded the idea of Murph asking for a union interview. Murph, who still ate his boogers right after he examined them on his finger. He was likely her only willing candidate.

Sabina had accepted she would either be alone for the rest of her life or be stuck in a union with someone like Murph. Solo sounded better. Sabina continued to argue with herself in her head and worked through her list of concerns. She decided she did not need to worry about standing out in her village for making a union declaration if she proceeded with her father's plan. According to the laws of Silvedome, a union was required before a tying. Although there was no mandatory minimum length of time for a union to exist before a tying, it was frowned upon to have a tying before a year of union had passed. Therefore, it was rare for someone as young as sixteen to consider tying.

Besides, that was not what he was asking her to do. He was asking her to consider a union. Even if she did enter a union, it could last years and never end in a tying. One could have multiple unions throughout their dating life. A union could be broken at any time by either individual without repercussions, and another union could be entered into immediately if chosen. Or the couple could decide to stay in a union and keep their possibilities open indefinitely. The fact was that a union was nothing more than an official public announcement that two people were exclusive and seeing what life would be like together . . . with the possibility of a tying. Validating her argument further, Sabina reminded herself it was common for unions to be declared at her age, especially for those who did not pursue studies in the Tradel, or for families with strong Moowins—like her father. The reality was that parents had the authority to secure a potential partner for their child through union interviews to protect their family's lineage regardless of the number of school years completed or the child's age. She didn't care what the laws of Silvedome said. It was her life and her decision, Sabina thought to herself. Nevertheless, she understood why parents set up union interviews.

Most families desired to align their household with another of similar status or level of Moowin. This ensured their future offspring would have the best life or chance of having a Moowin. The people of Silvedome were superstitious and believed two individuals tying with known Moowins had a better chance of giving birth to a child with one of the eight Moowins. They believed in this superstition even though research could not validate it. Sabina suspected the reality was that no one could explain why some individuals were born with Moowins and others were born without any Moowin.

Unless the child was completely independent, union interviews required the blessing of both sets of parents with a notification sent to the Ori—a nominated council of each of the rare Moowins and a person from each sector. These union interviews could be pre-arranged as early as birth. However, the law mandated that tyings required the blessing of the Ori, or a rare Seer. Even with the Ori's blessing, both sets of parents would still be involved if someone in the village wanted to ty with someone from outside the dome walls. Therefore, tyings were a serious matter and were the exception. In contrast, pre-arranged union interviews were a formality that took time to arrange. Every parent scrutinized and laboriously analyzed union choices before giving their permission for union interviews. Sabina's father would be no different.

Although Sabina avoided most people, she knew the village square was where union interviews were discussed. A topic of popular conversation, unions were something that one deliberated on. People were curious about what each family was doing and why one strategy may be more beneficial than another. Not to mention, union interviews provided entertainment when conflict existed, such as when one set of parents refused to give their blessing.

Often parents were more invested in the union resulting in a tying than the intended couple. However, the laws of Silvedome protected children's rights too. Silvedome prided itself on agency and the right to choose one's own path. Adult children were protected in three ways. First, union interviews could only be conducted between two adults. Parents had to wait until after their child completed their transformation into adulthood with the Birth Challenge ceremony, which was three days away for Sabina. Second, no one could be forced into a union or tying, no matter how much a parent insisted. The adult child was required to respect their parents' wishes by going on a union interview. However, it was solely up to the mutual agreement of the two adults whether they chose to enter into a union. Third, by declaring a union, parents were giving up their rights over their adult child on all matters from that day on.

～

Silvedome had three stages to adulthood that all villagers respected. The first stage was the Birth Challenge, which was the initiation and introduction into adulthood. In this stage, the adult child still had the protection and guidance of a parent. In the other two stages, the adult child was permanently separated from their parents. The next two stages could happen in any order, but once either one was chosen, the individual was considered independent of their parents from that point on, and a full adult. The other two stages were serving the village full-time, and selecting a partner or mate, whether in the form of a union or a tying.

Thus, parents lost complete control over their adult child's decisions once their child entered a union or began their servitude to the village. This was another reason why union interviews took a long time to form. Once parents gave permission, they were not permitted to interfere with their adult child's exploration of what their life would be like with that match. It was considered an experimental time where one could see if their intended partner made them a better person and made their life easier, or if the person complicated their life. All this was judged by how it affected one's servitude to the village, which was considered one's calling, their dharma. It also allowed everyone to transition from living by their parents' rules to finding the rules of understanding in that unique relationship. It was as if a union were a test to see if the relationship made each person thrive or suffer.

On the opposite perspective, if one or both parents refused to bless the couple's union, the couple could still go to the Ori and plead their case. The other option was to accept a full-time vocation and declare oneself independent. Two independent adults could enter into a union without their parents' or the Ori's permission. But no matter what, tyings required the Ori's blessing. If the Ori refused the couple's request to ty, the only other option was ignored for most people did not take the risk of going to a Seer. If the Seer did not see the couple's future together, the Seer would not bless them. Which meant no one would bless them. Seers were a last resort if one wanted to remain together in the village.

Silvedome village had one rare Seer. She could see outside her bloodline and far into the future of any person she willed. No one questioned her. Once the Seer looked into a couple's future and found no evidence of their life together, no one would bless that couple. To pursue a union or tying after the village Seer's bleak prediction meant the couple faced being exiled for their love, which hardly anyone chose to do. However, some couples would defy her words and continue to date each other. Eventually, those relationships ended, whether it was days later or several years later.

On rare occasions, the Seer did bless a tying, where two people's energy bonded together for eternity, not just this lifetime. Sabina loved those stories the best and would stay in the village square to hear all the details about the couple. She read all the books that had survived the nuclear war and savored the ones that told the story of two individuals falling in love despite tremendous odds. The concept of love being the most remarkable treasure seemed magical to her.

Raised in a village where the people valued Moowins above everything, Sabina found herself smitten with the idea of tying for love. Silvedome operated from the mindset that the greatest blessing was to have a village of talented Moowins, and that tying with a Moowin was of the highest status and achievement. Regardless of whether you were fortunate enough to ty with someone with a Moowin, the people of Silvedome taught that love was to be earned through respect, caring for one another, honoring each person's individuality, and helping each other toward their goals. Most people chose to be in a union because they found someone that made their life easier. Thus, love was a by-product of having a partner, not its reason.

∼

Sabina recalled when a neighbor girl stayed out past dark with her mate and how upset her parents were when she returned home for a visit, stumbling through the front door with her hair a mess and lipstick smudged under her lip. Had she not been in a union, her parents would have given her a week's worth of extra chores, but because of the union, her parents were forced to ignore the unpresentable behavior. Eventually, that girl disbanded the union. There were rumors she dissolved it because it caused her mother so much distress that she needed to stay in the Healer's hub for weeks.

Never having had a relationship yet burning with curiosity about them, Sabina wondered if the girl decided her partner was no good for her, or if their relationship lacked enough structure as it clearly didn't lack attraction or fun. Maybe the girl couldn't live with her parents' silent disappointment either. Sabina always questioned how much autonomy she truly had over her life, or perhaps she was the only one who felt the need for her parents' approval. The way she saw it, it should have been a promising match.

Now that Sabina thought of that memory, she was struck by how odd it was that Brom was asking her to consider a union. She couldn't picture Brom letting her go anywhere with a man without him escorting her, or having the Seer do a reading on each potential match's energy beforehand. That was how overprotective he was. From Sabina's perspective, Brom asking her to enter a union willingly was like asking an orangutan to walk away from her baby. Brom may have had a Seer's reading on every possible union interview, for all she knew. Sabina wasn't sure how he was protecting her, but she knew he had a plan, like always. She also knew Brom expected her to follow it.

Her self-doubt increased as she attempted to figure out her father's plan. Bitterly, Sabina recalled how many of her classmates were already in, or at least had, one or two unofficial relationships with someone without their parents' knowledge or permission.

Technically, the parents' consent was not required to date, but it was understood that you asked out of respect.

It wasn't surprising that no one had expressed an interest in Sabina, even though it was common to start dating as early as fifteen. How could she expect to date when no one included her in any activities outside of school? Believing that she would never be asked for a date, Sabina concluded this might be the only way a man would show interest in her, for she was always alone. And she was tired of being alone.

Sabina wistfully pictured her dreamy man hugging her as she completed her Birth Challenge. Sabina envisioned him waiting as long as it took to complete her ceremony. Then, he would embrace her in a way that told the world he didn't want to let go of her. She liked thinking about how he would only have eyes on her. Sabina could almost smile at the fantasy. At the very least, this thought comforted her and made her desire a relationship.

But . . . she wasn't sure she was brave enough to talk to a stranger. Sabina struggled to express her thoughts no matter who she spoke to. She became nervous and started analyzing what she should or shouldn't say. If her emotions were too escalated, she would begin to stutter. Sabina hated stuttering. Stuttering guaranteed unwanted attention. People would turn from their conversation and look at her with irritation. She would rather remain silent and unnoticed than be judged as annoying. Even with her father, she barely spoke, and Sabina loved him deeply. Surely her father had explained her shyness to these men, and these men accepted the possibility of a union with her anyway. It was likely that Brom thought of everything.

⌘

Brom leaned forward in his saddle as if he was going to dismount. He seemed impatient, and she knew he had a distance to travel tonight. She needed to answer him and now. With little time to think this decision through further, she relied on one truth she knew down to her core; she trusted her father more than herself. Sabina could do nothing more than nod and internally question her sanity simultaneously. She trusted her father, but this scared her in a way that made her question what she trusted more: that her father knew best, or that she lacked the courage to defy him. If he wanted her to meet someone, then Sabina would do so. She would worry about her shyness later. Besides, all tyings required both individuals in the relationship to agree to a lifelong commitment and to be blessed by the Ori, which was no small task. These union interviews were unlikely to result in anything but a chance to date someone.

Feeling like she could breathe more easily, Sabina focused on her father. Once Brom saw her nod of consent, he finally took his discerning eyes off her. Relief flashed across his face. Yet when he spoke, Sabina could hear the regret in his voice and maybe a little anger too. "You deserve a better life, Sabina. I know that." Brom slapped his leg and then rubbed the back of his head.

"What is it? Tell me, Father!" Sabina muttered, reaching her hand to rest it on her father's leg, giving him comfort despite her fear that his mare would trample her. She was automatically more concerned for her father than her own discomfort. Sabina didn't know what caused her father's outburst, and that concern helped her resist focusing on how large the muscles of the mare's hind legs were while they involuntarily twitched.

Looking down, with his hand still resting on the back of his head, it seemed Brom was grasping for control of his emotions. Sabina anxiously waited for him to tell her what was happening. Brom slowly lifted his head and looked into her eyes as if his head weighed a hundred pounds. There was an unbearable sadness in his eyes for a brief second. It was like looking into a man's face that was kneeling in the dirt hours after watching his home burn with his family inside of it. The tears dried, but the devastation already hollowed out his features. It looked like the face of a man who had lost everything he loved. Sabina didn't understand this look, but she felt his anguish settle over her. Then, one blink later, his demeanor changed back to business mode, and his spine straightened. He cleared his throat and pulled on the reins, causing his mare to step a comfortable distance away from Sabina.

"Your mother has the details," Brom went on soberly. He slowed his speech as if he didn't want to go on speaking but was obligated to tell Sabina the details before he left. "The first introduction will start one day after your Birth Challenge. Most of these men are from other villages."

Sabina groaned at hearing this news. Her emotions quickly shifted at the details of her union interviews, from concern over that fleeting glimpse of Brom's anguished face, to the knotting of nerves in her stomach.

"I know you don't like to do anything outside the norm," Brom admitted with a hint of urgency back in his voice. "But, because of my connections with other towns, you have opportunities that few are given. The villagers know me, and they will expect me to give you every advantage I can."

Sabina stared at her father with her eyebrows pinched, her arms crossed, and her weight shifted to her left hip, and she waited for this nightmare of a speech to be over. The anguished look she saw on his face was already pushed to the back of her mind. Sabina was in her you-want-to-bet stance. She may not have been able to tell her father with her words that she didn't believe this was 'normal', but nevertheless he seemed to understand her body language. Sabina trusted her father, but she wasn't buying into this fairytale that a union interview with an outsider wouldn't draw much attention to herself. Sabina would rather muck out these twitchy mares' stalls than be the town's talk.

"Plus, I have disguised some meetings so that no one will be suspicious of all the union interviews I have coordinated for you. You don't need to be concerned about unwanted attention."

This whole scenario just got better and better. Sabina looked at her father with apprehension as she pictured a strange man walking through the village and all the questions it would incite. People would want to know where this stranger was from and what he was doing here. They would want to know how this stranger knew Brom and why Brom was interested in him for a union with his daughter. They would want to know why he was special and *that alone would* draw attention to Sabina. The entire village respected Brom, and they would want their daughters to meet the man Brom had picked for *his* precious daughter. They would be waiting to pounce on that man as soon as they saw this stranger lose interest in her. And how many union interviews did he have set up for her? Sabina wasn't used to choices.

Seeming to mistake the look on Sabina's face, Brom switched tactics and looked out in a nonchalant demeanor. "Before you panic, the Ori knows of my plan, and they have approved these men to enter our village. I have taken care of everything. All you must do is meet these men. Get to know them," he explained. Leaning slightly toward her as if he was revealing a secret, he said, "Let them get to know you." He raised both eyebrows as if that was a novel idea.

Yeah right, she thought. What was there to know? *I sit at home by myself most nights. I like to go on long walks. I have taken up wood carving to pass the time. AND I spend a lot of time training by myself which I'm not allowed to talk about to anyone. It won't take long for them to get to know me.*

Brom straightened in his saddle, lifting one shoulder, and simultaneously tilting his head toward it as if his shrug silently communicated that all of this was no big deal. *Just talk to them. Smile at them and pretend you aren't terrified of making a fool of yourself.* Sabina had no idea what to say to these potential mates or how to entertain them during their interview. Maybe her father had thought of that too. Sabina decided that must be why he insisted she had nothing to worry about.

"May I suggest you give each of them true consideration? They will be staying in the village or near the village for the Ori's use as part of my arrangement with them. They are to become Silvedomeies."

Sabina's stomach clenched. Knowing she had to live in the

same village as her failed union matches rocked her to the core. She was hyperventilating on the inside.

Brom turned his horse toward the direction to leave once more but stopped. Sabina could tell he needed to go, but he was uncharacteristically indecisive about something. With his mind made up, he dropped his act of nonchalance and turned back to her a different man.

His stare was intense. It was as if his eyes were the intensity of someone fighting in the arena. Like he was studying his opponent's body for clues to his next strike. She had seen those eyes when Brom was ready to give the killing blow to the raiders that had attacked Silvedome in the past. Seriousness was plain on his face. It was as if he were in a different dimension. His body was there, but his spirit was not. His intensity was there, but his personality was not. A soft breeze of Brom's emotions enveloped her. She didn't think he was intentionally using his gift on her now. Sabina felt his energy radiating out of him. She could see the tension in his forearms and his clenched jaw. She knew how serious he was when he barked, "Don't. Leave. The. Village. No. Matter. What! This is the safest place for you. And don't show your talents to anyone unless it's an emergency. The men I have sent for you will help with that."

"Wha . . . Wha . . . what is wroooong?" Sabina stuttered under the warning. She knew these rules. He gave them often but not like this. Not with pure rage tickling the back of her neck. She had never feared her father before, but the anger encircling her wasn't his emotion. She was sure of it. It felt different from his energy. She had no idea what the tullom was going on, but she knew she wanted this conversation over. She started sending silent pleas to the universe that this rage would dissipate.

"You know how rare my talents are as an Influencer?" Brom didn't wait for her to respond, which wouldn't have mattered anyway. Sabina was too alarmed to speak. She felt even more unsteady on her feet than when he had first come rushing back to her.

"You know the stories of the Agni?"

Sabina nodded without hesitation. The eight Moowins fascinated her. Secretly, she desired to develop one of the eight Moowins, even if it was one of the abundant roles like Performer. She wanted a Moowin badly enough that she didn't care if it put her at risk of the Selector's attention. However, she was three days away from her Birth Challenge and she hadn't shown any signs or aptitudes for any of the eight Moowins. Sabina wholeheartedly believed she should have a Moowin. She had convinced herself that a Moowin would solve her problems. If Sabina had a Moowin, she could show all those that ignored her and made her feel insignificant that she was important. She was valuable. The closer her Birth Challenge came, the more she alternated between, on the one hand, berating herself for lacking a Moowin and, on the other, lifting her spirits by reminding herself that her Moowin could develop anytime over the Tradel years. Many before her had Moowins awaken in their Birth Challenge. She still had time, and she still had hope.

"The world is searching for the Agni, and villages are . . ." He broke off and gathered himself. The rage left her in a whoosh, as if the emotion had been sucked from the air around her. Sabina's hair flew forward for a moment. Then all was still. She felt dizzy with relief and struggled to listen through the spinning sensation she felt. Brom's no-nonsense demeanor had returned. His intensity was still there, but the tension in his body was normal.

Brom continued with the pertinent information, taking no notice of Sabina's unfocused eyes. "You are in danger for two reasons," he lectured quickly. "One, you were born from a parent with a rare talent with one of the eight Moowins. Two, in four days, you will enter your Tradel years. So far, the Seers have only been able to prophesy that the Agni will be born from someone with a rare talent and that the Agni should be around seventeen years old today. The age of someone in their Tradel years. That makes you a target based on those two factors. Thousands of individuals match that description, but I don't want to take any chances. Now, go see your mother. I will return quickly with the Messenger, but first, I must tell the Ori that the union interviews are beginning."

Brom didn't say goodbye. His mare sprinted off toward the village. He left Sabina standing by the pond, bewildered. The rollercoaster of emotions, the shifting of her plans, the uncertainty of her father's behavior, and the quiet surroundings made Sabina feel briefly desolate. Sabina was officially freaked out. What had just happened? She wanted answers immediately. Answers would give her some solid footing in this sinking sand of uncertainty. Starting with the possibility her father had been possessed by evil spirits on his last business trip. She didn't think that possession by a spirit was possible, but her body gave a tiny little jerk at the thought of the soft rub of rage against the skin on her neck. Her long, thick hair shielded her against the wind, and yet she was chilled at the energy that had touched her so intimately on her neck. Knowing she wasn't going to get answers by giving into her despair, and being crept out at the thought of lingering by the pond where she may never forget the grasp of rage all around her, she was ready to bolt.

Questions plagued Sabina as she made the long trek toward Sector Three of Silvedome village, where her family's stone tut sat indistinguishable from the rows of other tuts. She walked with her head hung low and her arms wrapped around, surefooted from all the times she had walked this path. Her brain was muddled with worry, so she ignored the burning in her calves as she walked with purpose. She processed and analyzed the bizarre conversation with her father as she walked.

Why did his demeanor change? Recounting the events, she recalled he was his no-nonsense and charismatic self before he had left the first time. Then he had returned to her with panicked actions. Then he had become firm with her, followed by pleading. That wasn't the norm. Brom was a man with great emotional control, yet he was suddenly frustrated enough to slap his leg.

Then that haunting devastation on his face. What was he thinking about at that moment?

She thought of Brom straining to lift his head, like some invisible giant was holding his head down in submission, only to look at her with that heartbreaking expression. The memory triggered a small stab in her heart. Brom was a rare Influencer, and with his talent, he could cause you to feel what he wanted you to feel without touching you. He was also disciplined, and he didn't spill his emotions like that. Yet Sabina could feel his emotions. She could feel his anguish through the touch of her hand, and with that touch came an image like a memory. She couldn't get the image out of her mind. Sabina could see a delicate thin knife stabbing through her skin.

The musky air brought Sabina's attention to her surroundings. She was getting closer to the hunting grounds. The path she followed was well-worn after years of escaping to the privacy of the pond, and with the sun setting, she would not see if any animal trappings had been moved. Some hunters may still be in the woods trying to catch some of the night creatures, but Sabina always had her bright orange scarf. She tugged it from her pocket and adjusted it around her face without a hitch in her step. Lastly, she pulled her pinewood scent from her tunic pocket and dabbed it on the inside of her wrist. Coming across a violent creature or even a hunter mistaking her for an animal was a low risk, but Brom's relentless drills made her discipline second nature. Sabina dropped the uncertainty she cloaked herself in. The worry over her father disappeared as she entered the forest. Sabina became the self-assured hunter Brom trained her to be. She slid the small hunting knife from her boot and stepped forward as she walked surefooted through her path. She walked with an awareness of her surroundings and in complete concentration. When she had crossed the woods without problems, Sabina tucked the scarf in her pocket, slid the knife back into its boot holster, and rubbed some dirt on her wrist.

Past the danger of the woods, her pace doubled. Her thoughts returned to her father. That's when she realized she had walked nearly two miles and it was the first time in her life that she hadn't watched her father leave town. She soothed herself. Had she not felt like she was boneless and struggling to breathe after feeling that burning rage, she would have watched him leave. She couldn't recall a time when she hadn't watched him leave but she also couldn't recall a time when her father had lost control of his emotions either. What had happened? Where had that rage come from and, if it came from her father, why didn't it consume her with a feeling of rage? She only felt the rage externally, not internally.

Brom's talents worked by making her feel emotions as if they were hers, but these emotions were clearly not hers. Inadvertently, her demeanor lost its hunter confidence, and she was once more wrapping her arms around herself, tucking her chin. Sabina bit her lip, worrying at it, and felt the crack of her dried lips. Then she tasted her blood. Her whole mouth was dry and hot. Her sandpaper tongue was getting stuck to the rough of her mouth. She was anxious to get back and drink some water.

After forty minutes of worrying about her father's shifting demeanor and trying to figure out why she was enveloped by someone's or something's rage, Sabina hadn't drawn any conclusion. To distract herself, she imagined the possibility of finding happiness with one of the men from the union interviews. She could allow herself the privilege to hope for happiness even if she would never admit it to anyone. She wanted love. Who didn't? she thought defensively. She wanted to be someone's whole world. She wanted what everyone seemed to have all around her.

It would be nice to have my fingers lightly intertwined with someone as we walk through the village. Or to cuddle with him as a cool breeze sweeps over us as we watch a performance at The Mox.

Sabina huffed. Who was she kidding? She would settle for a friendship. The simple joy of having someone she could confide in, instead of having all her conversations in her mind. Someone to share a meal with or someone to exchange gifts with on the Day of Giving. The chance to stop pretending she was content to be on her own wherever she went. Someone who would look for her at gatherings, or, when she was sick, someone who'd stop by her tut with a story to share about the day, or someone who would know that she liked dark chocolate above all desserts.

It was fun to think of the possibilities, but that small voice inside her wanted her to dwell on how easily everything could go wrong. She had never known a time when she didn't blunder under the pressure of attention. Admittedly, she didn't know what to expect from these union interviews or how much her father shared with these men about who she was. Did they know she was an inconvenience to her village? Would that embarrass them? Would they still want to be in a union with her if they knew what she was like? How old were these men? *What if they are way older than me, toothless, rude, or short?* The questions came faster and faster.

Who did Brom want her to meet from Silvedome? He said most of the men came from outside the village, which implied she would have a union interview with at least one person from the village, she reasoned. Sabina had no clue who it could be. She would have noticed someone paying attention to her. No one had ever approached her or watched her from afar . . . that she knew of. It had to be someone older than her. Someone she didn't see daily. Who was older than her and not in a union or tyed? Chi! Chi was quiet, six years older, and unattached. Chi was nice. He hadn't done anything nice specifically for her, but he at least helped clean up after gatherings. He wasn't bad looking either. He had a long birthmark that went along one side of his nose, but that didn't bother her. She knew he worked with land preservation, and he was always daydreaming. Could that be why her father thought he would make a good choice for her? They could both be lost in thought with no need for words.

She wondered where the other men were from. Sandi and Forge, probably. They were the closest villages to Silvedome. Why would they want to leave their families to be in a union with a stranger? Would their family transfer too? What did Brom have to trade to allow these strangers access to their reclusive village?

Sabina had reached the first signs of homes on the outskirts of Sector Two and Three with the sun setting before she finally asked herself, *What if I don't like any of them?* She may not have wanted to feel invisible, but there were times when she didn't want to be seen.

How many union interviews do people typically have after a Birth Challenge? Two, maybe three. This wasn't something she paid attention to. Many parents arranged union interviews that were pre-planned from a child's birth. Did Brom have a union interview planned for her since birth? One that he didn't feel like sharing with the village or with her? How many union interviews happened before someone was considered dating or a union took place? What was considered normal?

Parrot had four union interviews several winters back when she finished schooling. Sabina remembered Parrot had a list of qualities her partner would possess. A 'perfect' list. She would not tolerate anyone who did not match her perfect list. She slammed the door shut once when a suitor showed up to ask her on a date. He didn't even have time to ask her out. Sabina remembered her wearing the white toggle dress the next day when the story spread through the village. Those pursuing studies in beautification wore toggle dresses.

A growl erupted from Sabina when she was two tuts away from her home. She finally had an appetite, and it had to be two hours after dinner. Sabina untied her boots and slipped them off, resting them on the side of the steps where her mother and sister's shoes were. She approached the basin on the covered porch without a sound and poured a small amount of water on a clean, white cloth resting on the arm of a wooden rocking chair. Sabina considered taking a drop of water to moisten her mouth but thought better of it. She was beyond thirsty but didn't want to risk getting sick from the unfiltered water. Instead, she briskly washed her face and hands with the wet washcloth before placing it on the floor. She got her second clean cloth and repeated the process, but this time while standing on the wet cloth. Finally, she sat down and wiped her feet off with the second washcloth, throwing both dirty washcloths into the empty wash pan. Standing up and walking over to the plank door, Sabina took a deep breath before she faced her mother.

CHAPTER 2

Surprises

The door swung open with a creak into a dark, empty gathering room. Sabina turned to shut the door and saw two small duffle bags. One of which was her mother's, for her extended stays at the hospital, and the other bag was her sister's. *Oh no. I'm in trouble,* Sabina realized as she clicked the door shut. She wondered what she could say to make amends to her mother, who waited for Sabina to return home before she left for work. She could hear the angry clicks of the high-heeled shoes her mother liked to wear indoors when everyone else left their boots on the porch. The clicks stopped. Sabina stayed facing the door, her hand resting as she leaned into it and looked down. The hunger in her stomach quickly turned to acid in her throat at the anxiety of what her mother would say. Feeling sweat appear on her upper lip and a quick stab of fear in her heart, she promised herself she'd make eye contact, no matter what she faced.

Sabina's birth mother died before she turned one. Marigold was the only mother Sabina had ever known. She was a strict mother who took Sabina's failures personally, and Sabina had a lot of them. Her failures kept stacking higher and higher on top of each other like a volcano, ready to erupt. As Sabina grew older,

Marigold became more disappointed in her, and the gap between them grew.

To make matters worse, Sabina's nine-month-older stepsister, Fawn, was perfect. She was beloved by the town like Brom was, and it seemed as if she was his real daughter, not Sabina. Sabina never felt resentment toward her sister. She only desired to be like her. Marigold expected Sabina to be like Fawn: the ideal student, daughter, friend, and potential partner. People gravitated to Fawn. She was vital to Sabina, too, because she showed her affection. Her father understood her and made her feel calm. Her mother cared for her by wanting the best for her. But neither her mother nor father could be called affectionate.

She turned slowly to see Marigold standing at the kitchen entrance looking at her with contempt. The light shone behind her, casting a dark look across her frustrated face. She was a tiny woman with a slight build, but she always seemed taller when angry. "I'd ask you to explain yourself, but I don't have time for you to work up the courage to answer me." Marigold spat out in anger with her fist on her hips. She put her two fingers between her eyebrows, propping her elbow on the other forearm as she looked down. It seemed Marigold did this when she asked herself, *Why me?* With what looked like controlled anger, she said, "You *knew* it was my turn for overnight stays at the hospital and that I wanted to finalize your Birth Challenge order tonight." She threw her hands up and walked toward the kitchen, leaving Sabina standing on the thinly woven rug by the front door.

"Now I must rush to the hospital in-the-dark!" Marigold walked toward a kitchen chair and continued to speak. "You don't seem to understand that your world is about to be turned upside down." Marigold placed one hand on the chair and pulled it out but did not sit. "Sa-Bin-*A*," Marigold cracked. "Stop poking around and get in here."

She dashed to the kitchen and slid herself into the chair next to Marigold. She looked down at her fingers resting on the table, not daring to look Marigold in the eye. Marigold continued to stand. There was a moment of silence as it seemed Marigold stared down at her. She heard a slow, deep exhale. "I can no longer sit with you and discuss the best strategy for your Birth Challenge order." Marigold had calmed down. Sabina held her breath. She waited for Marigold to point out what she wanted to say, for she was a woman who did not waste time with small talk. She had a no-nonsense attitude, like Brom. When nothing came, Sabina glanced up, reading her mother's face. She quickly looked back down, focusing on the dirt under her fingernails. She could not resist fidgeting under the hard stare her mother gave her.

With her father leaving after a short visit and his mysterious behavior during his departure, Sabina had forgotten to worry about the Birth Challenge order. The reality was the Birth Challenge order didn't seem important anymore. Sabina had finally come to the inevitable conclusion that failure was her destiny. She accepted that even if she didn't like it. Sabina didn't think the order mattered anymore except to get the Protector Moowin test done first. If she waited to do the Protector test, she would be starved, tired, and have muddled thoughts, which would cause her to fall flat on her face with the first attack. No, the order didn't matter. Sabina had decided that the union interviews took priority over the upcoming humiliation she would face as she failed publicly at her Birth Challenge. Now she was more worried about the union interviews.

"I cannot decide *for you, Sabina*. Nor can your father or anyone else. The order is part of the test itself," she pointed out.

Sabina kept her annoyance hidden. Marigold contradicted herself, for that was what she had intended to do. Since Marigold couldn't control Sabina's choice on the Birth Challenge order, she turned to the next weapon in her tool belt. Marigold blamed Sabina for another failure to be responsible for herself.

Marigold pulled another chair out from the table and sat down. "Professor Tobe will expect your answer tomorrow, and you must figure it out on your own. Now! I have something else to tell you before I leave for work. Understand?" She leaned forward, bringing her face closer to Sabina's. It looked like Marigold was attempting to make eye contact despite knowing how uncomfortable eye contact made Sabina feel. Sabina knew she constantly did this to validate that she was understood.

"Yes," Sabina quietly answered as she looked down, annoyed her mother was in her face.

"Do you have an idea which fields you will pick?" she asked.

Sabina nodded, knowing this answer would require the least amount of interaction. She lied.

She had no clue what she was going to choose. She only knew she wanted to be tested on the strength of any Moowins. In all her years of schooling, she hadn't excelled in any area. The only exception was warrior training. Thanks to the hours of training over the years with her father, Sabina naturally excelled in this vocation. However, it happened to be the one strength her father forbade her from revealing. Despite excelling at fighting, Sabina did not want a warrior's job. Brom had convinced Sabina to want something safe, quiet, and away from people. She believed she only liked to train, which she could do alone.

"Good," she asserted. It was likely Marigold wanted to know more, but she was already late for work. She had to let it go even if she didn't trust Sabina to have a plan. Marigold got up from her chair and paced back and forth. She moved on to the next topic. "This should be your father telling you this, but here I am, husbandless once again," she complained.

Sabina squirmed at this old argument between her parents. It was an unsolvable conflict. Brom's work caused him to travel frequently. He was away more than he was home. Sabina didn't like it any more than Marigold, but she didn't blame him for it. She blamed the Ori, like right now; he was missing her Birth Challenge.

Marigold turned on her heels and faced Sabina with her hands forcefully clasped at her waist, a clear sign that she held back rage. "Your father loves you, and out of love, he has set up eight union interviews for you, which are spread out over the next two months, starting the day after your Birth Challenge." Marigold gave a tight-lipped smile while Sabina shot out of her chair, knocking it to the ground.

Eight! Sabina frantically thought. *Eight strangers I must meet with and have this awkward, uncomfortable, get-to-know-you conversation. Eight people who will witness me making a fool of myself in front of them; eight people I have to see again and again. I'm not ready for this. I'm not like other people. It's not easy for me to open up. I don't know what script to follow.* As Sabina's thoughts spiraled, her breathing became labored.

"Everyone will whisper behind my back, mocking me and my special treatment," she whispered. Sabina stood with her mouth hanging open; black spots appeared in her vision as heat flushed her face.

"Don't be so dramatic," Marigold stated with her fist back on her hips. She stood elegant and demanding, with hips slightly forward. Marigold waited for Sabina to pick up the chair and sit back down. "You know your father can **never** follow the rules. Besides, only Brom, the Ori, me, and you know about most of the union interviews. Brom arranged for them to be a private matter. No one in the village will know or suspect you are getting the opportunity to meet with Sky Above's most gifted young men," Marigold said with a hint of spite.

Marigold had never been a fan of how much favoritism she received from Brom. She was sure Marigold was angry with her for getting to meet potential partners with strong Moowins. Sabina searched her memory. She didn't think Brom had arranged union interviews for Fawn, but in her mind, Fawn didn't need the help. Fawn had received weekly requests before her Moowin developed. She could have anyone with her looks, her strong Moowin, and her status in the community. The problem was that she didn't want any of them, which irritated Marigold. Sabina knew she thought her daughter deserved to be with the best.

"All of them have Moowins?" Sabina's voice shook.

With her tight-lipped smile back in place, Marigold nodded. Sabina could practically feel her seething like the warmth of a fire.

Picking up the chair and putting her hands on the table for support, Sabina sat back down gently. She was scared to ask, but desperate to know more. Sabina breathed out. "Why so many?"

Taking a deep inhale through her nose, Marigold took one intentional, slow step toward Sabina at a time as she spoke. The click of her heel started the conversation. Click. "Your father convinced the Ori,"—click— "that you **needed** to have a union interview with someone from each of the Moowins." Click. "Bottom line." Click. "Brom's request benefits the whole village." Click. "Brom is bringing in more Moowins, which strengthens Silvedome." Click. "These Moowin individuals will be potential partners for the *others.*" Click, click. "Thus, his request helps our village by gaining more resources and giving the village the opportunity of new partners for others." Click. "The Ori see an opportunity to create more resources now and in the future, through additional Moowin children." Click. Marigold was back to standing over Sabina, looking coldly down at her.

"But, I . . . I . . . don't . . . have a Moowin," Sabina stammered.

With despise in her voice, Marigold hissed, "**No.** You. *Don't.*"

Sabina heard Marigold's unspoken words. She wasn't good enough. She didn't deserve the advantages that Brom gave her. She was unworthy. Those unspoken words stabbed her in the heart. Sabina longed to say this was not her fault and argue that she hadn't asked for this special treatment or wanted this kind of attention. She desired to fit in and be noticed only for her accomplishments, not her failures. She especially did NOT want attention for any privileges given to her. Suspicion filled Sabina. Marigold was probably waiting for her to fail at this too.

Pleasant and respectable as Marigold was toward her, she was never good at hiding her disdain for the special treatment Brom showed Sabina.

"Listen, *child,* don't worry yourself with these union interviews. The Ori doesn't expect them to result in a union or tying *for you.*"

"*Do you?*" Sabina blurted out in a small act of defiance as her cheeks burned with rejection. She could not believe she dared to challenge Marigold.

Marigold stared down at Sabina for a moment. The silence felt like hot humidity in the air.

Letting her nails click on her teeth, Marigold refused to answer Sabina. Instead, she scowled. "I have to go to work. Fawn is leaving in the morning for a special exhibition. She received the honor of being invited to go to Forge to find material for the upcoming Actalie celebration." For once, Marigold displayed a genuine smile in Sabina's presence. "She will be helping to design the attire for the performances. Her Moowin is flour-is-hing," she boasted.

"I will be a-a-alone?" Sabina swallowed hard, looking back at her grasped hands.

"*Is that all you must say*? You should congratulate your sister. Who, by the way, has exciting news to share with you, yet *she* is the one thinking about you. *That's the difference* . . . between the two of you. You are always thinking *about yourself*, and she is always thinking about others," scolded Marigold.

That wasn't the only difference, Sabina thought as she hugged herself.

With regret in her voice, Marigold instructed Sabina on what to do. "She will need your help soon, and you can congratulate her then. Let her work for now."

Biting on her bottom lip, Sabina wiped at her eyes. She shook her head obediently in shame, in answer, and in sadness. Marigold was right. She was only thinking about herself. Sabina had forgotten about her mother's overnight stay at the hospital and was late coming home. She had skipped dinner with her father because she felt sick to her stomach. Sabina hadn't even thought about what this exhibition would mean to Fawn. Instead, she thought of how scared she was to be alone as she faced these obstacles without her family. Sabina needed to be a better daughter and sister. Maybe she wouldn't feel so much anxiety if she thought about someone other than herself.

Marigold grabbed Sabina's chin lightly and lifted it up, causing Sabina's watery eyes to look at her. "You have much to think about. Use this time wisely."

Sabina looked into Marigold's stone face and knew she needed to pull it together.

"Wh-wh-whaaatt about the Bir-Bir-Birth Challenge?" Sabina stuttered out, unable to hide the wobbling in her voice as Marigold let go of her face.

"I will check in on you later," she answered with a one-shoulder shrug, ending the conversation as if to say it wasn't important enough for her to be there.

Sabina ignored the rejection and rushed to ask more questions before Marigold left. Breathlessly, she rambled, "What about the union interviews? Who, who am I meeting with? Where are they from? Do they know anything about me?" Sabina was standing without intending to do so. She was ready to follow her mother out of the house, but her mother wasn't going toward the front door. Instead, Marigold had walked away from Sabina but remained in the kitchen. Marigold's back was to her with her shoulders hitched. A sign of her annoyance. She paused briefly, seemingly waiting for Sabina's questions to stop. Then she spun on her heels to stare at her. **"Had you been home sooner, I would have had time to answer your questions.** *Now, I am out of time."* She turned back around with her hair swinging slightly and headed toward the kitchen corner, where she pulled out a drawer. "You have no one to blame but yourself for missing the time I had for this conversation. Next time. Don't. Skip. Dinner," she reprimanded, while keeping her back to Sabina.

"Mother," Sabina replied. Her stomach, quietly rumbling, now let out a loud growl. Marigold picked up a folded letter and closed the drawer. She strode purposefully toward Sabina with a blank look on her face. She avoided eye contact as she laid the folded letter on the table. Her fingertips remained still, holding the letter down as she continued looking at it. Sabina faced her mother's shoulder and peered at the letter with curiosity.

"The workers picked up dinner already," Marigold said in a distant voice, still not letting up on the folded letter. Sabina waited for Marigold to say more, but she remained quiet, staring off at nothing.

Uncertainty filled Sabina, so she softly addressed Marigold's concern. "That is okay. I'll find an apple or something."

Sabina felt the urge to pat her mother's shoulder and tell her everything would be all right, but the moment passed. Marigold walked away from Sabina and leaned her head toward the stairs. She shouted, "Fawn, love, I am leaving. Safe travels, and stop by the hospital if you need anything." Sabina heard Fawn answer, "I will," followed by, "Love you too." Marigold passed Sabina without a word or a look and headed for the door. She slipped her heels off and tossed them into her duffle bag before pulling it onto one shoulder. Before Marigold left, she half-turned toward Sabina with her hand on the doorknob, ready to go, and gave her final word. "Don't forget to fast from noon on the day before your challenge and figure out what you want, Sabina, because you are out of time."

Sabina looked at Marigold with her pose, strength, and firm, feminine hands. She let her words roll over her while she pondered other things. *Why was she leaving without saying anything about the letter? It must be important. Why would Brom be willing to use a non-renewable resource otherwise?* Sabina cringed at her selfish thoughts again. Marigold was already out the door and down the steps before Sabina thought to say goodbye.

Saying 'I will miss you or I love you' felt too uncomfortable for Sabina to say. They didn't have an affectionate relationship, so she settled for her usual. "I hope work goes well for you. See you in a few days," she shouted half-heartedly, like this parting was like all the others. Like it was insignificant. Like her world hadn't been turned upside down and her feelings weren't pressing against her rib cage. She took two slow steps back inside the tut and swung the door closed when she heard Fawn's light steps racing down the stairs, which made her pulse race. Her eyes narrowed on the folded paper resting on the kitchen table. She desperately wanted to keep that letter private. Sabina ran to the table, but Fawn got to the letter first.

She swept the letter up and unfolded it. Sabina watched her eyes scan the paper.

"Fawn! The letter is for me. Please . . ." Sabina stretched out her hand.

"I won't tell anyone! *I promise*," she retorted.

"I don't even know what the letter says," Sabina whined.

"All I want to know is who you are having meetings with, A-N-D I recognize only two of the names, which isn't very helpful. I cannot *believe* you are getting a meeting with Pond! I feel cheated." Fawn pouted.

"What? Really? . . . Why?" Sabina doubted this news. Pond didn't meet with anyone.

"Oh, come on, sister. You are beautiful and will be a powerhouse Moowin like our father after your awakening. **I know it**," she confidently proclaimed. Fawn looked up at Sabina, folding the letter and handing it back to her. "I have a thought!" she remarked with enthusiasm. "I'm going to make you an outfit for each meeting," she beamed, grabbing Sabina's forearm, and pulling her toward the stairs. Sabina fumbled with the letter and tucked it into her dress pocket while Fawn pulled her up the stairs. "I don't know that I can pull it off between my studies and traveling," she said, a little out of breath. "A dress a week will be tough under normal circumstances, but I can get friends to help," she announced as she got to the top of the stairs and let go of Sabina's arm. "Oh, wait. That won't work, will it?" she said rhetorically. She continued. "They will ask questions about what the dresses are for, and, with most of the union interviews being private . . ." She paused. She walked down the hallway to her room and turned her head over her shoulder. ". . . I'll have to lie, and I despise lying."

Following Fawn into the room, Sabina saw the elaborate white dress she was making, lying sectioned on the floor. She immediately wanted to leave.

"Do you love it?" Fawn grinned. Her positivity glowed off her skin, whereas Sabina was restraining herself from running out of the room and hiding. Fawn was a talented Performer who designed beautiful, detailed clothing, but that was not what Sabina liked. Sabina preferred simple attire with solid, earthy colors. Their styles clashed, but Fawn loved to gift her friends and family members with the clothing she made. It made her light up like the sun breaking through clouds after a rain shower to give loved ones what she had made. Sabina didn't have the heart to reject her gifts, but she didn't cherish wearing them either.

Sabina didn't take the time to consider the dress. She avoided the question by asking questions, not wanting to hurt Fawn's feelings. "How did you have time to make this? You must have spent the entire day packing and making arrangements for your exhibition."

Taking Sabina's questions for a compliment, Fawn beamed with pride and rushed over to pick up the body of the dress. She brought it to Sabina, lining the dress up to her body, lifting her arms out to the side. Satisfied with how it lined up, Fawn demanded that Sabina strip down to essentials. She was ready to make the finishing touches.

As Fawn worked, she told her all about designing the dress. Sabina attempted to listen to Fawn's one-way conversation, but Sabina was on autopilot manikin mode. Fawn pinned the dress to her until she was happy with how it lay, never questioning or paying attention to Sabina's quietness as she worked. In her element, Fawn didn't seem to sense the sadness in Sabina as she stood in the bedroom, numb with all that life had thrown at her tonight.

Sabina feared she couldn't face the humiliation of the Birth

Challenge or meet these potential mates. She was also ashamed to let her father down at the Birth Challenge. Sabina didn't believe she would achieve a union with one of these men or choose the right future vocation. In addition, she worried for her father while she simultaneously felt sorry for herself that Marigold didn't want to see her on her Birth Challenge. She thought it was her fault Marigold struggled to tell her she loved her. Plus, the fact she wasn't comfortable in Fawn's extravagant attire only made her feel more guilty for wanting something different. She didn't deserve her sister's love or Birth Challenge gift. Shame washed over Sabina like a glove too small for her hand. Here she was, thinking about herself again. A tear silently slid down her face.

"What do you think?" Fawn glowed with pride, turning around to see herself in a narrow mirror along the wall. Then she seemed to notice the trace of the single tear still wet on Sabina's cheek. Fawn's smile fell. She turned Sabina to face her, both hands on her shoulder. Never looking up, Sabina allowed her sister to turn her. Her eyes fell on the folded letter sticking out of her dress pocket, which was lying crumbled on the floor. Immediately, she wondered what that letter would reveal. Would it tell her why her father wanted her to meet someone from each of the Moowins? Would it give her advice on how to function in all this chaos?

"*Be in this moment*, Sabina, and you will find peace. Maybe a little happiness too," Fawn soothed, a smile forming as she spoke. Gazing at her sister's thin, manicured eyebrows and her big brown eyes, Sabina saw Fawn's steady faith that everything was okay. Everything was as it should be, she reminded herself. A mantra she used to calm herself.

"Why don't you do something for me?" Fawn coaxed. "*Believe in yourself as I believe in you.*"

"You see potential in everyone," Sabina responded in a monotone voice.

"I see potential in what is."

"Name one thing I am good at," Sabina challenged.

"Don't forsake yourself. You have greatness in you. You only need to unlock it," Fawn pushed back.

"Yeah . . . right," Sabina said with disbelief.

"You think my life is so great? It's not. Life is hard, and it's unfair, and it will tear you up if you let it," Fawn shot back fiercely. "You think it is easy for me to see father's devotion to you while Mom and I struggle for his attention?"

Sabina looked down, feeling her stomach clench. The silence lingered.

"*It's not your fault*, Sabina," she mentioned with kindness, "*but I want to matter to him too.*"

Uncomfortable with the truth, but desiring to hear something comforting, Sabina pressed on. "You didn't name one thing I'm good at."

Dropping her hands from Sabina's shoulders, Fawn adjusted the pins on the dress. "You are good at holding yourself back," she revealed. Her voice was quiet, and she avoided eye contact.

The words hurt. Tears fell freely.

Fawn inquired, "I don't know why you do it . . . I've seen you. When no one is looking, you are determined, strong, . . . confident."

She stopped messing around with the pins and looked up at her. The whites of her eyes were noticeable as she looked at Sabina.

"I want to be *you* in those moments," she admitted, casting her eyes to the side.

Sabina's toes tingled at her admission. Never in her life would Sabina have thought her perfect sister—who had everyone's admiration, who had stunning looks, talent others envied, and an aura of happiness—would want to be her: an unnoticeable, unwanted failure.

Jutting her chin slightly, Fawn remarked, "I tried to create a dress to resemble that."

Wiping her face of tears with the side of her index finger, Sabina looked down at the dress pinned to her and saw it was beautiful. She was expecting a dress with lace and shiny satin that revealed her figure. Although the body of the dress was form-fitting, it stretched with her, which allowed her to breathe and move freely. The corset was fitted and made of thick material with a faint brownish-gold trim with multiple diagonal lines from her waist to her chest. The chest was outlined in the same trim and covered in a white, stretchy material. The way the corset framed her chest gave the illusion of two mountains. It was sleeveless, with leather buttons along the center of the body. The buttons led to a pleated skirt of overlapping dark-brown worn leather that lay high on her thighs but hung longer in the back, reaching just above her knees. Turning to look in the mirror, Sabina marveled at how strong and brave she looked. She saw confidence and authority.

Stepping closer to Sabina, Fawn put her hands on the back of her arms. The top of her head only reached Sabina's shoulders, but she leaned in, giving her a little squeeze, a half- hug, as she announced, "This is who I see."

Sabina was unrecognizable. She stared at this person in the mirror and choked, "I look like one of the ancient warriors."

Sweeping Sabina's hair over one shoulder, Fawn glowed with pride as she looked at her in the mirror. "You know, . . . I've turned down all those requests for union interviews because . . . because I want to know who I am . . . when no one is looking."

Letting go of Sabina, Fawn played with a strip of fabric, repeatedly pulling it through her hands. Sabina looked over her shoulder at her sister in stunned disbelief. With her eyes down-cast, she explained, "You and I are a lot alike. We both comply and do what is expected of us in front of others. The difference is, you know who you are when no one is looking and . . . and I'm afraid to face who I am when I am alone."

"How can you say that?" Sabina whispered. *You have every-thing I want.*

She shook her head 'no' with a sadness Sabina rarely witnessed in her sister.

"I don't understand." Sabina turned to face her sister. Her sister, who she tried to be like, confessed to wanting something she had. Sabina couldn't even grasp what that could be. She didn't have anything. She didn't have friends, talents, status, looks, or good grades. What could Fawn want that she had? To be comfortable being alone? Well, that was no prize. Sabina was tired of being alone.

Fawn shrugged and started to gently remove Sabina's dress. She moved around her but did not speak of it anymore. Not wanting to get stuck with pins, Sabina remained silent and still as her sister worked. She didn't understand what Fawn meant by her statement. How could Fawn not know who she was? Fawn couldn't be anyone else. *Should I tell her I see her as someone who treats everyone with love and respect?* Sabina admired that Fawn saw goodness in everyone, and Fawn always found a reason to smile. That was who she was. That was not an act. Did she need to be reminded of that?

Breaking the silence, Fawn pried. "You have eight union interviews . . . I think it is wonderful you are getting this unique opportunity," she acknowledged with increasing warmth in her voice. "But . . ." She stopped working for a moment. "I don't want you to rush into anything or do something you regret."

Despite knowing her sister was talking out of concern, Sabina felt anger snap through her. "Just because you're not interested in being in a union with anyone doesn't mean I won't be interested," she proclaimed with some restraint. Sabina didn't know where her anger was coming from, though her anxiety over having these union interviews was building. Yet she secretly wished for a boy's attention or to be noticed. She didn't want that hope taken away, even if she feared it simultaneously. What did her sister know anyway? She could make the meanest boy's ice-cold heart melt and then he would fawn over her with the deepest desire to please her. Everywhere she went, she went with someone who wanted to be around her. She had it all: the success, the looks, the endless possibilities of love. She had their parents' approval and a

Moowin that grew stronger daily. She didn't know what it was like to be forgotten and left behind. Fawn didn't see how rejection plagued her or how Sabina sat in the dark corners of The Mox, watching her classmates having a great time together without her. Living with the hollowing out of her soul every time her classmates didn't include her. At night, when she sat alone in her room, she could hear her classmates laughing, teasing, and discussing whatever production they had seen through the open window of her bedroom as they passed by. She wished she could forget all those nights. Then it wouldn't hurt, and she could heal from feeling hollow.

Her family didn't even notice when she went to the productions alone. Of course, she went after they left. Still, her family thought she liked staying home. They thought it was her choice to be alone. As Sabina thought about it, she shrugged to herself. Maybe she did prefer to be alone. She didn't ask for what she wanted. Was it fair to hold them responsible for leaving her behind when she never stated what she wanted? She returned to the thought that no one knew her. So how could Fawn know her? Sabina didn't express any of these thoughts. She kept her thoughts to herself, but they brought up painful emotions.

Unable to hide the hurt in her voice, she crossed her arms and defended her decision. "I have never had someone be interested in me before. *You don't know* what I have gone through."

"Haven't you ever noticed that when you walk through the village, you walk with your head up no matter how much people beat you down? You are not like others who are shy or lack confidence. They keep their heads down. But not you."

"That's because *my* father taught me to be aware of my surroundings," Sabina shouted, feeling uncomfortable with this new perspective.

"Is that the *only* reason?" Fawn pushed.

"Why are we having this conversation?" Sabina practically growled.

"Because . . ." Fawn raised her voice with frustration and

cleared her throat. "Because I love you. Because I'm sorry I didn't do more for you." Fawn ran her hands along Sabina's arms. Sabina let her arms fall by her sides. "Because in three more days, you will have your Birth Challenge, and everything will change. Because I am worried for you," she mentioned with increasing concern in her voice. She squeezed one of Sabina's hands as she circled her. "I don't want you to have these union interviews and think this is the only opportunity you will have to find happiness in a partner."

At Fawn's words, the fear she would always be alone pulsed through her. A part of Sabina *did* think this was her only opportunity to find a partner. She took a deep breath. She had experienced so much mental chatter since she talked to her father. Brom offered her a solution, and she was contemplating taking it. Was that wrong? The fact was, the loneliness within her was ready to agree to a union with one of these eight union interviews even if they weren't a good fit for her.

Done replacing the pins with loose stitches, Fawn was ready for Sabina to take the dress off. She put the wristband pincushion and thread on the floor where she had worked earlier. Then she walked back to Sabina. Sabina pushed her fingers into her temple and looked down to concentrate. She needed to sort through the flood of thoughts.

Gently pulling Sabina's hands from her temples, Fawn soothed, "Even though Brom may know what is best for you, *he doesn't know your heart.*" Fawn brought Sabina's hands into a prayer position and placed her hands over hers. "I want you to allow yourself to live before you attach yourself to someone. You need a chance to be who you are without anyone telling you what or how to do it, before you—"

"That's-you-Fawn," Sabina snapped. Her temper flared as she pulled her hands away.

Fawn pressed on. "There is a reason why you get to choose the name you will go by when you transition into adulthood. Your life completely changes, and you become your own identity. *You don't understand . . .*" Fawn had sadness back in her voice. She was holding her arms and murmuring so quietly she could have been talking to herself. Her behavior made Sabina immediately calm down and squint at her to focus. She was looking down and shaking her head back and forth like she was denying a nightmare coming to life. "Most people don't come back to live with their parents once they go to Tradel school. Suddenly, you are expected to decide on every little thing for yourself. You, and only you, are accountable for every decision. There is no guidance." Even softer, she sniveled, "There is no help." Tears slid down Fawn's face, which caused Sabina to pause.

Sabina felt tired, hungry, and beyond thirsty. She didn't want this conversation. It was easier being alone than listening to her sister give unsolicited advice. Yet, Fawn's tears cut through some of Sabina's unwillingness to listen. Her sister never cried. Sighing to herself, Sabina asked, "Why are you upset? You may have left home, but you frequently see Mother and Father. They are always helping you and giving you advice. You are not—"

"Have you ever thought about what you want your name to be?" she interrupted. "Or have you only thought about what Father wants your name to be?" Her voice sounded defeated, but her eyes challenged Sabina.

"I don't know," Sabina responded with an attitude. "Rose, Autumn, Dove . . . What does it *matter*?"

"*It matters because **it's your choice**,*" she yelled as she wiped her tears and looked defiantly at Sabina. "It's the very *first* choice you get to make for *yourself*. It matters because, with time, our parents' hold on you lessens." Fawn turned away from Sabina and walked over to her bed. As she sank onto the bed, she said, "I wish I would have chosen a different name."

Sabina walked over and sat next to her. For the first time, she felt sorry for Fawn. Picking a name was important even if Sabina hadn't cared what people would call her. She understood people judged you for the name you chose, and it shaped the way people saw you. She had planned to pick a familiar name. One no one would think twice about or give attention to.

"I wish I would have chosen a name where people took me seriously instead of a name I thought would please Mother. I might as well be a delicate flower," she complained, hanging her head.

Rubbing Fawn's back, Sabina felt unequipped to handle such sensitive matters. She wondered if she should ask Fawn if she wanted to be called by a different name. *What name would Fawn choose if she could select differently, knowing what she knows now?*

Fawn sighed. "Maybe Fawn was the right choice. I was young and naive," she concluded, getting up and rubbing her face. Fawn mumbled, appearing to dismiss her emotions. "Whatever. A rose by any other name is still a rose." Then speaking up, she told Sabina, "It's too late for me, but it's not too late for you." Turning back to face Sabina, she signaled for her to stand up. She took the dress off Sabina and laid the material on the floor. Then, she sat cross-legged and stitched the fabric she had pinned as if she didn't have any more to say. Sabina pulled her tunic dress back on and hovered. She felt desperate to say something to ease the situation, but she didn't want to say the wrong thing. She was afraid to say what she wanted. "Fawn . . . I love the dress. Thank you." Fawn didn't acknowledge her, which wasn't like her. Sabina assumed she was pretending to be lost in her thoughts or work, so she continued to hover. The conversation with her mother flashed in her mind, and she sat down on the floor by Fawn.

"Are you excited about your exhibition?" Sabina faked interest.

"I am." She gave a small smile, glancing at Sabina. She continued to sew, and Sabina watched her precise stitch work. "I'm a little nervous too." She pulled a stitch through the fabric, stretching her arm out. "I am the youngest person invited to this exhibition and to have design approval. That means I am in charge of Performers who have been doing this for much longer than me. Not everyone is taking that so well."

"Your designs are amazing, and you must have earned the right to lead. I'm sure you'll do a great job picking out the right fabrics for the designs."

She nodded dismissively. "I am most excited about getting to see someplace besides Silvedome." She was smiling with mischief as she rested her stitch work. "This is my first time outside the dome. I might meet someone I haven't known my whole life. Maybe meet someone fascinating and rebellious." She wiggled her eyebrows.

"What?" Sabina snorted out a laugh. "You want someone who breaks the rules?" She shook her head in disbelief but was unable to resist a full-out smile. "I cannot see it, but I'd like to!"

Fawn brightened and smiled back. Focusing on her work once more, Fawn confessed, "I want to know what love is . . . not the love that Mother and Father have, but a passion . . . Everyone here is so focused on what they can gain," she trailed off, slightly humming to herself as she worked.

Pinching her eyebrows together, Sabina processed what Fawn had said. She never thought about her parents' relationship.

"What's wrong with what our parents have?" Sabina asked as she processed what Fawn implied. "They respect and love each other. They are loyal to each other. They talk about anything and everything without fighting. They take care of each other. They are best friends. That's what they both want."

"Nothing's wrong with their relationship. I . . . I want something different. That's all."

"Father says passion is for the young and foolish. It dies with time. He says it's important that you partner with someone you can envision being friends with for the rest of your life. That it's more important that your morals and values align than having someone you want to kiss." Sabina realized she had recited what Brom had told her repeatedly. Now she sat embarrassed for having said it.

"Mmm . . . Father's never had that conversation with me." Her face remained disciplined as she continued working.

"Oh." What else could Sabina say? She felt guilty that Brom had not treated Fawn the same way as he treated her. "What does Mother say?"

"She wants me to have a union with someone with a strong Moowin who will treat me with love and respect. She wants me to have the best. Honestly, that could be many people. But it's what she doesn't say that I'm more interested in."

"What do you mean? What's she not saying," Sabina asked with curiosity. Marigold hadn't talked to her about unions. Instead, she acted like it would be a miracle if someone asked her for a date.

She took a deep breath and sat the dress down as she exhaled. "I think Mother wishes she had someone who would hold her and kiss her hair when she had a bad day," Fawn admitted.

"Mother? She hates affection," Sabina rebutted.

Shrugging, Fawn said, "Or she fears it."

Sabina stared at Fawn, not sure what to think. Fawn had a better relationship with Mother, and she was more insightful than any other person Sabina knew outside of Seers.

"If she fears it, why do you think she wants to have it?"

"My guess is because my real father was affectionate, and she never wanted to open herself up to that again after his passing. I think our father is the same way." Fawn picked up her needle and stitched once more.

Sabina thought about it. There was truth to that statement, she realized. Brom was dedicated to her birth mother's memory still. She knew he held her birth mother in high regard. He didn't want to let go of her even though it had been nearly sixteen years since her passing. He didn't mention her often, but when he did, his emotions flared as if he was still grieving her loss.

Sabina's mind felt like it would crack in half. It was all too much.

"I think I need to go eat." Sabina got up, but Fawn quickly grabbed her hand and squeezed.

"Wait. I need to tell you something. This is important, Sabina! You need to hear me," she warned, tugging her down.

Putting her sewing project aside and squaring herself to Sabina, she declared, "I'm sorry. I haven't always been a good older sister to you. I could have defended you better when others made fun of you. I realize I didn't even try. I just watched, wishing they would stop. I'm embarrassed that I was no better than the villagers in making you an outsider. I didn't see the real you even though I thought I did. I let you walk through life alone. I'm sorry. I'm sorry, but I promised myself to do b—"

"Quit it, Fawn," Sabina hollered in distress. She looked out into the hallway before pressing her fingertips into her eyes. "I don't know what has gotten into you tonight, but you need to **stop it**. I have enough on my mind. I don't need your confessions on whatever you feel guilty about. I'm over it. It's fine." Huffing in aggravation, Sabina got up again, but Fawn grabbed her arm with desperation.

"After this Birth Challenge, you will go off to Tradel school and face a new world. You'll figure out things are not what they seem and you'll be pushed outside your comfort zone. Then you will realize our parents aren't perfect, as I did," Fawn uttered in a rush.

Feeling her heart beating in her throat, Sabina reached over to pry Fawn's fingers from her arm. A million thoughts were going through her mind, but one message pushed through the haze. What had Fawn gone through over the last nine months, and what did she need to know to protect herself? She had barely seen her sister. On the outside, she still seemed the same, but at this moment, Sabina thought she was barely holding on. Insecurity didn't look right on her sister. Torn between shutting down and needing to know how to protect herself from whatever Fawn was going through, Sabina bit down on her lower lip, thinking about what she should say.

"Did something happen to you at the Tradel?" she asked with concern, sitting back down.

"No," she blushed, sweeping her loose hair behind her ear. "Maybe. I don't want to talk about it." She ignored Sabina as she picked up her sewing project. She focused on her stitch work briefly and then rested it down. "I . . ." She swallowed. "It's just that you don't know what you don't know until you do," she voiced, looking down. "It's nothing. I grew up . . . that's all. I'm being dramatic." She shook her head and returned to her sewing. She continued. "I just want you to be prepared because no one prepared me." Pulling the stitch through, Fawn remained quiet and focused on her work.

Annoyance flashed through Sabina at the insult. Her sister thought she needed to grow up too. She didn't remember having a childhood. She certainly wasn't having a good time in life. If she hadn't gotten a dose of struggles and challenging times, then Sabina reasoned that she had at least practiced handling hardships. Burying her annoyance, Sabina reached over and put her hand on top of her sister's. "Stop for a moment. Something is bothering you, and I will listen. Please . . . tell me."

Her sister—with her bangs falling into her eyelashes, with her defined cheekbones—why would anyone want to hurt her? She was delicate, something to protect. Was she naive? Probably. Okay, most definitely. But she had everyone wrapped around her finger her whole life. Maybe it was different at Tradel school. Perhaps she had finally met someone who didn't think everything she did was perfect.

She gave in. "I want someone to love me for my flaws, my imperfections, not how perfect I am. And I want that for you too." It seemed to Sabina that Fawn pretended to be nonchalant as she sewed, but she saw her eyes flicker to the side to catch her reaction. Sky Above, she thinks she is so damn perfect all the time, Sabina thought, grinding her teeth.

"Is this about the union interviews, the Birth Challenge, or Tradel school?" she questioned, confused and irritated. Then she had a thought. "Is this about Pond asking me for a union interview?"

"Noooo," she rejected. "Although"—she leaned forward inquisitively—"Pond hasn't asked anyone for a union interview that I know of, and he has turned down all requests. Has he ever indicated that he likes you?"

"Nooo . . . wah," Sabina stressed, drawing out her answer. "I've hardly talked to him." She pinched her eyebrows together.

"Huh. Must be Father then."

"Yeah . . . must be," she agreed dryly.

"Father's letter is proof of his imperfections," Fawn announced quietly to herself as if Sabina wasn't in the room anymore. She looked deep in thought and frozen in action.

Sabina looked at Fawn in utter confusion until she came to the conclusion that she didn't realize she had said that out loud.

Fawn nodded toward the letter sticking out of Sabina's tunic pocket. "It's all in there."

Is she changing topics again? How am I supposed to keep up with this conversation? Is she upset about something that happened at Tradel, the eight union interviews, or Father's favoritism? "You're freaking me out, Fawn. I don't know what that letter says, but Father has always been honest with me, and I trust him. Besides, no one is perfect."

"I'm not saying you shouldn't trust him. I'm saying it's okay to want something different for yourself than what our parents want. *And . . .* the deepest type of love is the love that lets you be your whole self without making you feel less . . . without making you change." Shrugging one shoulder higher than the other as she lifted her palms, she added, "I guess I'm also saying I want you to stop holding back for others' sake." She locked eyes with Sabina.

Sabina dropped her head into her hands and groaned. Her head was pulsing. It was a day when she couldn't make anyone happy. Father told her to hide what she could do. Her sister told her to show her true colors. Her mother . . . her mother didn't believe in her. Pain coursed through her body at these thoughts. Sabina didn't know who she was supposed to be. In one way, Fawn was right. When no one was around, Sabina was a different person. A more confident and self-assured person. Yet, she fell apart when people directed any attention toward her.

"Go eat something. Your stomach has been grumbling this whole time," Fawn mothered, nudging Sabina's hands away from her face.

Sabina got up off the floor, feeling heavy and tired. She shuffled her feet to the door.

"I'll have this done for you tonight. I plan on leaving early in the morning. I'll lay this on my bed for you. But . . . I'm here for you if you want to talk after you read Father's letter."

Fawn finished her stitch and looked up with her bright smile, the sadness gone.

Too tired to answer, Sabina dragged her feet out of the room, one hand brushing the bumpy wall as she walked down the hall.

The Letter

Entering the kitchen, Sabina sighed in relief to finally be alone with her thoughts. The toll of the taxing conversations caused her head to ache. Plus, she had gone too long without food and water. Irritated, Sabina went to the first kitchen cabinet in search of food. She was looking for nuts, fruit, dried meat, or bread, typically found in the cupboard. Unfortunately, the cabinets were empty of food. *Of course, they are,* thought Sabina. It was Mother's overnight stay in the village. She wouldn't have wanted anything to spoil while she was gone.

Villagers prepared food in the town square, where most people ate their meals. However, dinners were delivered nightly, with fresh water for the basin. An hour later, a worker would come by to pick up the uneaten food and exchange the laundry. Now that Fawn was away in Tradel school and Brom was always gone on his scouting trips, Marigold didn't keep much food stocked in the kitchen. Marigold only needed one meal a day and the night meal wasn't one of them. Sabina had to fend for herself.

She walked outside and poured a cup of water, knowing the water would fill her empty stomach . . . if she drank enough of it. It would at least hold her hunger off till tomorrow morning. She finished her first cup and poured a second one. She smirked at the realization no one would complain tonight if she took her cup to her room. One advantage to being parentless was that there was no one to tell you what to do. She shuffled into her room and closed the heavy, red, patterned drapes that acted as a door.

The room was bare like all the rooms in Silvedome, but hers was particularly empty. The room lacked any personalization, as if it was a room designated for guests. Nothing in the room reflected who Sabina was or what interested her. There were no wood carvings or hung artwork. There were no decorative pillows or rugs. The only color came from the natural pine of the small chest and nightstand, a standard quilted blanket on her bed, and the red patterned door which matched the window curtains. Sabina hadn't even picked out her 'door' or curtains. Her mother had, and they meant nothing to her other than privacy.

Upon closing her door, Sabina looked up from the floor to find a large piece of bread and an apple sitting on top of a clean set of folded clothes. Marigold was a complicated person. It wasn't often that she saved Sabina from suffering the consequences of her choices. Smiling and grateful, Sabina silently thanked her mother for saving food for her. She grabbed the bread with haste and took a massive bite. Clenching her teeth, Sabina tore the drying bread apart. She put her cup down on the wood chest and sat on her bed. The curtains were open, which meant that her nosy neighbor could have been peering in as she sometimes did. However, the streets were empty.

She pulled her father's letter out of her pocket and took another bite of bread. She hardly noticed the crumbs fall off her lap onto her bed and the floor. She usually hated crumbs on her bed, but she was lost in thought. Sabina stared at the folded letter. She debated if she should read the letter now or later. Sabina knew she would fester if she read the letter before bed. She would toss and turn all night while she thought about what her father wanted her to do now. If she waited till the morning, she could read the letter alone in her sanctuary, where she felt safe.

Deciding, she folded the letter in half and stuffed it back into the pocket of her tunic. She held the bottom of her dress with one hand and the bread in the other. The crumbs gathered in her scooped dress. She sank her teeth into the bread again, not biting but using her teeth to hold the bread. She made her way quickly to the front door, attempting to keep the remaining breadcrumbs from falling onto the floor, and stepped outside, dropping the bottom of her dress as soon as she got to the edge of the porch. The breadcrumbs fell, some to the porch and some to the ground. She kicked the crumbs to the grass as best as possible, now holding the bread in her hand.

The village was dormant with sleep. Even the dirt settled on the street without the wind or foot traffic. She sat in the old wooden rocking chair and ate the rest of her bread. Her eyes were unfocused as she looked at the tut across the walkway. Her eyelids were getting heavy, and she struggled to keep them open.

She wanted to analyze tonight's conversations. She had to figure out why her sister was helping her when she had a big adventure waiting for her. Plus, she hadn't figured out why she felt the heat of anger sweep across her in the field with her father. She wanted time to feel sorry for herself that everyone in her family was abandoning her on the most important day of her life in this talent-obsessed village. It was useless. She couldn't hold on to a single thought. So her thoughts roamed, unable to focus on anything. Her eyes watered, and she stopped hearing the crickets. She absentmindedly chewed on her bread until it got stuck to the roof of her mouth. It scratched her dry throat as she swallowed. Dull pain at her temples flared each time she pried her eyes open. The air was crisp, and goosebumps spread across her skin. Sabina was too tired and numb to move. She needed to get a drink of water and go inside, but she remained sitting. The emotional weight of the day had drained her. The last thing she remembered before drifting into a deep sleep was a vision of her wearing her Birth Challenge dress to meet Pond. She went to hug him, but he stepped back from her. Then the bread dropped to the floor, and she was asleep.

She dreamed of her father's mare kicking up dirt and rock as it raced across the open clearing toward the village bridge. She felt herself fly backward as if the horse kicked her upon taking off. She landed in a pile of mud that was cold and dense. Her energy leaked out of her instantly as she attempted to sit up. Her bones felt like steel beams that anchored her down, increasing the speed of how quickly she sank into the mud. She panicked as she thrust her jaw above the ground. Her lips were cracked and bleeding. She was so thirsty that the inside of her cheeks stuck to her gums. She was unable to move. Her throat was too dry to scream to her father, who was racing off in the distance. She was alone, helpless, and incapable of doing anything. Inside her mind, she begged her father to turn around, see her, and come back for her. He would find a way to save her. He made the impossible possible. If only he would turn and look at her. But he didn't turn. She sealed her mouth shut to prevent the mud from rushing in. She struggled to take one last deep breath through her nose before the world went black.

Sabina was lost in the black void of sleep when Fawn pulled roughly on her arm. She had taken one of her arms and wrapped it around her neck. She had attempted to pull Sabina up but was unable to handle her weight and additional height. She lost her balance. She fell to the floor, letting Sabina fall back into the chair. Sabina hit the arm of the chair, and her eyes flew open in pain. She sat up.

"Whaaatt?" Sabina moaned.

"Who falls asleep outside?" Fawn muttered to herself testily, getting up and dusting her bottom off.

"Oh no, **DON'T** you fall back asleep," Fawn insisted, rushing over to Sabina. "Come on," she demanded, "help me get you to bed."

"Nuh." Sabina awkwardly waved her sister off, arms heavy and stiff from the cold.

Fawn dipped her fingers into the cold water of the basin. Then she brought her fingers above Sabina. She let the drops of water hit the back of Sabina's neck.

"Ahh! Why'd you do that?" Sabina howled, automatically sitting up and bringing her shoulders up to her ears. "I'm tired," she grumbled. Her eyes were already closing as she slumped back into the chair.

"You're tired?" Fawn said sarcastically, putting her hands on her hips. "I've been sewing half the night . . . for *you*, mind you. Now, put your arm around my neck and **stand up**," she bossed with Mother's authoritative tone.

Not waiting, Fawn guided Sabina's stiff, cold arm around her neck. "Tullom, you feel like an ice cube. What were you thinking, falling asleep out here?"

Rubbing her face with her other hand, Sabina tipped her weight forward and pushed off the arm of the rocking chair to stand up. She was a head taller than Fawn and forty pounds heavier. She staggered to balance Sabina's weight against her more petite frame, but she reached the door.

"Mother would *never* allow this behavior if she was here. What are you going to do without someone taking care of you?" Fawn criticized with what little breath she had.

Turning the handle and kicking the door open, she shuffled quickly through the door. She left the door open and leaned her shoulder against the wall to rest until she kicked the door closed behind her. Fawn squeezed Sabina's side as she positioned herself into a bear hug. She half dragged, half shuffled Sabina into her room, keeping one shoulder on the wall for support the whole time. The soft drapes rubbed Sabina's face, and she batted at them to clear them away. Fawn took five quick running steps, letting the momentum of her fall carry Sabina to the bed. Twisting slightly, she let go of Sabina as they both flew toward the bed. This time, Fawn was able to catch herself before she fell. Sabina, on the other hand, crashed into the bed. Her face hit the edge of her pillow, and she rolled to her side. Fawn lifted Sabina's legs onto the bed. Sabina opened her eyes to glare at Fawn. She pointed her finger to her cup of water on the chest.

Taking a deep breath from the effort of shuffling Sabina to her bed, Fawn fussed over her sister as she covered her up. "Ugh, you are heavier than a bolt of fabric," she complained. Fawn swept her fingers over her cupid's brow, looking in the direction Sabina pointed. She reached for the water as she talked. "I need to go to the spa and get a massage after all that. Here," she said matter-of-factly. She brought the cup to Sabina's lip and put her hand behind her head to lift it. Taking the cup with both hands, Sabina drank the water greedily. It sloshed out the sides of the cup and onto her neck and chest. After wiping it off, Fawn took the cup and rested it on her nightstand.

Sabina started to shiver now that she was warming up. Fawn worried over how Sabina's skin was ice-cold to the touch. She went to the chest and opened the middle doors, swinging them open and grabbing Sabina's only spare blanket. She tossed it over her, and after a moment, she told Sabina she would be back with an extra blanket.

Fawn came into the room and Sabina's back was to her, but she knew that she was asleep. With care, she placed the blanket on her and whispered a prayer of health and safety. Fawn stayed, not wanting to leave her sister. She felt responsible for her even though Sabina was technically older. Sabina didn't know that, but Fawn did. She had long known what Sabina would face in this upcoming Birth Challenge. The thought made Fawn squirm and a knot formed in her stomach. She placed her hand delicately on her sister's shoulder.

"I'm on your side," she whispered. "I hope you forgive me . . . I hope you will forgive us all." She stood motionless, looking at her sister's beautiful face with her strong jawline. She was mesmerized by her sister's ability to be so strong and independent. "I'm a coward," she cried as tears fell. Fawn jumped as Sabina rolled onto her back. The letter in her pocket made a crackling noise as she shifted.

Creeping forward, Fawn slowly pulled the quilted covers back and saw the edge of her father's folded letter hanging outside Sabina's dress pocket. She bit her nails in deliberation. Fawn desperately wanted to know what was in that letter. Earlier, she had glanced at the list of union interviews, but that was all she managed before she had to give it back to Sabina. Her father had been distant from her all her life to protect Sabina and keep this secret. Fawn thought of her younger self, full of envy toward her sister and full of self-pity for not having her father's attention. Fawn smirked at her more youthful, foolish self. Now, she felt grim thinking how Sabina stood at a crossroads of who she would be.

Fawn recalled the first time she realized there was something more to Sabina's odd behavior. Brom hadn't confided in her. It was by accident that she discovered the truth. For when Fawn was little, she spied on her father often. She was desperate to know why Sabina was so unique in her father's eyes and why she wasn't. Fawn had striven for years to be the perfect child, the perfect daughter. By village standards, she was perfect. Yet her weak little sister, who failed at everything and spent her whole life hiding in shadows, was Brom's favorite. Fawn wanted nothing to do with her younger sister until that one night when she had overheard her parents arguing. It was only faint sounds in the night with harsh s's and t's drifting down to her room. Fawn had slipped out of bed without a sound and put her ear to the wall, stealing her breath and closing her eyes. She had concentrated on hearing what her parents said. It came back to her now as she sat watching her sister sleep.

~

"You **cannot** leave. I won't *let* you," Marigold barked.

"Marigold, I beg of you, don't draw this line," Brom pleaded.

"This is not what I signed up for, Brom . . . I care about you."

Fawn could hear the strain in her mother's voice as if she was trying not to cry.

"No, don't. I don't want your sympathy. You don't get to hug me and then ride off during the night on some crusade." Marigold's voice was firm before spitting in anger, "You are playing a dangerous game that's going to get you killed."

"I am doing what I must to keep my daughter safe," Brom countered.

"What about *my* daughter? What about her safety? You are bringing harm . . ."

"Sssshhh. You are getting loud. You will wake the kids."

Fawn could hear shuffling noises which muffled what her father said next. "I promise you that no harm will come to you or Beatrice. **You are safe.** I have a million safeguards in place. It's Sabina . . . I must . . . all our sake . . . you must understand . . . she is sup . . . essed . . . Keep to Lan . . . it's wrong . . . trust me."

Fawn could not hear any movement, and she wondered if they knew she was listening. She hadn't made a sound. Guessing Brom must have finished packing his bag, Fawn waited to hear more.

Finally, she heard her mother say defiantly, "If you leave, I *won't* stay."

The room suddenly felt tiny. She wanted to scream "stop it" repeatedly but didn't move. Her parents never fought. Fawn didn't like it. She felt intense distress at the fact that her mother was being emotional.

"Oh, Marigold," her father pointed out in a defeated voice. "Cannot you see that you and Beatrice are only safe if you stay here?"

Fawn could barely hear the quiet "Yes" from her mother. Her mind was spinning with what this could mean. She decided they were talking about her mother going with him on his scouting trip. He was always going on scouting trips to find new talent. She agreed with her father. Her mother should stay. Where would she and Sabina go without their mother?

"Stay until Sabina's Birth Challenge. Then you and Beatrice are free to live your lives and go where you want."

"She will hate you for what you have done."

"I'd rather her hate me and be alive than the alternative."

There was a quiet thud as if he swung his backpack on his back.

"For what it's worth, I care deeply for you and Beatrice. You are my family, and I will protect you as you have protected Sabina and me."

The door creaked open. Fawn's heartbeat exploded in her chest. Paralyzed with fear, she felt like she had been caught spying, despite knowing she was unnoticed in her room.

"We saved each other once! Remember?" Brom reminded her mother in a gravelly voice. He waited a few seconds before saying, "I know you are scared, but I will live through this. Look for me in a few weeks." Brom's light footsteps were inaudible that night over Marigold's uncharacteristic sniffling, and then he was gone.

Unlike his scouting trips, which took two to three weeks, Brom was gone for months before returning home. Even though Fawn did not understand most of their exchange, she knew her parents held a secret between them. Fawn questioned everything her parents said and did after that. She knew her father was her stepfather and that her world no longer felt safe.

Bringing herself back to the present moment, Fawn reached out and carefully slid her father's note out of Sabina's pocket.

The following day, the sun blazed through the open curtains of Sabina's room. The sound of birds chirping aroused Sabina from her sleep. She lay with her eyes closed, wishing to drift off again. She felt the damp sweat on the back of her knees and lower back from the extra blankets stacked on her. She tossed the covers off. Sitting up, she placed her feet on the ground. Her arms were by her sides, elbows locked, and her fingers curled over the bed's edge. She let her head hang as she thought of last night's conversations with her father, mother, and sister. She turned her head toward her nightstand, noticing something in her peripheral vision. Through the sun's bright rays, she saw her bruised apple, a cup of water, and her father's letter on her nightstand.

Wait . . . Didn't I have that letter folded up in my tunic?

Still wearing the same tunic dress from yesterday, she stood up and patted both empty pockets. She was in disbelief that her sister would have removed her private letter from her dress.

"Burning Fires, Fawn!" she fumed as she reached over to her letter.

She could feel the heat of anger on her cheeks. She held the letter in her hands, dirt still under her fingernails. Unfolding the letter, Sabina recognized her father's beautiful, neat cursive writing. He wrote in tight lines with minimal spacing to make the most of the single page. At the bottom of the page was a different script.

Lifting the page to her face, Sabina read:

If you feel that Father betrayed you, then consider my perspective. Father gave you freedom from living up to others' expectations. You can live your adult life without pressure or fear of disappointment. That is a gift. Love, your big sister. XOXOXOXO

Looking at her sister's bubbly handwriting filled Sabina with disgust and annoyance. The childish part of Sabina desired to crumble the letter into a tight ball and squeeze the letter in her fist until she felt her fingernails dig into her skin. However, the more practical side of her knew she would be upset at herself later for ruining something that could be important.

"Freedom," she huffed in anger. *What does freedom mean?*

We are always subject to conditioning; if not from others, then from ourselves. She must think I'm impaired. I may be at the bottom of my performance, but I still complete my assignments. Does she think I am incapable?

Sabina dragged her fingers through her loose hair. She tossed the letter onto her bed. She went to her drapes, knowing before she looked that her sister would be gone. Even if Fawn were still there, Sabina wouldn't be able to tell her sister how she felt about this violation. Instead, Sabina griped to herself that being nine months older didn't entitle Fawn to mother her. She was always giving unsolicited advice that was not needed or wanted. Pulling the drapes aside, Sabina saw Fawn's duffel bag was gone. Free to be perturbed out loud, Sabina animatedly talked to herself. "Great, she left. I don't even know when Fawn will be back. How dare she read *my* private letter? I cannot believe she dared to write on it. Who is she to tell me how to think?"

She went to her chest, where her sister had moved the clean, folded clothes from the night before. Sabina wondered if she had moved them before she had tossed her on the bed or if she had to refold them. Perfect Fawn, she thought as she whipped her tunic off. She threw her tunic down to the ground by her feet. Then she grabbed her compression leggings and pulled one leg in at a time.

"What? Are all my secrets hers to have, but she hides all of hers from me?" she fussed, hopping in place as she pulled on her leggings. Next, she yanked her binder closed with little care or comfort. *"I don't even know what the letter says,"* she grumbled, getting more worked up. She carelessly tugged her hair free of the binder. "But, please. Go ahead. Look at my letter. I'd love to know your thoughts before I've had time to form my own." Grabbing the white, ribbed tank top, Sabina pulled it over her head and tugged it down. "I just *love* everyone telling me what to do and how to think. What would I do without someone treating me like a child?" She slammed her hand over the socks and palmed them in her fist. She grabbed the bruised apple and the letter from the bed. Walking to the drapes, she jerked them to the side and headed for the front door. Biting into her apple, she opened the door. The juices were already causing saliva to form in her mouth. She quickly flopped down on the porch and put her socks and boots on. Standing up, she bit into the apple, letting the sugar explode in her mouth.

Her stomach growled as she hastily made her way toward the pond. The apple was in one hand, and the letter was in the other. No one was around, which is what Sabina preferred. It was dawn. The mist was burning off the grass as she passed the rows of tuts without a sound. She headed to the private training grounds Brom made for her when she was a child. Sabina trained every morning before the village was up and starting their day.

As she walked, she recited the mantra, "I forgive my sister for unintentionally hurting my pride. I am humble and teachable." Eventually, she only uttered, "I forgive myself." She refused to let her sister's actions ruin her favorite part of the day. She loved walking alone in the peaceful woods. She never understood why she craved to be alone in nature, but hated being alone in public. She decided it was because she felt like a ghost around people. Most of the time, people forgot she was there. Being ignored was hurtful. She wanted to be seen and heard, even if people made her nervous and clumsy with their awkward, vacant stares.

The fresh air and quiet morning soothed most of Sabina's raw emotions. She would work out the rest of her feelings as she trained. She had finished eating her apple, but she waited until she was deep in the woods to toss the apple core. She wiped her mouth with the back of her hand and rubbed her sticky hands on her leggings. It was pointless. She would have to clean her hands before she read the letter. Avoiding getting it dirty, she carefully tucked the letter into her back pocket. Then she found a private place to pee. As she squatted down, she caught the slightest movement. She pulled her leggings up, not wanting to be in a vulnerable position as someone approached her. She took three steps backward and rested her back on a tree. Nothing happened. No sound, no movement, no smell. She waited until her heart was calm, and then she questioned if she had seen anything at all.

It was rare to come across another villager past the pond. Although there were workers up at this hour, only warriors scanned this deep into the woods. Most of the warriors knew Sabina because of Brom. They had never objected to her being alone, deep in the woods. She assumed it was because she had walked this path all her life with her father. She wondered if they thought her morning walks were a way to connect to her father when he wasn't home. Regardless, they ignored her despite the land being off-limits to villagers. She was happy to ignore them too.

When Sabina was five, Brom began to introduce her to martial arts. He brought her to a hidden training ground which she now referred to as the Loaded Hurricane. He assured Sabina that she didn't have to fear anyone suspecting what she was doing or where she was going. It was a secret place for the two to spend time together. She was safe here and could learn martial arts without anyone giving her trouble. He informed her that no one would notice or follow her because he paid someone with a rare Moowin to create a powerful shield to hide this special place just for her.

Sabina never questioned or realized how powerful the shield was. It was powerful enough that the Ori or rare Shielders couldn't detect it. Once she was close enough to the protective energy field, it would look like she had disappeared into the woods. The shield was designed to be invisible to others, to muffle the sounds within it, and to allow only Brom and Sabina to enter. If someone walked near the shield, their senses would remind them of something they forgot to do. The importance of that something would get stronger and stronger the closer they got to the shield. Sabina knew the energy field repelled people. At first, she didn't think that was possible, but she had witnessed it several times. People would be peaceful walking by, and then their stride would shorten. Their eyebrows would draw together. They might rub their head or appear anxious. Then they would turn around and walk away. Brom said it worked because it was true. There was always something you could not quite remember if you had done.

Sabina felt a shiver of energy run through her body. Goosebumps raised on her skin as a warning that someone was watching her. She knew this time was different. She continued walking, lifting her knees and placing her foot cautiously on the ground. The woods were quiet from the lack of animal movement. She didn't even hear squirrels jumping from tree to tree. Her eyes scanned the peripheral. She kept her head still. She didn't want to let on that she knew someone was there. She was perplexed with her sense which told her that someone was ahead of her. That was not possible. Her training grounds were ahead of her, and no one was ever on her training grounds.

She broke off her standard path and walked along the shield's outer edge, getting some distance between what she sensed but knew to be impossible. The tickle between her shoulders confirmed someone was watching her from her training grounds. She turned 180 degrees and scanned the woods. Standing still, she observed the beautiful forest as another shiver ran across her upper body. Sun rays occasionally broke through the trees, limiting her view, but Sabina couldn't spot any movement. She counted slowly to ten, listening to her own exhale. Sabina didn't sense any danger, just eyes on her. She reasoned that she had caught the attention of a fox.

She took a significant step to the side and crossed the shield. She had learned to detect the shield's faint energy buzz. Its tingle of power was as light as a mosquito landing on you. It was only noticeable if you were looking for it. She remained still for another ten breaths. Nothing changed. She continued to feel eyes on her, but there was no movement, sound, or pressing threat. It had to be a wild animal. They occasionally got through the shield. She told herself it was nothing to worry about. She took a deep breath and let the tension go on her exhale. Still nothing alarming. She had made a big deal over nothing.

Sabina smiled as she looked across her training grounds with its three acres' worth of obstacle courses, a shooting range, a gazebo, a weapon shed, an ice chamber, a solar-powered sauna, and a bathhouse. The Loaded Hurricane was full of challenges, and her favorite challenge was the ropes that dangled from the wooden platforms, towers, and trees. Sabina reasoned that if her heart couldn't soar with happiness, her body could at least fly through the air as she swung from rope-to-rope. Her father had even scattered booby traps, random pits, and potholes throughout the course. Sabina loved this magical place where she came to train her body. She had everything she needed but her training partner, Brom.

With no fear of being judged or hiding her talent, Sabina could be herself when she was in the Loaded Hurricane. She didn't have to guard against people's negative energy or ignore all the disrespectful ways the villagers treated her. Sabina could take a full breath without feeling the weight on her chest. Yes, this was her secret haven and was where she belonged. While her room was where she slept, the Loaded Hurricane was her home.

Closing her eyes, Sabina took a liberating breath. Her gratitude for this wondrous place filled her. Opening her eyes, she decided on her training intentions and walked to the pavilion. She placed her father's letter on the gazebo floor with a large rock on top of it to keep it safe from flying away. She dismissed her thought that she was procrastinating on reading her father's letter. She needed to train. She had a schedule to keep. She removed her boots and socks and ran through her yoga sun salutation routine, warming her body up. She moved through the standing and floor moves, allowing her breath to guide her. She stretched her limbs to the sun. Yoga was one of her favorite things to do. For the moment, all was right in the world. Warmed up, she moved through her ropes course. Afterward, she ran five miles. Then she completed her daily strengthening exercises of push-ups, pull-ups, and core stabilization. Finally, she finished with Savasana.

She lay on the wooden platform of the pavilion with her eyes closed. Her body was slick with sweat as she drifted to sleep in a complete sense of peace from her physical exhaustion. Feeling dryness in her throat, she rolled over to her side. Her father's letter was still lying under the rock close by. She eyed it. The temporary mental escape from training was gone. Now, the letter glared at her. It demanded her attention, and she dreaded reading what her father had to say. Letters were significant. Letters were for declarations of war, death, land, or transactions like unions and tying. Sabina let out a long, slow breath before she got to her hands and knees and headed over to the bathhouse.

She stepped behind the hung canvas curtains that lifted in the light breeze and peeled her sticky clothes off, dropping them to the floor. She opened the door to the bathhouse as steam met her. The moisture came from the warming beams at the corners of the walls and along the roof. A stream ran through the bathhouse deep enough for Sabina to swim. The water was warm due to the steam. However, it still had cool spots that caused goosebumps on Sabina's skin as she passed through them. She walked over the smooth rocks, allowing the water to carry her weight until she was floating on her back. She was entirely at peace with her eyes closed and her body limp. Sabina had forgotten about the letter once more.

As she floated, she listened to the muted sounds of the water until she felt like she could no longer procrastinate. She had to get dressed and make her way to school. Sabina submerged herself entirely underwater and then went to the river's edge. Breaking the water's surface, she placed her feet under her and stood up as water cascaded down her body. Sabina was squeezing her hair when she heard a branch break outside. She immediately squatted down and covered her naked body by wrapping her arms around herself. She felt like she had a small brick in her throat. Scanning the room, Sabina wiped the dripping water from her eyes.

Her heart raced with frustration that she didn't know what she faced because she could not see through the thick fog. She reminded herself she was safe. It was probably the animal from earlier. It would pass and go away. She wiped the water out of her eyes again. Cautiously, she stood up, grabbing a large, smooth rock in one hand. She groaned inwardly, thinking about being naked as she confronted an animal. Quietly as possible, she made her way to the bathhouse door. She listened for sounds to help her identify where the animal was. The rock she carried was near to her face. She was ready to launch the rock at it or use it to strike down. She placed the other hand on the door handle, closed her eyes, and centered herself.

In one quick motion, she whipped the door open, stepped out into a slightly crouched position, and yanked the canvas aside. She quickly scanned, spotting movement. She didn't think. She reacted like the thousand other times she practiced with her father. The only sound she could hear was blood pumping through her body. She released the smooth rock like a wound-up rocket, and it shot through the air. With a hit to the rib cage, the stranger crashed to the ground. It was a young man. He looked to be about the same age as her.

The pictures in Sabina's mind caught up with her. She saw a young man dressed in brown slacks, a creamy long-sleeved shirt, and a dark-brown tweed vest. At the sight of Sabina, the man's eyes bulged out. He seemed to quickly realize she had a weapon in her hand. He turned and jumped to the ground, but before he twisted, the thrown object slammed into him.

Sabina heard his grunt of pain, and more branches broke as he face-planted into the ground. For a moment, Sabina stood in shock, amazed that someone she didn't know was in her Loaded Hurricane. Sabina didn't see how that was possible. She began to panic at two realizations: she was naked and she needed to defend herself. She had a moment to decide. Grab another weapon and attack, or run to get clothes and hide.

"Curd, curd, curd, curd, curd," she heard herself say. She was flapping her hands in pure panic like she could shake off the adrenaline rushing her body. Embarrassment sent flames of heat to her cheeks. She needed to protect herself. This fear of being in danger circulated in her brain. She didn't dare take her eyes off him, so she reached back and yanked as hard as possible, ripping the canvas from the pole. Although some of the canvas ripped, it did not rip off the bar as she intended.

"Curd," she hissed. She gave up on the idea of attacking. Sabina decided she felt too vulnerable to do anything else but get on clothes. Breaking a rule in fighting, Sabina put her back to the stranger, and she ran low to the ground toward her folded clothes stacked on a shelf outside her curtained dressing room. Sabina grabbed a tunic and kept running until she was on the other side of the bathhouse. She stopped with her back to the bathhouse and whipped on her dress as best as she could. She was too wet to put the dress on without it getting stuck. She could hear him rolling over and grumbling.

"What the hell did you do that for?"

She walked to the other side of her bathhouse, lifting her dress high and wading through the river. Once she was at the edge, she peered out from her hiding spot. The stranger was sitting up, holding onto his side. Twigs were in his hair and on his garment, and a chunk of mud was on his cheek. His hat had fallen to the ground, and the stranger reached back for it, cursing.

"Bloody Fires. I think you broke my ribs, you wretched woman."

He was swatting his hat on his leg, and then with one hand, he tried to put his hat back on his head, but it kept slipping off. While he was distracted by his hat, Sabina picked up another rock.

The stranger managed to get his hat on and had one foot and the other knee on the ground, still holding his rib.

"A little help here. Tullom, this hurts . . . Hey, where are you?" He was looking around for Sabina, but she stood motionless. Her dress clung to her wet body, her hair was a knotty mess, her feet were caked in mud, and her eyes were unblinking. Not to mention, she was holding another rock. She thought he probably would not want her help if he saw her. She looked like a crazy woman.

"You can come out of hiding. I'm not going to hurt you, unlike you. Sky Above. Do you have something to wrap my ribs? I don't think I can get up without it." He leaned forward and put his free hand on the ground, squinting his eyes in pain.

"Sabina. Tullom. Can't you see I am in pain?" He paused for a bit, rubbing the sweat off his forehead with the back of his hand. "I'm Brom's talent. He sent me to you."

Sabina relaxed a little, letting the tension in her shoulders go. Thoughts rushed through her mind, and she moved so that her back was to the bathhouse. *Who is he? What is he doing here? How did he get through the shield? What does he mean Brom sent him? Why would Father give this stranger access to Loaded Hurricane? Why wouldn't he have said something? Tullom! Was that what the letter was about?*

In a mocking tone, he grumbled, "He sent me here to be your **puppet**."

That made Sabina look back at him. Puppet? Sabina swallowed hard and let her breath out slowly.

"Who are you, and how did you get into this area?"

"What? You must speak louder if you want anyone besides the birds to hear you."

Flushing at the criticism, Sabina swallowed again and shouted louder. "Who. Are. You. And. How. Did. You. Get. In. Here?"

"I'm Flann Alf from Aliward. The Messenger that your father sought. Now I'll explain the rest after you help me. No more talking," he dictated, slightly huffing.

Sabina recognized the name. That is why her father left yesterday. To bring him back. *How is it possible he is here now? That is a few days' travels from here. And if he is here, where is my father?*

"*Please,*" he drew out. "Take all the time you need. I am only hunched over in pain begging for your help *after* you attacked me," he quipped, full of sarcasm.

Sabina bristled and delighted at the split-second thought of hitting him with the rock in her hand. She discarded the idea immediately. That would not shut him up anyway. She walked out from her hiding place feeling an initial moment of vulnerability at her appearance before walking forward, feeling confused and angry. She walked, placing one foot in front of the other like a ballerina parading the stage.

Flann watched her approaching like a wild lioness with grace and fierceness radiating around her. Her beauty momentarily captured his attention before a flashback of her pale naked body brushed along his memory. She was like a siren calling out to sailors or, in his case, a wounded servant. Instantly irritated at the thought, he slapped his hat on the ground, looking down.

He muttered to himself in an agitated, low tone. "Sabina will **not** bewitch me. I swore to be married to Nora. She is the delicate flower I seek to behold." Flann thought he could handle Sabina's powers. Brom had warned him, but he had understated her gifts. What a pompous liar, Flann thought. Feeling misled by Brom about the depth of her powers, Flann wished he had kept his distance.

Sabina realized this could be one of her candidates to evaluate as a partner, and this thought caused her to feel butterflies in her stomach. Despite his muttering to himself, Sabina had partially overheard what this annoying stranger had said. Who was Nora? How could it be possible that he was sworn to Nora if he was her union interview? Did he have honor? AND . . . Who had bewitched him? Her, she thought questionably. What did he think she was capable of? Giving him leprosy? She wasn't <u>that</u>

repulsive, just plain. It was true people often ignored her, but no one ran, shrinking away from her.

Sabina wanted answers. "*Who* do you speak of?" she demanded to know. *What* did that tullom letter say???

~

Her tone suggested she was ready to slap him for his insolence. Flann hated his circumstance of being beneath this woman. No, girl! Irritated at himself, Sabina, and his injury, he gritted his teeth and sarcastically answered her. "Wouldn't you like to know? Now, what about the wrap for my ribs? Shouldn't you be ripping your dress or something to create that?"

~

She stood motionless along the riverbank, looking at this redheaded man who could not be that much older than her, holding his ribs and looking disheveled. She didn't care that she had hurt him. Hadn't he scared her by approaching her unannounced in the middle of a secured, private wooded area? It was unlikely Brom would have informed him of the shield and how it works. Sabina still felt suspicious of who this stranger was and what his intentions were. She didn't feel inclined to help him, yet the Ori would exalt his talents if he told the truth. Then, she would be stuck dealing with the aftermath of the poor treatment of such a valuable citizen. Plus, she didn't want him in her Loaded Hurricane. She thought this situation was wasting her limited time. She needed to get to school. She had other things to focus on.

Think, Sabina. Father trained you for this. What would he do? Yes . . . that is it. Come on, Sabina. Use your wits.

"What is my father's code word?" she asked solemnly.

~

For all that is right in this world, can this girl not see that I'm in pain? What tullom password?

Tired of waiting for her help and feeling frustrated, Flann straightened out his torso in preparation to stand, which shot pain through his ribs. He cried out while his vision went black for a second. Then, he saw bright, moving lights in his sight. Curling back into himself and propping himself over his thigh, Flann rested his hand back on the ground. Nope, that wasn't going to work, Flann thought as his pain settled. Realizing Sabina hadn't flinched at his painful attempt to stand, he calculated she wouldn't help him until she verified who he was. *Point for her. Well, curd. I think I need a Healer so let's get this over with.*

Flann had disobeyed Brom's orders by not staying away from Sabina until the stipulated time. However, he was bored. He shared a life force bond with her and he wanted to see what she was like. He knew Brom wasn't going to be happy. *Why hadn't the silly (and slightly dangerous) girl heard him? He was whistling, for curd's sake.* There was nothing left to do but confess his folly to Brom as he could see that Sabina was like a statue of resistance. And he was sure the stone in her hand wasn't there for leisurely skipping rocks.

Closing his eyes, Flann cleared his mind until there was only darkness. A void where he could use his talents to connect to anyone who shared the same Moowin as him. Brom was not a Messenger, but he had access to Flann's Moowin through their shared bond. It meant Brom could channel the Messenger Moowin as if he possessed it himself. No one knew this was possible because Brom was the first to experiment with shared life forces. Life forces were given to heal another, or as a death token to a loved one. Life forces were not mutually shared because no one wanted to give up their most precious gift.

Flann knew Brom would be cross with him for not following his plan. He was supposed to be introduced at his union interview. Until then, he was to watch over Sabina from a distance. That was before Sabina's gifts started leaking energy, and the

Selectors began attacking the dome walls. Flann may have resented his bodyguard role but wouldn't fail at his job. Brom would have to understand that he was doing what he thought was best. Still, he would rather not have this conversation with Brom, but there was no way to avoid it as he needed the password. Flann disliked Brom for several reasons, but he reminded himself that Brom had offered him an opportunity he couldn't refuse, which is why he agreed to take this job.

He mentally called out, "Brom Rockdin of Silvedome, Father of Sabina Rockdin." Remaining in the darkness, Flann waited for Brom's answering call.

"Flann?" Brom quested. Brom was not a Messenger, and therefore, the way his gift worked was unnatural. Flann shook his head at the disoriented feeling of Brom speaking through him instead of mentally to him. Brom could connect to any Messenger through this bond but chose to hide what he could do. Therefore, he didn't have much practice with it.

Already annoyed, Flann responded formally just to aggravate Brom. "Flann Alf of Aliward, your purchased Messenger and servant to Sabina Rockdin. I have interacted with Sabina, and I need your password to establish trust with her." *There! That was straight and to the point—no need to apologize or fret.*

Silence.

More silence.

Flann looked over at Sabina, who was looking at him with pinched eyebrows and a slightly open mouth as if she was considering saying something. She remained still with her head tilted and stared fixedly down at Flann. Sweat began to bead on his forehead from the pain in his ribs. Sabina made him nervous too. Truthfully, he felt her power even though she now looked frozen in place. The more aware he was of her power, the smaller and more fragile he felt, which was not a feeling he cared to have.

While Sabina stood there more confused than ever, Flann had closed his eyes with a bleak expression as Messengers often do when communicating with another Messenger. As he used his Moowin, goosebumps spiked on her skin like little razors. She could feel the faintest sensation of red, hot anger sending waves of energy toward her. It was the same energy she felt yesterday with her father but not near the intensity. Sabina had already concluded after a night's rest that the angry energy she felt yesterday was coming from her father, not around them. Sabina watched Flann as a theory formed, for she did not believe in coincidence. The only time Sabina had felt that ribbon of angry energy had been with her father right before he darted off in alarm. And now! She sensed it now.

Is he communicating with my father? Brom must be with a Messenger, but why did I sense the same energy being released from him yesterday? It's impossible for this weird energy to transport from my father through a Messenger and then to this stranger before me . . . Isn't it? I've never picked up on someone's energy before when they used a Moowin. None of this makes sense. I must be going crazy.

~

"What is the **tullom** password *Brom*? Sabina looks like she might snap and fly through the air like a vampire to twist my neck!"

Brom chuckled. "You must have gone to the Loaded Hurricane. Shall I remind you that Sabina's gifts are not blocked fully in that space?"

Flann could feel intense emotions coming from Brom due to their shared life force. He could feel Brom's fear. He imagined Brom pacing back and forth, rubbing the back of his head.

"You, of all people, know the importance of this plan. I trusted you to <u>keep your word</u>. You will make this right! . . . And stop with this nonsense of being a servant. I will not tolerate this poor-me attitude! It's getting old. You agreed to this commitment, yet you act like you have sold your soul when you and I both know I helped you."

Flann could feel his anger fizzing out before Brom asked with uncertainty, "Has she, has she read my letter?"

"No," Flann let him know, taking a deep, slow breath to calm his nerves.

"DO NOT LET HER READ THAT LETTER in the Loaded Hurricane," he commanded. "Do you UNDERSTAND what would happen if she read it without her gifts suppressed?"

Do I ever? thought Flann. "YESSSSS. I got it," Flann answered. He didn't need to be told twice. "Now, what is the password, and how can I fix this?"

"Sasquatch, and you will figure it out."

Brom disconnected, and there was silence. Figures! thought Flann. Keeping his eyes closed for a moment, he realized he had no idea how to handle this situation. Brom was a wise old owl who had little patience for hand-holding.

The angry heat was gone, and Sabina felt a tightening in her stomach. She didn't know if it was because she had to deal with this stranger or because she realized her father had lied to her. It could have also been her fear that something was wrong with her father's energy. Her gut said all three of those possibilities were true, making her feel like she was a physical and mental wreck.

"Sashquesh," Flann finally answered, wiping the sweat off his head with his hat and avoiding eye contact.

Sabina tossed the rock back along the edge of the river and lifted the rim of her dress to cross the river again. Sabina realized her body responded to Flann's words before her mind did. Like something drove her to be near him now that she knew he was safe. She didn't like that. He was not trustworthy to her yet. Therefore, she was grateful for the cold water splashing along her legs. It helped to clear the brain fog.

She stepped out of the river, and a shiver ran across her body. She looked up from the rocks to see Flann hadn't moved. She let go of her raised tunic and glanced at the gazebo where her father's letter rested under a rock. Then, she made her way to him, but his dark-green eyes and locked jaw made her hesitate. Sabina looked back at the letter, suddenly feeling a strong urge to read it. The desire was palpable. It made it difficult to think.

"Where is my father?" she inquired, speaking slowly, eyeing him with distrust. Regardless of his evidence to prove that he was safe, he was still a stranger to her.

She didn't know what to do in this unique situation. She was responsible for helping him get a wrap, but she didn't have anything she could use in the Loaded Hurricane. She needed this tunic to get back to the village. She didn't have any spare clothes here. She considered her white, sweaty tank as an option, but she grimaced at the thought. That would mean she would have to go shop in the square to replace it now that her sister and mother were gone. No. That would not do. The canvas from her dressing curtain? But that was expensive to replace. Distracted, she looked over at the bathhouse, and without knowing what she looked for, she walked toward it. She felt Flann's eyes bore into her the whole time, like he was standing right behind her and breathing on her neck. She didn't like the feeling. It made it even harder to concentrate and clear the fog from her mind.

"Brom had me stationed outside the town. He had planned to bring me into town so we could meet formally, but he had an unexpected family friend emergency."

That made her stop and look back at him. "Who?" she demanded.

"He didn't say. He just took off."

Continuing to look for wrap options, she asked, "Then how do you know he was helping a family friend? Did he stop and talk to you, or did he take off?"

~

Flann regretted his decision to spy on Sabina. He told himself this situation was more trouble than it was worth. She asked too many questions. Grinding his teeth, he answered, "During our time traveling together, Brom had a friend who he was helping with complicated issues. I saw him ride off in the direction of his friend."

~

While Flann spoke, Sabina looked around for something she could use to help him, but there wasn't anything she was willing to part with. She looked up and saw the sun rising over the trees. Sabina was late for school. She would have to ask more questions later.

Feeling the pressure of being late, Sabina gave up. "You're just going to have to go to the hospital without a wrap." Sabina used her fingers to comb through her tangled hair. It would be a ponytail day, even though wearing her hair up gave her headaches. She adjusted her mud-covered tunic, grimacing at her filthy feet. She grabbed her soiled clothes and hustled to clean them in the bathhouse, throwing them on the clothesline to dry. She pulled her boots back on and grabbed her clean clothes from yesterday. She hastily walked over to the letter and lifted the rock.

~

Flann watched her work quickly and panicked when she reached for the letter. He knew he was out of time to do something. Unfortunately, he felt like a rib would puncture his lung whenever he tried to stand. He couldn't go to her, and he couldn't let her read that letter. His only strategy was to distract her.

"Don't you believe in making amends for the injury **you** inflicted?" he said quickly.

~

Sabina had been lost in thought as she visualized the worst-case scenario of her day: her classmates staring at her as she walked in late. At Flann's coercion, the thoughts vanished. She was squatting over her letter with a rock in her hand, deliberating what to do, when Flann turned toward her, and her world shifted. Sabina saw the struggle on his face as he attempted to straighten up. Tension radiated from him, creating a beacon that pulled her into tunnel vision. The world was dark except for the brightly lit path that led to him. She couldn't take her eyes off his dark-green irises. She noticed how they softened at the edge and how his pain made his eyes more prominent. He looked directly at her, holding her gaze. No one had looked so intensely at her before. She swallowed hard, feeling seen by Flann. She looked away and tugged her dress down a little more, becoming aware of the skin she was showing.

She picked up the letter and stood.

Flann pressed on. "I was whistling and talking to you so you would not be alarmed that I was here. I'd never seen a smoking building like that before, and I didn't know what it was. All I was doing was checking to see if you were safe. We don't have rivers in Aliward." He coughed, a little out of breath as he struggled to talk. "I wasn't expecting a naked woman to jump out of the building and attack me. It doesn't seem right that I was attacked for waiting for you to come out of that building."

Heat flushed Sabina's cheeks. She crossed her arms in a moment of defiance, leaning back to glare at him. Who was this rude man who showed up in her private sanctuary and made her feel guilty for *defending* herself? She tucked the letter into the pocket of her tunic and picked up the clothes she had dropped. She stomped over to him, trying to stop herself from thinking about the fact that he saw her naked. She wished she could forget the surprise on his when he saw her. *HOW MORTIFYING*, she groaned inwardly. Flann visibly relaxed as she stomped over.

Sabina walked right up to him, ready to argue, but he didn't give her time to speak. "I need to keep hunched over. Can you come behind me and help lift me by holding me under my armpits?"

"HOW am I going to do that? My body cannot reach over yours," she argued, still feeling the sting of her mortification.

"Okay. Stand *in front of me* then and support the weight of my shoulders," he retorted in a low controlled voice. Walking in front of him, Sabina looked down at his sweat-stained clothes and his short, loose curly hair and thought, *Why me?* before bending over to grab his shoulders. He immediately tried to get his other foot on the ground, but his head pushed into her stomach. She rotated her grip and pushed him upright, causing him to cry out.

Huffing and puffing, Flann stood hunching over in pain. Sabina was already retreating from him. "Will you hand me my hat?" he requested. He had waited to ask Sabina for additional help so she would be too distracted to look at her letter. He asked when she returned to her clothes and reached down from them. He saw her stiffen, which made him smile despite the pain he was in.

Sabina felt her annoyance boil. She had no more time for his nonsense. She grabbed her clothes again and walked back to pick up his hat, wondering how quickly she could ditch him. She reached down and snatched the hat up, holding it out to him.

"Where is the Healer?"

"In the hospital," she answered, leaving him behind.

"Aren't you going to help me? I don't know my way around here?"

Fisting her hands, she turned and replied, "I'd love to, but I need to get to school. All you need to do is go through the town as all roads lead to the square. Then, cross the bridge over the river.

The low buildings are the schools. The hospital is behind them." She turned and swiftly walked away.

"Where is your hospitality?" he shouted as loudly as he could without causing himself to cough. He stood holding his rib, hunched over, smiling as he watched Sabina race off. This wasn't going to be as miserable as he thought.

CHAPTER 4

School

Racing through the trees, dodging objects, jumping over limbs, Sabina wanted distance between her and the eerie stares of that strange man. She was desperate to get to class, to the safety of her everyday unnoticed life. How much had she missed already? Had the Mistress already come to get her?

She was on the dusty street with her tut in sight. Usually, she would have stopped for a while before heading to the square for breakfast. But she didn't have the time or the tokens for the food. She'd have to work more hours now she didn't have anyone looking out for her. She made a quick dash into the tut. She tossed her clothes to the chair, opened the front door, grabbed her schoolbooks, and ran back out toward the village, her boots rubbing the inside of her ankle the whole time.

Due to Brom's elevated status in the village, the Ori gave him one of the larger, stone tut's that was closer to the village square. It took little time for her to pass the village square. She ran over the bridge and slowed down. Sweat gleamed on her skin, and she controlled her breath, slowing it down. She walked with her arms raised to shoulder height so the breeze would dry out her armpits. She walked past the school buildings and to the left, to the open-stage seating. She could see her class all gathered in their tidy, wrinkle-free white or black Shaolin uniforms with their ankle-banded pants and low-profile shoes. She never understood why no one took the privilege of standing out. They were granted the freedom to wear whatever they worked for, but she alone stood out in her khaki tunic dress. It was traditional to wear your hair tied back, and typically, Sabina did the exact opposite of what her peers did, which included letting her hair be free to fly around her face. Today was an exception. Today her hair was pulled back.

She could hear the teacher talking about the art forms of movement to music. She was a serious woman who didn't smile. She often stood with her feet apart and her hands behind her back. Today she had a long whip in her hand, and she was demonstrating how it could be used as a tool for discipline, or as a weapon. Sabina had slowed and dropped her arms. With the teacher's whip flying, her classmates hadn't noticed her. And she was to the teacher's back. Sabina made her way to the left of the stage where the teacher stood and headed for the side stairs. She noticed an open spot that was easy to get to. With her head down and her arms glued to her sides, she quietly but quickly made her way in front of the stage where the steps were. She got to the stairs no sooner than the whip's tip glazed the back of her ankle.

She was startled and jumped, but no one said anything to her. The teacher continued teaching without interruption to her lesson. Not willing to look up, Sabina hustled to her seat, getting as far from the whip as possible. She dumped herself into her seat and looked at her ankle. It burned, but her thick leather boots had protected her from the worst of it. Sabina was exhausted and hungry and annoyed at the teacher. *Of course, I'm late on the day that Professor Tiris brings a whip to class. Let me show you what I can do with that whip, and then the class will have something to talk about.*

Brom taught Sabina all forms of defense, weapons, etcetera. He was fanatic about her safety and drilled her in several combat styles. When she was younger, he brought her on shorter trips where he met and trained with others.

Grumpy and slouched, Sabina looked up to see the professor in a tiger crouch, holding the whip over her hand, folded and taut. Brown-noser Markus was on the stage, jumping in the air and slashing his sword toward the whip. Markus was the professor's favorite because he never held back. Even though the professor was externally calm, Sabina could almost see the excitement in her eyes as Markus attacked. Professor Tiris was either proud of him or living her glory days as a warrior, Sabina told herself, as she watched the action unfold before her.

The sword hit the taut rope, and the professor released one hand, twisting the other with a downward slash, and the whip unfolded. In one smooth motion, the professor was standing, her whip wrapped around Markus's sword arm. She twisted his captured wrist, disarming him while he was stuck like a fly in a spider web. "Tullom," Sabina whispered with appreciation. *I don't like her, but I cannot deny she is impressive.*

By the end of class, Sabina had made hundreds of notes. She had made little sketches of the actions to help her interpret her notes and was so preoccupied that she didn't notice the Mistress walking to the stage. Oddly, she realized she was enjoying the class.

"Sabina Rockdin," Professor Tiris called out in a deep voice.

Sabina looked up to the stage and saw the Mistress standing next to Professor Tiris with her long, draping, velvet dress. Her skin was wrinkled and stretched across her face, and her arms were folded as if she was about to present something in grand fashion.

"Don't waste our time, Sabina. Gather your belongings and follow the Mistress," Professor Tiris said as she walked to gather candles for citations. "Students, it is time for citations. You know what to do."

Sabina fumbled to get her belongings and catch up with Fog Fourshul, who demanded to be called Mistress, not Mistress Fourshul. Mistress had left Sabina, trusting that she would catch up with her without a glance behind her. Sabina was forced to wait for her classmates to file down the stairs before she could descend. She kept an eye on Mistress's black and silver bun in the distance, unsure why she had come for her. She was expecting Professor Tobe to call for her to discuss her Birth Challenge.

Once she was able, Sabina went down the stairs and weaved her way anxiously through her classmates, who acted like she was not there. Clearing the crowd, Sabina caught up with Mistress but kept a three-step distance behind her as she preferred.

She was a finicky woman who had earned a great deal of respect from the villagers. She was on the Ori, and she worked for the school. Plus, she had a rare Shield Moowin and helped maintain the dome around the village. She was powerful, even in her old age. At her Birth Challenge, she named herself Fog because she believed she had control over the climate. One could argue she was correct as the dome was a force field that could block out weather. Every day in Silvedome had the perfect temperature.

"Your time has come, Sabina," Mistress calmly said as she strode forward with purpose, passing the long row of classrooms and heading to the office facilities. "I have been most interested in your Birth Challenge."

Sabina followed slightly to the right of the Mistress's path to hear what she was saying. "Why?" Sabina asked, genuinely curious.

The Mistress waited a long time to answer before she said, "At my age, you see things that cannot be seen, and by that, I mean, I don't need to be a Seer to know things. Your father is up to something. He is clever and diplomatic, make no mistake, but I am a rare Shield, a master of my talents, and a powerful one at that."

They made it to the office building, and the Mistress opened the door for Sabina. She studied her with a discerning eye as she walked through the door. Sabina stepped to the side of the doorway as soon as she was through. She was ready to follow the Mistress to her office, but the Mistress stopped once she entered the door. Looking up at Sabina with one eye barely able to open fully, the Mistress said in a questioning tone, "But there is something off about your energy. I've never been able to identify it."

She walked on, letting the door slam behind her, and Sabina followed down the dreary cement-gray corridor. "It's quite maddening, really."

"Why does my energy concern my father?" Sabina asked, puzzled.

"Who said it did?" the Mistress answered with a coy smile, opening her office door, and gesturing for her to take a seat.

Sitting down and not wanting to answer any more questions from the Mistress, Sabina focused on her breathing and counting. This normally calmed her, but she felt like the room was dimming today. *I should have eaten something,* she thought to herself.

The Mistress shuffled past her tall stack of books propped on the floor near her desk and then flipped through a file. *I bet that's about me,* Sabina thought to herself, glancing down at her outfit. Her tunic had mud dried on the bottom of it. The dried mud flaked to the floor, and her black boots also left muddy marks. Her hair felt like straw and was clumped together. Her breath probably stank too. She hadn't had the time she needed to freshen up. *How embarrassing.* Sabina scolded herself, cringing.

Here she was before a high-ranking member of the Ori, school, and village, with a known expectation for tidiness, and Sabina looked like she had run through a bush and a pile of mud. *Not too far off the truth, really.*

"Tell me, Sa-bina, do you know why you are here?" Mistress asked without looking up from her file.

"Fh . . . fh . . . for the Bir-th . . . Challenge," she stuttered out. *Pull it together, Sabina. You don't want to be doing push-ups all day. Calm and steady. Nothing has gone wrong here. Everything is fine,* she told herself.

"Would you like to explain why you did not assist Master Flann Alf—one of our newest members of Silvedome, a Messenger, and your potential partner—to the hospital for broken ribs?" she said, putting down the file and looking regally at Sabina. "Is he **not** a guest in your home until further notice?" she asked, a little more authoritatively.

"What? Sabina asked incredulously, sitting up on the edge of her chair. Her stomach was boiling with nausea. *Oh, horrid nightmares. What did that tullom letter say, and why am I avoiding it?* Sabina felt the weight of the letter in her pocket and wished she had read it.

"This is a serious offense, Sabina. Do you understand that?" the Mistress stated as she sat down and folded her hands in front of her. Sabina was sure that her olive skin had turned green with nausea.

"In Brom's absence, your mother working in the hospital, and your sister in Tradel, you are responsible for your guest's well-being . . . now that you are of age. Well," she said, fanning her hand in front of her, "I consider you of age since you are two days from your Birth Challenge."

"He just got into town today, Mistress. I had no idea I was responsible for him or that he was a potential partner. Or that he is a master. A master? . . . I was not informed, Mistress. Please, I will correct this. May I be excused to check on Flann in the hospital?" Sabina blurted this out in a rush, as her foot shook.

"Excuses, Sabina, and I have little time for excuses." Opening her one eye as much as it would allow, she asked patiently, unfazed by Sabina's plea, "You do not deny knowing about his injury, then?"

"No, Mistress," Sabina answered quietly, looking down.

"Recite the guest laws to me now," she demanded, pursing her lips in a thoughtful gesture.

Sabina's mind went blank. She hardly cared about these matters, but she knew the basics.

"It is a privilege and an honor to welcome a guest into Silvedome . . . All Silvedome guests must be pre-approved by the Ori before admittance. Guests may stay temporarily and be the responsibility of the household making the request. As such, the household will share tokens with their guests to feed them, entertain them, and care for them.”

“Enough. That was poorly done. It was out of order, and it lacked confidence. But . . . it proved that you understand the law.” The Mistress drummed her fingers on the desk. Sabina remained apologetic with her head down, waiting on her consequence. *I should have known I was responsible for that redheaded, irritating Messenger.*

“I understand that Brom left late in the day yesterday to visit his friend, and on his way out, he requested to activate your union interviews. It would be *irresponsible* of Brom not to inform you of your interviews or fail to inform you that some of your interviews would be out-of-town guests transitioning to permanent residence in our village.” She drummed her fingers.

“I highly doubt that Brom failed to inform you of these matters. However, no one expected Master Alf to arrive this early, and I understand he would not have done so had it not been for the injury he suffered during his travels. Nonetheless, until he is acclimated into our village, he is the Rockdin’s guest.” She continued to drum her fingers.

“But it is also true that you are technically not an adult. It is also clear that no one formally introduced you to Master Alf . . . I was never a fan of Master Alf staying in your tut while going through union interviews,” she said, letting out a long breath, “but I was outvoted.”

Standing up, the Mistress said, “Brom will pay the price this time. But make no mistake, in the absence of an adult, you are, here on out, responsible for him.” The Mistress briskly walked to the door, ending the conversation.

Panicked, Sabina stood up. She didn’t want her father to get into trouble.

“I will return when I have conferred with the Ori. Sit down and wait,” Mistress Fourshul ordered.

“Mistress, I accept responsibility for Ma-Ma-Master Alf”— but there was no need to finish speaking. The Mistress was already striding down the corridor with her long, black velvet dress dragging behind her.

Plopping down in her chair, Sabina put her head in her hands. *What am I to do now?* Her stomach was rumbling, and her head was spinning. She wanted to close her eyes, fall asleep, and pretend nothing had happened.

There was a light tap at the door, and Sabina lifted her head from her hands, turning to look. There stood Seer's apprentice, Scholar 'Crystal' Sheb, Sabina's only friend. Crystal waited at the door. Her beautiful, short, tight curls bounced. She looked elegant in her pale-green, cotton long-sleeved shirt, with ribbon that laced up her arm, a belt around her thin waist, and her loose brown pants tucked into knee-length boots. Sabina thought she was beautiful. She looked fierce, confident, and beautiful, with skin that glowed and a strong collarbone. Her index finger was against her lips, indicating not to talk.

Sabina nodded that she understood. The office buildings were not a place for unescorted residents to walk through.

Crystal walked into the room and bent down to whisper into Sabina's ear. Sabina despised that her hair felt like straw and cursed the day she was having. She wished she looked more presentable.

"Master Dub sends a message. She requests to see you today but also says not to worry. She will speak to the Ori." She stood up and pulled wrapped dried meat from her belt satchel, putting it in Sabina's hand with a wink of her eye. She slid her hands off Sabina's slowly, smiling brightly the entire time. Then Crystal, soundless, left the room and was on her way.

Sky Above, Crystal had a way of making you wish you were into women, if you weren't already. There was no question that Sabina appreciated her beauty, grace, and confidence, but what she really loved about Scholar Sheb was that she always made her feel noticed and normal, even if it was because she was a big flirt.

Crystal was one of Brom's recruits, and she came to Silvedome almost three years ago with her younger brother. Recruits stayed in the home of the Scouter until they were settled and comfortable with Silvedome's way of life. Therefore, Crystal and her brother had stayed in Sabina's home for a few weeks. Although Brom was responsible for teaching guests how Silvedome operated until they were independent, Sabina ignored them. Brom loved helping the recruits by introducing them to the people that needed their services. It's one reason he was beloved by villagers. Brom understood what people in the village needed, and he matched skill sets where there was a need. As charismatic as her father was, he wasn't much into entertaining the recruits, but Fawn loved it. She was the one who entertained them. Fawn showed them where to shop and how to get food. She took them to performances and befriended them. She could relate to anyone. But Sabina wasn't the only one who ignored their guests. Marigold never cared to entertain or host, either. If there was a recruit in town, Marigold volunteered for overnight stays at the hospital until they were gone.

Despite avoiding the guest, Crystal was one of the few recruits that Sabina liked. Crystal informed Sabina that after her sixteenth birthday, Selectors attacked her family, believing she was the prophesied Agni. Even before her sixteenth birthday, Crystal was known in her region as a powerful Seer, but other than her being a powerful Seer, it was unclear why the Selectors thought she was the Agni. She was older than the prophesied age of the Agni. When Brom brought Crystal to Silvedome, injured and scared, the Ori demanded their ritual Birth Challenge—expected of all newcomers—after she had seen the Healer. The ritual revealed she had a few mild Moowin talents and was a powerful Seer. In theory, her Moowins could have strengthened until they reached a rare status, but she did not possess all eight Moowins of the prophesied Agni. Her suffering was unnecessary. Sabina's father wouldn't stand for this and he'd become passionate about helping find and protect young Moowins.

Sabina didn't see much of Scholar Sheb now she lived and apprenticed with Nana Honey.

Crystal studied with Nana Honey, helped her around the house, and ran errands. She was fortunate to work with a Seer as sharp-minded, kind, peaceful, and powerful as Master Dub—to use her formal title. She was like no one else in the village, and her power seemed to vibrate off her. Sabina reasoned it was because her visions let her know what to expect and what would inevitably happen. She was blind now, but it didn't faze her one bit. Her visions let her see as if her eyes were open. Crystal was to take her place, assuming her talent grew strong enough to be considered rare and if Nana Honey ever passed on. The Scouters were still looking for someone with rare Seer status, but there were fewer Seers than any other Moowin. Crystal didn't have a rare status, but Sabina had heard the Ori were concerned about Nana Honey's age.

Sabina sat back in Mistress's wooden chair, thankful for the snack Nana Honey probably saw she needed. She smiled and relaxed as she chewed the salted, dried meat. Sabina didn't spend much time with Nana Honey, few did. But Nana Honey had always shown her kindness. She believed it was because her father worked with Nana Honey frequently to find recruits.

As she ate, she wondered what Nana Honey saw that she wished to tell Sabina. Nana Honey often said that visions were neutral. She said it was in the eye of the beholder, and how one perceived them caused them to be one or the other. Nana Honey understood that perception could alter with time too, so what was once a blessing could become a curse. She'd explained that the Seer could not be responsible for one's perception or interpretation. That is the way it worked with Seers.

Nana Honey's rule was that she didn't offer unsolicited visions. Therefore, Sabina wondered if Nana Honey summoned her because of a vision or something else. She had never been contacted by Nana Honey before. With the odd day she was having, she guessed it could be many things: her union interviews, her Birth Challenge, the recruit, Brom?

One minute she was wondering about the request to see Nana

Honey, and the next, she was jerking awake, hearing the chair slide backward. Rubbing her eyes and looking down at the mess on the floor, Sabina quickly reorientated herself. With her senses waking up, she could hear Mistress and Professor Tobe coming down the hall. Sabina straightened up and cleared her throat softly, thirsty again. It seemed like she was always parched.

"She gets too much leeway," Mistress proclaimed.

"I agree, Mistress, but this is the way it is for now," answered Professor Tobe in a rumbling voice. Sabina could hear him pant out his breath as he walked.

The Mistress pushed open the door and sat down in an aggressive manner. She took a moment to compose herself.

"It is settled," she announced pretentiously, with her chin elevated. She looked at Tobe but addressed Sabina. "Brom will be excused, as will you, for failure to comply with Silvedome's guest policy, with a *warning* and a *proclamation* you are responsible for Master Alf until his job placement. When we finish our discussion, Professor Tobe will discuss the financial expenditure and allowance of Rockdin's recruitment funds. Now"—she paused, slowing down and taking a breath—"you are further <u>notified</u> that several guests . . . that should be Brom's responsibility"—she emphasized in a higher pitch, then softer—"are headed to Silvedome or have, in fact, arrived early at our village. Buuutttt"—she drew out her words—"out of the kindness of several of our villagers' hearts, they have taken it upon themselves to help you by accommodating your guest. You are released from being responsible for these guests, except for Prince Zoel Alpheus of Morten, his Healer Master Viggo Nadel, and Viggo's sister, Fabia Nadel. Fabia will stay in Fawn's room with Master Nadel and Prince Alpheus staying in your parents room. Master Alf will stay in the guest room. Understood?" she asked, nodding to Sabina as if her nod was both an order and Sabina's corresponding consent.

Sabina stared unblinkingly at the Mistress, completely perplexed and aware that her brain had shut off as soon as she had mentioned the word 'Prince.' All she could think about was how she was supposed to suddenly be responsible for not only one guest but now three additional more, one of whom was a Prince. She? The outcast who wasn't credited for accomplishing anything of significance and spent her life in isolation. She didn't know about caregiving for herself, let alone another person. *Geez, what have I gotten myself into now?*

"Sabina? We would all be interested in hearing your questions or your agreement to this matter so we may proceed. We have much to accomplish today," the Mistress pressed as she looked across at her.

Sabina longed to ask for help but knew it was not wise. Mistress would never accept that Sabina didn't know what to do with all her guests in her home or accept the 'excuse' that she couldn't handle the responsibility of it when she was two days away from 'adulthood'. Sabina really needed Fawn right now. Who else could she ask for help?

"Ma-, ma-, Mistress," she stuttered. She closed her eyes and counted to ten to calm her nerves. "I have much to do to prepare for my Birth Challenge, and with my fasting starting soon, I, I—" She took a deep breath. She didn't know what to ask for and had hoped it would come to her as she spoke. She concentrated on making her request, one that was logical and would not be perceived as an excuse. "I won't be available to my guests on the day of my Birth Challenge. How can I be responsible for my guests when I am unavailable?" she spat out.

"Nonsense. Your guests can attend your Birth Challenge. They may find it fascinating. Not all villages perform such elaborate rituals." She reached out, grabbed a file, and looked up to peer at the door. "Scholar Sheb, I believe that is all you needed to hear for Master Dub. Sabina has been informed and agrees to her role. It has been witnessed by two of the Ori and a bystander." She nodded toward Professor Tobe. "Everything is in accordance with our bylaws. Is there anything else you need?" she said, looking bored.

Jerking her head to the door, Sabina finally noticed Crystal's thin stature behind Professor Tobe's thick arm. Crystal's face was flat, expressionless. She nodded wordlessly, making quick eye contact with Sabina.

"Then you are dismissed," Mistress declared, looking down and waving her arm in a dismissive gesture, but Crystal was already walking away. Sabina didn't know that Crystal was part of the Ori. *Wow. She has moved up in status.*

"Professor Tobe?" Mistress snapped with her eyebrows raised. "You are dismissed too. I will come get you when I have finished speaking to Sabina."

Professor Tobe raised his index finger like he had a suggestion or a question, but decided better of it. He turned and shuffled away, huffing with the effort. Mistress rested her forehead between her index fingers and thumbs and looked down. Sabina could feel a slight energy shift, but sat still. Mistress was always composed, and this was the first time Sabina had seen her not be collected.

She got up, walked to the door, closed it softly, and slowly walked back to her desk. Sabina shifted, and her boots slid in her pile of dirt, making a squeaking sound. Mistress sat down, folded her hands on top of each other, and looked at Sabina, remaining quiet. She squinted at her. Feeling like she was being examined, Sabina dropped her head down and took a deep breath as quietly as she could, holding her breath. She felt her heart beating faster and faster against her ribcage. She held her breath until she couldn't hold it anymore. Then she let her breath out as slowly as possible, feeling her brain panic for air. The desperate need for oxygen helped her to focus on something other than being spot-lighted by Mistress's gaze.

"Yes, there is definitely something odd about your energy."

Sabina looked up to see Mistress looking at her, but not at her face. It was as if she was looking through her. Sabina hugged herself, holding onto her elbows.

Mistress opened the file and picked up a page. "Why have you failed at almost everything?" she asked rhetorically. "This is unprecedented. You are a capable girl. There are no deficiencies in you." This term always made Sabina bristle, but the Mistress took no notice as she continued to review her file. "The Healers have examined you several times at the request of your professors. Your brain is functioning at optimal levels. You have no physical impairments. You have suffered no trauma. It says you are disengaged, which is only seen in foreigners who become members of Silvedome." The Mistress drummed her fingers and thought.

This was news to Sabina. No one had ever told her she was disengaged. What did that mean? Sabina leaned forward and spoke softly, looking down, avoiding eye contact. "What does 'disengaged' mean?" she asked tentatively.

"What? Oh, yes, it means a disconnection between mind and body. Something is a barrier for you. Something that is not associated with trauma as with the foreigners." She answered mostly by talking out loud to herself.

Sabina leaned back and thought about that. *That was why I had to go to extra lessons on meditation and report all those articles on self-awareness. Why didn't they clue me in on what they were doing? It might have been more effective. So this is what is wrong with me! This explains why I am an outcast.*

"There is nothing wrong with you," Mistress rejected, interrupting Sabina's thought without looking up from her reading. Sabina's stomach dropped, and her cheeks flushed at her thoughts being so readable, and then she realized the Mistress never looked up. Sabina wanted to know how the Mistress knew what she was thinking. She was reading her chart and talking to herself out loud. Of course. This realization caused Sabina to feel ridiculous for overacting. She bit her lower lip and watched Mistress with curiosity.

"What's your association with Master Pond?" she inquired, setting the file down, folding her hands on top of it, and staring directly at Sabina.

Sabina was taken aback by the sign of disrespect Mistress showed Master Vela by calling him by his first name. It was one thing for the Rockdins to call him Pond because they had been family friends since Brom recruited him, but Mistress's relationship with him was strictly professional.

"Master Vela is a close friend of my father's," Sabina explained, unsure why the Mistress had asked.

"I'll ask you again. What is YOUR association with Master Pond?" she said impatiently.

"I don't know what you mean." Sabina answered defensively before correcting herself and politely saying, "He is a family friend. Nothing more."

The Mistress, who always sat up straight as if a steel rod was attached to her back, looked away and swallowed. Her eyes were closed, and Sabina could feel a wave of the Mistress's anger flash over her skin. She squirmed in her seat. The Mistress snapped her attention back to Sabina. Her eyes were glassy with age but sharp. Sabina felt nausea roll over her. What had she done wrong?

Sabina waited for her to say something, but the Mistress only glared at her. Her anger dissipated. "Have, have I done some-some-thing . . .?" Sabina asked nervously, not even wanting to say 'wrong'.

"There is *no reason* you should stutter. **W-h-y** do you stutter?" she demanded to know, making her eyes larger and pressing both palms into the desk, fingers spread wide.

"I, I don't understand," spluttered Sabina, getting upset but trying to close her eyes and give herself a mental pep talk. *Curd, she is intimidating. I cannot help my stuttering. Does she think I am doing this on purpose?*

The Mistress placed her head between her hands, her index and thumb supporting her head, elbows on her desk. She took a deep breath and sighed in frustration, looking up.

"I apologize, Sabina," she said in a controlled manner. "This is not your fault. I am angry at myself, not at you. It is my job to ensure that all the youth of Silvedome excel. Somehow, I have failed you. It is my fault." She scolded herself. "I am taking my anger at myself out on you," she remarked slowly. She closed her eyes briefly and opened them. "I am sorry," she said with conviction and sincerity.

Shifting uncomfortably in her seat, Sabina nodded in response to the apology, afraid to speak for the lump in her throat. She felt cold and drained from the day and wanted to go home, curl up in her blankets, and let today be over. *No, I cannot. I must see that bossy Messenger in the hospital. Oh, and Nana Honey. What dreadful news is she going to tell me? When will today be over? I feel like I have aged ten years.* Sabina bit her lip as she thought.

"Please help me understand your relationship with Master Pond." She tried again with more patience. "I'd like to know why he looms around you."

Frowning, Sabina thought about the Mistress's question. "He attends meals in the village with our family but outside of that, the only time I see him is when he stops by the tut to visit my father," she responded, thinking about all the times she had seen him over the last couple of years.

"What about your union interview with him? Since his Birth Challenge, he has told the Ori he will consider only you for a partner. So I ask you again, what is your relationship with him?"

Sabina practically choked on air. "What?" She felt like someone had smacked her hard on the forehead. "No," she conveyed, stunned and unsure she had heard the Mistress right. Why would Pond be interested in her? He barely acknowledged her in front of her father.

"Very well. Let's move on," Mistress stated, as if she didn't believe Sabina. "I'd like to discuss your studies with you. Do you intend to continue with Tradel or choose an apprenticeship?"

Finally, she got a question she had anticipated, even if she hadn't figured out the correct answer. "Tra-del," she responded, as if it were a question. Sabina tugged her tunic and sat up straighter, biting her lip.

Mistress nodded. "Good, I'm glad to hear it. At least you are smart enough to continue your studies, and if I were you, I would not get distracted by these union interviews." Pulling a sheet of paper from her drawer and grabbing a pen, she asked, "Do you know what you would like to study?"

"I, I," Sabina stammered and sighed. "I was going to request a test in all Moowins," she said. She knew it was an odd request since she hadn't shown any signs of possessing a Moowin, but she clung to the possibility of having one.

Mistress looked surprised, but hid a partial smile. "Interesting-ggggg. And. Why. Is. That? You understand that if your ritual shows any power toward a Moowin, you will be tested auto-matically?"

"Yes." Sabina nodded.

"So why test for Moowins you may not possess?"

She shrugged. How was she supposed to answer? That she believed she was special even if no one else did?

"That is an interesting request, Sabina, but it supports some-thing I have been thinking about."

"What?" Sabina asked curiously.

"Before we get to that, what are the three areas you wish to study?"

"A warrior makes sense. Out of all the skills I have learned, it is what I do best, but I'm not interested in the work a warrior does."

"I see," Mistress commented.

"I was thinking about land preservation, educator, and . . . a Healer Aide to the adult Ducklings." Sabina looked at her hands in her lap. She was waiting for the disapproval and the verbal objection she knew she would receive for asking for something that was not possible.

"I can see you working with the Ducklings. I understand you visit them when you stop by the hospital for your mother. You have a special spot in your heart for our Ducklings, and they adore you."

"I've spent a lot of time with them since I have been tested routinely to see if I am still a Duckling. Besides"—she shrugged—"if it wasn't for the Healers, I might still be a Duckling."

Mistress clarified, "You know those positions are for mild Healers, Influencers, and Persuaders?"

There was her objection. Feeling annoyed, Sabina didn't answer. Instead, she looked out the door numbly.

"What is your backup plan if you do not test into one of those Moowins?"

Hugging herself, Sabina moved her gaze from the door to the pile of dirt on the floor. Her toes were pointed, and she controlled herself from drawing the infinity sign with her toe.

"Sabina?" the Mistress called to her. "Sabina, I understand your passion, but you need to have a backup plan."

"Why?" Sabina cried out, surprising herself and wiping at her eyes. "This is what I want to do."

"Then you will either test into it or volunteer there," she clarified, unfazed, her tone firm.

Drying her face, Sabina continued to hug herself and look down, pouting.

Giving Sabina time, the Mistress went on. "I can see why you chose land preservation. I don't know anyone who goes on more walks to the pond or the trees than you. But why the educator?"

Shutting down emotionally, Sabina shrugged. She didn't understand why the Mistress was interrogating her. This was not a part of the process. No one else had to meet with the Mistress. This was Professor Tobe's job. He didn't question why people chose what they chose. Wasn't this part of the challenge, making decisions for yourself that you must live with?

"You are stronger-minded than your professors give you credit for," she pointed out. Sabina avoided eye contact, but she looked up to see if the Mistress was smiling. Her voice seemed pleased.

"I brought you here today to offer you an opportunity I have never offered anyone before, and I don't do it lightly." She paused to watch Sabina, who maintained eye contact. "I'd like to offer you an opportunity to study being a Shielder with me as your mentor. We would work one-on-one like an apprenticeship, but with no obligation to pursue this as your service."

Confused, Sabina questioned, "What if I don't test for a Shielder Moowin?"

"No matter," the Mistress remarked dismissively, waving her arm. "I've already told you that your energy is unusual. That is what we will work with. It will be a learning experience for both of us."

"I don't understand." Sabina spoke slowly, her eyebrows pinched. "How can I practice for a Shielder but not a Healer Aide?"

The Mistress smiled. "What do you know about rare Shielders?"

"That they can camouflage a person by making their appearance different. They can cast an invisible shield around someone to protect them from various elements, like Silvedome's dome. The stronger they are, the more shields they can cast and maintain at once."

Mistress added, "And a select few can make someone invisible, even if for a few moments."

Sabina nodded her understanding.

"I am a rare Shielder, and I help maintain Silvedome's shield," she said with pride. "I also help the warriors in battle to keep our people safe. I can cast several shields simultaneously, but I could never make anyone invisible. Until today! I made you invisible today while you sat here in my office."

"I was invisible?" Sabina doubted what she was hearing.

The Mistress nodded and watched her.

"How is that possible? Why didn't I notice?"

"You won't notice your invisibility as you are inside the shield. You will always see yourself, but others will see the shield. Depending on your talents, you may feel or sense the energy shift when a shield is placed on you."

"Does this mean I have a talent for shielding?" Sabina asked with delight.

"No, I am afraid it neither confirms nor denies any shield talent. The fact is that anyone can be shielded regardless of their capabilities, and until your Birth Challenge, we will not know if you have any talent for shielding. I am interested in discovering why I can perform this rare talent on you alone."

Disappointed that she didn't show a sign of this Moowin, she slumped back in the wooden chair. "So, if I don't have a talent for shielding, what good would it do for me to study being a Shielder? I don't see how I could be of use or how I could use the knowledge without the talent. Wouldn't it just be a hobby?"

"I suspect you must have some talent for it, much like Healer Aides have some strange infinity to healing despite their level of talent being minimal." She tapped her chin, thinking. "I wonder if you may be an amplifier to a Shielder Moowin. That could explain why I made you invisible. But an amplifier has not existed since the nuclear war."

That got Sabina's attention. She felt a little tickle in her stomach at the idea of being needed and possibly having any association with a Moowin. Then she considered working with the Mistress, which led to catastrophic thoughts. The thought that worried her the most was feeling like she didn't matter.

"You don't even like me," Sabina whined, avoiding eye contact.

"Not true. I am quite fascinated by you. It is widely known that I do not like your father nor that *gnat*, Master Pond, but I have nothing against you," she stated matter-of-factly.

"Why don't you like my father?" Sabina asked defensively, wishing she hadn't blurted that out.

"That is my business, but I will entertain your question. I don't trust him. I think he is hiding something from me."

She knew her father guarded information but didn't think it was possible not to like him. He was a powerful Influencer, after all. Not knowing what to say about that or how she should feel about the Mistress's response, she moved on. "Is this approved with the Ori?"

"The Ori may dismiss this idea. They may say it is far-fetched, but something needs to be done. There are fewer and fewer

Shielders. This could be an advancement in the field. There are no known Shielder Aides or studies. It has purely operated on apprenticeship status."

"What if I don't have any talent for the Shielder Moowin and the Ori doesn't approve my request to study with you? Then I have lost an option to test for studying in a different field." She bit her lower lip.

"Let me worry about that. I have a feeling about you, and I think I can prove the validity of this . . . unusual request. I promise I will make this work for your best interest. You have my word."

"Professor Tobe is expecting my answer today. RIGHT NOW. What if things go wrong?"

Pursing her lips, Mistress stood up and walked to the front of her desk. She leaned against the desk inches from Sabina, who wanted to slide her chair backward to create space. The Mistress was almost at her eye level, eliminating the difference in their stature. "Sabina, I will level with you and be vulnerable. The way I see it, we need each other. Without my help, you will serve Silve-dome by collecting animals from traps in the field, replacing the water basin, or doing other tasks aligned with your school scores. Shall I remind you that you haven't shown an aptitude for anything except average fighting skills, which you have confessed you aren't interested in pursuing?" She paused to let her words soak in. "You need me to help you petition on your behalf to be a Healer Aide, and I need someone who will . . . potentially follow in my footsteps."

Sabina immediately objected but was cut off.

"There are a few people who believe I am getting old," she huffed, waving her arm. "As if my age somehow makes me obsolete when I am quite capable and active. A few prominent people are pushing for Master Pond to take my place on the council since there isn't another person with my skill level beside him. In my humble opinion, Master Pond has his best interest at heart, not the villagers'."

The Mistress rose, turned her back to Sabina, and took a few steps. "I will not stand idly by and let Master Pond desecrate everything I have worked for, even if his power makes him worthy of his service." She turned back to Sabina, arms taut by her side. "With you as my apprentice, I can soothe their concerns about my ability to continue to serve. Do we have a deal?"

"Mistress, you just reprimanded me. How am I supposed to be an apprentice if I'm always afraid of making a mistake?" she asked, genuinely concerned about this idea.

"Make no mistake, Sabina. I will follow, uphold, and enforce the rules of Silvedome. I made an unbreakable oath to do so, and I will not spare you or anyone else," she promised gravely. "However, I can show compassion and give forgiveness where forgiveness is due. Remember, I want you to succeed."

"I don't know," Sabina hesitated, shaking her head and wishing she had time to consult with someone, wishing she knew what her father would say.

"I will not push you into this agreement, Sabina. This is at your discretion, but opportunities like this don't come around often. Let me know your decision after you speak with Professor Tobe, as I will need to seek approval from the Ori for both the apprenticed Shield and the Healer Aide course. If I may make one suggestion about your studies . . ." She waited, raising both eyebrows.

Sabina nodded dully.

"If you work with me, I think our focus should be on warrior training for a Shielder. No one will argue about bringing someone who can amplify the strength of Shielders to protect our warriors. Plus, I can make you invisible to keep you safe," she vowed solemnly. "If you agree, tell Professor Tobe you wish to study warrior training. I will speak to the Ori." The Mistress nodded to Sabina and went to the door. "I will get Professor Tobe."

Sabina felt she could practically melt into the chair. She let her head fall back, and she closed her eyes. Her head was pounding. *What should I do? What would Father want me to do?* At that, the conversation with Fawn flashed into her mind. Fawn had warned her about the changes that come from the Birth Challenge, but she also encouraged her to think for herself. This is what the Birth Challenge was all about. Stepping outside your parents' shadows and taking full responsibility for yourself and your decisions. Tullom. This was harder than she expected it to be.

Slowly, sitting back up, Sabina prepared herself for the next task. She knew she had moments before Professor Tobe would be here. Sabina analyzed her choices and found she was stuck on two ideas. One, she knew she wanted to work with the adult Ducklings, and two, she liked the idea that she could make a difference as an amplifier. The Mistress had sold her a long-time wish to be needed and valuable. It was too enticing not to lay down all her fears and to take the leap of faith it would all work out.

She was standing in the pile of dirt she had created on the floor, with her bag swung across her shoulders, facing the door, prepared, when the Mistress came into view. She was a few steps ahead of Professor Tobe huffing along.

"I agree," Sabina confirmed firmly, feeling like she had a purpose for the first time in her life, and it felt good. She felt powerful at that moment. She was standing up with as much dignity as she could muster, with her hair clumping, her tunic muddy, and the pile of dirt on the floor.

The Mistress gave a small, half smile that was barely noticeable. "Very well." She turned to face Professor Tobe, who had finally made it to the door's entrance. "Professor Tobe, if you will excuse me. I'm on my way to discuss Sabina's Birth Challenge with the Ori. She will be approved to study as a Healer Aide. Sabina, once you complete the arrangements for your Birth Challenge, you are to go to the hospital to show Master Alf around Silvedome."

"What's this?" demanded Professor Tobe to the Mistress's back, but the Mistress did not stop.

She was already three steps down the hallway, striding with purpose as her long dress robe draped on the floor.

The professor's face was drawn back and confused. "Mistress?" Professor Tobe hollered louder, but she continued to the door. Sabina heard the crash of the door slamming shut. Frowning, Professor Tobe turned to Sabina.

"You, come with me," he barked and waddled to his office a few doors down, panting the whole time and taking a cloth to wipe his forehead.

Walking one slow step at a time, Sabina followed him into his office, which was more significant than the Mistress's despite her status. However, Professor Tobe needed the extra space to move around. He shuffled sideways to his desk and sat down, wiping his forehead with his cloth and tucking it into the pocket of his dress tunic. He licked his lips as he picked up Sabina's file. She sat down, keeping her satchel on her shoulder.

"As you know," he grumbled, muffling his words, "we are here to finalize your Birth Challenge. This is a requirement of all citizens of Silvedome on their sixteenth birthday or the date they become citizens of Silvedome, blah, blah, blah. You get the formality," he stated and dropped her letter to the desk. "So, what will it be, Sabina?" he asked, picking up his pen, preparing to write, and leaning over her paperwork before looking at her.

Unprepared for the lack of formality, Sabina was startled to realize he was already asking her about her studies. Butterflies were in her stomach, and she felt like static electricity was drumming through her. It was as if her ears blocked out the sound, and she couldn't hear her voice when she answered.

"I, I, I want to be tested for all eight Moowins starting with the Protector course. Then it doesn't matter."

"That is not how it works. If the ritual shows you possess any talent for a Moowin, you will be tested to see the strength of that Moowin. Now, what are your three studies?" He licked his lip, head down. Sabina didn't answer and Professor Tobe looked at her with a bored expression.

Swallowing hard and feeling cotton-mouthed, Sabina gripped her satchel strap harder. "With all due respect," she said, trembling and looking down, "I want to be tested for all eight Moowins even if the ritual doesn't reveal I have any Moowins." Sabina got quieter with each word.

"Are you done?" He yawned.

Sabina nodded. She bounced her leg.

"Good, shall we continue?" He picked up his pen. "What are your three studies?"

"Warrior training, land preservation, and . . . Healer's Aide," she answered softly.

"Huh." He glanced up, but he wrote down her request in the appropriate spots on the form.

Sabina could tell that the professor was done recording the Birth Challenge. Her cheeks were flushed, her mouth was dry, and her stomach was practically cramping with nerves that caused her spine to curve. She huddled in on herself and reminded herself she could be brave. She could do this. She could ask for what she wanted. She had a right to request this. She recalled the rules of Silvedome's Birth Challenge in her mind.

"What is this nonsense about studying to be a Healer Aide?" he pried, dropping his pen and leaning back in the special chair made for him. He had interlocked his palms at the crest of his belly, eyeing her with disbelief. "I haven't heard anyone tell me you showed any signs of a Moowin. It seems more like you might work with a Healer Aide. You could be on cleanup duty or the sterilization team," he offered.

Ignoring his questions because she wasn't sure how to respond, she changed the topic. "Professor Tobe, it is my right to request to be tested on eight Moowins regardless of the ritual. I have requested at the appropriate time, under the laws of Silve-dome's Birth Challenge," she declared in a shaky voice. She avoided eye contact and kept her eyes focused on her paper. Counting slowly to herself, she tried to relax her muscles mentally.

Professor Tobe was quiet for a moment as if he was processing what she had said. Perhaps he was slowly boiling over like a pot of water. He picked up the pen, agitated. "Fine. If you want to embarrass yourself and waste the professor's time to prove something to yourself, so be it," he complained as he wrote it on the paper and dropped the pen.

Sabina could feel acid in her throat as Professor Tobe stood up, but she was secretly proud of herself.

"Come on then. YOU have given me a bunch of work to do. I must get this all coordinated and to the Ori," he spat as he waddled sideways around his desk.

With his office door open, Sabina stood up quickly and hustled outside the door in front of him, waiting for him to walk her to the exiting door. They walked in silence down the hallway, minus the sound of Professor Tobe struggling to breathe.

CHAPTER 5

Guests

As soon as she and Professor Tobe were outside, Sabina quietly thanked him and took off toward the hospital with her mind racing. A breeze swept across her, and she realized her tunic was damp with sweat. *Great,* she thought. *Perfect. I'll meet Master Alf, looking like a buffoon.*

Arriving at the hospital, Sabina quickly went in and used the restroom. Not only was she desperate to pee, but she also wanted to finger-brush her hair. She did the best she could and wiped down her boots and tunic, getting as much mud off her attire as possible. A Scholar Messenger was at the door waiting for her when she walked out of the bathroom.

"Sabina," Scholar Sandalwood said, wrapping his arm through hers. "You have been holding out on me." He patted her hand. "Master Alf," he said and then leaned in and whispered, "I'd butter him up and put him on my plate if I wasn't spoken for. You luc-keee girl. Mmm." Pulling away, he continued without missing a beat. "He's right over here." He showed her a booth where Master Alf was lying back, propped up on one elbow, smiling mischievously.

"Now you be sure to tell me how your union interview goes," he said, walking away slowly.

"She is already taken with me, Scholar Sandalwood," Master Alf called out.

Scholar Sandalwood pointed his index finger at Sabina and smiled. "I want details, lots and lots of details," he said.

Controlling her reaction not to roll her eyes, she walked forward and crossed her arms.

"Are you healed?" she said, bobbing her head in annoyance.

"Better than ever," he asserted, swinging his legs off the bed table, standing up, and putting on his hat. "I'd say it is time for lunch."

Sabina's stomach dropped. Curd, Professor Tobe forgot to go over Brom's guest account. Sabina had no idea how it worked.

"Ah, would you wait right here? I'll be right back."

"Oh no you don't," he said, catching up with her. "Some feisty older lady in a black wedding dress made it clear we are inseparable for the next two weeks or until I'm settled," he said, leaning in toward her with a chummy smile.

"Fine." Letting out a breath and trying to hide her annoyance, she walked through the hallway to the stairs that led to the second floor. She made her way to Marigold's area, where she worked as a Healer Aide to baby Ducklings. Flann kept up and remained quiet, mostly looking around with his hands in his pockets like he was on a leisurely stroll, especially with that hat on.

"I'm going to speak with my mother. I'll be right there." She pointed to Marigold across the room, who was burping a baby in a rocking chair. It always amazed Sabina to see her mother at work. She became a different person when she held those babies. Her face softened, and her spirit seemed to sing.

Smiling while heading toward Marigold, Flann started to say, "Brom's partner—" before Sabina put her arm out to stop him. "What?" he said, raising both arms in an innocent gesture. "I want to meet her."

Noticing the commotion, Marigold stood up with her no-nonsense expression on her face and placed the baby gently down in her crib. She was the only one in the nursery, yet she would still consider this 'disturbing' her while she worked.

"Congratulations, you get to meet her," Sabina said through gritted teeth, already feeling like she had been slapped in the face with the disapproving look her mother gave them.

Marigold eyed Master Alf as she crossed the room. She walked between them, and as she passed, she grabbed Sabina's arm hard, dragging her outside the room. Flann started to follow, but Marigold turned to face him with her palm out. "Privacy," she said in a low, authoritative voice. Then continued to drag Sabina outside the nursery while Flann stood with his hands in his pockets, looking around.

"What are you doing *here*? You should be in school and **who** have you brought with you?" she spat in an angry whisper.

"That's Master Alf from Aliward. He arrived early with an injury. He is now my responsibility, and I have been called out of school to retrieve him from the hospital."

"That explains the unplanned ritual bells," she said, leaning around Sabina to look at Master Alf again. "He is your union interview," she said with a serious face.

Sabina nodded.

"I assume you need my help, or you would not be here. What is it then?" She crossed her arms and leaned back as if to say she would expect no less.

Biting her lower lip in embarrassment and feeling the shame of bothering her mother at her work, Sabina said, "How do I access the tokens for Father's guest and how much does he get per day?"

"The villagers will know he is a guest. There isn't a stranger in this village. Brom gets thirty tokens daily for guests for the first seven days, then fifteen for the next seven days. That is more than enough to feed him, entertain him, buy him clothes, get his necessities started, and begin his savings. After that, Silvedome expects him to make his own way, so tell him to save up. Once he is serving, he will earn ten tokens a day, the same as us. He is a Messenger, no?"

"Yes."

"Silvedome has plenty of Messengers," she said, moving past Sabina to approach Master Alf.

"Greetings." Marigold gave a slight bow. "Welcome to Silvedome. We have a room prepared for you in our home until the Ori places you in your own place. Sabina will attend to you as I reside at the hospital, and Brom is traveling. I'm sure you will find your life here much simpler than where you are from. Aliward, is it?"

"Yes, and thank you—" Flann answered pleasantly, poised to ask a question.

"May I ask what you did for work in Aliward, Master Alf?"

"I was a bookkeeper—" he replied.

"Sabina must introduce you to Flood Parvat then. He runs Silvedome's token system." With a baby crying, Marigold gave a tight smile. "Excuse me."

Walking out of the nursery, Sabina felt relieved that her mother didn't criticize her about her attire or hair. She didn't bring up her studies either, which would have been a chance for Marigold to remind Sabina of her place in the village. *Blessing for me that she was distracted,* thought Sabina.

"She was pleasant," Flann announced sarcastically, dropping his smile.

"You wanted to talk with her," Sabina responded dryly.

They made their way down the hallway to the stairs with silence between them until Flann asked, "Do you have a **p**roblem with me? I'm sensing some mental interference from you."

Sabina chose to ignore him as much as she possibly could.

"Your thoughts are like tiny pebbles hitting against my mind," he claimed, showing the smallest space between his thumb and his forefinger. "So, what is it? Can't resist my good looks?" he suggested, pulling at his vest with self-importance.

"Please." She rolled her eyes, taking the bait.

"Please, what?" He raised one eyebrow. "Grant you the privilege of being in my presence? Yes, and you are welcome."

"Ugh," Sabina sighed, raising her arms in surrender.

Flann gave a genuine smile, seeming to enjoy her frustration.

"I don't think we *need* to have a union interview," Sabina confirmed out of annoyance.

"Tsk, tsk, tsk." Flann mocked her. "You can only make that judgment when you have entered a-dult-hood." He smiled ruefully and bounced his head from side to side. "You must wait until after your Birth Challenge before you can declare your intentions, and you are required to entertain one formal meeting with me. You are stuck with me, kid."

Insulted and annoyed, Sabina took a breath to respond, but at that moment, a group of Ducklings walked across the intersecting hallway. The Ducklings immediately recognized Sabina.

"Bebe, Bebe," was heard from the group as they gathered around her, touching her hair, and trying to hug her. Unnoticed by the Ducklings, Flann was pushed aside.

"When you going to visit?" one asked.

"Too long, too long and no Bebe," another shouted.

"Come with us. We go to BBBIIIGGG tree," another announced, stretching his arms out as wide as he could.

"Ducklings. My loves," the Master Persuader called.

Sabina felt the pull of energy from the Master Persuader. She was most sensitive to energy shifts around the Ducklings.

"Come with me. We have much to see and do," she explained excitedly. The group shifted their attention from Sabina to Master Tulip Frock.

Master Frock smiled, waved, and blew a friendly kiss goodbye to Sabina as the group gathered around her. She guided them gently by their shoulders back into a straight line.

"What is that about?" Flann uttered, apparently baffled.

"I spend a lot of time volunteering and playing with the Ducklings. They are like family to me," Sabina said, still smiling from her interaction with them. "They miss me."

"No, I mean, your village doesn't put them to sleep at birth?"

Sabina's stomach rolled with nausea at the thought. She stopped in her tracks and was ready to punch him in the stomach. But, when she turned to face him, she saw he was asking out of confusion and not condemnation. Sabina's whole body relaxed, and her drawn-back arm dropped by her side. Flann was oblivious of her preparation to strike him. He was still staring, puzzled, at the group of Ducklings and hadn't moved forward with Sabina.

She breathed deeply through her nose to center herself. Her emotions got carried away. She was fiercely protective of her family. This was his first day in Silvedome. Other lands had different principles and beliefs, she reminded herself. He didn't know better.

"Ducklings are a blessing to our people. They are a source of joy. They have the best magic, for they are light and free from conditioned darkness. Even when the Healers are unable to heal their ailments, they are full of love of life and others. It is considered an honor to serve them and be around them."

"Oh yeah, and how did you get that honor?" Flann taunted as they walked forward.

"I was *born* a Duckling," she confessed defensively, but then softened. "But the Healers were able to heal me completely . . . with time. That is how Brom came to know my mother, Marigold. She is not my birth mother. I never knew my birth mother. She died when I was an infant. Marigold cared for me in this nursery when Brom first became a citizen of Silvedome."

Sabina knew very little of her own story. Flann walked with his hands in his pockets, looking down in concentration. He was meshing together the story Brom had told him over the course of last year. Marigold was exiled from Silvedome for her relationship with another man before meeting Brom. It was during Marigold's banishment that she started caregiving for Sabina. Flann chose not to say anything. That was not his place, and he had a job to do.

"I've never seen an adult with limited capabilities. Why do you call them Ducklings? Are they like pets?"

"No, they are not pets. In case you haven't noticed, there are no pets in Silvedome. One would think you were raised without . . . never mind. Ducklings has a double meaning. It is a term of endearment like sweetheart and also symbolizes a connection to family, intuition, and emotions."

Flann shrugged.

About to exit the hospital, Scholar Sandalwood shouted to their backs. "Remember. I want details. And Master Alf, visit me an-y-time."

Flann shook his head. "I think I am going to like it here. Silvedome treats their Moowins like heroes instead of slaves."

He said it jokingly, but Sabina felt her gut clench at the words. She felt compassion for him in that moment. He probably was enslaved. Most of the world outside Silvedome treated Moowins like slaves. Sabina never understood it. Moowins were powerful, yet they gave all their power away and were subject to cruel treatment by others.

Not knowing what to say and feeling obligated to teach him the ways of Silvedome, she corrected him. "No, not heroes. But they are admired and perceived as special. Moowins make our village stronger, and they make people's lives easier and more enjoyable. You will find that we treat everyone as one, for Silvedome believes we are all connected. People with Moowins have a better status in life, but everyone is respected for their work and paid the same. Everyone has the same opportunity to serve on the Ori or earn a better sector with a nicer, bigger home. You can even earn a home closer to the village square. But everyone serves Silvedome."

"Yeah, like I said. Moowins are heroes here. They make your life better and they are admired for it. What is a hero if he is not someone who is admired for what they can do?"

Sabina ground her teeth. Her immediate thought was he was so tricky, but then she started to slow down her pace as she considered his words as they crossed the bridge into the village square for lunch. *Shoot, he has a point. But then again, so do I. Huh. Perhaps we can both be right.*

Sabina bit down on her lower lip and pushed back the hair that was blowing in her face. "What do you want to eat? The booths are organized by plant, and then mildest to strongest meats, starting with white meats to red meats." She pointed to the half circle of food booths. "Over at the end, there is fish. Everything is good and everything costs the same number of tokens. Meals are two tokens. Each booth comes with a serving of your main course and three sides, so you can choose extra meat as one of the three. Sides are a vegetable, nuts, dried or fresh fruit, roll of bread, or dessert. Do you see the booth labels overhead? They tell you what main course they serve. Oh, and they only serve one main course at each booth, but they change what they serve each day."

"I see. I'll take the rabbit then."

Nervous at how this would work, Sabina followed Flann toward the booth. They were serving buckeye rabbit in wine sauce with peas. There were only three people ahead of them. Flann observed the process. There was a bored Messenger sitting at the corner of the booth shooting messages to another Messenger. As Flann wasn't addressed in the message, his mind was not open to receiving them, but he could feel the energy exchange.

"What is he communicating?" he asked, leaning into Sabina and speaking softly.

Sabina glanced in the direction Flann nodded. "The token exchanges. He is identifying who the person is and communicating to the Messenger who works in the bank to subtract two tokens from his account."

"Why don't you just carry the tokens? Seems like a waste of a Messenger's talent," he whispered.

"We have an abundance of Messengers. This gives the mild Messengers work and makes life simpler. Plus, we don't have physical tokens."

"What? What do you do if you leave Silvedome?"

"We don't. I mean, a few do, but they are expected to bring supplies with them or trade." Sabina shrugged and stopped talking as it was their turn.

The Messenger stood up as Flann approached with his index finger lifted, as if to say 'just one minute'. Sabina shifted her weight back and forth, not sure if she needed to say anything. She didn't know exactly how this all worked. Flann felt the energy exchange and knew he was talking with someone. Hands in his pocket, he rocked back on his heels as he waited.

"Name," the Messenger said, bored in his role.

"Flann Alf of Aliward," he answered while Sabina grabbed her satchel bag, too slow to speak.

"Correction, Master Alf. You are of Silvedome now. Welcome. You are a guest to Brom Rockdin?" The Messenger spoke almost robotically.

"Yes," Flann answered. Turning to Sabina, he whispered. "I better get that right next time."

"You have two weeks under Brom's account. See Flood Parvat before the end of the two weeks to set up your account." The Messenger sat back down.

"Sides?" the worker called out impatiently.

"Right. Extra meat, bread roll, and if that's cherry pie, I'll take that." The worker handed Flann his food on metal plates with metal utensils and a folded cloth.

"Nothing for you?" Flann noticed that Sabina let the person behind them order.

"I'll go to the duck line," she responded, following him to a seat. "I'll be back."

"Where's the drink?" Flann shouted after her, looking

around. He shrugged and sat down to start eating when Sabina didn't stop to answer.

Sabina ignored the question and realized she had made a mistake. She should have stopped by the market to pick him up a canteen first. She would do that next. As she got in line, she glanced over at Flann to see him digging into the food without reservation. *Everything is okay. Everything is fine. It is all working out,* she told herself. As she waited in line, Markus approached and pulled her father's letter out of her pocket.

"What's this? A love letter from your new admirer?" he teased, waving the letter in the air. Another classmate joined the mockery while Sabina dropped her satchel and reached for her father's letter. Despite her height advantage, he moved backward and toyed with her.

"Yeah. We heard you have a union interview. *Who's* the special REJECT?" Dormancy sneered.

"Alf, or is it Elf like all those fantasy books you are always reading?" Markus taunted, pushing Sabina back and keeping the letter out of reach as he laughed.

"What's an Alf?" Dormancy played along but stopped. Suddenly, he quieted as a tall man with short hair ran with speed and power toward them.

Markus's smile was still on his face as he started to look backward at what Dormancy was focusing on. The man slowed his steps and then stepped right up to Markus, squeezing his wrist with enough pressure that Sabina was sure she heard his bone pop. Markus was now hopping on one foot in pain and yelling at the man as he let go of the letter.

The tall man took the letter from Markus as soon as he released it. "Where I come from, letters are a *private* matter," he said in calm authority. Power was radiating off him, and Sabina had to tilt her head to look at him.

Sabina saw Master Lockin approach. "Ooooooohhhhh my. You run fast," she huffed. She was giggling and exuberant while she placed her hands on her chest, indicating that she needed to catch her breath. She took the scene in. Her puffy skirt shifted back and forth as she looked around.

Sabina saw the villagers in the square eating slowly and watching them. She looked for Flann, who was easy to find because he was the only one standing. He seemed torn between helping her and remaining where he was.

The strange man finally let go of Markus's wrist. His face was redder than Sabina had seen it. He was holding his wrist and giving death stares at the stranger. It seemed likely that Markus wanted to challenge him. Markus was clearly going to be a Protector Moowin.

"This is *ALL* a misunderstanding," Master Lockin stated, placing her hands affectionately on the arm of the stranger who was buttoning his jacket back up from his sprint. Her smile was overenthusiastic, as if she were watching a dramatic scene being performed at The Mox.

"Markus, Dormancy, and Sabina, I'm pleased to introduce you to **B**enford **Tulk** from Pux. He is here for a performance at The Mox to celebrate Actalie." She beamed with joy. Her tone was upbeat. "He is *MY* guest for the next few days. He is an incredible **Master** Performer. Aaaannnddd, he has some talent for Protector, too," she gushed like she was a baby adult. She was wiping under her eyes as if she had sweat on her cheeks, but there was nothing there.

Benford Tulk stood straight and tall, with his feet apart. His hand grasped his other wrist, which was the hand holding Sabina's letter. He had a gray-and-black textured wool suit. At the introduction, Benford stepped forward and held out Sabina's letter to her, still folded between his index and middle finger.

Sabina took her letter back slowly, making sure their fingers didn't touch, and she didn't make eye contact. She stayed focused on her father's letter, as her hair slid forward, covering her face. Retrieving it and putting it back in her pocket, she pretended to be interested in the tunic. She forgot to say thank you or show any gratitude. She was too stunned by the iconic Performer who was standing before her tall and good-looking. Benford Tulk, the famous actor from Pux who was a triple threat and a proficient Protector. Sky Above. Sabina had seen him perform shortly after he became an adult. He was incredible.

"Oh curd. I knew you looked familiar," Dormancy said, looking like he was going to eat his finger as he used his hand to hide how big his smile was. Moments before, he was probably ready to defend Markus from this man; now Dormancy was bouncing around in excitement, completely forgetting what he had just done. Markus was rubbing his wrist and looked not at all impressed with the revelation that a star was in front of him.

"You do me great honors," said Master Tulk. "It is my pleasure to be here and to help . . . Sa-bin-a, is it?"

"Oh yes, I'm sure that Sabina appreciates your assistance as I do. Markus and Dormancy, I think you can move on, or do I need to report you to Professor Harren? I'm sure he would like to give you some lessons on peaceful behavior," Master Lockin said to them as if they were eight years old.

Not staying to hear more, Markus and Dormancy went to a different line for food. Master Lockin wrapped her arm around Master Tulk's arm and started to pull him back toward The Mox. She was chatting with him about how he enjoyed his lunch.

Sabina went back to her satchel. She pulled it on her shoulder and got back in line. She crossed her arms and counted to ten slowly. *Everything is as it should be,* she reminded herself. *Nothing has gone wrong.* She looked over to Flann, half standing with his knee resting on the chair, taking large bites out of his bread roll. She noticed his food was almost finished. She thought about skipping the meal but decided otherwise, since she had already missed breakfast.

With her food in hand and feeling sluggish, she headed back to Flann. Her cheek still felt red from the embarrassment of Markus almost reading her letter, and her awkwardness around Master Tulk. She couldn't even say a word. *So embarrassing. I just stood there, looking down.*

"You need to read that letter and burn it," Flann declared before she could even sit down.

Flicking her eyes to his, she questioned, "How do you know that's what I *need* to do?" This man-child was so bossy.

"Your father is in my head. I know what he wants."

She sat down and took a large bite of duck, using her fingers, ignoring etiquette. Juices ran down her chin, and she closed her eyes. Food felt so comforting right now. If she could only block out this bossy redhead, she could enjoy her meal.

Flann sat down and seemed to wait for her to chew.

"You eat like a child," Flann criticized, handing her his cloth.

"I eat like . . ." She stopped talking and let it go. But she wanted to say she eats like she wants to. Too bad she wasn't confrontational or bold.

"You eat like what?"

"Never mind," she grumbled. "What do you mean, my father is in your head? He is no Messenger."

Flann shrugged. "He has unlimited resources. The man is in good graces wherever he goes."

Sabina smirked for a split second before taking another giant bite and wiping her hands free of juices. *Brom probably does have a Messenger at his side.*

"You are making a mess." Flann got up, took her napkin, and laid it across her lap. He handed her the utensils. "My baby sister, who is six, can eat with less of a mess than you."

Bug off, reddie, Sabina thought, annoyed. Instead, she mumbled, "I'm sorry I am offending you." She stood up and wiped her hands and face, uninterested in eating in front of him.

"What are you doing? Sit down and eat."

"No thanks. I'm finished." She grabbed her bread roll and dried mangoes, dumping them in the food container in her satchel.

"Don't be like that. Sit down, please. Enjoy your food."

"Let's go get your canteen for water. I need to stop by the tut, so let's pick up your things."

"Good. Then when we get to your home, you can read your father's letter, and I'll burn it for you."

"I am capable of burning it myself." She grabbed her tray and walked over to the dish bin.

"I never said you weren't." He followed her with a pleasant smile.

"Why do I need to burn my letter, and when did my father tell you that?"

"So many questions from someone who is described to be quiet?"

"Did Brom tell you that?" she snapped.

Flann nodded.

Sabina brooded.

As they walked to the shops, she recalled their conversation from this morning. "Didn't you say you were sent here to be my puppet?" she asked triumphantly.

"Oh, is that what you heard? Sorry, I don't recall what I said after I saw you naked. I could have said anything," he claimed.

Cheeks flaming hot both from anger and embarrassment, she glared at him as if she despised him.

"Don't be angry with me. I'm the one who should be angry at you," he said jovially.

"What? How? Why? What have I done to you?" Sabina spat.

"Where I am from, any adult non-eloped male who sees another adult non-eloped naked female is required to elope. So, your act"—he toyed with her hair—"cost me my right to choose my bride-to-be."

"No. N-O-," Sabina insisted, raising her palm toward him to stop him from playing with her hair. "That is not going to happen. First off, you shouldn't have been there. Secondly, we are not in your land. We are in Silvedome. AND thirdly, no. I'm not entering a union with you."

"Look, I get it. You are embarrassed by your overwhelming desire for me. But we both know I made my presence known to you. It could have gone down any number of ways. You *chose* to present yourself to me N-A-K-E-D," he embellished with a mocking curtsy. "Then you freaked out when I didn't respond the way you wanted. It's okay. I forgive you for throwing that rock at me. It wasn't gentlemanly to look at you with surprise on my face. I wasn't prepared for your forwardness. Now I know what kind of woman you are, and I am prepared. You can surprise me *any time you want*." He smiled.

"My head was *un-der* WATER. I didn't hear you. AND YOU SHOULDN'T HAVE BEEN ABLE TO GET IN THERE," Sabina fumed.

Raising his hands in a peace offering, Flann teased, "No need to explain. I won't tell your father, but you should tell the other union interviews. It's only fair to let them know where we stand."

Sabina stomped up to the trader's door and opened it for Flann. He walked in smiling brightly, declaring, "Why, thank you. You shouldn't have!" As he walked past her, he breathed, "Your secret is safe with me."

"I hope lightning strikes you," she whispered through gritted teeth when he was out of earshot. In disgust, she decided she wasn't going to help him. Instead, she shouted to him that he had twenty-six tokens and should get what he needed. Then she shut the door and sat on a bench outside the store. Her arms crossed, her satchel resting on the dirt, her mind was full of visions of beating Flann up until he was whimpering. He was so infuriating, but even agitated at him, she still felt guilty for not helping him.

~

Flann turned to see her shut the door, engrossed in anger. He was enjoying his assignment much more than he thought he would. Sabina had a hidden temper, and she took the bait every time. Flann realized it was way better than pestering his little sister. He smiled with pure delight. He didn't know if he liked her, but he enjoyed making her angry.

~

Twenty minutes later, Sabina had simmered down. She no longer envisioned Flann with his hands bound up and tape over his mouth. She wished she would have finished her meal and ignored him. Now she was hungry and tired. Plus, she still needed to go to her last class, get Flann settled in his room, and visit Nana Honey. Uncertainty surfaced about what Nana Honey wanted, and she felt a million different emotions playing in her body. One was a pang of mounting guilt for leaving her 'guest' to figure things out.

Opening the door to the store, Sabina felt a tension in her shoulders, and her jaw locked at the sign of Flann laughing and conversing with the young Messenger behind the counter. Flamingo Ura swept all her beautiful, long red hair over one shoulder as Flann laughed at whatever she had said.

Good grief, why does everyone like him? He is like a pesky red ant. Sabina walked up to them and dropped her satchel on the floor with a thump. Her normal shy character was overridden by exhaustion and worries over her upcoming obstacles.

"Sabina." Flamingo blushed, looking down but smiling. "I'm sorry to hear you have a headache and don't have time to go to the Healers. Flann was explaining the circumstance while you rested outside. I understand how it is with your Birth Challenge coming up. They really overwhelm you, don't they? Plus, having a guest! I can't imagine." She batted her eyes at Flann while placing her hand over her heart. "You poor thing. I was happy to help you. I have Flann started with all the supplies he'll need."

"And I thank you for your help," he commented, smiling, and leaning on the counter. "But we must be on our way." He feigned disappointment and picked up the purchased items.

Even though Flamingo directed the conversation toward Sabina, it was like she wasn't there. She picked up her satchel, which was feeling heavier by the moment, and grabbed a few of Flann's items.

"You have to be going so soon? That's a shame. Come back

and see me," she invited, smiling sweetly. "Sabina, I'd be happy to help anytime. In fact, I'd be happy to take him to The Mox tonight for the performance so you can rest. You skip those performances anyway, and Flann should see it."

Again, the conversation was about her and seemed to be directed toward her, but had very little to do with her. Flamingo had all her attention on Flann, who was making his way around the merchandise and to the door.

"That is kind of you, Flamingo, but what type of guest would I be to leave my host home alone not feeling well. Thank you for your offer." With that, he was through the door.

Sabina shuffled through behind him, feeling exhausted and hungry. She was completely puzzled and annoyed that Flann made an impact with so many girls. She didn't know what they saw in him. Couldn't they tell he was faking niceties?

Flann waited until they were a few feet away from the store before speaking to Sabina. She looked down in a daze, thinking about whether her studies were going to get approved, what Mistress would have her do, and when she could get rid of him, when he interrupted.

"I really thought you were going to be better at this, but you are not. I can see I'm going to have to take care of things myself."

"What are you talking about?" Sabina questioned.

"Are you going to let everyone flirt with me? Am I not your union interview and guest? I'm new to the customs here and don't know what is acceptable behavior and what isn't," Flann complained.

"What? Am I supposed to chaperone you?"

"Yyyyeeesss. That is exactly what you should be doing." He sighed, looking up at the sky, raising his hands up as much as he could while carrying the bags. "You finally get it."

"What do you want me to do?" she challenged.

"Tell people to bug off or tell them I'm your union interview. Claim me, for tullom sake. Like that bright, bubbly woman did in the village square with her guest."

"You heard that from where you were sitting?" Sabina doubted that. "And I don't want to claim you. How can I anyway? Aren't you already in a union interview with someone else?" She demanded to know, turning to see his reaction.

He debated what to say. He had a job and a role to play. But he had made an unbreakable promise to two people, and those promises conflicted with each other. That was the gamble he made when he took this job. Now he questioned how he was going to honor both people. He shook his head as he thought to himself.

"So, you deny what you said earlier?" she pressed, watching him closely.

"It is true that I love another person back home, but she is above my station. Even though we live in the same area, we live in two different worlds that can never be together," he confessed grimly. He kicked a rock as they walked. "She is shy, sweet, and wholesome . . . She is too good for me," he stated, getting lost in his memories and realizing he had said more than he wanted to. He panicked at what Sabina might think but saw her processing what he said in a neutral manner. She seemed to believe that story. Flann was relieved, and he reminded himself it was always good to tell partial truths.

Sabina thought about Flann's words. Assuming that he was enslaved and that the girl was a citizen, Sabina decided. She figured this meant he was in love with the idea of her but didn't have a relationship with her. He dreamed of being with someone his governing system would never allow him to be with. *Who knows, maybe they know one another and like each other, but does it matter? He is now a citizen of Silvedome.*

But Sabina knew deep down it mattered to her. She didn't want to compete with an illusion of some perfect girl he could never have. Then she scolded herself. *Why am I even thinking about this? He is a bossy, self-important person who loves someone he cannot have.*

"You know what you are telling me?" she said instead of thinking. "You cannot have the person you love so you will settle for me, likely for the opportunity to become a resident of Silvedome," she explained.

~

That was too close to the truth, Flann thought. She was an insightful person, and he worried the magical bindings placed on her were getting worn thin the closer she was to her Birth Challenge. It was out of character for her to be this forthcoming. He needed to speak to Brom about this unfolding, but for now, he decided to distract her.

"Listen, your father found me and chose to help me escape from the Selectors. He would have brought me to Silvedome with or without our union interview. And . . . you don't hear me complaining about the fact that you are having several union interviews. I don't know if you have the hots for one of them while you are considering me. I'm not judging you. Why are you holding my past against me?"

"I'm not judging you," she retorted, stopping, and looking at him, seemingly appalled that he would come to that conclusion.

"Yes. Yes, you are," he confirmed, stopping and glaring at her.

"I'm the least judgmental person I know," she refuted. "I'm simply making an observation."

"Oh, is that what you call it?" He swung his bags over his shoulders, and walked forward. "An observation. Call it whatever you want, but you are still pegging me as some lowlife man using you to get into Silvedome."

"I never said you were lowlife," she rejected, trying to catch up to him. "I would never say that."

"YOU DON'T NEED TO," he shouted. He stopped and put down his bags to adjust his hat. He needed to shift his attention because he was getting worked up. This was a sore spot for him. Coming from a lifetime of being treated like a tool to be used and not worthy of having what was so readily available to others. That was his past. That was not him anymore, he reminded himself, closing his eyes and grounding himself. He was a person who was freed from slavery and could have the life he wanted, including the girl of his dreams.

Sabina caught up with him and shifted the uncomfortable bags in her hands. Noticing he was standing in the path with his eyes closed made Sabina feel guilty. She wasn't being a good hostess and wasn't making him feel welcome. She wasn't going to apologize, she told herself. She wasn't judging him as he accused, but she vowed to be a better hostess.

With his eyes still closed, Flann informed Sabina, "You know your father picked me out of all the Messengers he met to fulfill his desire for you to have a union interview with someone from each Moowin with rare talents." He opened his eyes and stared intensely at Sabina. "Why do you think that is? Do you think he would have picked someone who wasn't suited for you?"

She dropped the lighter bag and rubbed her arm. She felt small at that moment, not only physically but emotionally. Her father loved her, and he cared so deeply for her safety. He would not have set her up with someone awful. Flann reminded her that her father met countless powerful Moowins every day and he would have picked someone else if he wasn't satisfied. Besides, her father had a skill for matching people up for the right beneficial relationships.

Quieted, Flann suggested, "Let's start over. We started off

with an . . . unusual meeting. Perhaps it has set the tone for our relationship, and I'd like you not to hate me over the next two weeks while I get settled in."

He seemed so reasonable, and that made it worse for Sabina. She still felt he was rude and arrogant, but she could admit to herself that she may not have given him a fair chance either.

"Fine," she decided reluctantly.

Flann smiled. "I'll make a deal with you. Help me get settled and I'll return a favor for you. It sounds like you want out of the union interview. I can claim it happened," he offered, shrugging.

"That's not much of a deal and I'm law bound to help you get settled in."

"True but you don't seem to want to do it."

"Come on." She ignored him and started walking. "We can talk about 'deals' later. I need to get back to school."

"Where is your tut, anyway? I thought you lived close to the village square."

"Right here," she announced, walking to the front porch and kicking off her boots. "Welcome to your new living quarters for the next two weeks." She opened the door and sat the items by the front door. "This is the gathering room we never use. My room is right here." She pointed to her red drapes. "The kitchen is through here. Wait, you need to go back outside and take off your shoes. You never bring shoes in the house."

Wordlessly, Flann went outside and took off his shoes.

Grabbing the bags, Sabina continued. "Let's take this upstairs. Your room is the first one upstairs."

Flann followed asking all sorts of questions. He hadn't realized that Silvedome operated without electricity and he was shocked to see such a bare home.

"Silvedome assigns homes. We can be reassigned to a new living quarter at any time. I expect that we will be reassigned a new home shortly now that Fawn, my sister, is living at Tradel school."

"You don't own your homes?"

"Nowah, silly. Why would you own your home? They are just where you sleep," she said, shaking her head.

"What do you own?" he asked, puzzled.

"Not much. A few pieces of clothes, blankets, a canteen, necessities really."

She had opened the door to his room. "Here you go. Be careful of the furniture. It belongs to Silvedome, so no carving 'Flann was here'." We had someone do that once," she told him, shaking her head, and biting her bottom lip. "That wasn't fun to repair. No holes in the wall either. You can tack decorations if you like. Extra candles are in the kitchen with matches."

Sabina felt weird to be giving Fawn's guest routine speech to Flann. She knew Fawn would have shown Flann where the extra blankets were, but she needed a break. "I'll be downstairs changing. Drapes closed means Do Not Enter. I have to get to school. Dirty clothes go in the bin on the front porch. Someone comes by to pick them up. They are returned the next day, clean, pressed, and folded."

Sabina started to close the door.

"Why don't you have a door?" Flann wanted to know. He stood with his hands on his hips, looking lost.

"My room is meant to be a workshop for people who do crafts out of their home," she answered as she closed his door.

Flann immediately opened it again. His short, red wavy hair was shaped oddly on his head from wearing his hat. "You cannot get rid of me that easily. I'll be ready to go with you to school in a few minutes. I just need a moment to get settled." His green eyes communicated he was a serious man, but his smirk said he didn't take much seriously.

Biting her bottom lip, Sabina didn't respond except to flee from him. She went down the stairs, already imagining how good she would feel after she freshened up. She was thinking how confusing Flann was when she heard a knock at the front door. Sighing to herself, she went straight to the door and opened it unenthusiastically.

"Ah good, you are home. I can stop searching for you," said the Runner, who looked like a tiny girl with thin baby-blue appendages and a center crest bone on her forehead. A Tory. She could be fifty years old, or she could be fifteen. Tories were forever frozen looking like a twelve-year-old.

Sabina didn't recognize her. Tories were from lands across the ocean. Only a few lived in Silvedome, and they served as Runners because their bodies stayed youthful. Their birth wasn't celebrated like the others either, and they never reached adulthood or went through puberty. Therefore, they didn't participate in Birth Challenges. Since their bodies didn't age outwardly, it was shocking when one passed away. It was as if their spirit was ready to move on. Sabina had heard that even under a microscope, their body resembled a healthy child.

"You are called to see the Ori immediately. Here is your pass," said the girl with a nasally young voice, pulling out a glowing neon-green marker from her waistband satchel. She placed it on the back of Sabina's left hand. The marker made six simultaneous sharp stabs into her skin.

Sabina drew her hand back quickly.

"What is that?" She swallowed, looking at her hand.

"It's your pass into the Ori's building. It's a tracker too so I would not waste time getting there." She snapped her waist satchel closed and smiled brightly before jogging off.

The Ori

Sabina stood there holding her hand as it throbbed painfully. Despite the pain, she still felt the anger energy's invisible red ribbon approaching her as if she could see it in her mind. Sabina looked behind her and saw nothing unusual. But her mind saw, and her body sensed, the invisible angry energy coil around her waist. Sabina stood frozen on the spot. She felt paralyzed as her pulse lodged into her throat. The ribbon settled around her, not squeezing but clinging to her. After a moment, Sabina relaxed, seeing nothing was happening.

She reminded herself that nothing had gone wrong. Everything was okay. She closed her eyes and counted to ten, focusing on her breath, aware of the energy clinging to her. Coughing a laugh after attempting to center herself, Sabina decided she was insane. How could everything be okay?

She realized her body had moved, and she made a sound with that desperate laugh, but nothing happened. This energy was harmless. It was not doing anything except attaching itself to her. Barefoot, she stepped forward cautiously. Nothing happened except the ribbon shifted. She took a larger step, reaching out with her toes and placing them down, followed by her forefoot and then her heel. Her feet were wider apart and again, nothing happened except for the ribbon adjusting.

Even though she could not see it with her eyes, she sensed the energy of the ribbon, and the ribbon was coming from upstairs. Her father! That had to be it. Flann was talking to her father. Without a second to consider it, she ran up the stairs, the ribbon coiling even more around her body. As she hit the stairs, she heard Flann shuffle. No voices were exchanged, but she clearly heard him move. She continued up the stairs, and the ribbon vanished from her before she reached the top, causing her to pause. With a slowed breath, she continued calmly to Flann's door. He opened the door before she reached it.

She intended to ask about her father, but Flann's eyes were immediately drawn to her glowing left hand.

"What's that?" he seemed to ask out of curiosity, but then he immediately shifted his emotional state. "What happened?" he demanded, like he was ready to defend her against someone who had harmed her.

"Nothing. I need to see the Ori. What did my father say?" she responded, thinking, *Is this what it is like having an overprotective brother?*

"What does the Ori want? Who sent for you?"

"How am I supposed to know? What did my father say?"

"Who. SENT. For. YOU?" he insisted.

"Why do you care? YOU don't know anyone anyway. You have only been in Silvedome for one day," she shot back, feeling prickly.

"What has gotten into you?" Flann suddenly had a vacant stare and an authoritative voice. His tone reminded Sabina of Brom. Like when she asked too many questions, or when he made it clear what he wanted her to do. Angry energy flowed out of Flann and coiled around Sabina. "Answer the QUESTION," he barked.

Sabina stepped back, hitting the wall, and slid down to the

floor. She pulled her knees into her chest as the coiled ribbon of energy struck her once again.

"Father?" she asked in a small voice, scared. She was looking at Flann, but could not see the green of his eyes. How was that possible?

Flann snapped out of his trance and squatted down next to Sabina. His eyes shone bright green once more. "I'm sorry. Brom was so loud in my head. I couldn't think straight. I didn't mean to scare you."

The coiled energy around Sabina was immediately gone. Flann held her upper arms, and she looked down at her waist for the energy that had disappeared, before the shock wore off. Coming around, she shook herself out of his grasp and stood up.

"STAY AWAY from me," she asserted coldly, already crouching and angling her back to the open stairs to bolt.

"It wasn't me. It was your father. I would not speak to you that way."

"THAT'S NOT POSSIBLE," she yelled, feeling her world spin out of control. She moved the clumping hair blocking her vision, preparing to make her move.

"Yes. Yes, it is. Read your father's letter," Flann insisted, mimicking her crouching stance.

"How? How is it possible? What is that energy attached to him?" she asked, reaching back with her barefoot for the first step.

"I'm bound to your father," he stated with shame all over his face. His green eyes were no longer shining but dark.

He spoke those words with such regret that Sabina believed him. She discerned the unbearableness of his binding. At that moment, a memory that did not belong to her flashed in her mind. It was of Flann as if she were in Flann's body. This vision revealed Flann shaking her father's hand. She saw the look of triumph and the certainty in her father's eyes when they shook on their deal.

"What does that mean?" she asked, squeezing her eyes shut. She tried to be aware of her foot on the floor, noticing the smell of

Flann's light—sweet, smoky aroma—and the sound of Flann's breath, slow and steady. That flashed image made her lose her sense of where she was, but now, she was back.

"I don't know," he stressed. Neither one of them blinked as they stared at each other in their crouching, fighting positions. It was as if they were in some Latin dance instead of a potential death match. "Like in the stories of old. He figured out how to do a blood oath with our Moowins. I'm connected to your father through a shared life force that binds us together. He can use my talent as if it is his own. I don't know how to explain it. He doesn't have the gift, but he is sharing a link within me," he explained, keeping his hands out, palms facing her.

Even though she believed those words, Sabina latched on to a particular thought. Her father wasn't just talking to Flann through a Messenger, he was talking through him. Fear flooded Sabina at the thought of such power. A power she didn't know, understand, or want anything to do with.

"I don't *know* you, and I don't *trust* you," Sabina acknowledged as she twisted her body around and ran down the stairs. She didn't look behind her, but the angry red invisible ribbon was at her back. She threw open the door and ran barefoot down the path to the village square. Her feet pounded into the dirt, kicking it up. She listened for Flann, pumping her arms as her hands flew into her vision. She needed to control her breathing so it wouldn't be so loud. As it was, she could not hear him, and she was too scared to look.

The path was deserted; there was one hour left of the villagers' typical hours of servitude. Sabina ran over the bridge, hearing the thump of her feet hitting the wooden planks. She headed straight to the Ori building. Not only was Flann unable to enter that building without the marker, but the Ori could help her.

This was her first visit to the Ori. She had never done more than look at the building in passing. She reached the building but had no idea where the entrance was. She didn't recall ever seeing one. She rounded the corner and stopped abruptly.

"My child," said Nana Honey in her strong accent, apparently unconcerned about Sabina running her over. Nana Honey stood with a blanket draped over her shoulders and her hand resting on a walking stick.

Sabina glanced behind her and didn't see Flann. She realized she didn't sense the ribbon of energy either. She relaxed a little. She returned to look at Nana Honey, who stood patiently as she waited for Sabina's attention. Sabina swallowed and took several big breaths.

"You vorked yourself into tizzy . . . Come, I valk you to meeting."

Sabina glanced behind her, her clumped hair swinging with her head movement. She was sweating, her armpits damp, and her feet and calves covered in dirt. She was a mess, and she would have been embarrassed if she weren't relieved to be safe.

"He'll beeee along," Nana Honey said.

Confused and not knowing what she meant, Sabina said, "Sorry?"

Nana Honey stopped and turned to Sabina. She looked at her with cloudy eyes, raising her arm that was holding the walking stick. "You see this?" She held her arm, shaking with the effort to lift the stick.

Sabina's eyes flicked back and forth, not sure what Nana Honey was getting at. Slowly, she answered, "Yes."

"Vhat is it?" she inquired patiently in her short, harsh accent.

"Aaaaahhhh walking stick," Sabina answered.

"And? Does age of stick change vhat it is?"

"Nnnnoooowwwwaaahhhh," Sabina claimed.

"If not age, vhy, my child, vould you think a Seer like me vould not know exactlee vhere you and frrrriend are?" Pointing at her forehead, Nana Honey clarified. "I see exchange that took place?" Her lips were a firm line, looking disapprovingly at Sabina. Sabina thought she was waiting for an answer.

"You know what happened?" Sabina whispered, bringing her fingers to her lips, feeling like her breath had been sucked out of her. "Does that mean you can explain how it happened or what is going on?" Sabina burned with a desire to know what was happening.

"Yas," Nana Honey confirmed, and turned to walk. "But not now, my child. No time. The Orrrri is expecting us. Now, ve have different task."

Sabina walked beside Nana Honey and kept pace with her. She moved slowly. She was assumed to be the eldest among all the villagers and the only one with such a distinctive accent. No one knew where she was from or exactly how old she was, but her wrinkly face, blindness, and missing teeth indicated she was ancient. Despite her age, Sabina found Nana Honey terrifying and fascinating in her ability to read the past, present, and future. The old woman was simultaneously scary, powerful, and comforting.

"Vhat you need to know is . . . you trrrust him. Let us not speak anymore." She placed her hand on the cement wall. The wall slid open. She walked through.

Sabina realized it was an optical illusion. She knew there was no way she could find it with sight and she couldn't fathom how Nana Honey found it without sight. The door opened to a hallway. A Master Healer was waiting inside the doorway. Although Sabina wanted to ask questions, the Healer, normally a gentle woman, grabbed Sabina's elbow, placed her finger to her lips, and pulled her a few steps away. They entered a bathroom and the Healer immediately got to work. Nana Honey followed to supervise the Master Healer.

Master Songbird Fis didn't give Sabina a choice. She pushed her right down on the toilet seat.

"That's disgusting," Sabina objected, trying to get up, but Master Fis kept a firm hand on her shoulder.

"As is your tunIK, my child. I have **new** outfit for you."

Sabina stopped fussing and Master Fis pulled a bowl of water closer to her knees. She lifted one foot at a time, cleaning Sabina's feet efficiently. As she cleaned, Sabina discovered she had received minor cuts from running blind with fear through the village. It's remarkable how they stung now she was aware of them, when moments ago, she hadn't noticed.

Once Sabina's feet were clean, Master Fis lifted one to her chest. Her long, silver hair framed the foot, and she hummed a lovely melody she must have heard at The Mox. As she hummed, Sabina felt her healing energy enter the bottom of her foot. Within minutes, her foot was healed, and she started on the next one. Master Fis stood up and left Sabina without a word. She gently bowed to Nana Honey and left, holding her bowl in one hand at her chest.

Sabina stood up, but Nana Honey, who wasn't in the stall with her, said, "Vait. Scholar Sheb bring new outfit vith shuess."

There was a moment of silence, and all seemed quiet. Too quiet. Sabina kept her feet lifted off the floor and, by the time Nana Honey opened the stall door, her thigh muscles burned with the effort.

"Vhere is necklace? Thee necklace from grandmother. Thee am**let**?" she interrogated.

"What?" Sabina queried, confused, automatically reaching for the amulet that wasn't on her. She always wore her amulet. She never took it off except in the bathhouse. *Where was it?* She dropped her feet to the ground in her concern for her amulet and as soon as her feet touched the ground, she anxiously picked them back up.

She needed to calm down and focus. She only needed to recall the last time she remembered having it and then recount what happened from there. She had it this morning. She remembered being angry with her sister for writing on her father's letter, which she still hadn't read. Then she went to the Loaded Hurricane like usual. She took it off when she got in the bathhouse. But then there was the bathhouse 'incident'.

"My eyesight cannot lo-kate it. You need it. Vhere is it?"

No one knew about her private training ground. Maybe her eyesight couldn't see into the shield that Brom had put there.

Sabina didn't feel comfortable telling her it was in the Loaded Hurricane, and she considered what to say to keep it private.

"Ah, Crystal, ve have problem," she announced as the door opened. "Can you see it?"

Crystal shook her head 'no' and walked around Nana Honey, who took one large step to the side. Crystal sat Sabina's boots on the ground before her. She immediately reached for them, placing them on her feet. Crystal stood up, holding a folded tunic.

"Find Sabina's amulet," Nana Honey ordered Crystal.

Crystal remained silent and nodded.

Sabina stood in her muddy tunic and clean boots. She looked at Nana Honey and Crystal and they looked at her. Everyone was waiting. Sabina was more awkward by the second. Candlelight flickered on the cement walls and the room was warm from stifled air. She wanted Crystal to step back and allow her to close the stall door, but she wasn't brave enough to ask for that space.

"I see you. Crystal sees you. Let's be on vith it," Nana Honey barked.

Reaching for the bottom of her tunic dress, Sabina pulled the garment over her head, concentrating on the candlelight dancing on her skin in an effort to ignore the uncomfortable feeling of being watched by someone she considered a friend. It was discomfiting to witness Crystal bluntly staring at her. It made her feel like a spectacle. Sabina exchanged her old tunic for the clean one Crystal had brought, which was a deeper brown with a multi-color blue Aztec design at the bottom of the dress. Crystal handed the dirty tunic to Nana Honey, whose hand was outstretched.

Sabina heard Crystal speak to Nana Honey when she was in her most fragile moment, with the dress blocking her face and her arms sliding through the openings. "She does not have the amulet," Crystal confirmed to Nana Honey. Sabina quickly pulled the clean tunic down and noticed Crystal in her trance state, seeing through Sabina. "Her last visual of it is taking it off and placing it on her pile of dirty workout clothes before getting into the bathhouse." Crystal finished talking, but her eyes were still distant.

Meanwhile, Nana Honey located Sabina's father's letter. Dressed, Sabina stood with her arms wrapped around herself. Her eyes flickered between them, watching their silent exchange before she felt a painful pulse from the glowing green marker.

"The countdown has begun," Crystal verified, turning to Nana Honey, taking the tunic, and exiting the bathroom. Before she left, she announced, "Master Alf is waiting outside the door." Then she was gone. No flirting, no smile, all business.

Cornered in a bathroom stall, Sabina was alone with Nana Honey. "My child. Do you realize how unaware you are?"

Sabina pouted at the insult, but she didn't understand.

"Vhat vould happen if letter read by someone other than you? Young, tall man saved you today. How many chances you need?" she inquired, tucking the letter in a layer of clothing near her chest. "Never mind. Ve see Ori. I keep letter safe. You see me tonight. Ve discuss letter," she said, nodding in agreement as if the matter was settled.

"I don't understand what is happening. Why is Flann here? If the letter is so private, why didn't Father give it to me himself? Why do so many people know about this letter?" Sabina's questions spilled out as Nana Honey shuffled to the door. *Why do you think it is okay for you to have MY letter? My private letter! Will you give it back?*

Sabina sucked in air as the marker pinged once again, but this time with increasing pain.

"Hush my child," Nana Honey said, soothing Sabina as she drew her close. Nana Honey spoke so softly that Sabina crouched down close to hear. "Flann hired servant. By your father. To look after you. He is bound forrrrever to you and temporarily to Brom. He is unable to cause true harm, bodyguard."

As Sabina attempted to protest, Nana's hand found her forearm and squeezed hard.

"Nooo. Ve speak tonight. You trrrust. You trrrust me and you trrust Flann. Flann rare Messenger. Powerful Protector, Persuader. He is skilled. Your father work one year to prepare him. He knows. You don't. You trrrust. I explain later. Tell no one who Flann is to you, his extra talents. Only Messenger. Tell others Flann is your guest. He is frrriend. Maybe lover too!"

Appalled, Sabina yanked her arm back. *LOVERS?!?! . . . How dare she talk about lovers like that makes it all okay?* Sabina pressed her hands into the side of her face. *This is unreal. Trust? Trust what? What the tullom is going on? Is this my father being psycho about my safety again? Yes. That's it.* Sabina sighed with relief.

Everything is fine. Father probably realized he wasn't going to live forever and be able to look after me in my adulthood. Sabina suspected Brom bought Flann and created some legal contract. Nana Honey was not the best with the English language. She misunderstood the meaning of certain words. This was likely another secret like the Loaded Hurricane or using resources from outside of Silvedome.

Wading through her thoughts, Sabina concluded Flann was her puppet after all, and likely too ashamed to admit it. That concept made her smile. Everything made sense. Then guilt trickled in. She had a slave! What kind of person was she? Silvedome didn't allow slaves. That made her a lawbreaker. Sabina bit her lip. Anxiety swelled as she contemplated doing something she didn't agree with. She hoped the letter revealed something about the contract. Thinking this, she no longer felt resistance toward reading the letter.

Nana Honey, seeming to sense the shift in Sabina's energy, said, "Must go. Ve collect Orrri news for you. My eyesight blurry. Decisions not firm. You understand?"

"Yes," Sabina confirmed, barely audible.

Nana Honey struggled to pull the door open, but Flann was there. He stepped to the other side of the door and used his arm to prop the doorway open. Flann looked deeply saddened; his fiery spirit dimmed. *Docs he know that I know?*

Walking through the door after Nana Honey, Sabina didn't

resist the temptation to look into his eyes. She wanted to read what he felt. She willed his eyes to look at her. Moments ago, she ran fearfully from his presence, but now her mind played tricks on her. She suddenly felt a pull toward him. Her gaze locked on his downcast eyes as the rest of her body turned and walked left down the corridor. At the last moment, his eyes lifted from the ground, and she saw hurt. A ripple of energy radiated through her. The spark between them was alarming. Sabina looked forward and followed Nana's slow progress.

The door creaked closed, and Sabina sensed Flann at her back. They walked single file. The only thing Sabina could think about was his eyes. The deep green of them, framed by bushy eyebrows. She knew she should focus on what the Ori wanted from her or what Nana Honey would explain later. However, she was satiated by the information she had received. Now she was sorting through every exchange she'd had with Flann throughout the day.

Flann had known the feeling of freedom would be short-lived. He had enjoyed today, for the most part. But the old woman had spoiled it for him by telling Sabina his true purpose for being here. He didn't hear their conversation, but he trusted his intuition and suspected Sabina knew.

Flann lived a life where he had no choice or rights, and the shame of being a slave was fresh on his mind. Memories of being shoved down to the ground and laughed at because he was unable to protect himself haunted his daily experiences. He gritted his teeth at the memory. He reminded himself that was the past. He had a new owner. He also had Moowins. No one would treat him that way again and no one had since Brom purchased him over a year ago.

Originally, Flann had wondered if Brom got lucky purchasing a slave boy with no family trace of a Moowin or if he'd had the ability to know Flann would develop Moowins. He was purchased when he was fifteen years old, which was a year before his talents presented themselves. By the time his Moowins came in, Brom had bound him permanently to Sabina. He now contained seven percent of Sabina's life force and she contained twenty percent of his. What did it matter that Brom had a contract for his life when she owned twenty percent of his life force? For it was more than being a slave when someone owned a piece of his spirit.

He thought he'd made peace with the cards he was dealt, but he was plagued with the knowledge that if he had not accepted Brom's offer, he could have freed himself when his talents surfaced. He could have escaped or earned his way out of slavery. However, he was the only one in his family to have a Moowin. His family would have continued to be slaves without Brom's help. He chose to bind with Sabina in order to free his sister and pay his parents' debts. He made the right decision in accepting Brom's deal, but he had to remind himself repeatedly that it was his choice to sacrifice his life to free his family.

Frustrated, he glared at the old woman, sensing her power. Rage exploded in his heart, knowing for certain he was cheated. The Seer must have helped Brom to locate and take a naive boy under his 'protection'. Flann scoffed. Brom told him to trust and rely on this Seer. Yet this Seer was the reason he was enslaved to serve this strange girl who wavered under all the bindings, putting him and everyone else in danger. How dare they expect him to blindly trust what they said? For it was evident this old woman was on Sabina's side. The thought made his fist clench in fury. Who was on his side?

Flann stalked down the cold, dreary hallway and felt his fury steam off his body. His shame had turned into a feeling so much sweeter: anger. He knew Sabina had been informed of his role to protect her. The old woman tried to use a sound shield to prevent her words from being heard. But it was a weak cast, and she didn't have any talent for it. Even though Flann couldn't hear her words, he sensed Nana Honey's energy to hide them. He knew! Then the intensity of Sabina tugged on his soul as she walked out of the bathroom. Her desire to see the truth called to him, but he refused to give her the satisfaction of it. He fought that desire until his willpower gave in. It was as if that twenty percent of him within her compelled him to meet her gaze, and he did.

Flann wanted to hate Sabina. He wanted to hate Brom. He could taste the righteousness of his anger. It was undeniable that he was hurting at this moment, but he was not willing to give in to his emotions. He had broken the habit of being angry when he became responsible for his choices. He was tired of feeling jaded by his destiny. He chose to *work* as a bodyguard, protecting a girl who had been lied to her entire life. He was not a slave, he told himself fiercely. He was a paid worker, and he had a job to do.

This is my choice. I am not a victim. This is not Sabina's fault either. Brom was right. We both benefit from this deal. Even with these affirmations and reminders that Brom had protected him from the Selectors who hunted people like him down as if it were a sport, Flann found his brain looping on the unfairness of it all. Brom and this old woman had found him before he knew he had a Moowin.

He sighed with the weight of his conflicting internal struggle. Regret filled him for not having more time to be free and to be anyone he wanted. Scorn settled into its familiar place as he felt sorry for himself. It was a shame Sabina knew he was her puppet. He had enjoyed being free of that. At least he was given a life of possibilities and unlimited barriers for one year. Now it was gone. His only solace was that Brom had given him a sliver of freedom.

The green marker went off, pulling Flann out of his internal dialogue. Sabina drew her hand into herself, immediately going into a squatting position as if to protect herself. Flann grabbed her armpit and pulled her up to her feet. His reaction to her pain was instinctual. His anger vanished, and he felt true concern for her. He was staring at her green marker, curious about what that contraption could do. He pushed aside the déjà vu. Two years ago, he had played with one of his sisters and had helped her to her feet after she had fallen.

~

Sabina noticed a tingling surge of energy at Flann's contact. It made her think of a black octopus with long tentacles attached to her and making a sucking motion. It was unnerving. She looked at him to see if he noticed, but his eyes were on the brightly glowing neon marker now flashing in a warning.

Had she ever been touched by him before this moment? Was this her imagination playing tricks on her? Was the awareness of this binding thing getting to her? She didn't recall anything except for a shoulder bump when they were in the village square and she hadn't felt anything then.

"Hurry," Nana Honey bossed without stopping.

They rounded the corner of the empty corridor and proceeded down a wider hallway. Flann stepped back behind Sabina. This hallway led to an open room with the twelve Ori at their individual desks. An entire glass wall separated them from the room. The members of the Ori had their heads down, working on assignments in utter silence as the light spilled in from the square windows that framed the ceiling. The only candles Sabina could see were on the window frames beside the doors, but it was beautiful how the light filled up the room.

Sabina marveled at the Ori all together in their private chamber until the council shifted their attention to her. They all looked up as one, which sent an eerie feeling through her stomach. She chewed on her lower lip and shifted her weight. The Ori stood up from their desk in unison. It was like a synchronized dance at The Mox. Nana Honey nudged her.

"You guide. I see re-flections. I follow."

Sabina placed her palms on the glass to push the invisible door she assumed was there, but there was nothing. Space. She stepped forward with her hands outstretched and walked forward until she finally hit the wall. The illusion of what she saw not being there gave her a sense of motion sickness. *What is this?*

Her hands pressed into the surface, but it did nothing more than leave her fingerprints on the pristine glass. She perceived Flann close to her back, ready to follow her into the room. Her palms were sweating, and her heart raced as she felt the pressure of the Ori's scrutiny. They were all sitting on top of their desks, with their legs outstretched and crossed. Each one of them had one hand on their chin and the other arm wrapped across their body. Sabina stood there feeling like a deer at the other end of a rifle.

"It's not glass. It's a reflective mirror," Flann informed her in a low voice, standing behind her.

Nana Honey tapped her palm with the neon-green marker. *Why doesn't she speak and tell me what to do? She has been here a hundred times.* Sabina waved her arm foolishly around, squatting to the ground, and hopping up to higher spaces, knowing the green neon marker was given as her key into this room and that the outside wall was an illusion. *Why doesn't one of the Ori come to help me?*

Flann tapped the floor with his foot. Sabina thought he was getting impatient with her, which caused her to become even more frantic in looking and feeling for an opening. She kept glancing at the Ori, getting distracted until she convinced herself that their eyes were turning red and glowing. She bit her lip and decided to avoid further eye contact with them.

"Sa-bin-a," Flann hissed.

Sabina turned around to see Nana Honey and Flann looking to the wall, not the Ori.

"Why are you looking at the wall?" she asked, feeling flustered and huffing her hair out of her eyes.

"My child, you engross**ed** in fear. Unable to feel mar-**kerrrr** go off. Look, palm bleeding."

Sabina's eyes immediately went to her palm and realized a small line of blood was coming from the marker. The blood dripped down her palm to her elbow and onto the floor. She didn't want to wipe the blood on the beautiful tunic Nana Honey had given her. She considered her options, but realized she didn't have any.

As Sabina drew her elbow to her hip, Flann stepped in front of her and used his undershirt to wipe the blood off. His eyes stayed on the task, but her eyes roamed everywhere. She looked at him, at Nana Honey who stood looking at the wall and leaning on her walking stick, and she looked at the Ori who were now all turned to one of the side walls, talking with their hands up as if in argument.

Flann pressed firmly on the green marker, slowing the blood, which brought Sabina's attention back to him. Her heart was racing, and her mind was spinning, feeling overwhelmed. She closed her eyes, and centered herself. She heard Flann's exhales and Nana Honey's walking stick scuffing the floor. She felt the physical contact of Flann pressing on her hand, and she smelled his light smoky aroma. Feeling calm, she opened her eyes. She was taller than Flann and she looked down at him; he clenched his jaw in frustration. Her heart softened toward him and she felt gratitude for his help.

"All you had to do was ask for help, but you refused." He looked up at her, jaws prominent, with eyes that seemed to move in and out of deep shades of green. She could feel the warmth of his breath on her neck as he spoke. "You didn't even notice that I found the opening."

Immediately, Sabina bristled at his comments and pulled away. But he held her palm. She felt immense pressure to get to the Ori and get this green marker removed. She wasn't thinking at her best and Flann's gaze wasn't helping her either.

"Where is your amulet?" Flann asked in alarm.

"That's enough, Master Alf. It's end of workday and Orrrri ready for her vith or vithout thee necklace."

Flann looked at Nana Honey and held her milky gaze for several moments before dropping Sabina's hand. He turned to face the wall, creating enough space for Sabina to approach between them. Flann whispered in an angry low voice something that was too low for Sabina to hear. She didn't see why they were turned to the wall, but then she saw a sliver of light between the tiles on the floor. She stepped forward, reaching her hand casually toward the light. Her fingertips hit the light, and she immediately felt an electric shock. Nana Honey was holding onto her forearm again. "Scan mar-kerrrr first. Ve have thirty seconds to cross barrier."

No wonder no one comes to the Ori, thought Sabina. It's a bloody booby trap. She now understood why so many meetings were held in the village square. Sabina let her eyes go unfocused until she finally saw a silver button among the reflective image being cast on the side wall. She brought the back of her hand to the silver bottom and the strength of the magnet whipped her hand to the metal device. In one instance, the green marker was removed and had vanished behind the metal plate. Sabina looked down to see six red, angry marks on the back of her hand.

The light on the floor disappeared, and all three shuffled forward at once. They walked toward the wall and then turned left, all huddled together. They were still seeing the cast of the mirrors, but they only needed to take a few steps in before they were in the Ori's main room. Sabina pushed the glass door open, feeling the shift in temperature from the hallway into this much cooler room. The room was in full discussion and Sabina's senses shifted to take it all in. Her vision shifted from the illusion presented on the reflective mirror of all the Ori facing the wall, arms up in argument, to only one Ori member making that gesture while the others faced him in a semicircle.

The Ori went by their first names as if their names were so legendary that the formality of 'Master' or a last name was unnecessary. All except for Master Fog Fourshul who demanded to be called Mistress. The Ori consisted of twelve people. Out of the twelve, seven represented each of the Moowins, and there was also one citizen without a Moowin from each of the four sectors. The only Moowin not represented in the Ori was the Seer who was a consultant of the Ori. To replace the Seer, someone with multiple Moowins was chosen, and that person was Bagger Tols.

Bagger stood with his arms raised. He was talking confidently as if there was no other perspective to consider. "This is more important than **one** individual's rights. She needs to sacrifice for Silvedome. This will give our warriors the best fighting chance and could save countless lives."

"You make a fair point, but this is not *our way*," proclaimed Smoke, Professor Tiris's wife.

"Vhat happened?" Nana Honey demanded to know as if she was a mother who had just walked in on a food fight.

The Ori all turned to Nana Honey who was slowly shuffling forward and gazing at each one of them. Her question had interrupted their discussion, and the Ori gave the smallest bow. The room was now quiet. No one dared to speak. Mistress walked around her desk and approached Nana Honey.

"I have petitioned the council to consider a special assignment for Sabina Rockdin," she explained with her hands grasped in front of her. "I have recently discovered I can shield Sabina, which is an exception to my talents. I have proposed to the counsel that I mentor her on Shield work to serve our warriors. Her Birth Challenge is in two days, and when—"

"No." Nana Honey objected, holding up her hand in protest. "Explain vhat you expect Sabina to do. How exac-tly does shielding her help our varriors?" she challenged, looking Mistress in the eyes as if she could see. "Vhere is this connection between this because I do not see it?"

"Mistress has proven she can shield Sabina, <u>so</u> Sabina must have some talent for shielding. This needs to be researched further," encouraged Bagger, looking eager to push forward with his decisions.

"Excuse me, Bagger. I vill hear Mistress explanation before vee proceed."

Bagger scoffed and turned around to lean on his desk, looking impatient to jump into the conversation.

The Mistress, always poised, stepped toward Nana Honey. She looked confident she would win this challenge. "It is my opinion and now a fact that Sabina is an amplifier like the original survivors from the nuclear war. We will know if she has the talent for shielding after her Birth Challenge, but she has already proven that she has amplified my shielding capabilities. With her on the battlefield, I can shield countless warriors."

"Which is why I propose that you step down from your Ori service and be one hundred percent committed to this endeavor. Our people's safety should come before a girl's right to choose three studies. And it should come before the dream of a retiring member of the Ori to continue on with the council," Bagger specified, wasting no time to take control of the conversation.

"I AM FIFTEEN YEARS YOUR SEN-IOR," the Mistress stressed, looking disrespected. "That is hardly an age differ—"

"Enough," Nana Honey said low, but firm. "Mistress. Vhat did you mean, you proved Sabina an amplifier?"

Raising her chin up and composing herself, the Mistress paused before returning her gaze back to Nana Honey. "While we waited for you to enter, I shielded all of you, which was impossible for me until Sabina."

Nana Honey's skin turned pale, and she seemed like she would lose her balance. It was as if an invisible object plowed into her, and she lifted one arm to the side to steady herself. Flann was there by her side so quickly that it was unnatural.

The room erupted into questions as each spoke over the other. Sabina could make out a few things. Someone asking, "Are you okay? What did you see? Is there a problem? What did you say your talents were?" Bagger shouted an order for someone to pull the paperwork on Master Alf's Birth Challenge.

~

Nana Honey realized the mistakes she'd made by not seeing this event in her eyesight, and that Sabina wasn't wearing her amulet throughout the day. There was nothing that could be done about the Mistress's discovery, but she could use her loss of balance to her advantage by claiming she had received a vision. She didn't have time to find the right solution to this issue, so she used the one thing all people were controlled by—fear. She would use fear to control the Ori's decision and keep Sabina safe.

Sadness welled up within her at this crossroads. This lie would be her funeral. She knew she was sacrificing her spiritual gift for this act of love. She was reluctant to give her gift up, but she did not see another choice before her. Internally she told the universe she was sorry for her betrayal.

Nana Honey lifted her hand for silence and one by one the room quieted. As she waited for everyone's attention, she saw Sabina through her third eye and could see the shock on her face. Master Flann stood strong, immovable, with his jaw locked. He was analyzing. He was grounded in himself and not at the mercy of the waves crashing on the rocks as Sabina was. *I chose him well,* thought Nana Honey.

Once she had everyone's attention and the room was still, Nana Honey spoke. But before she did, she went inward to her main spirit guide. Nana Honey was surprised to see and hear her without having asked for her. She listened.

"Why do you rush home when you are needed there?"

The answers she gave her guide were that she was tired, old, and had served long enough. This was the best way to protect Sabina. But her spirit guide helped her shift her viewpoint. She was focused on herself at that moment and not what was best for Sabina.

"Do you so easily turn to fear and let fear steal your values without the aid of your sight?"

Nana Honey felt the guilt of seeing herself reflected. Her spirit guide called her out. She was taking the easy way out of this situation and staying in comfort despite what it would cost her in the long run. She had given in to fear and was not trusting. She was not using her resources to solve this problem. Instead, she was allowing her fear to keep her trapped.

"Do you see? You are the one in fear and fear likes to be shared. It tricks you. Do not listen to its sweet lies. Stay true to your values. Stay in alignment with your dharma and it will guide you."

Internal peace built within Nana Honey like the sun rising over the land and she smiled. Her soul spoke to her and told her to trust that Sabina was having the journey she was meant to have. It reminded her there was a purpose in pain and suffering and without that struggle, growth could not blossom. Her soul whispered to her: "Do not deny Sabina her journey because you cannot bear it."

"Thank you for quiet time to consult vith guide. My visions are trrrue and accurate. They have nev-er failed in my years of service. You knew this to be trrrrue. But vhat my third eye sees is no vision. This is unique and unprecedented. Ve are in unknown time. Vhat my third eye and guide tells me is no vision. This is omen. Omen of var."

She paused and let her words settle. The room was intent on every word that Nana Honey said. Sabina wrapped her arms around herself and bit her lip. Bee looked to Bull who was always the calm one in the group. Bull stood tall with his arms hanging by his side but he was excessively blinking as if he couldn't take this in.

"Thee Mistress is correct. Sabina is amplifier. This lost art is thee omen. As you know, my visions are neither good nor bad, but this is no vision. This is omen with visdom from my guide. Premonition. If you use Sabina's talent, you bring var to our people."

"What happens if we do nothing with Sabina's 'talent'?" Bagger probed.

"That is yet to be seen," Nana Honey responded as if that was answer enough.

"What does that mean?" implored Smoke. She seemed to

trust Nana Honey's input over the politics of the Ori. "You cannot see a vision?"

"Ovce you surrender to one path or other, I vill look again. Then, I can tell you vhat I see."

"What you are saying is that either way, Silvedome could face a war?" Bagger simplified. Nana Honey suspected he was almost eager for the chance to show the world how mighty the Silvedomeies were.

"No," Nana Honey answered but Mistress moved in front of her. She turned to face the Ori. "This is why Silvedome does not have a Seer on our council. This goes beyond the consultation of a Seer and goes into self-fulfilled prophecy. We must take wisdom in our ancestors and not let these words persuade us any further."

"Nana Honey has never led us astray." Smoke defended her in a clear, theatrical voice.

"We must prepare for war either way. That is the safest course of action. It is better to be prepared than sorry. I suggest we move forward with Mistress devoting herself to Sabina's ability and that we bring another Shielder"—Bagger looked over at the Mistress, and said with disdain—"Someone to temporarily fill in for her while she trains Sabina."

"We don't know there will be war. I suggest we move forward with Sabina picking three studies to pursue that are outside of Moowins and continue to train our warriors as we have always done. Nothing needs to change," Dove, the Messenger, proposed.

"You are too young to understand the implications of not taking every advantage you can," huffed Bagger, getting in Dove's face.

The room erupted in chaos.

Nana Honey blocked out the Ori's argument and reflected on the situation. She spoke the truth. She was a spiritual guide. Yet she had resisted this day for so long. She had worked for years with Brom. She had taken so many precautions to ensure Sabina's safety that she was ready to forsake herself to stop something that was unstoppable. Now, she trembled with fear. Her stomach knotted at her dread of what Sabina would face, but she also felt it was right to allow Sabina to face these burdens. *Heaven on earth, protect her as I could not.*

"Nana," Bee beseeched, putting her hand on her arm and rubbing it lovingly. "Are you okay?" Moon was standing next to Bee with light tears sliding down his smooth, cream skin. He was an Influencer and perceived all of Nana Honey's emotions. "Moon can feel a lot of shifts in your energy," Bee declared, projecting her voice over Bagger and Dove's argument.

Nana Honey looked around her and took stock of the situation. Bagger and Dove were in a heated exchange like normal. The young woman had a fiery spirit for someone so small and delicate looking. Bagger, thinking he was all-knowing and superior to the rest of the group, constantly dismissed Dove's perspective, which inevitably instigated her to get in his personal space and blast him with her thoughts. That was nothing new. Dove stood on her toes, trying to gain height and get closer to eye level with Bagger. Bagger, who had a balding spot in the center of his hairline—creating the impression of two cut-off bullhorns—was frothing with agitation. Bull and the Mistress stood by their conversation, chiming in, and attempting to de-escalate the two. The four sector representatives were quietly huddled in a circle talking to themselves. Smoke was sitting on her desk, twirling a necklace around her finger, completely unbothered by the chaos. Berry had his hand on Master Alf's shoulder and engaged him in conversation. Sabina stood alone, looking down with her arms wrapped around her. Moon and Bee, who were natural caregivers, were looking at her.

Nana Honey patted her hand. "I'm fine. I'm tired. Too old for battles of vills." She turned toward Sabina. "My child, come take me home. I'm tired."

～

Sabina was lost in self-pity, thinking about why she had ever asked to be special. This was not how she chose to be special. It was unfair how she was finally recognized by her community for something rare, but to claim what made her matter meant she brought war to her people. She heard Nana Honey and looked up. Nana Honey called most people 'my child', but Nana's milky eyes gleamed at her.

She walked over, not sure what support Nana Honey needed. She was too tall to comfortably put her hand under her arm, so she settled by putting her hand on her shoulder and walking next to her. They made their way to the door, which could be clearly seen from this viewpoint. Moon and Bee followed behind them asking Nana Honey to stay. Telling her to sit down and rest at their desk.

"Bullocks, where are you two going?" Bagger shouted across the room, his cheeks heated.

Nana Honey in her cool, authoritative way, didn't give him much attention. She simply turned her head to the side to address the Ori.

"It appears ve are not needed. You made it clear you intend to violate Silvedome's upheld laws of giving Sabina the right to choose her path for vhat suits you. Vithout my visions, my vords are not counsel."

"Wait a minute," cautioned Bull, coming forward with his palms held up. "Let's slow things down."

"You cannot leave," Bagger bossed. "A decision has not been made."

"I'm not Ori. I'm consultant. I've informed you. Now I go home. Sabina's future lies in your hands. If you cared for her input, you vould have asked. Yet not one asked. You have ignored her." She turned and shuffled forward to the exit.

Flann disengaged from Berry and walked behind Sabina who was following Nana Honey.

"Bee, the silencers," Bagger ordered, flicking his finger like she was his servant.

That stopped Nana Honey. Bee popped up, putting a bright smile on her face.

"I would appreciate knowing how you would vote, Nana Honey. If we could have more time with Sabina and Master Alf, I believe we can all come together with a plan. Smoke, would you be willing to see Nana Honey home?" inquired Bull in his calm voice.

"Sure thang, sweetheart. You know my vote is with Na-na Honey anyway." In her theatrical way, she catwalked up to Nana Honey, wrapping her arm around hers. "Shall we, my Queen of Magic?"

"Why are you even on the council? Can we not get a more actively involved Performer? We all know she got this position because of her status with Professor Tiris," Bagger proclaimed.

"Quiet, old man. All the Performers are this way or have you forgotten that?" Dove smirked. Turning to go to her desk, she bellowed, "They are here to learn how to act like a fool by watching you anyway."

"What did you say? TELL me!!!" demanded Bagger.

Smoke wiped her shoulders off for illustration and said, "Dove, my young sister. I would not be here if I did not care about what happens to Silvedome. But I have better things to do than listen to you squabble," she said with confidence.

Dove rolled her eyes in response. "Or maybe you can't think for yourself."

Smoke squinted her eyes at the remark but let it go.

"Let's not forget this is all confidential information and Master Alf is only here because he is Sabina's guest. He should not be privileged with this knowledge," informed Buck from Sector One.

"About that. Master Alf has a mild reading on his Protector Moowin and since we don't test outsiders further than the Moowin ritual, we don't know more about his talent. He is only sixteen though and by what we saw tonight, his Protector skills could be developed into a greater skill. I'd be happy to work with him myself," Berry smiled. "His rare Messenger capabilities could be useful out on the field with Mistress and Sabina." Looking around the room, he continued. "Not too many Messengers agree to be on the battlefield," he reminded them while he leaned with one butt cheek on the desk, chewing on a thin wisp of wood.

"Point taken," said Iris.

Buck responded. "How can you be a powerful Protector and seem so carefree all the time?"

"Now let's not get carried away by these ideas. Master Alf is a stranger," Bagger pointed out.

"Master Alf is a newly acquired citizen of Silvedome," Dove hotly retorted.

"I've heard enough. My spirit longs for peace. Thee corruption of ego drains me," Nana Honey stated, preventing another debate. "Sabina, my child. Follow your heart if given a choice. Pay no heed to vhat others vant from you. Valk your path." Moving her gaze away from Sabina, Nana Honey looked toward the exit. "Smoke, take these old bones home."

"Nana Honey, what is your will?" inquired Iris, getting to her feet, looking ready to interfere with Nana Honey leaving.

"My vill is for Sabina to pick three studies. Live her life as should be her right. Not be your *secret* veapon."

"You heard the badass WITCH." Smoke credited Nana Honey while doing a little victory dance as homage to her.

"Ah, my child. Stop vith these imaginations. Too many stories in your heart."

"And what do you want Sabina? How do you cast your vote?" said Mistress with her eyebrows stretching up.

Sabina watched Nana Honey and Smoke walk out of the room, feeling like she was losing her voice with every step they took away from her. She flickered her gaze to Flann, who studied her with his watchful eyes, but she couldn't read his expression. She turned to face Mistress and saw a look of pleading in her eyes. They had made a deal. Yet Nana Honey told her to follow her heart and not be influenced by others. Nana Honey also said to trust herself. It was clear to Sabina that Nana Honey didn't want her to use her amplifier skill. How was she supposed to choose?

Should I trust Nana Honey and choose the three studies that didn't use my amplifying skill? Or should I trust the Mistress and explore the gifts given to me? Keep it simple Sabina. What matters at this point? Has anything changed? I value keeping my word and isn't that following my heart? But my heart's desire is to be a Healer's Aide, which would also allow me to keep my word. But logically, I cannot do that. If I follow that path it means I could bring war on my people. I don't want to be responsible for bringing war to my people. That is selfish of me. But I don't want to choose a life of not mattering and serving Silvedome doing something that doesn't matter to me. Tullom.

"Sabina," called the Mistress softly.

Adrenaline was slowly increasing in Sabina's veins as she considered how to answer. She felt like she would pass out. Her eardrums were flooding with a roaring sound, and she felt like she couldn't catch her breath.

"She is having a panic attack," stated Moon and Bee together, both rushing to her to calm her down.

The Decision

Sabina's pulse slowed, and warm, comfortable energy spread from Moon's touch. She felt so peaceful, like she was sleeping. Her muscles were relaxed, and her breathing slowed. Her eyes became heavy, and she blinked slowly, refocusing each time.

"Probably not the best idea to combine our gifts simultaneously," mused Bee, looking sheepishly at Moon.

"Give her a minute, she will bounce back," soothed Moon, who, for an Influencer, didn't show a lot of facial emotions.

Master Alf brought a chair. Moon and Bee lowered her into it.

As a discussion ensued, the Ori formed a circle away from her. Master Alf waved Bee and Moon off to join the discussion. He squatted next to Sabina, one hand on her thigh, the other on her shoulder, examining her. Sabina could feel the weird tingling sensation of Flann's touch, but she felt too heavy to care.

~

Flann attempted to draw upon the twenty percent of his life force within Sabina to send a mental message to her. Brom would not want Sabina to do this study. This whole incident would not have happened if she had been wearing her amulet, which he felt was his fault. He should have stayed away, like he was told to. If she had not been distracted this morning, she would have been wearing the necklace.

"Let's make a list. Each person makes one con and one pro," Violet suggested.

"This isn't grade school," said Dove, dryly.

"For once, I agree with you. This is simple. Silvedome has been on the brink of war for years. We have more Moowins than any other territory. We have kept the Selectors out of our dome but as each day passes, we are at a greater risk. The Agni is out there. The time of the prophecy is now. We need to take this advantage. Now I'm sorry this denies Sabina her right to choose, but we have a moral obligation to protect all our people," Bagger declared, pushing the vote in favor of approving Sabina's training.

"We have tested each person in our village for Moowins. We have no reason to fear the Selectors. They are a bunch of singular groups that our warriors can handle," Bull reassured, reminding the group of the facts.

"Yes, but any sixteen-year-old getting tested could be the one," said Bagger, bending his knees and leaning back, clearly frustrated that the group did not get the risk.

"Normally I agree with Nana Honey, but the Mistress discovering this amplifying talent is no coincidence. The universe delivered us a gift, and we need to receive it with open hands," Iris instructed.

"Exactly." Bagger practically jumped.

"Mistress, why are you being so unusually quiet? This affects you too," Bull asked. The group all turned to look at her.

"I'm allowing you the freedom to figure out what is best in your eyes. I know what I want. I would not have petitioned for this if this was not something I wanted."

Bull rubbed his hands together as he thought. "You are saying that nothing has changed for you, knowing that Sabina's talent is an omen, a premonition of war?"

"There are no guarantees in life. There is only one decision after the next. Nana Honey wasn't able to see a vision on this situation, only an omen. In other words, we *don't* know the consequences of our choice today. Personally, I do not think it is wise to ignore this opportunity to work with Sabina's talent." Raising her index finger as if to say 'but', she added, "I understand that you are trying to decide based on what our gains or losses will be, but the fact is, none of us has the talent of being a Seer. We cannot predict the future. I am making my decision based on what serves me best, which is what I believe will ultimately serve Silvedome best."

"This selfish behavior is exactly why I consistently and unashamedly vote for you to be kicked out of the Ori. You have gone senile in your old age." Bagger folded his arms.

"Lay off," Berry requested, looking completely relaxed. "It is the villagers who decide who is on the Ori, not you."

"Exactly. You do not have the authority to make that call," chimed in Buck.

"As I was saying, isn't that the goal in life?" Mistress said rhetorically. "To find out who we are and then give it all back to the universe. I do not find anything selfish about that. Quite the opposite. But to answer your original question more thoroughly, I choose to believe that everything will work out regardless of the outcome I desire."

As their discussion continued, Sabina regained control over her limbs. She still felt content and at peace, as if she were waking up to a beautiful sunset on a perfect day. Flann was by her side. She rolled her head toward him, fairly sure drool was sliding down her cheek. She lifted her arm to wipe the drool, but Flann put his arm over hers.

"Don't draw attention to yourself," he whispered. "Don't do this. Don't train. Brom . . . would not like it."

Swallowing the intensity and the nearness of his face, she stared back. Desperate to use her tongue to remove the drool but worrying it would send him the wrong message of how she felt about him, she didn't register his words at first. Then his words floated into her consciousness, and she jerked from him.

"I am my own person. I have authority over my life." *Why, oh sky above, does this man irritate me so much?*

Flann felt her words sting like a slap on his face. He was torn between doing his job, which was to see her safe, and his personal desire to get her away from Brom who oppressed her. He didn't like Brom and how driven Brom was to keep Sabina safe. Brom didn't see what it was doing to her. Yet, by Flann pushing his desires onto her, he was making the same mistake as Brom. He sat back on his heels, giving Sabina space.

"Ah, you are feeling better." Bee made her way to Sabina and felt her cheek. She was smiling and pleasant. "Yes, you are! I can see you are feeling well," she remarked as she used her thumb to wipe her drool. "Ready to stand?" Sabina lifted her arms for the assistance and was pulled to her feet, Flann raising with her. Bee rubbed her back and smiled brightly when Bagger pushed his way forward.

"So can we get on with this vote?" Bagger pushed.

"Give her a moment." Bee advocated for Sabina. With an idea apparently coming to her, Bee walked off, saying, "I have something that will help her feel more centered."

Iris crossed the room and grabbed both of Sabina's hands, squeezing lightly. "I've had a panic attack in the past too. It happens sometimes." Pulling Sabina closer to her, she leaned in to say, "When you want to do something you are afraid to do, you should do it anyway." Pulling away, she continued in her natural voice, "For me, the best thing happened after my panic attack. I accepted this position on the Ori. I must admit, I was terrified to accept this responsibility, but it was the best decision I've made."

Bee walked back, holding a thin slice of tree bark in the air. "I have it right here. Just suck on this for a minute and it will dissolve in your mouth, helping you feel as right as rain."

Berry walked over and tossed his arm over Iris's shoulder. She had released Sabina's hands. Bee placed the tree bark on Sabina's tongue while Berry confessed to Iris: "You were a pleasant surprise. Someone who sided with me needed to join the Ori." Iris smiled and playfully pushed Berry away.

"You two could take life more seriously," Violet advised.

Sabina's tree bark quickly dissolved in her mouth. She felt a warm, glowing sensation in her heart, and she felt super alert. She felt ready for anything at that moment. She felt like she could climb a mountain or do any challenge, including challenging Markus to a duel or asking that cute boy from land preservation on a date. She felt in control of her life. *What has Bee given me and can I get more of it?*

The Ori chatted with one another, distracted in the teasing conversation that Iris and Berry had started.

Bee was still standing next to Sabina after administering the tree bark and was away from the group. "Feeling good, right?" Bee wiggled her eyebrows and smiled. "My treat, love, but keep it between us." She turned around and Flann was there. "Oh, slide back. You are like an overbearing mate. She is fine now," she told Flann, grabbing his jaw and playfully giving it a shake.

"Not a mate," Flann clarified.

Sabina smiled. She thought it was amusing and didn't feel any need to correct Bee, who made light of the situation.

"Oh, I see you all hot and bothered. You cannot hide that

energy from a Healer. Brom did well arranging you two for a union interview."

"Can we focus on why we are here?" Dove called the group to order.

"Sabina, are you ready to answer?" Bull inquired.

Sabina was ready to answer. She waited for the fear, guilt, worry, self-judgment to surface, but it was gone. That tree bark had rescued her from her internal prison of saying no to herself. She thought of Iris's words: 'Do it anyway.'

"I want to train with the Mistress and as a Healer Aide," she said without any uncertainty. She waited to feel the guilt or to receive visions of her village in war, but she only felt the warm glowing sensation in her heart. Her highly alert mind saw several of the Ori's faces and felt the stiff movement of Flann who was slightly behind her. She heard Bee say to herself, *That's my girl* in a proud voice and she wondered if that was a hallucination.

Several people spoke at once but not to Sabina, at each other. After a minute, Bull shouted over everyone, but he wasn't loud enough. He walked over to Moon's conversation and gestured for him to use his talents. Moon stood still and expressionless, but his energy spread out of him like an enchanting lullaby. Sabina could feel its effects, but the tree bark was too strong for the lull of Moon's talent.

"Alright, Moon. That is enough," Bagger asserted, annoyed.

"Violet will record the votes," Bull announced. "Bagger, we will start with you as always," he said calmly, rubbing his hands together.

Violet had gone to her desk and pulled a sheet. "Ready!"

"Your vote is yes or no for agreeing to the Mistress's petition to train Sabina on Shield work. Bagger," Bull indicated to start the voting process.

"Yes," he said with a confident smile.

"Mistress?"

"Yes."

"Dove?"

"I vote NO." Dove glared at Bagger when she answered.

"Bee?"

"No."

"Moon?"

"No."

"Smoke's vote was no," Bull informed the group. "Berry?" Bull asked.

"Yes."

"Trout?"

"Yes."

"Violet?" called Bull.

"No," she answered, without looking up from marking her sheet.

"Iris?"

"Yes." She smiled at Sabina.

"Buck?"

"Yes."

"My vote is no," Bull confirmed, looking down and rubbing his hands.

"That is a split vote among the Ori and as is custom, our tie breakers are decided either by calling upon the Seer or a citizen, and we have done both. The Seer's vote is no, and Sabina's vote is yes. That poses a problem. We are still in conflict if we consider Sabina's vote," Bull thought out loud.

"The Seer is not council. I move that her vote be disregarded," Bagger interjected.

Dove sighed loudly.

Smoke walked back in at that moment. "You cannot discount a vote once cast even if it was not in an official manner," she said coolly.

"She is right," Iris agreed.

"Let's call upon another citizen then," Bee purred. She was smiling and twisting her shoulders as if she was in a fine mood. She was clearly looking at Master Alf.

"Mmm," Smoke hummed.

"I like it," said Berry.

"Fine by me," Iris chimed in.

"No. He cannot be trusted. He is hardly a citizen," Bagger pleaded in frustration.

"What makes him a citizen? Wasn't it our vote this morning where you gave your blessing for him to be one?" Dove stated.

"He hasn't been a citizen for one day yet." Bagger raised his voice.

"I agree with taking Flann's vote for the simple purpose that I don't want another citizen dragged into this confidential conversation," Buck complained.

"Mistress, do you agree with this? This is your petition," Bull asked.

Wringing her hands for an instant, Mistress straightened up and walked over to Master Alf, circling him. The room grew quiet.

Sabina felt her dreams slowly become crushed. Flann had told her not to do it. She could feel the tears surface in her eyes as Mistress walked around him. She could not believe her luck. She finally had the courage to ask for what she wanted and now her fate was in this irritating man's hands. Sabina silently pleaded for the Mistress to say no.

As Mistress circled him, Flann locked gazes with her. He wasn't willing to look away. The Mistress's face was sober.

"Why are you parading around him? If you asked me, we should make this discussion open to the villagers," Dove advised.

Buck immediately protested Dove's comment. "We cannot do that. That would alarm everyone."

"Maybe they should be alarmed, **Buck**. We are talking about WAR," Dove asserted, cutting him off and placing her hands on the back of her hips with her long, sleeked-back hair cascading down both shoulders. Turning to Mistress, she said, "My point is you said you have faith that everything will work out, but now you are judging whether he will answer in your favor or not." Dove looked unapologetically at Mistress, calling the Mistress out on the integrity of her words.

The Mistress stopped walking, sighing to herself. "You are right, Dove. Thank you for that reminder. The final vote is yours, Master Alf." The Mistress surrendered. She lifted her chin and glanced at Sabina as she walked back to her spot in the circle.

"Now wait a minute. Let's think this through. Master Alf is probably a fine man, but he doesn't know Silvedome. He doesn't love our people," Bagger argued.

"All in favor of Master Alf being our citizen that breaks the vote?" Bull said, not letting Bagger continue.

Almost everyone looked around, waiting for the first person to raise their hands. In the end, they raised their hands at the same time, except for Bagger who kept his arms crossed in clear defiance of this choice. The rest seemed resigned that this was the best choice, given the circumstances.

~

Sabina dropped her chin to her chest. All hope crashing down. Her imagination took her to working in the field, reseeding the land, and being covered in dirt. She looked at her curled-up fingers and saw the dirt still under her nails. She huffed to herself. *Maybe that is the omen.*

~

Mistress kept her chin lifted and waited for Master Alf to answer, knowing his answer was outside her control. She comforted herself, reasoning it was always a big ask of the council to go against Nana Honey's words, and an even bigger ask when Nana Honey predicted war. She was proud of herself and of Sabina for fighting for what they wanted.

The Mistress did not know how Master Alf would vote. War was familiar in other lands, but not here. She knew little of him, but she had performed his Birth Challenge ritual to confirm his Moowin capabilities, as was custom to all visitors or recruits. Flann was hurt and cocky then. He seemed broody now, but his energy felt more solid too. When she circled around him, she wondered if he hadn't been healed enough to do the ritual, for his energy did feel stronger to her now. Maybe his anger made his Moowins stronger. She considered that he might need to be retested as he aged. Berry might have been right about him. He was only sixteen and their lands had more spiritual energy than other lands. He could develop into a stronger Moowin than his ritual had revealed.

The room suddenly felt hot to Flann, who'd originally thought it was cool. Out of the corner of his eye, he watched the Mistress walk away from him and Sabina's head drop. Shame raced through him. He was the reason she gave up hope so quickly. He did not think this should be his decision to make. The Ori were crazy for putting the final decision in his hands. He agreed with the wound-up, old man called Bagger. Flann didn't know Silvedome's customs, and he hadn't been there one day. But as Sabina's head fell in disappointment, he was grateful to the universe that it was his decision.

Trust was a pivotal concept that did not carry through equally in all areas of Flann's life. Each area had to be evaluated and considered. He trusted Brom to help him develop his skill, to get his family to safety and out of debt, and to get him into Silvedome so he could start his life with Nora, the woman he could not marry in his lands. Yet he didn't trust that Brom was making the best decision for Sabina, even if his motives were of good intentions and out of love.

Being a slave, Flann knew what it was like for someone to tell you who you could or could not be and what you could or could not have. Flann recognized how limited Sabina's life had been under Brom's authority. The saddest part to Flann was he knew he was a slave, but Sabina had no idea she was one too.

Flann was at a crossroads. His fist was clenched, and he rubbed his thumb across his index finger lightly as he considered. It was his duty to protect Sabina and honor his word to Brom. At the same time, Flann needed to honor his soul, which said he would not be an oppressor. He would not commit the same injustice to another person as was done to him. He refused. A flame burned in his heart, calling him to seek justice.

He looked around the room. All the Ori were staring at him, waiting for his answer. All in different moods, different temperaments. He didn't care. He cared about one thing right now. Doing what was right to him.

"She trains with Mistress, and I work with them as their personal Messenger."

∼

Berry immediately made a fist and yanked his arm back in excitement. Sabina smiled to herself and brought her hands to her face, covering her smile, her head still down. She couldn't believe it. Flann had taken her side. She wondered why he had changed his mind, but the thought was fleeting. She was too engrossed with a powerful, uplifting emotion that made her whole body tingle in excitement.

"That's not your decision, boy," said Bagger, getting up in arms.

"It makes sense. I don't have a job yet. Messengers don't like the battlefield. I need to choose three studies myself. Plus, I can help keep this work in secrecy."

"OHHH, I like the way this boy thinks," Smoke praised.

"You have no business coming in here and putting stipulations on your vote. It is a simple yes or no," shouted Bagger, with

Buck shaking his head in agreement. "Since you don't know how to do that, I'll handle it for you. Let the record show he voted 'yes', Violet."

"Yeah, I got that," Violet remarked.

"Fine. My answer is yes," Flann firmly said. "How would I **petition** that I will work with the Mistress and Sabina?"

"I knew you were all hot and bothered about her." Bee winked in her playful manner.

"This conversation is done," Bagger blustered.

"What are you proposing?" Looking over at Bagger, urging him to settle down, Bull continued. "It's the end of the workday and I think everyone here has had enough excitement. What are you proposing? We will consider it later."

"No, I am sensing he may have a more powerful Moowin than the ritual showed. I'd be interested in working with his aura to see what I can discover," requested the Mistress with her finger on her chin.

"That boy can move fast. He must have a stronger Protector talent than the ritual picked up. His Protector skill barely registered on the scales and to move that fast would make him strong at the very least." Berry looked around excitedly.

"Maybe they are twin flames, and they make each other's energy stronger," Bee teased. "You did say you were unable to put a shield on Sabina in the past. Then Master Alf arrives in town today and you happen to exhibit a skill you have never possessed before. Maybe it's not you, but them causing you to have access to this talent."

"Bullocks," grinned Smoke excitedly. "I love twin-flame couples."

"That is a possibility, and it would explain a lot," Iris remarked.

Twin Flames. Sabina had read plenty of stories of old about twin flames, but she didn't believe it was possible for her to have a twin flame. She looked over to Flann, still feeling the strong influence of the tree bark, and stared openly. She wrapped her arms around her waist. He looked annoyed by this conversation with his jaw clenched and the challenging gaze he gave Bagger. Plus, she had decided that they were not compatible. *But what if Iris is right? Being twin flames would explain a lot.*

Sabina found Flann irritating, but twin flames often triggered each other. If she was willing to admit it, which she wasn't, he was good-looking. However, he didn't make her have butterflies in her stomach. *No, he makes me feel like throwing more rocks at him.* That thought made her smile.

"Please . . . let's call it a day and reconvene on this tomorrow when we have had time to consider this request," Bull beseeched.

"We have gone this far, and I'd rather get this over," Dove declared with her arms thrown up in the air. "Can I get a motion?" she snapped.

All raised their hands but Bagger, Bull, and Moon. Bull shook his head and sat down, yielding to the group, but Bagger fumed. "This twin flames idea has gone to everyone's head. No one will vote against that and there is no way to prove it until after Sabina's BIRTH CHALLENGE!!!!"

"You will vote against it," Dove contradicted quickly and quietly.

"One could argue it has already been proven," added Violet. "Sabina has low performance and unremarkable growth toward any talent. Yet, she is clearly marked by the Seer as an amplifier which is a lost talent. Master Alf scored low in the Protector skill on our ritual, which has a ninety-nine percent accuracy, yet he moved with the speed of a strong Protector. What more proof do you need?"

"Those poor men that your father worked so hard to arrange union interviews with don't stand a chance," Bee stated to Sabina with pretend sorrow.

Wanting to dispute this far-fetched idea that she and Flann were twin flames, Sabina gathered her thoughts on what she wanted to say but paused at the realization that Flann wasn't disputing it. *What does that mean? Does he think we are?* Sabina felt nauseous and sat down. All her life, she wished for someone to show interest in her. Granted, he had not shown interest, but she knew she didn't want anything to do with him. Since he came into her life this morning, everything had gone wrong.

How am I going to tell him I don't like him?

~

Flann held back from interrupting the direction of the conversation, not caring what the Ori thought as long as it got him what he wanted. These were suspicious people, he thought, smirking. There was more than one possible reason to explain Sabina being an amplifier, but they were blinded by the desire for magic and for the impossible to be possible. He looked over to Sabina sitting down, her head close to her knees. Man, her father did a number on her.

"Moon, what are your thoughts?" the Mistress inquired.

"Yeah, buddy? I get Bagger doesn't trust Alf and Bull wants time to analyze the situation. I don't know if I believe this twin flame thing, but you already know I think Master Alf's Protector talent should be further trained. Why didn't you raise your hand?" Berry asked.

Moon shrugged. "I have felt the energy between twin flames, and it was intense." He shrugged again. "I don't feel it," he said, as if he was sorry.

"Flames take time to burn but once they catch fire, there is no stopping that love," Smoke said.

"Maybe." Moon shrugged.

"Do we need a formal vote, or can we do hands?" Violet asked, getting a new sheet of paper.

"Hands," most of the room remarked at once. Bagger stood with his arms crossed and sucked on his teeth like he wasn't going to participate in something so ridiculous.

Seeming to worry, Buck commented, "Do you think this should be common knowledge? Sabina's unusual talent, war implications, twin flames . . . I think we should have a vow of silence."

Bull, still sitting at his desk with a disapproving face, wasn't participating in leading the call, so Violet stepped in for him. She announced, with a note of fear in her voice, "Raise your hand if you agree to approve Master Alf working with the Mistress and Sabina in a Messenger capacity and developing his Protector talent with the condition this training be done in secrecy. Furthermore, only the Ori, Sabina Rockdin, and Master Alf will know about the suspected twin flame possibility. A silencer will be implemented. All in favor?"

All raised their hands except Bull and Bagger. "That makes the vote in favor of Master Alf's training. This is approved and recorded. This concludes our meeting." Violet smiled, standing up and tugging at her shirt.

"Silencers," Bull remarked, barely lifting his hand to motion to Bee.

Relieved, Flann was pleased he'd worked out a way to keep Sabina near him. He didn't argue with the Ori for wanting a vow of silence. That seemed like a fair exchange. Actually, it worked in his favor, but as Bee approached him with a tiny microchip with legs on it, he stepped back.

"What's that? What are you doing?" He backed up with his hands raised.

"This is your silencer," she explained, looking completely at ease with the task before her.

Alarmed, he grabbed her wrist to stop her. He didn't want to hurt her, but he didn't know what this chip did. He had seen the neon-green marker on Sabina's hand and the pain that it inflicted.

"Shhh. It's fine. This won't hurt. You won't feel anything but the smallest pinch," she soothed, keeping still. "I'm going to put this chip on your neck. It will bury into your skin. That is when you will feel a slight pinch. Once the chip is inserted, it will separate into two halves. One half will attach to your vocal cord and the other half will travel up to your brain and attach where your thoughts form. The chips communicate with each other. The chip on your brain will read your thoughts and if you are going to communicate something about twin flames or your training, it will have the chip on your throat stop your breathing until your brain shifts thoughts."

"Does this chip allow you to read my thoughts? Can this be removed? What happens if it malfunctions?" he asked, clearly unsure about this technology.

"No one can read your thoughts," she assured. "Your thoughts will always be private. In fact, we will not know if your chip is activated to silence you. Chips never malfunction. Any proficient Healer can remove this, but it's marked as the Ori's property. It requires a Healer to get the Ori's approval to remove the chip."

"What's stopping me from writing it down or from using my Messenger talent?"

"It doesn't matter what form of communication you use, essentially your air will be cut off and if you continue to ignore the lack of oxygen, it will sever your artery," she smiled, her short, wild hair making her look a little less than reliable.

Repulsed, Flann kept her hand away from his neck. He rebuked her. "I don't think so. How about I promise not to say anything, and you trust my word?"

She laughed lightly. "This *is* your promise and naturally we will trust you to keep your word because the consequences will ensure it. Now relax. You have already agreed to this, so nothing is happening against your will. And no one has ever died from a silencer or had any major incidents. At most, people slip up and the chip causes them to cough."

Deciding he could have a Healer outside Silverdome remove this chip, he let go of her wrist and dropped his arms by his sides. His hands were in fists, and he squeezed his eyes shut. Moon placed his hand on his shoulder while Bee's fingers touched his neck. There was a small pinch, but it was hardly noticed with the flooding of calm rippling through his body. He opened his eyes and Moon's back was already to him. Bee was looking at him.

"Perfect. Everything is in its place." She patted his shoulder and turned to squat down to Sabina. She rolled her head over to one shoulder. Bee placed her finger on her neck and without any fuss, Sabina was silenced.

~

The only ones left were Sabina, Flann, Bee, and Moon. Everyone else had left, trusting that Bee and Moon would take care of administering the silencers. Sabina was still sitting in the chair, unmotivated to move. It had been a long day. Flann stood in front of her while Bee and Moon walked over to the door and waited.

"Let's get out of here," Bee declared, tossing her head toward the door.

"Do you need help?" Flann asked Sabina, unsure what to do.

"No," she moaned, reaching down to pick up her satchel that wasn't there. *Oh right, I left that at the tut when I ran like a possessed person was chasing me.* She slowly got to her feet and waited for Flann to give her space. He stepped to the side, and she walked unenthusiastically to the door. Bee was watching her with concern.

"What's wrong, pumpkin? Your energy is all off."

"It's her mood. You guys may have been right about them. Her mood is tied to Flann," Moon revealed, much to Sabina's dismay.

"Of course, I'm right," she said. "I can spot love a mile away."

~

Not having thought about what twin flames might have meant to Sabina, Flann turned to look at her questionably, but she slouched, looking depleted of willpower. She ignored him. Her eyes were forward but unfocused. He wondered if what Bee had given her was making her ill. She didn't look good.

"Do you think Bee should look you over?" he asked quietly as they walked down the hallway a good pace away from Bee and Moon.

"Huh, what? Oh, no. I'm fine. I'm great. Never better."

"What's that?" Bee had heard her name and hung back, letting them catch up.

"Does she look alright to you?" Flann questioned.

They were close to exiting the building and Bee only glanced at Sabina. "Humm, I don't sense anything wrong."

"It's Flann," Moon responded in a flat tone. "Do you want me to help?" he asked, stopping in front of the door.

"No, you two go ahead. Let me have a minute with Sabina." Bee waved them on.

Flann looked between the door and Sabina. He couldn't leave without her, but he didn't need to be *right* by her side.

"Flann's energy says no," Moon revealed dryly.

"Stop reading my energy. Have you heard of privacy?" Flann shot back, flustered.

Moon shrugged. "Sorry. Now I'm interested to see if you two are . . . connected. I cannot help myself."

"Got it *bad* for each other." Bee smiled to herself as neither Sabina nor Flann were in the mood to be teased. "Just wait outside the door for her. We won't be long."

"Come on, buddy. You can tell me about Aliward while we wait," offered Moon.

Taking his eyes off Sabina, who had wrapped her arms around herself and bit her lower lip, he followed Moon out the door. He was aware Sabina was avoiding eye contact with him. He felt pity for her and what she was going through. He could only imagine how she felt. He could faintly feel her despair through the binding they shared. He figured it must be because of the twin flames story. He vowed to himself to tell her the truth and set the record straight.

Bee lightly pushed Sabina into the same bathroom she was in earlier where she had learned that Flann was her slave. Less than an hour later, the same candlelight flickered low as the candles were almost burned out. Just like the dying candlelight, Sabina had less light within her. She wanted to go back to believing that Flann was simply her slave. That was easier. She didn't want to believe they were twin flames.

Taking a big breath and sighing, Bee put her hands on her hips. "I cannot fix your thoughts. Nobody but you can. All those thoughts causing you trouble are thoughts you are choosing to think about. So out with it because I'm not giving you anymore of my precious tree bark." She looked expectantly at Sabina.

Not wanting to talk about her personal issues, Sabina looked up and asked in a thin voice, "What was that tree bark? It made me feel different."

Bee answered swiftly. "It is something that blocks your brain responses to fear. It affects the back of your brain. The cerebellum. Now, are you going to tell me, or do I have to guess?"

Looking off to the side, Sabina avoided eye contact and refused to speak. She pretended she wasn't there.

"Sabina Rockdin. I have known you since you were a baby. You have spent half your life in my hospital hiding from everyone. Don't think I don't know you," Bee said firmly.

"I don't like him," she whined, instantly giving in to Bee.

"Is that it?" She waited for the rest to come out.

"How am I supposed to tell him I don't like him when he thinks we are . . . connected? Why would I be connected to someone I don't like and who irritates me so much? And what if I only have these abilities if I am connected to him?"

Bee answered, "Have a little faith in the universe. Everything will work out. It always does. People are put in our life for a reason. The ones that are the most challenging are the biggest blessings to us because they *reflect* to us what we need to work on."

Sabina scoffed.

"Tell me a time he got on your nerves," she probed.

Thinking she was proving her point about how wrong they were for each other, Sabina said, "He indulges the girls flirting with him, he is bossy, he asks too many questions, AND he is always looking at me too," she huffed.

"Is that so? Sounds like any other relationship, so the question I have is why does it bother you what he does? What are you making it mean?"

"I'm not making it mean anything. I just don't like it," she fumed.

Putting both hands on her shoulder, Bee waited for Sabina to look at her, but she stubbornly kept looking to the side. Bee pulled Sabina's chin slightly toward her.

"What you are telling me is you don't like him *now*," she said mischievously. "Pumpkin, love yourself *enough* to **trust** yourself in what you know to- be- true- for- you-. No one says you must like him or mate with him, and it would not matter if any of us did. YOU have authority over your life. And let me explain something to you because I know Marigold has tight lips when it comes to teaching you about love. You- don't- owe- him- anything- but decency and your honesty. So let go of these expectations you are putting on yourself and on him," she pleaded. "When you are ready, things will become clearer to you. Until then, you keep following joy and learning *who you are*. Have fun dating all these men your father has lined up for you. Go wild. Be free." She laughed lightly, looking up at the ceiling with joy on her face.

Feeling calmer, Sabina smiled back. Bee helped her to see she had choices.

Bee offered her a little extra advice. "And trust me when I tell you that the universe has a way of providing you with exactly what you need, and not necessarily what you want," she claimed with a knowing smile. "Funny thing is that what you need most, often turns out to be what you want in the end so be OPEN to the experience. But for now, speak your truth and tell him how you feel. Then move forward."

"How do I do that?" Sabina moaned with distress.

Bee shook her head. They had a shared kinship with the Ducklings and before Bee's career took off, she had spent a lot of time with Sabina and the Ducklings. Bee realized back then that Sabina had nowhere else to be. Her momma barely talked to her, and her father was always gone. Although Sabina was happy at the hospital with her friends, Bee wanted a different life for her. She vowed to be her secret and wacky aunt that would look after her, but she didn't keep her word. She had let her career take over, and she forgot to check in with Sabina. Recalling that vow she made herself over ten years ago made her heart fill with regret.

This was a conversation that her parents should have had with her. As Bee decided long ago to be Sabina's secret, adopted wacky aunt, Bee filled in where her parents failed to teach Sabina ways of life. It was a shame they failed to raise Sabina up in a way that allowed her to freely express herself without guilt or shame. *This poor girl is riddled with insecurities. It's not right. I cannot change the past, but I can be here for her now.*

Putting her hand on Sabina's cheek, Bee said gently, "You talk to him like you are talking to yourself."

"I, I don't know. Cannot I just ignore him? He will eventually go away."

"What, do you love misery so much you are willing to suffer rather than to have one challenging moment where you are uncomfortable speaking your truth?"

Sabina shook her head 'yes'.

"You understand that you are essentially silencing yourself?" Bee pointed out, looking at her.

～

Sabina let her words sink in. She had been willing to be silent about how she felt to spare herself from feeling rejected or hurting Flann's feelings.

"What is the worst that can happen if you tell him you don't like him? He says he doesn't like you either. Well, good. Then you are both in agreement and that makes things easier."

"What if he does like me and I hurt his feelings?" Sabina mumbled.

"Are his feelings your responsibility?"

"Well, yeah. If I hurt his feelings, then it is my fault."

"Umm, it must be nice to have the power to choose what feelings Flann feels. Why did you choose for his feelings to be hurt? Why not choose for his feelings to be peaceful and make it easier on yourself?"

Confused and trying to catch up with what Bee was saying, Sabina responded. "I didn't choose for him to be hurt. I caused him to be hurt."

"That's odd. I thought you said you were responsible for his feelings," she said putting her fingertips toward her chest, "which means that you have control over his feelings. I don't understand why you don't control what he feels now. Wait," she replied, like she had just figured something out. "Unless what you are telling me is you only have responsibility for fixing his feelings after he makes a choice on how he wants to feel?"

"Oh, Bee. Why do you have to be soooooo confusing?" whined Sabina.

"Sounds like you have a problem. Because what you are telling me is that you are accountable for fixing his feelings when you have no control over what feelings he chooses to have."

"Yesssss." She sighed, relieved Bee had said something that made sense.

"He gets to pick. You get to fix," she sang in a pleasant, happy tone. "How do you fix the emotion he picks? Do you tell him to pick a new one?"

"Nowah. I don't know. I find a way to make him happy." Sabina pinched her eyebrows together.

"Does he get to pick whether or not he is happy with what you do for him?" Bee inquired.

"Ugh, yyyeeaaahhh."

"Teach me. How does this work? Because I don't understand. How do you *make* him feel the emotion you want him to feel when you don't get to pick his emotions? He could always pick a different emotion. It sounds exhausting. And when does he become responsible for causing you to feel exhausted? I mean, when is it his turn to make you feel, let's say, energetic? And does that cycle continue? Do you continue to make him happy, while he continues to make you feel energetic?"

"He cannot cause me to feel energetic," Sabina rebutted in a tone that said Bee was absurd.

"Why?" Bee asked.

"I don't know," she uttered.

"Let me ask you this and then I'll stop trying to understand," she replied. "Why are you not allowing him to have the feelings he may need to have? AND *why* are you not accepting the feelings that come up for you?" she asked gently.

Shutting down, Sabina looked at the door, longing to leave. She felt small and childish.

"I suspect you want to be busy fixing his emotions, so you don't have to feel yours." Bee held the silence for a long moment.

Eventually Sabina stopped pretending to ignore her and looked up.

"I just don't want to hurt another person's feelings, okay!" Sabina responded.

"Let me save you some time figuring this out. You are assuming responsibility for his feelings. The truth is you have no control over another person's feelings. Honestly, most of us have a hard enough time managing our own feelings and it is not your place to manage someone else's. He is a grown man, and you are not his mamma," she said with her hands on her hips.

"Beeeee, I've wronged him. You are supposed to make amends when you wrong someone," she complained.

"How did you wrong him? By telling him your truth? I- don't- think- so. You have nothing to amend."

"You don't get it. YOU don't get me."

"Being honest with someone about what is best for you is how you show love to yourself and to others. If you cannot tell him this relationship is not for you then you are lying to yourself, and you are misleading others about your intention. THAT's when you will have a mess to clean up."

"But what about hurting him?" Sabina still wouldn't allow herself to let go of being responsible for Flann's expected feelings.

"What you need to understand is that feelings are created by the thoughts you think. Unless you can crawl into his head and rearrange his thoughts to cause you the least amount of suffering, I suggest you stop focusing on his emotions and deal with your own. So, let's get to the bottom of this, shall we? What emotion are you resisting when you tell him you don't like him and what thoughts are you having to cause you those feelings?" she coaxed.

Knowing that Bee was relentless, Sabina gave in. She took a moment to think about what Bee said. Sabina responded. "I don't know. I guess I don't want to feel uncomfortable or awkward."

"And what thoughts make you feel uncomfortable?" she pried.

"I'll just be standing there not knowing what to do with myself. I won't know how to react to whatever he says to me. I'll look foolish and then every day, I'll have to see him after that. He'll think, there is that girl who doesn't like me."

"Stop right there. All those are made-up stories. Unless you are a Seer, you cannot predict what will happen."

"That's what will happen. I don't need to be a Seer," she remarked defiantly.

"You're telling the universe what you want to happen, so I guess so."

"I DON" T want that to happen. That's just the way it will go," Sabina declared, getting upset.

"Remember, the universe works on its timeline, not ours. But the words you speak into your life are in your control. Every word you speak is creating something, even if it is a feeling within you and those feelings affect your actions. Now I have had enough of your pity party. NOTHING good comes out of feeling sorry for yourself. Master Alf showed up in your life at this time, for a purpose. That purpose may be for you to teach him a lesson or two. Or maybe it's a lesson for you to speak your truth. All I can say for certain is that your energies are connected. What you make that mean—or what I make that mean—is all made-up stories, like the story you are telling yourself right now." Bee dropped her hands from Sabina's shoulder. "Come on. We have two men waiting to be graced with our presence," Bee chirped, changing the subject.

Dropping her head, Sabina followed Bee out of the bathroom. She felt better knowing she was not responsible for Flann's emotions and was relieved she didn't have to 'be' with Flann. But she felt worse having her insecurities and self-doubt brought to her attention. She didn't want to acknowledge those parts of her. There was a sense of darkness in her mood. Silvedome believed in living your purpose, your dharma. She was two days away from entering adulthood where she would have to figure it out on her own. She should have a sense of who she was and her purpose. She should know what lit her up. But all she knew was she wanted to be included, and that was with the Ducklings.

As she followed Bee, she reflected on why she was so scared to listen to that inner voice within her. Why did she not have the ability to let go of her desires to please others? Everyone was thriving around her, and she was a dull rock with no shine. She didn't want to think or feel anymore. She was hollow and she wanted to sleep. She was exhausted, and ready for everything to disappear so she could shut down.

Bee looked back at Sabina, registering her emotional struggle. She was suffering but Bee knew from her years of experience working in the hospital that she needed to let Sabina work through these emotions. Despite knowing this was a valuable lesson for Sabina, Bee felt pulled to cuddle this incredible girl, too often unnoticed by others.

"It's tough love but it is still love," she empathized. "You are my girl," she said affectionately, wrapping her arm around Sabina as they walked through the exit, "and I believe in you."

Feeling the need to say something, Sabina mouthed: "Thank you." They walked quietly together, noticing Flann and Moon talking a few yards away. Flann kicked at the ground and Moon lounged with both hands in his pockets.

What The Seer Had To Say

"Bee, earlier when we were voting, I heard you say, 'That's my girl' when I chose to train, but when it was your turn to vote, you voted against me." With every step they took, they were closer to an audience, and Sabina didn't want anyone else to hear. She sighed, thinking Bee would not answer before Flann was in earshot.

"And? Do you have a question?" Bee pushed back.

"Why?" she struggled to say, feeling betrayed that Bee had supported her decision but didn't agree with her. Sabina was confused. She felt Bee's pride for her asking for what she wanted. Yet she chose for her to pursue something else.

"Why indeed?" she uttered in delight, looking unfazed by Sabina's negative state. "Oh, pumpkin. You have much to learn. Things cannot always be easily explained. Let's just say I want you to follow your heart, and what brings you joy, but I also want to do what's best for me. Sometimes, our paths in life don't align, but that never stops me from rejoicing when I see you advocate for your desires."

Flann looked up, disregarding Moon's polite small talk. His intense green eyes read Sabina's mood, who turned to look over her shoulder. Growing up in a house full of girls, Flann didn't need any talents to perceive Sabina's unhappy state. He realized this would be a long walk home. He comforted himself with reassuring words. He could handle whatever was thrown at him, including her not wanting anything to do with him. Regardless of how she responded, he vowed to tell her the truth. Maybe a partial truth. No need for her to know everything.

"Master Alf, it was a pleasure making your acquaintance. I would have loved to witness your Birth Challenge and see for myself the strength of your Moowins," Moon acknowledged.

"It was nothing special, I assure you."

Smiling, Bee remarked, "Oh, I think it's *quite* special to meet someone whose energy connects to my girl," and she pulled Sabina in closer to her.

Glancing up briefly, Sabina made eye contact with Flann and looked away, biting her lower lip.

"Right. Master Alf." Moon nodded. "May I walk you home?" Moon held out his arm for Bee.

"Moon, you take all the fun out of it," Bee teased. "Yyyy-eeesss," she responded, rolling her eyes playfully.

Moon almost smiled with half his cheek raising.

"You are such a handsome, *mischievous* fox," Bee cooed, coming up and grabbing his chin. She gave him the lightest peck on the lips and wrapped her arm around his. "Is he not?" she asked, looking at Sabina and Flann, who stood opposite each other.

Neither answered the rhetorical question. They watched the enchanting, fun-loving Bee cause Moon to stand a little straighter with her on his arm. Before Moon proudly escorted her home, she leaned her head back and said, "I've got a good feeling about you two!!!" She laughed as Moon patted her hand.

"Alright, alright. I'll behave . . . For now," she purred as they walked away.

~

Looking down at her tunic, Sabina focused on the blue Aztec design. Her heart was racing with fear, considering telling him she didn't like him. *No, maybe later. Maybe tomorrow. It would be better to do it after I have at least eaten something.*

"Are those two an item, a couple, or whatever you call it here? Are they in a union?" Flann wondered, watching them disappear in the distance.

Grateful for a safe topic, Sabina looked at him. She saw he wasn't watching her. *Good.* "No. Bee is a free spirit. She, she loves too many people to settle for one flavor. That's what she says anyway. She has a lot of suitors though. They are just friends. Moon likes her because she is always happy. He is super sensitive to everyone's energy with his Moowin. He is exhausted most of the time from feeling other people's feelings. Bee is like an energetic shield for him." Sabina tucked her hair behind her ear.

"But your people are big into marrying for life, or mating for life," he said, correcting himself. He was looking at her now.

"Yeah, sorta. Tying is rare. It is a permanent spiritual bond that binds a couple across multiple lifetimes. That person is called your mate. But, if you find someone who makes your life easier, and you mutually make a commitment to love each other, then you enter a union, which is comparable to marriage in your culture. That person is called your partner."

"Ah," he said awkwardly. "Can I talk to you about . . . us?" His voice was rough, but he sounded firm.

The world seemed to dim, and Sabina's heartbeat thumped furiously against her chest. She took a deep breath to steady herself and recalled Bee's advice. *There is nothing wrong with telling him how I feel,* she chanted to herself.

She nodded as they quietly approached the bridge.

Flann took three running steps to close the distance. "Slow down and let me think. I'm trying to tell you something I don't want to tell you and, frankly, it is not easy for me."

She slowed, wrapping her arms around herself. She kept her head down but kept eye contact.

"I lied to you, okay. I lied . . . I lied and I'm sorry. I know it's not right. I didn't know what else to do, and I didn't expect things to go this direction." He sighed heavily. "I didn't think about your feelings and I'm sorry," he admitted.

Sabina felt confused and her confusion pushed away her fears. She was staring at him, watching him fidget in his discomfort. Flann was looking up to the sky as if he was confessing his wrongs to the universe and not to her. She admired his bravery in pushing through his discomfort.

She put her hand on his upper arm, attempting to draw his attention back to her. She was not used to touching people, so her automatic response came as a surprise. A zing of energy forced her to drop her arm to her side. "What are you saying? What did you lie about?" She was relieved to hear her voice was calm as she questioned him.

His focus had shifted to her touch, and he seemed calmed by it. He swallowed and returned to looking her in the eye. Sabina absorbed his emotions, maintaining eye contact.

His eyes revealed conflict. "I'm not your tw . . ." He started wheezing, unable to breathe. His face turned quickly to a shade of purple and he scratched at his neck.

She grabbed his arm, spinning him toward her. She realized what was happening as she saw him turn purple. He must be still trying to say it, she thought. She was responsible for him! An alarm went off in her body. She moved her hands to his face, feeling the prickle of his shadowed beard. "You **cannot** say that. STOP. Stop," she yelled over his wheezing. "Say connections. Replace it with connections. Breathe," she commanded.

Eyes locked, her face inches from his, she suddenly let go of his face. Adrenaline was pumping through her veins. She felt shaky. As she saw him regain his breath, she closed her eyes. "You cannot say that word. Don't even think it! Bee told you what would happen. Burning Fires. I thought I would have to give you oxygen or something. Why did you keep trying to say it?"

Rubbing his throat, he coughed. "I forgot. Tullom. That works fast and swift. I thought there was a gentle reminder before they suffocated you."

"It does," she said, standing with her feet apart and looking at him like he was a fool. "You are just too stubborn to pay heed."

"Yep. Sounds about right."

"Do you need the hospital?" she asked with a little more compassion in her voice.

Clearing his throat, he said, "No. I've got it." He was still making sounds to clear his vocal cords. "I can guarantee you I won't be making that mistake again."

"Let's go home and get some water," she quietly replied.

They walked side by side in silence. The sun was at its highest point of the day and the weather was beautiful as always, but Sabina felt cold. She knew it was irrational, but she felt wounded that Flann had tried to tell her he didn't like her. She knew it didn't make sense because she didn't like him either. But his rejection was a reminder she was unlovable, and she didn't belong.

Flann was deep in thought, considering what to say but desperate to clear his conscience. He was determined to tell her the truth so she could move on to someone who would make her happy. But next time he would avoid saying 'twin flames'. *Tullom, I must get this contraption out of me.*

As they crossed the bridge to the village square, people were out. Most people worked the same hours, but a few worked earlier or later, depending on their profession. Stores stayed open for two hours after the traditional work hours and the square was buzzing with people. No one paid particular attention to them as they stayed on the main road to Sabina's tut. There was a lot of noise and commotion, but Sabina seemed to focus on watching her boots swinging one foot in front of the other in a methodical way.

Once they got into the home section, Flann continued with what he had attempted to tell Sabina earlier. He had thought it through to the best of his abilities and had concluded that Brom would forgive him for whatever issues his communication caused.

"I am not connected to you in the way you think," he continued once it was quiet. He didn't look at Sabina. He looked forward with his gaze taking in the scenery.

Sabina looked up from her boots and squinted at him. The sun was hitting the other side of his face and he was casting a shadow on her. She mused to herself at the irony of being in his shadow physically and emotionally.

"Are you listening?" Flann prompted.

"Yeah," she responded distantly. She felt detached. Her thoughts were on the awareness that this was her first break-up conversation and the relationship had never even started. She sniffed.

"When you read your father's letter, you will understand more, but you have some of my life force within you and I have some of yours in me. Our energy is connected. We literally share an energy link."

"Nothing you are saying is making *any* sense. How do you have my life force? I've never given it to **anyone,** and you must have my permission to have it. Plus, a super rare Healer is required for this kind of transaction. And we have never met before today."

"I'm surprised you know so much. Most people don't know anything about giving one's life force to another. It is kind of frowned upon."

"I read," she answered, looking down at her boots again. "I spend a lot of time reading," she said, with loneliness etched in her voice.

"Well . . . we do. I cannot explain how it happened for you, but to say a decision was made for us."

Pinching her eyebrows together, she gawked at him. *Is he unbalanced?* But she was curious, so she played along. "Ooookaaaay. Why did you agree to give up your life force?" *At least this will help me understand him more*, she decided.

"Aahhh. Short story, I did it to help my family." He was looking down now.

Sabina glanced over at him and noticed he looked glum.

"Honorable," she replied, not sure what to make out of this whole story. "So how did you lie to me? Because, so far, you have only told me what I didn't know."

~

Tullom. She heard what wasn't said, thought Flann, clenching and unclenching his fist. "I . . . am . . . involved with someone," he stated quietly, still looking down.

"And you agreed to be in a union interview . . . with me? Why? I mean, what does that mean? Is this relationship not serious or is it serious and you are a liar?" she blurted out.

Taking a large breath and holding it, he finally said, "I'm a liar." The words were hard for him to say. "I'm sorry. I plan to marry Nora Fanfield soon."

~

They were three tuts away from Sabina's tut but that announcement stopped her in her tracks.

"You *are* a li-ar," she whispered, staring at him. Some part of her felt betrayed and angry.

"Only about this and it's because your father would not have helped me if I didn't agree to be a potential . . . partner for you. I needed help. My family needed help."

"How CONVENIENT for you," she spat in a low tone. She

walked off quickly, eager to get home and have privacy. She was breathing fast and shallow with emotions she was not accustomed to feeling.

Flann followed. He reached for her elbow to grab her, but she yanked her arm out of his grip. "Hey. That's not fair. Why are you getting upset with me? We just met today and unless I am mistaken, you don't like ME," he argued, taking a running step onto the porch of the tut to cut her off.

"Leave me alone," she said, looking at his chest and folding her arms.

"Truce?" he asked with his palms out to her.

"Why would I make a truce with a liar?" Sabina growled.

"Just read your father's letter," he pleaded.

"I don't have my father's letter anymore," she snapped.

"What do you mean you don't have it? Where is it?" He seemed to panic.

"The Seer took it when we met the Ori," she explained, confused by his concern.

"Come on." He grabbed her hand and pulled her toward the village. "We need to get your letter back."

"I don't *want* to see the Seer. I'm tired and I want to sleep and pretend this day never happened. Besides, my letter is safe with the Seer. She basically knows everything." Flann didn't let go of Sabina's hand as he hurried down the path. Her foul mood was escalating as she toddled behind him like a child. She tugged harder to free her hand.

"Quit it. Come ON," he demanded.

Feeling her fingers and knuckles being squeezed together and being unable to pull her hand free, she put her weight on one foot and swept her other leg at his ankles. Flann anticipated her move instinctually and jumped. He must be a more skilled Protector than he tested, Sabina thought. The good news was that her hand was freed when he jumped out of the way of her leg.

"Why are your hands so rough?" she questioned, feeling like her hand was sliced open by his rough calluses.

"Your emotions are becoming unstable. Where is your amulet?" he cautioned.

"My amulet. Why do you want *my amulet*?"

"I don't want it. It's yours. I want you to wear it."

She reached for it as if she was wearing it. She didn't know where it was and that gave her a moment of panic, as it was sentimental to her.

"This isn't you, Sabina. This isn't how you normally behave. You are ready to charge me. You are not the prey but the predator right now. Isn't that odd?" Flann seemed to hope logic would help calm her down.

She looked up at him, feeling feral with angry, confused energy. She never felt this way. Where was her fear or her loneliness, which was her constant companion? *Is this an after-effect of the tree bark Bee gave me?* That thought calmed her. She stood up straighter, not realizing until that moment she was in a fighting stance. She looked at Flann. He looked worried. No, he looked scared. *I caused him to feel scared.* A knot formed in her stomach. This was not the person she wanted to be. She was a person who loved, not hated.

She started trembling. *I am behaving horribly.* She scolded herself. It was no excuse that she was tired and hungry. She had allowed her emotions to overtake her, and she was ready to hurt him. It was as if her brain shut off and she could not reason when she allowed her emotions to take over.

As the fog cleared from her brain and her emotions settled, she rationalized what Flann was saying. Of course, his hands were rough. He was a slave. He probably had lots of work that was labor intensive. She recalled some of the books she had read about a slave's life. It dawned on her what it must be like for him to be a slave to her. Pain lurched in her stomach, hard and fast. *He can't hurt me. He may not have even been able to protect himself.* She needed to get to the Seer and read her father's letter. She needed to understand the terms of this contract and discover how to free him.

Calmly and with as much dignity as she could muster, she said, "You were saying something about a truce?"

"We need to get you to the Seer and find your amulet. I think you will feel better once you have your amulet?"

She nodded. She was shaking too much with unused energy to sleep anyway. She looked around, relieved that most people were in the village square, and no one witnessed her behavior. She tucked her hair behind her ear, bit her lip, and glanced at him quickly.

"I'm, I'm sorry," she mumbled, feeling too embarrassed to make eye contact. "You are right. I don't normally behave this way." And then she thought it was odd he knew what her behavior was like and the fact she wasn't being herself. Was it because of his communication with her father? She didn't feel that red energy.

"I'm curious. How did you know I wasn't . . . myself?" she questioned.

"Come on. Let's walk and talk. Walking will help me clear my head." Flann started walking past her and Sabina joined him.

"Your father found me before my Moowins came in. I was a slave. My entire family were slaves," he said, monotone. "Classic story of parents who had low-income jobs and too many kids. My father was injured, and he didn't work for a period of time. My parents borrowed money until one day, we were all slaves working to pay off the debt. It's an odd sensation going from being a working-class citizen to a second-rate citizen whose voice no longer matters. One day you can think for yourself, the next you cannot."

Listening quietly, Sabina didn't understand how someone could become a slave because of owing money. Money was never the focus in Silvedome.

"Anyway, I was a smart boy. I quit school and worked in the bank during the day. After bank hours, I worked in the horse stables. That is where I met Nora. She is a shy girl but loved horses. We were fast friends and our relationship grew into something more over the years. Being a slave, I didn't have the right to be with Nora. She was from a wealthy family. Therefore, our relationship was always one of secrecy. Long story short, outside of being free again, marrying Nora was my one wish. Everything in my life would be better with her by my side. So . . . when your father found me and offered to pay my entire family's debt, relocate them to new lands where they could start over, and give me a job that would provide me with income throughout my life all in exchange for twenty percent of my life force," he huffed, "I thought it was worth it. Either way, I was a slave and my life expectancy was going to be shorter. With your father's offer, my family could be free, and I would have the opportunity to bring Nora here to Silvedome. Once we were together, I planned to marry her. The choice was easy."

"Why did my father want your life force?" she puzzled out loud.

"Where are we going? We are almost to the village square." Flann slowed down.

"Oh right. Nana Honey lives in Sector Four by the square," she said absentmindedly. She led the way, cutting across the tuts to get to Sector Four, which had large homes on private lands. Nana Honey's home was the first house. "So?" she pressed.

"Let's see what your father's letter says about that."

"You have not read it?" she inquired

"No. But I know about it. I know about a lot of things," Flann mentioned.

She pinched her eyebrows and walked up the path to Nana Honey's front door. "Yes, but how do you know a lot of things?"

"My child," Nana Honey called through the window. "You early. Vhat caused this?"

Crystal had opened the door and was leaning casually into the doorframe. Her intelligent eyes gleamed and her cheekbones glittered. She wore a tank with a long pendant necklace.

"I didn't tell you a time, Nana Honey," she returned.

"Didn't need to," she said from her chair.

Crystal stepped aside to let them in, but before Sabina entered, she stopped, shocked to see the Performer from earlier and Master Lockin.

"Oh, you have company. We can come back later."

"They arrre not staying. Come, my child. Master Lockin honor me. In-tro-duced talented Master Tulk." Nana Honey rocked.

"I'm most pleased to have Master Tulk staying with me. You must all come to The Mox tonight and see him perform. He is simply magnificent," Master Lockin beamed.

"Of course, my child. Love to see performance," Nana Honey said with little inflection in her voice.

"WONDERFUL," Master Lockin said, obviously delighted.

"And will I see you there?" she asked Sabina.

Sabina was sure Master Lockin didn't even know she existed, yet she felt obligated to say yes despite how tired she was. She probably should go. That is what Fawn would do for her guests. *Remember, I'm supposed to entertain our guests*, she said to herself. But she didn't want to. "Yeah," she answered weakly. The uncertainty was clear in her tone.

"We should be off, Master Tulk. We must give you time to prepare for tonight."

Master Tulk was silent and followed Master Lockin. Both gave an honorable bow to Nana Honey sitting in her rocking chair and a nod of respect to Crystal as they left.

"I'll see you tonight," called Master Lockin cheerfully as she walked down the steps.

Stepping back on the porch to give them way, Master Lockin passed as her large skirt swished merrily by. Sabina glanced at Master Tulk's face as he passed, but was startled to see him step toward her.

She took another step back automatically. Master Tulk reached to pick up Sabina's hand with no resistance. She felt too shocked to move. Out of the corner of her eye, she could see Flann at the bottom of the stairs, making two strides up to the top step as her hand was drawn to Master Tulk's lips. Master Tulk looked at her hand, giving it a kiss, and said, "Until tonight."

The image and associated feeling of the octopus with its sucking tentacles registered once again. Her nerves tingled, but this time, it was fainter than what she felt when Flann touched her. Sabina flinched at the sensation. He dropped her hand. Whether that was because of her flinch or Flann, Sabina didn't know. Flann attempted to step in front of Sabina but only managed to get half his body in front of her. The two stared at each other. Flann, shorter than Master Tulk, looked tense, whereas Master Tulk looked amused. Master Tulk's eyes were a smoky gray, and they were mesmerizing. Sabina had an intense desire to get a closer look at them.

"We haven't had a chance to meet." Flann ground his teeth, holding out his hand with his vest unbuttoned. His loose, red curls were shining in the light and Sabina noticed his forearm muscles were flexed. Yes, she could see that he did hard labor.

～

Flann stared up at Benford, wishing he was taller. *So Benford thinks he can win Sabina over! He is such a pretty boy with the perfect jaw to punch.* Why Brom chose him didn't make sense to Flann. He was batting for the same team, and Flann didn't trust his agenda.

"My apologies," responded Master Tulk in a smooth voice, taking his hand. *Oh, you think you are her Protector. Pleaaaassseeee. We will see what she wants and it will most likely be someone like me. Someone that allows her to rescue herself.*

～

Both men stared at each other, leaning slightly toward each other in cross-examination. Crystal shifted, looking ready to step in. Sabina froze.

"Ah, you know each other." Nana Honey's voice drifted through the open door. How she saw them was beyond Sabina.

"What's going on?" called Master Lockin, who had finally turned around and noticed that Master Tulk wasn't following her. She was pouting and then her face lit up.

"Oh yes. How exciting! Master Tulk, this is our newest member of Silvedome. It's . . . Master Alt or something. Oh . . . that's not right," she said, barging up the stairs, happy to take up space.

The two men dropped their handshake. Flann stood where he was, but Master Tulk turned to face Master Lockin with a little smirk.

"He arrived today. Like you," she said, batting his arm playfully. "I'm Master Lockin, the manager of The Mox." She extended her arm and smiled brightly. "Now, I've heard you are a Messenger. Is that right?"

He took her hand lightly for a quick shake, then forcibly drew his hand back, rubbing it on his pant leg with disgust on his face. "Yes. That's right and it's Master Alf," he corrected.

"I wasssss close." Her voice raised as she talked. She was clearly pleased with herself.

Crystal rolled her eyes, turned, and sauntered away.

"All these young new men," Master Lockin blustered.

Nana Honey interrupted Master Lockin. "My child, don't keep me waiting."

"Excuse me." Sabina slipped through the door feeling like the universe saved her from witnessing what desperation looked like.

Not giving Master Lockin a courtesy goodbye, Flann followed Sabina into the house. Sabina heard Master Lockin mumble, "Did I miss something?" and Master Tulk's smooth answer, "No, I don't think you did." Sabina tried to hide her smile. She liked Master Tulk.

Although there were chairs and a couch, Sabina plopped on the cushion on the floor by Nana Honey's feet. There was only one cushion which forced Flann to find a different location, away from Sabina, to sit. Sabina liked this seat. Nana Honey had a comforting but scary presence. Like a flame of fire that was beautiful, warming, comforting, and powerful, but likely to spit and burn.

Over minimal chatter, they heard Master Lockin and Tulk's footsteps descend the stairs, and Flann continued to wipe the hand that touched Master Lockin like he couldn't get her perfume off him. Crystal was gone and Nana Honey had both eyes covered in an eye wrap.

"Thank you for brrrringing Sabina, Master Flann. I see vhat happened. You did smart thing. I am pleased. But vhy I ask for help?"

Settled in his seat, Flann scooted forward, elbows on his knees. "I am not asking for your help. Sabina is here for her father's letter in your possession."

"Stand down, boy. I know eve-ry-thing about you. Ve serve same purpose," said Nana Honey looking forward when Flann was sitting to her left. "You came for let-ter. Trrrrue. But also trrrrue, you came for my help. Do not mix vords with me. Does no good," Nana Honey pointed out.

"Okay, what help do I seek," he said with disbelief.

Sitting on the floor, Sabina looked back and forth between them feeling like she was a fly on the wall. Sabina was curious to know what help Flann needed.

"You need much help. Hiding your Protector Moowin. Keep promise to Norrrra. Ori's permission for Norrra to come to Silvedome. Brom's forgiveness. Sabina's trrrrust. Keep Sabina's energy safe. Shall I go on?"

Flann stared at Nana Honey, looking slightly white-faced. "How powerful are you?"

Nana Honey shrugged. "Much, little, no matter, Tokey. I am vho I am. How you perceive me is how you perceive me."

"What is a Tokey?" Flann asked, confused.

"That is, you. You are Tokey. You are lost one found."

"Oooookaaaay. Let's say I need your help—"

"No say. You do. You mix vords again, Tokey."

"Flann."

"Flann, Tokey. You have no name. You don't plan to give yourself a name. No authority over vhat you call yourself. Sabina calls you 'Brick'."

"Ooaa," Sabina moaned, covering her face.

Flann looked at her. Her face was beet-red between her fingers.

"You call me . . . Brick?" He was clearly appalled.

"Not to your face," she meekly said into her hands.

"Uncover your face, my child. Be proud of vho you are. I see Tokey has brick qualities. You spoke trrrue to you."

"What is this?" Flann flustered, getting up. "I'm not a brick or a Tokey," he claimed confidently. "We came for Sabina's letter. Hand it over and we will be on our way."

"No," Nana Honey declared. "I talk to Sabina. You find Crystal. She needs your help."

Flann shook his hands at the ceiling, getting nowhere with Nana Honey. "Nooooo. I'll stay here with Sabina," he protested.

Nana Honey started rocking her chair. "Fine. Suit yourself. You stay, and I rest. Let-ter is safe. My life easier not helping you." Nana Honey relaxed back.

"It's-her-letter. Give it to her." He raised his voice.

"You think you have authority over me, Tokey?" Nana Honey remained calm and rocking.

As the two battled with wills, Sabina was lost in random thoughts. *Why was I upset that Flann loved someone before he met me? When I think about it, most union interviews don't result in anything anyway. How can I blame him for deceiving my father? He wanted a better life, and he paid a large price. Yeah, he used me as an excuse to get Nora into Silvedome, but I would have lied to get out of slavery. I would have agreed to a union interview. Besides, I don't like him that way anyway. And if Nana Honey saw Nora in her sight and was willing to help, then their relationship must be special. What karma is this? He is self-sabotaging his future for my letter.*

Sabina squirmed, uncomfortable with how this conversation was going. She closed her eyes and took a few breaths, asking herself what she should do. "Nana Honey? If Flann is my slave, isn't he obligated to . . . help me?"

"Trrrrue," she spat.

"Is it possible Flann is fulfilling his obligations by demanding that you give me my father's letter?"

"Possible, yes. Probably, no."

"He has asked me several times to read the letter. It seems to be a great source of anxiety for him. And I don't think he is opposed to helping you or Crystal; I think he only knows how to trust himself," Sabina said as she searched for words.

Nana Honey continued to rock, and Flann sat back down, rubbing his thighs.

Sighing and surrendering, Flann exclaimed, "I do need your help, but I also want to make sure Sabina gets her letter. I don't know you and you are not bound to Sabina as I am."

"I am bound to Sabina in other ways, Tokey. She is safe with me. Always vill be. I give my vord. My vord is source, my power."

Flann understood that the integrity of her word was what caused her to be the gifted Seer that she was. "Thank you." He nodded. He relaxed a little, pinching the pressure point at the bridge of his nose. Relenting, he said, "How can I help you?"

"Crystal needs help. Ve must find Sabina's amulet. Crystal searched with her sight. She is gifted. She finds objects, but cannot locate it. Your connection to Brom and Sabina vill help her."

"Why didn't you say so. I am all for Sabina having her amulet back. Where is she?" he asked, standing up, putting his hands in his pockets.

"It took you long enough," Crystal huffed. She was at the

entryway between the living room and kitchen, waiting for Flann. "I thought I would have to hog-tie you and drag you into my spell work."

"How long have you been standing there?" Flann fretted.

~

Crystal smiled. Her face was radiant and her eyes, finding Sabina's, were still as mischievous as when they were kids playing in the fields. "I wasn't," she said innocently.

"I'm seriously rethinking living in Silvedome." Flann raked his hand through his hair.

Crystal laughed out loudly. "We are sand in the water, my friend." She slapped him on his back as she guided him out of the room.

Waiting for them to leave, Sabina calmed her nerves and tried to stop thinking about whether she had said the right thing.

"You know vhy I'm so powerful?"

"No," Sabina answered, looking at Nana Honey.

"Because . . . I believe an-y-thing is possible. I am not bound to limitations. And I trrrrust the universal laws."

"What are the universal laws?" Sabina said.

"Everrrrything energy. Ve all connected. Ve live in dream, not reality...."

"How can we be living in a dream?" Sabina questioned.

"Trrrruth is fluid. Personal trrrruth is perspective. My personal trrrruth is not your trrrruth. Your trrruth is not your neighbor's trrrruth. But rrrrreal trrrruth evolves you. I understand multiple realities happen simultaneously. Time is circular, not linear. This is trrrruth."

Sabina was used to Nana Honey teaching her about the universal laws. She changed the subject. "Why is everyone upset about my amulet? Shouldn't I be the one who is upset?" she asked and rushed on to say, "which I am. But I find it odd that others care about my sentimental token." She lifted one shoulder.

"Your amulet is important. All amulets are. Carries an energetic connection to great-grandmother. Amulet's prrrrotect the vearer. Your amulet is special. It is inscribed to contain energy and . . . let certain energy in," she answered.

"Other amulets don't . . . contain energy? Is that a good thing or a bad thing because I—"

"My child, ve have little time. I vill speak to you about other matters." She cut Sabina's curious mind off. "Here, pour a salt circle around you."

Sabina took the bottle of salt. She didn't understand all the magic Nana Honey exercised but she trusted there was a good reason. "Like this?" she asked Nana Honey, so used to Nana Honey using her third eye to see everything.

"That vill do."

She dug in her pocket and pulled out the folded letter. She held it in her hands and whispered over the letter in a language Sabina did not understand. The room's temperature dropped noticeably but not uncomfortably.

"I don't agree vith Brom, but I accept his motives are out of love. I suggest you do same." She handed the letter to Sabina who took it with trepidation.

Once the letter crossed the circle of salt, all the candles in the room lit and an incense burned. The sudden action startled Sabina, and she looked for reassurance from Nana Honey who sat so calmly Sabina felt her presence wasn't there. As if she drifted asleep.

Looking at the letter in her hand, Sabina told herself everything was fine and that she could handle whatever important information she read. She relaxed her shoulders and she shifted to read the letter with her back to Nana Honey.

Her father's tiny cursive was difficult to make out, and she brought the letter close to her face to read it.

Biny, it is cowardly of me not to say this directly to you, but I lied about leaving. You may feel abandoned in your time of need, but it is out of love and my calling to protect you that I leave now. It is time for you to walk this path alone. I don't expect you to understand. All I can do is ask for forgiveness. There is much I have kept from you since you were a child but now you are an adult. What I write puts your life in danger. No matter how you feel, burn this letter after reading.

When you were born, you were deathly sick with most of your life force missing. It was a miracle you lived with only twenty-one percent to sustain you. Opal was mystified by your lack of life force. Once she, your great-grandmother, and I donated life force to you, and your energy increased to forty-two percent. However, when friends gave their energy, nothing happened.

Your mother believed it was her fault you struggled to live. While she carried you in her womb, she donated her life force to save her best friend's pregnancy. There was no research or stories of anyone else doing what she had done. Despite your mother being one of the most gifted, rare Healers across several lands, she was powerless to help you. She knew you were dying. No matter what we tried, you were not thriving. You needed a specific source of energy.

Opal noticed there was no distinction between your life force and ours as if it was always your life force to begin with. She had a theory you could only gain life force from someone who shared your blood. We didn't have any more living relatives to go to, but this theory gave your mother a plan to save you by asking past recipients of Opal's life force to share blood and life force between you and their male newborns or young sons.

After that first dosage, you immediately thrived. We were thrilled until we tried to give you the next dose. Your body rejected the second one. Your great-grandmother used her third eye to seek a vision of the future. She discovered you could only receive one dose each year, causing you to remain a Duckling until you had sufficient life force within you.

We soon discovered that when you nursed, you drained your mother's life force without gaining any of hers. When she stopped nursing you, you stopped growing. Opal had a decision to make. She could nurse you and allow you to drain her life force which allowed you to thrive, or let you die.

~

The words sunk down into Sabina's heart and shattered it. She caused her mother's death. She was a mistake and should have never been born. She was a weakling who drained her mother's life force.

~

Nana Honey sat rigid in her chair, siphoning as much of Sabina's energy as her body could handle. She exhaled forcefully with each breath, bearing the weight of the energy. Every candle flickered with the rocking of Sabina's body. Sabina was wailing in her pain and gripping the letter tightly in her fingers. Nana Honey trusted that her wards on the house would keep the sound and the energy away from others' attention. To be safe, she grabbed a couple of her crystals and sent energy to them. The crystals vibrated until they turned to dust. Despite Nana's efforts, Sabina was barely keeping her energy within her circle. Nana Honey called out to the universe for help.

~

As Sabina read, her body racked with pain and tears flooded her eyes, spilling down her face and blurring her vision.

Your mother knew you were special, and her belief was confirmed when each child's energy changed after receiving your life force. They all revealed one of the Moowin abilities. This led me to fear you were the Agni. I vowed to protect you at all costs.

I have taken several steps to ensure your safety. These are my confessions: I brought you to Silvedome where the dome and all the strong

Moowins would keep you hidden. I kept your great-grandmother a secret from you. I placed a shield around you that caused you to be easily forgotten by others. You are invisible unless someone specifically focuses on you. When I first brought you to Silvedome, your low life force caused the villagers to believe you were a Duckling, and I encouraged that misbelief. Meanwhile, I gave you each vial of life force with the help of Marigold every year until you were healthy and functioning. I also lied about your age. You are actually a few months older than you think which is why some of your power leaks out when you feel strong emotions. Your talents have been suppressed by your great-grandmother's amulet. And finally, I have trained you on all forms of self-defense and martial arts.

Over the years, I have kept all those who share your life force safe and hidden. I have arranged for all those individuals to come to Silvedome under the pretense of being your union interview. You will have eight union interviews; each one has a rare Moowin. Their names are Pond Vela, Benford Tulk of Pux, Kean Dagston of Ole, Tevin Okar of Spur, Zoel Alpheus of Morten, Viggo Nadel of Morten, Flann Alf of Aliward, and Felix Dorven of Erest.

I do not expect you to ty with any of them,

but you are stronger with them by your side. Your shared bond drives you to protect each other. Plus, their powerful Moowins will mislead others on detecting your talents. It is my belief you can remain safely hidden but to be cautious, I have hired Flann as a bodyguard, which is why you share more life force with him than any of the others. I've spent the last year working with him to prepare him for this day. Trust him. He is incapable of harming you.

There is one complication. One of the individuals you share a life force with is a twin. The twins are cursed. Flann will tell you more. Rely on Flann as your source of information. I have seven percent of his life force, allowing me to use his Messenger capabilities as my own.

I must warn you that once you go through your Birth Challenge, your amulet will be unable to contain all the energy of your awakened Moowins. Your energy will shine like a beacon to the Selectors. I have a plan to help diffuse it, but they will come for you if you are not careful with how you manage your energy. I will keep as many Selectors out of Silvedome as I can. Which means I may never see you again. I love you and I wish I was wrong about all of this. Find joy and peace so you may live. Be safe! Until our spirits are reunited. Your father

Her father's letter dropped out of her fingers. She realized he was positioning himself to be a martyr for her. When the letter hit the floor, it instantly caught fire.

"NOOOOOO," screamed Sabina, immediately reaching for the letter that had already burned to ashes. The ashes floated up in a spiral motion toward the ceiling. That is when she noticed her circle of salt had the shimmery look of a bubble. Every chain-filled crystal that hung from the walls was pulled toward the salt circle, floating in the air. The flames from every candle stretched into the air, yet there was no smoke. Nana Honey's face looked strained like she was lifting a heavy weight and her face was beet-red with perspiration.

The scene caused Sabina to feel afraid. The change in that motion caused all the crystals floating on their chains to vibrate.

"Peace, mmmmmmyyyyyy ch ch ch child," Nana Honey said with difficulty.

"What's going on?" shouted Flann as he entered the room with Crystal by his side. He sprinted to Sabina.

"STOP," yelled Crystal and Nana Honey simultaneously but it was too late. Flann crossed the salt circle and grabbed Sabina's shoulders, ready to draw her to him. But his hands only reached her shoulders before his body was flung across the room, where he smashed into the wall.

Sabina jumped to her feet. "What happened?"

Her attention on the letter shifted to concern for Flann. She squinted, covered her face with her arms, and walked through the shimmering wall. Nothing happened to her, but the crystals clanged, the candles went out, and Nana Honey sighed in relief. Crystal was at Flann's side when Sabina rushed to him.

Flann tried to sit up, reaching up to rub the back of his head.

"Just a moment." Crystal responded calmly, putting a hand on his chest.

"I'm too tired to see," Nana Honey said to Crystal without having been asked a question.

Sabina looked back to see Nana Honey's head drooping and

to the side. She felt the cool temperatures of the room and shivered. In that moment, she felt displaced as if time had lapsed and she was only now aware of it. Her eyes burned as tears surfaced. She hated feeling helpless and vulnerable, and not knowing what to do. One side of her face ached. Her gums were throbbing, and she wondered if she had been grinding her teeth. The tension headache was getting stronger by the second. She pushed away those thoughts and focused on Flann.

Emotional Poison

"I'm going to get him something for his head. Then I'll make a judgment call on if I should get him a Healer. He will need to see a Healer either way, but it will look less suspicious if he can walk to the hospital."

She lingered, looking at Sabina whose eyes were red from crying. "I'll make something for you too. It will help," she said softly. She placed her hand on Sabina's shoulder as she got up. "DON'T MOVE," she commanded, deepening her voice.

Crystal walked off, and light snores came from Nana Honey. Sabina sat on her heels, looking at Flann. He was trying not to stare at her. Eventually, he broke the silence.

"I've never seen anything like that before. Are you . . ." He wanted to ask if she was a witch or if she was a human. Logic made him stop though, as he knew he had her life force. Whatever she was, he was also in some small way. ". . .Okay?"

She didn't seem to have the energy to pretend otherwise. "No," she answered in a small voice and her face contorted as if to stop herself from crying. "I read my father's letter." She burst into tears. She covered her face and wiped her snot on her clothes.

Lying down with his head propped up, hands resting on his chest, Flann felt the pull of her emotional pain and his instincts to fix it surged. When he tried to sit up, he felt dizzy. Sabina was sobbing uncontrollably and all he could do was put his hand on her thigh, which was all he could reach. It was awkward physically and emotionally. He wasn't sure if he should ask about her letter or if that was too private.

He had sisters and the default words spilled out of him. "It will be okay. Everything will work out. It always does."

Her head nodded as if she heard him, but she cried harder. When her tears were done, she asked, "How could . . ." She swallowed and took a calming breath, letting the air out slowly. She wiped her face again. "How could he do this to me? Why didn't he trust me? He could have told me all along. I think I could have handled the truth. At least then I would have understood why everyone ignored me."

"I don't know," Flann answered helplessly.

"How many people know? Do all the union interviews know about me?" Her arms were wrapped around herself and she curled into a small ball.

"Not many." He didn't want to make her pain worse. He felt so compelled to tell her the truth and worried at the same time that the truth would hurt her more. "They know about you. The binding doesn't allow us to tell others. There is an inherent need to protect you as much as there is for us to protect ourselves. Don't you feel that way?"

Sniffling and wiping her nose, she defensively wanted to answer 'no', but she was concerned that he'd been hurt. Now she knew he wasn't there to hurt her. She had wanted to touch him, even when she thought of him as a blockhead or super annoying. She didn't like to touch people; that was always awkward.

"Maybe." She bit at her lower lip as she tucked some hair behind her ear.

"What do they . . ."

"Here we go," Crystal called pleasantly from the other room.

She stepped over Flann to get to his other side, raising his head slightly to give him a thick neon-green drink.

"That smells awful," he said once his nose came close.

"Yeah, and it will taste awful too but it will make you feeeeeel pretty damn special. So drink up." She didn't give him time to argue; she tilted the glass further so the slime slid forward and hit his top lip.

He nudged her back and Crystal adjusted the glass. Flann swallowed noisily and almost gagged, but he took another drink.

"Nicely done. Give that a minute to work." She sat the glass down along the wall before pulling a vial from her pocket. "This is for you," she said to Sabina. It seemed she couldn't hide her smile.

"What's *in this*?" Sabina asked suspiciously. "Don't forget, I lived with you. I know your shenanigans."

Crystal smiled and shrugged innocently. "It's a birthday wish. Now drink up or I will. I haven't had a night off in some time." She tilted her head to Nana Honey, who was asleep. "That woman works non-stop and I like a little work with my play."

Sabina eyed Crystal.

"What? Alright give it to me." She reached for the vial and Sabina handed it over.

Crystal put the vial to her lips, watching Sabina the whole time. She tilted her head back and took a sip of it, closing her eyes once the flavor hit her tongue. Her whole body gave a ripple of delight, and she opened her eyes.

"Here. Take this. I better check on Nana before this really hits me." She stood up and stretched. "If I wasn't so worried about her, I'd thank you. You had her channeling the full strength of all your Moowins."

"What do you mean the full strength of MY Moowins. I have *Moowins*?" Sabina asked incredulously.

"YeAAAH. Isn't it obvious?" she spat out as her body became

visibly more relaxed. "You know what? You need more of your playmates here to help hide all this energy coming off you."

Lingering, Crystal stared with bright eyes for a moment before Flann interrupted.

"Oh yeah, that reminds me. Here is your necklace." He dug into his pocket and he retrieved her amulet. "It better not be broken after all the trouble we went to get this."

Crystal shifted her attention from Sabina to Flann and squatted down. "Let me see it." She held her palm out expectantly. Sabina didn't remember her wearing those tall heels before this moment. That was unlike her, Sabina noted. Was she wearing those tight leather pants earlier? No, she was wearing a tank and boots.

Handing over the amulet, Flann sat up, amazed he didn't feel dizzy anymore. His bright green eyes fixed on Sabina. He regretted not having his hat to shade his face. Though Sabina was pale, with puffy eyes, she had an attractive quality about her. Her raw state made his gut clench. He noticed the way Crystal looked longingly at Sabina and he didn't like it. Sabina was unaware, but Flann saw it clear as day. He was relieved to have an excuse to draw Crystal's attention away from her.

Crystal rotated the amulet in all directions, holding it up to the light. "Smithsonite," she announced and then closed her eyes, enclosing the crystal in her palm. "No. It's fine." She turned to Sabina. "Here." She placed the necklace over Sabina's head. She slid her long hair out of the way, allowing her fingers to skim across Sabina's cheek in the process. Crystal shut her eyes and let out a breath. She knew the potion was flowing through her and she was being careless.

"Ahhh, I better check on Nana. I am sure she is just tired, but I'll feel better *after* I check on her. Be sure to drink that up." She nodded toward the vial. "You look fine," she stated to Flann as an afterthought, avoiding eye contact. She was pretty sure he saw the desire in her eyes and she didn't want that being brought to light.

~

Flann watched the light in Sabina's eyes dim like a fire reducing to soft embers. Her energy was swallowed and, with it, her brilliance. She almost looked sickly now. What a contrast, he thought. He had only ever known her without her amulet. Her smooth olive skin flashed through his mind. He pushed away the thought and reminded himself he wanted to be respectful to Nora.

"Do you think we can go?" he asked.

~

After examining the amulet in her fingers, she looked at him with sadness in her eyes. The smithsonite crystal was embossed with a protection symbol etched into its surface, and although she felt older after this eventful day, she welcomed the familiar soothing energy the necklace provided. She glanced at Crystal fussing over Nana. "I think so." She looked at the vial in her other hand. "I'm not sure about this." She held up the vial. "She'll never tell me what is in this, but I don't like how she acted after she took it."

~

Clever girl, Flann agreed in his head. But he knew better than to say that out loud. "It's your choice," he remarked calmly. He waited for her feisty comeback. He expected her to say, 'Of course, it's my choice. I don't need your permission.' Instead, he was disheartened with her response.

She meekly responded as if talking softly to herself. "Thanks."

Standing up, she held her hand out for him, letting her amulet fall between her tunic and chest while holding the vial in the other hand. Flann took her hand and pulled himself to his feet. There was no energy exchange this time and his concern spiked.

"Are you *alright*?"

"Yeah. Fine. Just thirsty and it's time for dinner. What about you? Do you need to go to the hospital?" she asked in a monotone voice.

"No. I'm done with the hospital for today, but I could eat."

"Okay." Sabina yawned.

She walked out of the house without saying goodbye to Crystal or checking on Nana Honey. Flann stood, confused at the change in her behavior. She walked off as if she was sleepwalking.

~

"She'll be fine," Crystal announced as she wrapped a blanket around Nana. "But she needs to drink that vial." She walked up to Flann and looked out the door at Sabina's autopilot mannerism.

"What does that stuff do?"

Using her tongue to poke the inside of her cheeks in contemplation, she considered whether he needed to know and replied, "It smoothers your nerves and detoxes emotional poisoning, but it makes you crave touch because your body is seeking an energy source to aid the spell."

~

She turned away and walked out of the room, ending the conversation. Her cool, calm behavior was back. Well, it is quick-acting, Flann decided and ran after Sabina who was quietly walking down the path. The sun was setting in the distance.

The village square had cleared out and despite the events that took place, he was hungry. He had asked about dinner, but Sabina didn't hear his questions. Then, when they reached her tut, he saw a tray of food sitting on the porch of dried meat, fruits and two rolls. She went through the door and closed it as he went to pick up the tray.

He had to set the tray down in order to open the door. After opening the door, he picked the tray up again and brought it into the kitchen, leaving the door open. The house was quiet and cool. The light from the sun was disappearing fast. He decided to check on Sabina, light some candles, and eat.

Knocking on the wall outside Sabina's room, he waited for an answer. Since there was none, he cautiously pulled the red heavy drapes to the side and looked in. She had slipped her boots off and was curled in a ball in the bed. He remembered they weren't supposed to wear shoes in the house.

He crept quietly into her room and picked up her boots. When he bent down, he noticed the vial in her hand, slowly dripping onto her sheets. He set the boots down and took the vial from her hand. He gently rested it on her nightstand using some folded blankets to keep it propped up. While his back was to Sabina, he heard her mumbling in sleep about 'Shielding Aide' and Flann smiled to himself. He turned back to her. She was a shell of herself and his smile fell. He stepped over to her and put his index finger on the amulet which was resting on the bed. He didn't feel any magic. "How can a rock take away your essence?" he whispered.

Sabina shifted and turned to her other side. Her hair was close to the potion that had spilled on her sheets. He used his hands to wipe the spilled potion from the bed, but it only spread the spill so he gave up. With one hand wet and sticky from the potion, he used the other hand to grab the boots. He slipped through her drapes and out the open door, placing the boots on the step. Kicking his shoes off, he went into the house. His hand had already dried, and he focused on finding the candles. Ten minutes later, he was sitting down to a candlelit dinner for one. He took a bite of the hard, dried meat. It had a sticky teriyaki sauce on it, but it was delicious. He was about to take another bite when he heard clunky footsteps. His back was to the door, and he spun around effortlessly, already standing.

The door flew open and Master Tulk walked in, bowlegged with funny boots, a gigantic blinged-out belt, and tan cowboy hat. "HOWDY PARTNER," Master Tulk bellowed in a chipper mood, his thumbs tucked into his front pockets. "Don't mind me, good fellow. I'm here to check on our gal. Please . . . go back to eating," he offered, nodding his head to the food at the kitchen table.

Sucking the sauce off his fingers, Flann asked, "Why are you talking funny?"

"Wwwwhhhhyyy, haven't you heard? I'm performing in the Western classic *The Good, The Bad, and The Ugly* at The Mox. I'm Blondie."

Agitated, Flann quibbled, "Why would I have heard about that? I've got more important things to do."

"That may be, but Sabina agreed on your behalf for the both of you to come." Slipping out of character, he took the bend out of his knees and asked in his own voice, "Where is she? I'm concerned. I felt a surge of her energy and she went dark. I can't feel her," he said, concerned. "I don't have much time. I am expected on stage."

While Master Tulk talked, Flann started to buzz with energy. He felt like a joyous kid who could make the impossible possible. He felt like he could dance on the ceiling. That is how much energy was buzzing through him. He walked up to Master Tulk, barely able to concentrate on what he was saying.

"Put it there, partner," he smiled and held out his hand. "That's what they say, right?"

"Ahhhh." Master Tulk took a step back at Flann's offered hand. "You licked your fingers."

"Don't be shy," Flann persisted, grabbing Master Tulk's hand and shaking it vigorously as he pulled him closer. He threw his arm around his neck and pulled him down to him. "Boy, do you have soft skin. It feels really nice." Flann was too short to comfortably have his arm around Master Tulk, so he settled for grabbing the back of his neck.

Master Tulk pushed Flann back and said, "You're not my type. **Don't touch me like that again.**"

The drapes were pulled back and Sabina's drawn face appeared. "I can't sleep. Will you keep it down, please?" she pleaded.

Master Tulk gasped. He seemed to be appalled at how haggard she looked.

Affectionately, he said, "Sssiiilllkkie, what happened? Tell me everything." He walked over to her and held the drapes open. Grabbing her hand, he led her to the couch and gently tugged her to sit down.

Zombie-like, Sabina followed and flopped into the chair, boneless.

Flann wasted no time and sat on the other side of Sabina, picking up her hand and placing the back of it on his cheek. "She feels cooled," he purred with his eyes closed. He felt blissful.

"What's wrong with you?" Master Tulk snapped, pulling Sabina's hand out of Flann's.

His bliss disappeared and he felt agitated until he picked up Sabina's hand again.

Ignoring Flann, Master Tulk continued. He sighed and focused on Sabina. "How can I help you?"

Her hair blocked her face, and he tucked a piece behind her ear. "Flann, have you called a Healer?"

"Master Flann to you," he grumbled and then leaned his shoulder into Sabina's. His bliss was back.

Sabina slid into Master Tulk, and she rolled her head onto his shoulder, closing her eyes with her mouth falling open as she drifted back to sleep. Master Tulk scooted off the couch, letting Sabina shift into a comfortable position. Flann slid with her, resting his head on her hip, resting his hand on her thigh; completely content.

Master Tulk stood up and mumbled, "This is useless. He is

drunk." He grabbed Flann's arm and fisted his shirt to pull him up.

Popping his eyes open, Flann complained, "I'm not drunk. What gives you that idea?" He jerked his arm free and placed his other hand on Master Tulk's, holding his shirt. He immediately relaxed, keeping his hands on top of Master Tulk's.

Master Tulk wasn't prepared for Flann to go limp in his hands, and his free hand reached for the arm of the couch to balance himself. His chest bumped into Flann's face, and Flann rubbed his cheek. Master Tulk slammed his hand into the side of Flann's neck, jumping back.

"You are drunk." He rubbed his chest.

With pain throbbing in his neck, Flann got to his feet in an instant as Master Tuck continued to rub his chest. "What did you do that for? I told you. I'm not drunk." Flann felt like he was waking up from a dream and slightly disoriented. Despite feeling groggy, he recognized that Master Tulk was irritated, but kept his distance. This wasn't a fight, but Flann would have preferred if Master Tulk was enraged. He'd like to get a few punches on him.

"*Oh,* did I knock some sense into you? I'll remember that for next time. Can you not SEE that Sabina is ill and needs a Healer?" he retorted, his arm extending with his palm up to indicate Sabina's state.

Holding the side of his neck, Flann looked at Sabina, whose energy level had plummeted further. Her beautiful olive skin looked green and drool was running down the side of her mouth. She almost seemed lifeless. Looking at her, his stomach dropped and panic built within him.

He spoke out loud in a serious tone. "Yeah, okay." He immediately called out to the only Messenger (by default) that knew about Sabina: Brom—he could communicate with Viggo, a rare Healer. Flann had met Viggo a few times over the last year, as he was the son of Brom's childhood best friend. He was also one of Sabina's bonded candidates for union interview. Viggo, his sister, and the nasty Prince Zoel Alpheus were outside of Silvedome waiting to enter.

"Are you getting help?" Master Tulk inquired as he squatted down to wipe Sabina's chin.

"One second. I'm calling Viggo," he said with his index finger lifted in concentration. It was actually a three-way conversation, which drained a lot of his energy.

~

"Brom, get Viggo. Sabina read your letter in the Seer's home without the amulet. Once the amulet was placed on her, she deteriorated in personality and health."

"Got it," Brom responded in a deep, clear voice.

A moment later, Flann heard, "Here," in a slow, expressionless voice.

"Have you been caught up?" Flann questioned.

"I have," Viggo claimed.

"And?" Flann prompted.

"Have you tried taking the amulet off?" Viggo responded calmly.

"We don't want to do that, Viggo," Brom reminded him.

"It's probably emotionally poisonous to her right now. My guess is the amulet needs to be realigned. I felt her Moowins. You cannot revert to old ways once you have outgrown them. It doesn't fit her. I can feel her suffering. You—"

Brom cut him off. "Take it off," he demanded. "We will risk it."

~

Not wanting to lose the conversation, Flann snapped his fingers at Master Tulk and spoke out loud. "Take the amulet off." He ran back into the conversation in his mind, trusting that Master Tulk heard him.

He watched as Master Tulk looked back at him and asked, "What?" Flann was already back in the space of his conversation and then saw his words register. Master Tulk gingerly gathered Sabina's hair and lifted her head enough to move the chain from her. She immediately gasped for air, her back arching, and her head falling back before she relaxed.

~

"She gasped and relaxed back asleep. What does your connection say?"

"She is in less pain, but I'm afraid that too much energy was drawn from her. She will need something and until I set up shop, it will be difficult for me to make it."

Taking charge, Brom gave orders. "Tell Benford to get the amulet realigned with Nana Honey and have him send Crystal to talk to the council for me. We are approving Viggo and his sister to enter. Then Benford needs to get to his show. We don't want to anger the council. Viggo, I'll talk to Zoel and get you moved into Silvedome tonight. Get your stuff ready. Flann, sit with her and take care of her. Notify me if she worsens. Everyone got their orders?"

Viggo answered, "I understand."

As Brom gave his orders, Flann thought about the potion Crystal had given Sabina. Whatever it was, it made him feel incredibly good . . . And embarrassingly touchy.

"When can I expect Viggo?" Flann inquired, thinking about Sabina's weak state.

"An hour or more," Brom responded for Viggo.

Taking into consideration his limited knowledge, Flann decided to inform them of the potion. "Crystal made a potion for Sabina that she said would help her, but she wasn't thrilled about taking it. It has a side effect of making you seek contact with others. Should I give her that while we wait?"

Hesitating, Viggo answered, "I'm not familiar with what that is and, as a general rule, I don't trust other people's work. I'd prefer we wait so I can investigate it myself."

"Give it to her. I trust Crystal. Now, let's take action."

~

Brom hung up, which meant Flann lost connection to Viggo. He relayed the conversation to Master Tulk, who took to his orders with minimal clarification. He left the tut with the amulet in his hands.

Grabbing the vial, Flann settled next to Sabina. She was resting across the couch but it was wide enough to give her perch. He attempted to scoot her toward the back of the couch to make room for him, but she was in a deep sleep. Her body was heavy, and despite his intrusive maneuvering, she barely moved. He grunted and gave up. How was he supposed to give her this medicine if she wasn't alert enough to take it?

He twisted his body and lifted her head, but it fell back. He laid her head back down and kneeled alongside the couch, trying again to lift her head, but the drop that hit her lip rolled down her chin. He used his finger to swab it up and gently placed that finger on her lips, wiping the medicine along her mouth. She didn't stir. He wanted to give up on this fruitless task but worried that her state would worsen if he did. He decided to get personal and he would have to suffer his discomfort. He splashed a small amount of the liquid on his pinky finger and, squirming, put his finger in her mouth. Her mouth fell open, and he quickly wiped his finger on the inside of her cheek.

He released his hand from the back of her neck and stood up, watching, waiting to see if anything would happen. She lay peacefully asleep. He decided to give it a minute. He was hungry and he could think better on a full stomach. He grabbed his dried meat from the kitchen and pulled the chair into the living room, lightly watching her as he ate.

As he ate, he thought. What if she is the Agni? He didn't

believe in that prophecy. It was just a silly ploy for people to have a reason to hunt and kill what scared them. It was an excuse to kill what was different. *We are unnatural to them.* Many Selectors enslaved people with Moowins to control them. To date, no one had more than four to five rare talents and so it seemed impossible to think anyone could possess them all. Admittedly, the energy he felt from Sabina was intimidating and he wondered if that was how the Selectors felt. Then he considered her amulet. Was a pretty rock really able to soften her energy levels to the public eye? He didn't know that he believed all that either. His logic reminded him she hadn't shown any Moowins, only intense energy. He finished his meat and got up to get his bread.

Out of the corner of his eye, he thought he saw her move. He grabbed his roll of bread and came back to the couch. Taking a bite, he saw her wipe at her face. She didn't look any better, and she had been sleeping for close to thirty minutes. He decided to try again. He took another bite of the bread and set it down on his chair. He grabbed the vial and placed his knee on the couch, leaning over her as he lifted her head and placed the vial to her mouth. He placed a small amount on her lips. Neither hand was free to do anything else but hold her head and the vial, so he placed her head back down, prepared to wipe a small amount into her mouth. As he laid her head down, the liquid dripped into her mouth and she swallowed.

Her eyes opened, and she licked her lips, smiling. He froze, looking at her, momentarily concerned for her until her arms lazily reached up, wrapping around his neck. Pure panic set in. He felt an alarm shoot to his feet, his hands, and his head all at the same time. Close to what he felt with Brom when he pushed him over a cliff to get him over his fear of heights. Only in that case, there had been a safety net. He didn't see a safety net to land in; he saw sparkling eyes, soft lips, and a bright smile that seemed to be just for him.

This was a lie, he told himself. This was the medicine and its side effects. He shut his eyes. He went to stand up and pull away.

Her hands moved from the back of his neck to the sides and then to his face, and she hummed as if in pleasure. He opened his eyes and she was arching her head back in delight. Visions of kissing her flooded his mind. He was seeing double like when he heard two different realities when using his Messenger talent. But deep down, he knew that neither was a reality. No, he was seeing two fantasies. One of a beautiful girl in bliss at his touch and another of a passionate kiss between them.

He jumped two feet in the air, or at least that is what it felt like. He breathed hard and fast, and he paced. He wanted to shake the images out of his head and yet, he froze again at the sight of her long body stretching in delight. "Nora," he said firmly to himself. Fiercely, he reminded himself, "I am with Nora and I am a man of my word," and he pictured her shy smile. He talked to himself, reminding himself his relationship with Nora was what was real. Further confirming this, he replayed a scene of Nora shyly asking him to unsaddle her horse.

Calmed down, he saw Sabina slowly shifting to a seated position. She was rubbing her arms and not paying attention to Flann. She looked better. She looked a lot better. Tullom, that stuff is powerful. He only gave her a small dose. What would have happened if he had given her the full amount?

"How long have I been sleeping?"

His voice gruff and deeper than normal, he tried for indifference. "Not long. Are you hungry?"

"A little bit. I thought I was sleeping in my bed. How did I get out here?" Sabina rubbed her toned arms and Flann shifted his view to the fruit on the kitchen table.

He was frustrated with himself and his poor self-control at the images of Sabina slipping repeatedly back into his thoughts. "Ah, don't you remember Master Tulk stopping by?"

Keeping his focus on the fruit, he still managed to notice the sudden stillness of Sabina's body. He flicked his eyes over to her and her arms were by her side. She was gripping the side of the couch with worry on her face.

Slowly and with concern, she said, "Nooooo. Why would he have stopped by?"

Not wanting to talk about Master Tulk and feeling resentment toward Brom for putting him in this position, Flann spoke bluntly. "More breaking news for you. Master Tulk is one of your union interviews. He is your Performer. He is into men, so don't get too excited." As soon as he said it, he felt regret. He was losing his patience, mostly with himself. "I'm sorry. I could have said that nicer."

He actually turned his body to fully face her, but her hair was too drawn forward for him to see her face. She was quiet. Too quiet for him. Her body started to shake and he crouched in front of her. He repeated himself. "I'm sorry, Sabina. I was cruel. There is no excuse . . ." He stopped talking when her shaking turned into laughter.

"Let me get this straight. My father lined up all these interviews for me and not one of them is going to be truly available to have a relationship, right?"

She laid back down on the couch, her long beautiful hair scattered all around her, and she pressed the heel of her palms into her eyes. "I've dreamed for so long of having a loving relationship. Wishing and hoping. And I fooled myself into thinking that one of these union interviews might turn into something. *But* you are in a committed relationship. Master Tulk is gay. Will the next person be married? I mean, come on." She slammed her fist into the couch by her sides and rolled to face the back of the couch.

Flann, who was squatting down by the side of the couch, was at a loss at what to say. He went through the list. *Ram, widow unable to move on, not that he was one of the eight Brom wanted her to meet. Pond, in love with himself. Benford, gay. Kean, pretty sure he was possessed. Tevin might be an option. Zoel is a narcissist creep I'd like to go a few rounds with. Viggo, depressed. Felix, not the settling type.* And him, sworn to Nora. He realized she may not be wrong and he couldn't help wondering if Brom knew about Nora all along. *Tullom; he was a strategic genius.* Flann could appreciate

Brom's work and also be concerned about the role he was playing in Sabina's life.

He sat at the edge of the couch where her knees bent and looked out the front window. He thought of rubbing her back but didn't trust himself, so he reached out and grabbed the bread roll from the chair. He studied the bread as he talked. "Who am I to know the future? Anything is possible but I can tell you Brom wanted you to ty with one of us. He must have seen something in all of us." Under his breath he commented, "Except Zoel."

The couch shifted as she turned. "What did you say?"

"Nothing."

"No. I heard you say 'Zoel'. What about him? No more surprises," she said with firmness. "Please." She reached out and put her hand on his wrist. Flann looked at her strong hand. "Help me." Her voice was soft and pleading.

He cleared his throat and took a bite of the bread, which forced her hand to fall away. She moved her hands to her shin. He chewed, thinking. She dropped her head toward her knees.

"Zoel was a union interview before you were even born. Your mother, Opal, was best friends with Zoel's mother, and Opal saved Zoel's life when he was still in the womb. It was always arranged for you to meet him." His voice lost fluctuation as he refrained from influencing her. *She should have a right to choose for herself what she thinks of him.*

~

"Oh." Sabina was quiet and conflicted. Here she was talking about meeting these other men and the idea of having a loving relationship, yet she was fighting every impulse to reach out and touch him. *What is wrong with me? He is taken.* She didn't dare risk touching him again. "Flann, I . . . I don't feel well. I think I'll just go lie down in my room."

Before she moved, Flann popped up. "Here, let me get you some food. You mentioned you were hungry." He took off toward the kitchen while she swung her legs off the couch and prepared to stand up.

"I'm hungry but I can't eat." She stood up but felt wobbly. Closing her eyes and taking a moment to check in with herself, she told herself she was fine. She took a step forward and her knee buckled.

"Tullom. It's okay to ask for help," he scolded as he grabbed her arm.

Blissful warm energy shot through her arm at his touch and she felt a smile spread across her face. She wanted to rub her face in that feeling. Even as she had that thought, her body started to fall forward. She heard Flann say "Tullom" and then a thump on the floor. Warm bliss touched her back, and she wanted to dive into that but her body was already going the opposite direction.

Flann struggled to grab Sabina as her body went limp and fell forward. He dropped the bread, cursing. His other arm wrapped around her back and side. He yanked her toward him to counterbalance the fall and she slid on the ground. *Well, that is better than falling.*

The color she had gained was already disappearing. *Is she asleep or did she pass out? Should I call Brom again or should I give her more of that medicine?* And then it hit him like a two-by-four; the medicine needed touch to work. It must pull energy into you so you feel better. This whole time he had been running away from her touch. As humiliating as it was for him to admit, he recalled pawing at Master Tulk. He felt queasy at his actions but he undeniably did those things.

Well, he had a plan this time and he could control some of the elements now he understood. He picked up Sabina from the floor with the intention of taking her to her room. But after trying to pick her dead weight up from the floor, the couch seemed just as good as her bed. This way, he could keep an eye on her, he told himself.

He settled her into the couch and pulled the chair alongside. He had the vial in his hand and poured a small amount on her lips. Then he rested her head back down but this time, the liquid didn't fall into her mouth. It slid down her cheek. He wiped it off and wiped his hands on his clothes. He wasn't taking any chances with this medicine again. He repeated the action and this time, some fell into her mouth. He quickly set the vial down and placed his hands on both sides of her face.

~

Her eyes were closed but a gentle smile spread across her face. Her hands found his and she rubbed his hands as she hummed. The humming seemed to vibrate in him. She rubbed her hands along his arms toward his elbows – reaching.

~

Flann closed his eyes when she arched her back. He decided that not seeing her movements would be easier for him. It wasn't. Even with his eyes closed, he felt her touch like erotic electricity through his veins.

Chanting Nora's name over and over, he used all his willpower to think of her. Although it helped, he knew he was reacting to Sabina's touch, her hum that vibrated to him. He let go of her face and pulled his hands back from her. He fisted his hands under his arms. He didn't think this through far enough.

He sat with his eyes clenched, waiting for her to touch him, but she didn't reach for him. He opened his eyes, and she lay still, already falling into this boneless, green state. She was going after what she needed, he thought. She would receive the touch but not take it for herself. "Well, tullom," he groaned. He was going to have to do this again.

In the back of his mind, a voice said to him: *Or I could wait for Viggo?* He dismissed it even though it was super appealing. "Tullom, for being tied to you and knowing you are not well," he said out loud.

He scooted her to the back of the couch and carefully lay down next to her. He propped himself up on his elbow and turned her face to him. Concerned about her possibly choking, he poured the smallest amount into the cheek area of the inside of her mouth and let her head roll back to face the back of the couch. He corked the vial, put it in his pocket, and wrapped his arm firmly around her stomach.

He felt her belly expand, taking a deep breath. Her free arm found his. She held on tightly to his bare arm. Her bare feet wiggled until they hiked up his pants and found contact. She curled her body into Flann's and he found himself pressing his face into her neck as she settled. He lay on his side, holding on tightly to her, preventing her from moving around and arousing him further. The last movement he remembered was her relaxing into him and intertwining her hands into his.

He meant to stay awake, but he could feel her body absorbing his energy. He grew tired, comfortable, and then too relaxed in the warmth and smell of her. He was too deep into his relaxation to care when he heard the door open and shut with an obvious clang. He knew his back was to whoever walked through that door and a thought surfaced that at least he was shielding Sabina, before he drifted back to sleep.

His arm stiff and hurting, he opened his eyes to see Sabina's hair and the back of her neck. Thoughts came rushing into him and he untangled his arm from Sabina's and slipped off the bed. She lay peacefully asleep. The candles had burned out, and he wondered what time it was.

His ankle made a clicking noise as he got up and made his way to the dark kitchen. He still felt tired but his senses made him stop and focus.

"I'm in here," a familiar female voice said, and he heard a chair drag across the floor. He relaxed, seeing Crystal's shape in the dark room.

"What are you doing here?" He yawned, making his way to the candles.

As he crossed Crystal, she stepped in front of him and pushed him into the wall. His hands immediately went up. ***"You. You don't deserve her,"*** she growled in a low tone through a voice that was full of tears and sorrow. She walked away and came back at him. She pointed her finger at him and clearly wanted to say something. She turned back around, throwing her arms up. "Gosh. It hurts so bleeding much."

He could see her wipe her face. He stayed where he was. He had sisters and when his sisters were upset, he learned it was safest to stay out of their way.

Going back to the kitchen table, Crystal palmed the necklace in her hands and walked back over to him. She pushed the amulet into Flann's lifted hand. "Here. Her necklace has been realigned as best as I could manage." She used the back of her hand to rub her cheekbone. "This is temporary. I couldn't wake Nana. Come by tomorrow to have Nana work on it."

She stared at him. She seemed unashamed of her tears and there was a fierceness in her face. "I don't know why I got so upset. She won't choose you anyway," she reported with conviction. She snorted. "She was most likely too sick to even remember what you did for her," she said, dismissing his energy-giving deed. "As much as I want to hate you right now for lying with her, I thank you for helping her." She walked confidently out of the dark room.

His back was pressed against the wall and he looked at the amulet in his hand as he heard the door shut. "Well, that was strange," he said to the necklace. "I guess you were the excuse she needed to come over." Love triangles, mused Flann. He pulled out a drawer and placed the amulet inside. "Whatever secret power you have, don't use it on me. I'm putting you in this drawer for now," he whispered.

He grabbed a few candles and lit them in the kitchen and living area. He looked over Sabina, feeling assured now that she looked healthy again. He sat back down in the chair and stretched out his legs, wondering what time it was. Uncomfortable and cold, he decided it was a new day and Viggo wasn't coming. He reasoned that there was no one available to do the Birth Challenge ritual on them at the time they came through.

He got up and went to the door. "Who doesn't lock their doors?" he whispered, shocked to realize that there was no way to lock it. He picked up his chair and jimmied it under the door knob. He went to Sabina's room and grabbed her blanket. Then he tossed it on her, and he rested on the couch. Part of him wanted to lie back down with her and feel the peace and warmth of her body. He knew better than that and he wasn't going to toy with those desires.

He blew out the candles and went upstairs. He lay on his bed and promised he'd contact Nora tomorrow, wishing she was here; falling asleep, dreaming of her.

He woke up to the sun spilling across his face and blinding him. He threw the covers off and made his way down the stairs. He walked into the living room expecting to see Sabina to ask her about breakfast, but the couch was empty. The blanket was back on her bed and the tunic Nana brought her was resting on the floor. *Where is she?* The Loaded Hurricane. The thought snapped his fingers. *Tullom, she is disciplined. She looked like a cancer patient on her deathbed and now she is training. Where is the sense in that?*

He still had the same clothes from yesterday and he took the time to change into his new Silvedome attire. He was tempted to leave right away to go talk some sense into Sabina about taking it easy, but he imagined she would struggle to veer from whatever routine she followed. In less than five minutes, he was out of the door, and headed to the Loaded Hurricane eating his fruit from last night. He was relieved to see that Sabina's dinner was taken, and he assumed that she had at least eaten something.

Despite being new, he already had a feel for the town's setup and he knew where to find the Loaded Hurricane. After all, he had trained there for months in preparation for watching over Sabina. Funny, he no longer thought of it as babysitting now. *Is that the power of this bond?*

Crossing the invisible energy barrier, he could see Sabina dive from a post in the air, arms reaching out for the rope and accurately timing the transition from one rope to the next object. Her face was determined, her muscles were taut, and she moved with complete trust in herself. She was mesmerizing to watch. She twirled in the air like a fine-tuned weapon. He admitted to himself that he did enjoy watching her train.

She over-rotated on her flip and took a running step forward, letting her momentum carry her into a roll on the ground, grabbing a small tree branch and popping up in a tiger crouch, weapon lifted like it was a planned movement. It wasn't. She had just trained herself to use all her environment for her gain.

"I can feel you and you are distracting. Where are you?" She huffed out of breath.

"You need to train with distraction. It's good for you," he called back.

Sabina's body shifted in his direction, her eyes scanning. She stood up and threw down the branch. "What are you doing here?"

Bemused, he smiled. He liked this side of her personality. "Aren't you testy this morning?" He could almost feel her rolling her eyes. "I was on a peaceful stroll. Care to get some breakfast with me?" he asked innocently.

～

Annoyed at her training being interrupted when she was so close to being done, she flippantly asked, "Care to spar with me? I'd like to show you JUST how testy I am."

"That would not be fair. You were feeling unwell last night and I'm a proficient Protector."

She looked at him. Her arms hanging loose, her hair falling forward, sweat rolling down her face; annoyance vibrated off her. She kicked up the branch without breaking contact with him and charged. "Advantage leveled," she screamed. She twisted as she passed him and swung the branch around to hit the back of his calves.

"Tullom." His knees buckled at the impact and he dropped his playful attitude and switched gears to combat.

She whipped around him and placed a hand on the ground and kicked him. He dodged, barely missing being kicked in the face. She spun low on the ground and made for another attack at his legs. Flann had the same trainer and he had not forgotten Brom's instruction on opponents that liked to fight low to the ground; he saw her strategy. He countered. He cartwheeled over her kick and, using his hands on her shoulder to bear his weight, landed behind her for a choke hold. She bucked back and tried to roll them both over his back. He resisted the move. She twisted to the side and created enough space to pull her hand through his choke hold. He moved with her to prevent giving her the window to pull her arm through. Sabina switched tactics and used her arm to pull away from him and then suddenly drove her whole body into him, taking them both to the ground. She once again attempted to shove her arm through the chokehold to create more space while he adjusted from the impact of the fall. He wrapped his legs around her and used his leverage to pull her back into a chokehold. She grabbed his foot, yanked it up and toward her, driving her elbow hard into the inside muscle of his knee.

Flann felt the burning pain of the muscle and the force of his body twisting into a position his body didn't go. He let go, and they both tumbled. He got to his feet. Sabina threw herself at him and jabbed an elbow to his face; he blocked. She moved with incredible speed, force, and relentlessness. She was not holding back. He was on defense. Blocking and watching for an opportunity to counter. His heart pumped and his nerves tingled at the force of her hits. She knew where the pressure points were.

Sabina attacked, letting go of her thoughts and moving with speed. All the anger she felt at the life she was denied was at the surface. She was ignored for years. Invisible. She had to pretend to be a poor fighter. Her whole life was a lie. The only place she could be herself was in the Loaded Hurricane. It was the only place where she existed without the amulet blocking her natural abilities.

She had all these feelings and now her father wanted her to shove down all her potential, all her possibilities, so she could be safe? What does safety matter without the joy of living? She punched Flann hard in his side. He took it without a flinch and moved into a better position. She screamed in her head. She wanted to live! *No one gets to tell me who I am anymore.*

Feeling Sabina's emotions escalate, Flann moved in closer, taking a punch to his side. He saw his moment. As she went to kick him, he squatted under her and grabbed under her thigh, lifting her higher in the air. She turned the kick into a twist and let her head drop toward the ground. Flann saw immediately she was going to land on her head and a painful flash of concern tore through him. He immediately grabbed her and flung them both backward, letting the air get knocked out of him as he hit the ground. She landed on top of him. Her head by his feet. She punched his quad as she got up.

"Gugh." Flann exhaled at the hit.

"I had that," she screamed as she walked away.

He lay on the ground, recovering. He had not been that challenged . . . ever. He needed an ice bath for all the bruises he was sure to have. He rolled over to his side, watching her. Her brokenness called to him like a siren. She was angry, upset, and emotionally hurt. Even as she struggled with those emotions, she looked wild and free. She looked exotic and beautiful to Flann. He could feel the desire to wrap his arms around her, like he did last night. Memories of holding her tingled along his arms, along with the memory of her smile as she arched under him. Despite his wish not to recall those memories, they flashed into his mind anyway. He blocked the mental images and focused on watching her stomach muscles contract and release with each breath in the wrap she wore that exposed her entire abdomen. She was lean and strong, quite the opposite of Nora who was soft and slender. Flann knew he should look away, and he wanted to. But not as much as he wanted to see what she would do next.

On the verge of tears, Sabina focused on her breath as Flann lay on the ground watching her. She wished she had a weapon in her hands as she felt a different kind of vulnerability than she had ever felt before. He saw her like no one else had. He was the first person she was around without her amulet. A necklace that prevented people from witnessing her. A battle fought within her at his observation of her. Part of her wanted to turn away and hide as she had done in the past . . . Whereas another part of her reveled in the way Flann looked at her. She felt powerful, even with tears brimming in her eyes. She had never had someone watch her with an intensity that made her want to walk toward that someone. It was like gravity.

He had a stick in his short curls and she envisioned herself walking over to him, pulling the stick out of his hair as his hands made their way to her back. Sky Above, she wanted to do that, but then Nana's voice floated in her head that she would find a way to bring Nora to Silvedome. With that thought came emotional shards of ice.

He is taken. I'm lonely and getting drunk on attention I have never received before. That is all this is.

She turned and walked away. "I'm taking a bath." Her somber voice drifted back to Flann.

~

Rolling onto his back, Flann put his hand to his head, gripping his hair. He didn't trust himself to move because part of him wanted to follow her. He recited his promise to Nora in his head and fixed his thoughts on his dream of bringing her to Silvedome, getting married, and sharing his life with her sweet, gentle soul.

Even as he felt the peace of being with Nora sweep over him, his thoughts were filled with concern. He never expected to feel this. This sense of energy charging through him like his body was full of electricity and every nerve in his body was reacting. With Nora, he felt peaceful and special, like he mattered. She was delicate and shy. She had a sweet nature, and it was easy to be with her. He longed to talk with her and hear her laugh.

But with Sabina, it was raw. Raw emotions, like his body was on fire with need and desire. Whatever this relationship with her, it was simultaneously delightful and infuriating. He had a lot of fun teasing her, yet she triggered him. He wanted to fight with her and protect her. He wanted to hold her, and he wanted to run from her. He didn't even know her and yet, a part of him did. Was that the shared life force, he wondered? He lay on the ground, a few yards away from Sabina and couldn't stop his body from desiring more interactions with her, even as he schooled his mind to believe that whatever he felt for Sabina wasn't real.

When You Don't Know Who You Are

The cool water enveloped Sabina, and she welcomed the coldness. She hoped it could numb not only her skin, but her emotions. Her mind drifted through too many thoughts starting with the amulet necklace, previously a token of love and affection. Now it felt like a curse. The amulet stripped her of her essence, to which she was completely blind until this experience. Her thoughts shifted to her father, who she always idolized, and now she wondered if she really knew him at all. Then her thoughts shifted to why Flann looked at her like that and why she wanted his attention. She took a breath and submerged under water, holding her breath and feeling the pounding of her heart. She wondered what her life would have been like without the amulet withholding her true, authentic self from being seen by the world. Who would she be if she had gotten to make choices without this blocking force? Who would she have been friends with? What subjects would have fascinated her? What would she have excelled at? Who would have asked her out?

Needing air, she popped up to the surface, and she pushed all the thoughts away. There was no way of answering any of those what-if scenarios, she told herself. Whatever answers she came up with would only be stories. The question she really needed to ask herself was who did she want to be now? Sabina stepped out of the water, ran on the balls of her feet over to her towel and threw it around herself, burying into the warmth.

Today was her Birth Challenge preparation day. Her last meal would be this morning, or maybe afternoon, if she could eat her lunch early. Then she would go into fasting. She was meant to spend the day in silence and stillness, to reflect on who she wanted to become as an adult. Perfect timing, Sabina thought to herself. She supposed most people had their vision figured out and spent the day dreaming of what it would be like in their new adult role, like Fawn. She knew Fawn had mapped out her career ambitions as a fashion designer and had spent her time in silence designing several new outfits. The silence had confirmed Fawn's dharma. Whereas Sabina had a lot to figure out today. She had lived unknowingly in silence and had just awakened to the truth about who and what she was. She had a whole new viewpoint to grapple with as she struggled to reconcile her past with this present identity. An identity others feared and prevented her from seeing.

Except for the Mistress, who encouraged her in this adventurous, new amplifier role. It's funny how yesterday she was afraid of this path. She was afraid of stepping into a role for which she neither felt qualified nor special enough, but now, she no longer feared this path. She felt ready to take control of her life and to see what she was capable of when no one was holding her back.

As she thought about this new beginning, her spirit warmed. She felt excited—maybe for the first time—which was a welcome feeling compared to the insecurity that had plagued her previously . . . As she hopped on one foot, trying to pull her pants over her wet legs, she thought about how Flann would be with her in her Tradel training. The thought made her smile. She wanted more fights between them. She felt a sense of wild power around him and it felt good to feel so free. Plus, she enjoyed the satisfaction of landing a few punches on him.

She walked out barefoot with her shoes thrown over her

shoulder to see Flann lying in the same spot, a stick still in his hair. "Let's go eat. I'm starving," she said, feeling a sense of peace and purpose.

Flann got to his feet without looking at her. Sabina sensed his dark mood as he began to walk a good arm's length from her. She was curious whether he was hurt or tired, but didn't feel like having a conversation when his mood might spoil hers. She snorted to herself, thinking about how their emotions had flipped. Now he was the emotional one, and she was the pleasant one.

"We need to stop by and get your amulet. Crystal tried to fix it while Nana Honey slept, but Nana really needs to be the one to re-align it," he informed her, making a disgruntled face.

Sabina reluctantly commented, "Right," as she put her boots on. She didn't want that necklace back on. It was a living hell when she wore it. She felt muted, and the world seemed colorless. She lost her ability to connect to her senses. Not to mention how deathly ill she felt last night when she put it back on. She knew that was an accident and with Nana's help, that would not happen again. This time would be better, she told herself, leaving the Loaded Hurricane. She wasn't sure what she wanted to do about the necklace, but it wasn't worth discussing right now.

After a long silence, she stepped over a large fallen tree and said, "Today is my Birth Challenge preparation. I cannot eat after noon. I'm not supposed to talk or see anyone. I basically need to spend the day being bored, alone, and in silence. Do you want to hang with someone else today while I do my mental preparations?"

He didn't want to be with her *AT ALL* as he blamed her for his cheating thoughts and he was starting to feel resentment. At the same time, he didn't want to be away from her either. He gritted his teeth. He was <u>her</u> bodyguard. With conviction, he told himself, *I have to do my job. End of story. I'll just have to keep my distance and not allow myself to think about her.* "No," he mumbled. "I'll sit in silence too. It's not a problem. I do it all the time."

Sabina seemed to bristle at this reaction but he didn't know why. He didn't say anything wrong. Maybe she wanted to be alone. That is what she was used to. Or maybe she was reacting to his mood.

Irritated at himself, Flann walked alongside Sabina, keeping his distance from her. He had decided she had bewitched him into some weird space. Being with her made him feel like he was cheating on Nora. Being without her caused him to long to be with her. He was silent as they walked. In his head, he practiced mind over matter. He was doing his best to honor his role as bodyguard and his relationship with Nora, which seem to be at odds with each other. No matter what he told himself, in his gut, he felt he wasn't being fair to Nora. She deserved better. That thought made him resolve to see Nana Honey immediately about bringing her here. Being around Nora would fix things. It had been too long since he felt her touch and helping Sabina last night was too much for any touch-deprived person.

They made their way to the house, picked up the amulet, and headed to the village for breakfast. Both ate in silence. Both were stuck in their heads, thinking about what they needed to do. After breakfast, Sabina calculated that they had enough time to stop by Nana Honey's prior to going to school, so they headed there.

They walked up the front porch steps and knocked on the door. It felt odd to Sabina that Crystal hadn't anticipated her arrival and wasn't at the open door to welcome her. Nana Honey called them in. She was ready for them with a few objects on her stand by her chair. One of which was a beautiful, dark-green crystal. Nana Honey must have seen Sabina notice the crystal.

"It's malachite, chosen crystal to represent Tokey here. I vill have Crystal add it to my vall. This vill help me co-nnect to him."

Apparently miffed, Flann corrected her. "I'm not Tokey."

She ignored his foul mood. "Tokey, please pic-k up crystal. Silently tell it something about you. You need to in-tro-dduce yourself to it."

"Yeah, no thanks. I don't believe in talking to rocks."

"Sabina . . . vill you excuse us? I'd like to hear vhat Flann vants to tell me . . . prrrivately." Nana Honey started rocking in her chair, her peaceful state unfazed by Flann's sarcasm.

"Oh," Sabina said, jumping up from the couch that she had just sat down on. *I wonder what this is about. Will he tell me later?* She looked over at Flann, who had his hands in his pockets and was looking down. She felt his foul mood, and it seemed like he was trying to avoid her. *You know what? I don't want to know. The less I know about him, the better for me.*

Nana Honey offered Sabina a solution as she stood there looking lost. "Crystal is in the garden. Vhy don't you visit her?"

"Yes. I'll go do that," she said, looking at Flann the entire time. He continued to look down. She didn't know why it bothered her that he was avoiding her, but now she was aware of it, she was tempted to shoulder him as she walked past. It took effort, but she walked past him without knocking him over or saying a word to him. As she did, she told herself he didn't matter. It was none of her business what he was feeling or why. It did her no good to waste her energy on him.

Walking out the back, down the steps and into the scent of lavender, Sabina entered the garden to find Crystal sitting on the ground, with a small basket of herbs by her side, playing with a flower. She could tell something was wrong. Crystal was sulking. Sabina was about to ask what was wrong, but Crystal talked first.

Her spirits seemed low. She said, "I sensed you were here. Is Nana working on your amulet?"

Standing for a moment, watching her, Sabina decided to sit

down next to her. "She probably will, but Master Alf and Nana are talking right now."

Crystal lifted her head, eyes tired and dull compared to her normal, confident self. "Good. Maybe she will talk some sense into him." She looked back down after making eye contact.

"Did something happen last night?" Sabina inquired.

Playing with the flower, Crystal asked, "Do you remember anything from last night?"

"Yeah. A bunch. My father's letter in the salt circle; Flann flying across the room; me feeling super tired; the vial of stuff you made; going home and taking a nap; feeling so sick and miserable." Sabina did a one-shoulder shrug. "Then it gets fuzzy. I think I dreamed about Flann and me *being* together. All those union interviews must be getting to my head because I know he is with someone else." Sabina was confused, slightly embarrassed to admit that to her friend. "Why do you ask? Did I do something I don't remember?"

Crystal sat up from her slouched position and swung her legs crisscross in front of Sabina, completely focused on her. She seemed calm when she asked, "All these union interviews are with men. Have you ever thought about being with a woman? I mean, we have never discussed it before and now you are becoming an adult . . . You get to decide what you want."

She waited for Sabina to answer with her heart open. Crystal hoped for the answer to be what she longed to hear and feared Sabina's rejection at the same time.

Sabina never talked about being attracted to anyone. Crystal believed Sabina was asexual and settled for friendship. The truth was Crystal had fallen for Sabina when she was a guest in her home and since then, she had looked for signs her feelings were returned. All this time, she had never been brave enough to have this conversation, and she fooled herself into believing Sabina's union interviews would result in nothing more than casual conversation. But after seeing Flann hold Sabina last night in such an intimate way as if their bodies fit together like a puzzle, Crystal had to know how Sabina felt, even if the pain of hearing the truth hurt.

Sabina paused. She knew Crystal was into women. And she knew Crystal wasn't asking if she was into women in general, but was asking if she was into her. Sabina wanted to smile at Crystal's question because she was embarrassed and uncomfortable, and for whatever reason, her natural bodily response was to smile at the wrong moments.

Crystal was one of the few people in this village who she would consider a friend. Sabina valued their friendship even if they were not the type of friends who did everything together. Crystal was independent and three steps ahead of everyone else. She was confident, strong, and attractive in a fierce, untouchable way . . . She knew what she wanted, and she went after it. All these traits, Sabina admired. She was grateful for how Crystal always looked out for her. Sabina schooled her face as best as she could. She was not going to smile at this inappropriate time. Crystal was important to her, and she didn't want to lose a good friend because she was being emotionally immature.

Tentatively, Sabina answered truthfully. "I've always imagined myself being with a man, but I haven't honestly given being with a woman much thought. Have you thought about being with a man?"

Crystal looked away. A moment passed. She swallowed and let out a jagged breath. She almost laughed as tears fell down her face. "Touché. No, I haven't. It doesn't appeal to me at all."

Sabina laid her hand on Crystal's shoulder and placed her head on top of her hand. "If I was into women, I'd be into you. You have so many qualities I admire and looks that don't compare to any other woman. I don't think anyone compares to you, actually."

Crystal continued to look away and quietly composed herself. She was nodding to indicate she was listening but not talking.

Pulling away, Sabina looked at her. Gently, she said, "I love you, but I love you like a cool, older sister."

Crystal took a large breath and held it. After slowly releasing the air, she seemed to attempt a smile. She looked at Sabina. "I'd like to be alone, if you don't mind." She placed her hand on Sabina's..

"Sure. I understand," Sabina answered affectionately and got up, feeling a sense of loss. She knew Crystal had tried to reassure her everything was okay with that touch, but she was uncertain how this conversation would shift their relationship.

Not wanting to go in, Sabina walked around the house as slowly as she could, thinking. She could not be sure, but she wondered what effect not wearing her amulet was having on others and what her amplifying abilities caused others to feel.

While Crystal and Sabina had their conversation, Nana Honey and Flann spoke. As Sabina walked out the door to talk to Crystal in the garden, Nana Honey opened her third eye to talk with Flann.

"You have something to say to me. It burns off you. It is not necessary for you to say anymore. Let me put your mind at ease. I promised to help you and I vill as you have helped find the amulet."

Flann's argument deflated at hearing Nana's words and he relaxed. He didn't know what to expect except resistance. That was what he was used to. He was used to fighting for what he wanted, not someone giving him what he wanted. He attempted to calm his nerves and to shift his train of thoughts from the argu-ments he had prepared in his head to the present moment. He sat down on the edge of the couch, fingers interlocked, trying to shift his thoughts to prepare for the next phase of his plan.

It seemed Nana Honey waited for him to settle before continuing. "Yesterday, you vished to bring Nora into Silvedome. Is that vhat you still vant?"

Joy welled up inside of him at hearing her question. With hope in his voice, he quickly answered, "Yes. Absolutely."

"I ask because last night changed things for you. Do you realize that?"

He could feel a tingling sensation rush over his body at Nana Honey's words. A vision of holding Sabina as they slept surfaced in his mind. His joy was displaced by this threat. He pushed the thought of Sabina away. He wasn't going to let the effects of some potion derail him from what he had strived for and desired for over a year.

He retorted with conceit. "Last night changed nothing. My heart belongs to Nora."

Nana Honey felt disappointment sting her heart, and she found herself saying to Flann: "Tokey, you are lost and barely know yourself. You haven't *allowed* yourself to know vhat your heart vants."

Flann snapped. "You don't know me. You see parts of me, but *I* get to decide who I am."

Sorrow for this young man filled her heart. "Very vell. If you cannot be honest vith yourself, then I cannot help you. Give me time to think of vhat I can do for you."

Flann flushed with anger. "You promised to help me! Now you cannot??? Is that what you are saying?" He pulled his hands through his hair in agitation. "Stop talking in riddles and give it to me straight."

Her tone shifted. "Mas**td**er Alf . . . You stand at a crossroads. Because of that, I cannot bring Nora into Silvedome for union as

I foresaw before. Nor does she have a Moowin. I need time to consider other options for bringing her into Silvedome."

~

Nana Honey's words revealed to him that she didn't see them being together anymore. He shouted, "What are you saying? I chose Nora." He felt like his dreams were being crushed at Nana Honey's announcement. In frustration, he knocked the crystal that supposedly represented him off Nana Honey's stand. "I *had* to help Sabina last night, but nothing happened."

Nana Honey began to rock in her chair and didn't say anything. She folded her hands on her belly and allowed Flann to process his frustrations.

He lowered his voice, seeing her lack of response. "I love Nora. I love being with her and she loves me. She is to be my wife. NOTHING you say can change that."

He was up, pacing, feeling like he was coming undone. He wanted to yell and demand to get his way. When one year ago, he would not have dreamed of asking for what he wanted. He was not the same person. No, he didn't need her approval, he told himself. He was no longer a slave with no rights. He was a rare Messenger and a citizen of Silvedome. But, somehow, a logical thought broke through his emotions. He didn't need her approval, but he needed her help. He had no idea how to immediately bring Nora into Silvedome without Nana Honey's help. The original plan of waiting until he was established in the village and asking the council wasn't going to work. Not with how things were going with Sabina.

Huffing out a breath, one thing became clear to Flann—he was losing. He was losing control of his emotions and his thoughts. He was losing sight of what mattered. It didn't matter that Nana's words made him feel the threat of losing what he wanted. What mattered was the results. He was a warrior and warriors practiced controlling their emotions. That reminded him of who he was. He had choices. He always had choices. He needed to stop thinking about proving he was right and start thinking from a different perspective.

Crossing the room, he picked up the crystal and placed it back on Nana Honey's stand. He sat down on the couch. He slowly looked up, steeling his emotions. "I'm sorry . . . for acting childish. Nora is important to me and I felt defensive. Is the crystal harmed?"

Absentmindedly, she answered, "It is as it should be. I thank you for retrieving it."

She was looking out the window whereas normally she looked toward him. He swallowed, thinking through his words. "You said something about me being at a crossroads. To me, a crossroads in my physical life is about choosing a direction. If that same theory applies to my . . . heart," he said awkwardly, "I'm choosing Nora."

She continued to look out the window, a sad disposition across her face. "Mastder Alf, you are new to Silvedome. You are new to vorking vith me. Forgive me for not explaining to you that I must *always* follow vhat is in my heart, even if others do not understand or agree. I can be no one else but me. Do you understand?"

Unsure where this conversation was going, Flann reluctantly replied, "Yes."

"Vhat I say to you may not make sense. I appreciate your struggle. Thee problem is you hear vhat is said, but you do not hear vhat is unsaid." She turned to look at him. "**I** hear vhat is unsaid. Your heart has spoken to me and your vords have spoken to me. They are misaligned. So I say-again-to you: I cannot help you in the vay you vant me to help you, until you are honest vith yourself."

What in the fires is this woman talking about? I don't hear . . . my heart? All Flann wanted was to understand if she was willing to help him. He tried again. "What do you need from me in order to help me bring Nora to Silvedome?" he asked.

"To trrrust me. Now go sit vith your struggle in your day of silence. Sabina is on her vay back to us."

Feeling his control of his emotions starting to slip with the pressure of the conversation ending, he fisted his hands. He felt like crying but held on to anger instead. "So you will not help me? I don't understand *what* you are saying, but what I am hearing is that NORA **isn't** the right person for me. *What about my free will to choose?*" He was standing now. He realized he had taken a step toward her.

Though Nana Honey sat in her chair, and hardly moved a single muscle, Flann felt the weight of her words. She spoke with power and deliberation. "I said no such things. You have the power to choose, not me. I'm saying you don't know vhat to choose because your head is so full of fear that you cannot hear vhat your heart vants. Vhat you need is to stop holding onto Nora like a comfort blanket. You need to stop resisting your emotions. You may very vell choose Nora after you have sorted it out. Now be done with this obsession. I vill keep my vord and bring Nora to Silvedome, even if that makes you unhappy in the long run."

Flann sat back on the couch, resting his head on the back. He pressed his head with his hands. He felt like he was hit by a two-by-four. "I guess I've earned my name today."

"Yes, Tokey, you have."

He felt clarity in that moment. Nana Honey wasn't going to buy the bullshit he was selling to himself, and oddly, that realization made him trust her. He wanted to confide in her to sort out these thoughts and feelings, but he was not sure how close Sabina was to returning to the house. He didn't want to risk her over-hearing.

"No more questions. I need my energy for Sabina's amulet."

Even as he realized he was confused and conflicted about Sabina, she knocked on the door and walked in. It was as if spring air wafted into the room. Her energy seemed to pour over him and he felt the shift through him, though he still wanted to deny it.

"Sorry to interrupt. I need to get to school. Do you have time to work on my amulet?"

"I'll only need a moment. Grab your crystal from the vall," she said, pointing to the crystal on the wall by her side.

Sabina took her crystal and amulet to Nana Honey.

"Sit next to me . . . yes. Now clear your mind and think of something that you love. Hold on to that feeling for meee."

Sabina sat on the floor and Flann watched her in silence. He wondered what she was thinking about. He didn't know what she liked. He didn't know much about her, which was more proof that what he felt was lust or this life force bond.

Nana Honey held the crystal on top of Sabina's crown and the amulet close to her heart. She whispered prayers that Flann wanted to remember, but they drifted from his awareness as soon as they came. Within minutes, the prayer ceased and Nana Honey drew back from Sabina.

"Tonight is an important night for you." She handed Sabina the amulet and moved her gaze to Flann as Sabina put the necklace on. "Silence is necessary to trrruly hear our heart. Allow it to come. It vill prepare you for your Birth Challenge. I must admit I am curious to see vhat name you give yourself."

"Why wouldn't you look into the future to see?" Flann asked.

"To me, time is not linear. I see multiple timelines vhen I use my sight. To you, as you mentioned earlier, you have free vill. You are free to change the course of your path any time you choose. It does no good to look vhen transformation is at play. Besides, privacy is integrity in my line of vork. Vhen I use my sight, it is out of service to others and not out of personal gain."

"I don't feel good," Sabina said, resting her head on the couch.

Nana Honey frowned. Flann automatically rested his hand on her arm. He could sense the apathy coming from her.

"I don't like what happens to others when I don't wear my amulet, but I don't like what happens to me when I do." She sighed and said in a whiney voice, "I have a lot I need to do today."

"Enough with thee fretting. There is no space for that here. I vill vork on the amulet some more. Go to school. People vill notice you today. That is how it vill be. If you both agree, you may consider having Flann's arm around your shoulder. That vill buffer the energy coming off you. They vill read it as his energy."

Seeing that Sabina wasn't moving to take off the necklace, Flann nudged her. He could see drool leaking out of her mouth and panic hit him. He quickly moved and grabbed the string from the back of her neck. He moved around her and worked the necklace off. He turned to hand the amulet to Nana Honey.

"Good choice, Tokey. Vill you put her crystal in one hand and yours in the other? That vill help ground her."

He did as he was asked, and then he felt a call coming in. He answered.

"This is Master Alf."

"Master Alf, this is Scholar Daffeney. We have three guests at the council, approved to visit Silvedome, who are requesting an audience with Sabina Rockdin. They are to be her guest. Will you see to it that she comes immediately to Ceremony Hall?"

"She has school."

"Yes, we will notify the school of her approved absence."

Looking at Sabina, he felt concern and didn't want to rush her out the door, but he heard Nana Honey in the background. "She vill be fine. She is starting to stir."

"Fine. We will make our way there," Flann continued, eyeing Nana Hone and marveling at her abilities.

"See you soon."

The conversation ended. He moved his focus to Sabina. She had let go of the crystals and was wiping her mouth. "I have such a headache."

It occurred to him that Viggo was here. He finally had someone who could help Sabina feel better that he knew and trusted. "We are actually on our way to meet another one . . . well two . . . of your union interviews, but one of them is a Healer," he informed Sabina.

Lifting her head from the couch, she said, "What?"

"Yeah, we talked about this last night. You know, when you weren't feeling good."

Slowly, she got up. "I don't remember any of that conversation."

Flann reached out to help her, but she ignored his offered support.

"You tell Fabia to come see me vhen she can. I miss that beautiful soul."

Sabina turned to look at Nana Honey. "You know them?"

"Oh yes. In my youth, I used to travel vith Brom to help recruit young Moowins. Ve often stayed at the Nadels' home. Viggo is Brom's godson and Fabia is Viggo's younger sister. Truth-sayer is that one. Strong and powerful." She smiled.

Flann had forgotten Nana Honey knew them. "Rrrright. Can you walk yet?"

She seemed confused and answered, "Yeah. I walked in here, didn't I?"

Yeah, that was Sabina without the amulet, Flann thought. Unwilling to ask for help. He wanted to smile at the comeback he thought of, but he was smart enough not to say anything. "I'm ready to go when you are," he chose to say instead.

"Thank you for your help, Nana Honey. How will I get my amulet since I'm in silence for most of today?"

"I don't know if I can fix your amulet," Nana Honey responded. Seeing Sabina's concern, she continued. "Be at peace, my child. All vill vork out. Vhen one learns to fly, their soul longs for it. Keep your soul partners close. Flann, let Brom know about the amulet. Sabina, your father left his initiation note vith me." She looked down at the note on her desk.

~

Sabina picked it up. It hit her that this was her last day of her childhood. A thought of regret surfaced in her mind: All the mistakes she could have made while it was safe to make them were gone. She spent her whole life hiding, feeling insecure about herself. Now the day had come when her mistakes would most likely change the quality of her life.

Looking down at the note, she felt paralyzed. She would leave her nest of safety and face the world, dependent on herself. She would serve and earn her place in the village. Doubt surfaced within her at the heaviness of this new expectation. Where did all that bravery and excitement for life go that she had felt in the Loaded Hurricane? She could use that strength now.

The initiation note was a part of the Birth Challenge ritual that symbolized parents saying goodbye to the child. Most thought of it as a way for loved ones to give their blessing. A way to say that they understood the person was no longer a child—a child who believed what their parents, teachers, and council told them. This letter meant tomorrow she would be responsible for answering for herself. This required a level of trusting herself that she had never practiced before but would have to depend on immediately. There is great freedom in getting to choose what you believe, but there is also accountability for standing by these beliefs. Sabina didn't know what she believed in anymore.

The pressure in her head throbbed, and she felt the bones in her face ache. She wasn't ready for this. She didn't get a chance to enjoy her childhood, and it was gone. A desire to be wild and reckless swept over her and another thought pulled her back. She only had a few hours before her silence. She needed to get ready. There was a lot for her to do today.

She looked at Flann and Nana Honey. She desperately wished they would tell her what to do. A bitter thought of 'Welcome to adulthood where you are responsible for deciding for yourself', popped into her head. Tullom. She wanted to melt into the couch and pause time. She looked at the note in her hand and hoped her father had given her excellent send-off advice because she needed it.

Out of habit, when all seemed to be going wrong, Sabina said the words of affirmation that helped get her through past times of pain. *I am exactly where I need to be. Nothing has gone wrong.* She took a deep breath and decided she was going to do something for herself today. She was going to have her own goodbye party to Sabina, the girl who wore an amulet necklace that snuffed out all her joy. That girl deserved to have more fun than she did.

Feeling a sense of purpose, Sabina said, "Okay. Let's go meet these . . . Partners."

They left Nana Honey's house and walked to Ceremony Hall. Sabina's mind was brainstorming bold moves she could take, repeatedly coming up with the idea of kissing one of her partners . . . possibly that good-looking Performer. She thought of challenging Markus, who always put her down—but that was revenge. She wanted fun. Besides, he had his Birth Challenge today. He would probably be bragging about his Protector score. The other thought she debated was swimming naked in the lake. The other kids did it as a way of daring themselves. Isn't that what she was doing? She was daring herself to do something she would never have dreamed herself brave enough to do before this day.

As Sabina asked herself what would make her happy, Flann thought about what Nana Honey had said. He needed to work out this . . . temptation he felt toward Sabina. The sooner, the better. Then he could bring all his focus back on Nora.

By the end of the walk, Flann had come up with three reasons for being at a 'crossroads' as Nana Honey had put it. One, he was resisting acknowledging his interest in Sabina. In fact, now he had acknowledged it to himself, he didn't feel any connection to her. The evidence was in the fact that he was walking next to her without one ounce of desire. That proved the saying he had often heard: 'What you resist, persists.' Two, he was convinced that sharing a life force with Sabina caused him to feel something for her. It made sense. He liked himself and she had part of his essence in her so naturally, he would be interested in her. He planned on watching Sabina interact with the other bonded partners to see their reactions to each other. Third, the distance in his relationship with Nora was affecting him. He had not seen her in so long and their conversations through a Messenger were not the same. They were not investing enough time with each other to keep their connection strong. That would be fixed. He was bringing Nora to Silvedome.

Ceremony Hall was an outdoor, tiered sitting arena with a massive, lit center stage. They walked down the slope to the stage where Viggo sat on the floor, his head resting on the wall. His skin looked more ashen than the normal bright green color of the Forddin race. Fabia stood, looking at her nails, bored. Zoel's voice could be heard from the back of the arena.

"I will accept nothing less than the best."

They heard soft mutterings from Dove.

"I should not have to repeat my request. It is ridiculous that you are unable to accommodate my wishes. I won't hear of it."

Dove walked away from him as he bolstered his demands, completely ignoring his rants.

"You have taken enough of our time, sir. I appreciate your status . . ." remarked Bull.

"Yes. And as a Prince, I deserve the best. It's about time you finally saw reason."

Calmly, Bull addressed Zoel. "Prince or civilian, all outsiders receive an abbreviated ritual. Markus is a resident. Residents receive the full ritual. Those are our rules."

"I am a rule maker. I do not follow the wishes of subordinates. I dictate what rules subordinates are to follow."

"And you are not in your land. You are in ours. We are not subject to your rules."

"If you didn't want me to ask for the full ritual, then you shouldn't have shown me what the full ritual looks like. *This is your fault.* Now I know there is something better and I will not settle for some dismissive ritual," Zoel criticized.

The Mistress walked swiftly toward Bull and Zoel with Markus trailing behind. "May I remind you that you are a guest here and not entitled to the privileges of your land. Now, this discussion is officially over. Your company has arrived to escort you to your places. If the council finds any further challenges or demands, our warriors will gladly escort you outside of our lands."

"And I'll be guarding the dome walls ready to Knock You Down . . ." Markus smiled as he flexed his arm muscles.

"Enough, Wolverine," the Mistress said, looking at him with her squinting eyes.

At Markus's threat, Zoel spat on the soft black boots that Markus was wearing. "You are nothing more than target practice for me. Not even worth the spit I valued you with."

Markus lunged. Bull grabbed him by the collar and pulled him back. "Get to the wall. Your training starts immediately." Bull pushed Markus toward the stairs, pointing his finger in a 'go' motion.

Meanwhile, the Mistress stepped in front of Zoel. Her short stature was not intimidating but the power of her shield was. "You will treat our people with respect. There is no other alternative for you if you wish to remain here."

He looked down at the Mistress, his upper left lip pulling up. She remained a firm statue, not breaking eye contact. Rubbing his hands together watching him seethe, Bull seemed to have decided Zoel had got the message and walked off, waving to Sabina.

It was no surprise to Flann that the high and mighty Zoel Alpheus was arguing with the council about his unfair treatment. Sabina slowed as they approached, listening to the conversation. She turned to Flann and whispered a question.

"My father wants me to have a union interview with him . . .?"

"No. Not really. Your father cannot stand him but he is the son of your mother's best friend. The one that she saved. He had your life force from your mother's womb. The union interview was a gift to your mother."

Clearly disgusted at the thought, Sabina said, "I'm connected to him?"

"Yes, yes-you-are. I have news I think you will be glad to hear later though."

Markus, leaving the Ceremony, walked by with a smug expression on his way out of the arena. "I had the *pleasure* of meeting your next buffoon partner. I would have thought your father loved you more than that. I guess I was wrong," he mocked.

Flann didn't like the smartass, but on this subject, the kid had a point.

~

"Huh, that's odd. I thought today was your Birth Challenge but I guess I was wrong because you are still acting like a child," Sabina said with more confidence than she felt. She couldn't believe she had just said that. *That is stuff you think, not say, Sabina.*

"Watch it," Markus said with his thumb pointing to himself. "You don't know who you are speaking to now. I was reborn as Wolverine and as the name implies, *I'm dangerous.*"

"Wolverine?" Sabina whispered out loud to herself, squinting her face and drawing back like she had just been sprayed by a skunk. *Gag me.*

"You are looking at one of Silvedome's gifted Protectors. I scored so high that they asked me to serve immediately. I already have my first assignment. I'll be defending the dome, keeping everyone safe. The notorious Borax is outside Silvedome as we speak." He smiled with a cocky expression. "We will see what you are made of tomorrow."

"Why are you needed immediately?" Flann asked.

Wolverine stepped past Sabina and walked up too close to Flann.

"First night in Silvedome rough? I see you got some bruises on your forearm." He glanced down at where Flann's arm was beginning to develop a bruise. "I could offer you some protection *for a price*."

~

Flann hadn't noticed the bruises though he wasn't surprised to see them after sparring with Sabina. "Oh, that was just a little bit of fun wrestling, but you won't know a thing about that would you?" He winked toward Sabina as he spoke. His foul mood gone, he smiled.

Sabina flushed. Wolverine's jaw muscles flexed. Flann took a step toward him, keeping his mood light.

"If I had known Sabina liked to play, I would have shown her what real skill looks like. Maybe I still will now that I know she likes to *play*." He turned back and looked at Sabina with his cocky smile.

Sabina crossed her arms, visibly irritated at this conversation. She looked like she wanted to give his ego a kick in the ass but settled for, "If I wanted to be with someone who thought of themselves as a dirt burrowing, aggressive animal, I would be. **But** I don't. Let me be clear: I'm not interested." She turned and walked away.

Flann chuckled. He patted Wolverine's shoulder. "Better stick to fights you know you can win."

"I AM A WINNER." Wolverine snapped his arm up but Flann had already taken a step back.

"Easy. I was making light conversation. Seems a little strange to me that you are skipping training and going right into the action. You must have scored extremely well in your ritual. Not many can say they are that gifted."

Wolverine yanked his shirt down in a movement of dignity.

He seemed irritated with Flann and Sabina but it also appeared he liked getting the recognition he deserved.

"I did score high," he said, lifting his jaw. "Several of our men were hurt yesterday defending the wall and while they are healing, I am skilled enough to step in and help keep *OUR* people safe. That is what a person of honor does." He looked Flann up and down quickly and took off toward the village.

Flann shouted at him. "Wait, I'm not questioning your honor. HOW many were HURT?"

Seeing that Wolverine was done talking, Flann turned back to walk to the stage. He saw the Mistress speed-walking up the ramp with her short, fast steps. She stopped Sabina and grabbed her arm.

"If you have any trouble with *that Prince*, have Master Alf contact Scholar Daffeney. We will handle it." She took a deep breath and stood up taller. "It's not my place but as your mentor I'd like to say that Prince is no frog in disguise. You be careful with him." She spoke sternly. "I'll see you here tomorrow morning. I have requested to do your ceremony. Now if you excuse me, I have to catch up with Wolverine."

Flann heard most of the conversation as he met up with Sabina.

"What does she mean, the Prince is no frog?"

"I think she means love won't turn him into Prince Charming." She turned to look at him. "You know, like in the stories before the nuclear war."

"No, I don't know. I have not read any stories from prehistoric times," he remarked.

"Really? I love them. We have a whole library section of them if you are interested."

～

They approached Zoel who was furiously talking to himself, pacing back and forth. Sabina heard him say: "I demanded a proper Birth Challenge. It's **my** birthright. I have waited years to have this . . ." He stopped complaining as Flann knocked on the stage floor. He took Flann in and then shifted to look at Sabina with an expectant eye. "*You* are my next lover? More muscular than I like but you will do." He jumped off the stage in front of her.

Taking a step back out of Zoel's reach, Sabina cringed at his assumption of her.

Zoel's hair was shaved short on the side with the top of his head thick with short black hair. He had a beard that wrapped into a well-manicured mustache. He was groomed to perfection with flawless skin. His thick eyebrows framed his intense eyes and he had a plump bottom lip. Sabina would have considered him eye-catching if it wasn't for his attitude.

"*Don't be shy? I am here for you after all.*" He took a step toward her.

Flann grabbed Zoel's forearm. "Give her space. She is not obligated to you," he reminded the Prince in a firm tone.

"Lay off, guard dog," Zoel said, ripping his arm away from Flann.

Flann smiled.

Fabia walked up behind Zoel. She showed the full length of her legs as she walked. She had a curvy body, wide hips, and prominent breasts cinched in a brocade corset with dangling fur embellishment. She had a significant amount of black paint around her eyes and blonde, ratty hair with black roots. Her skin was luminous and shone bright green, which perfectly complemented the black and cream colors she wore. Sabina had only ever seen Performers wear outfits like this in their shows.

She was mesmerizing to watch as she sauntered over full of power and command. Sabina had never seen a woman so . . . provocative. There was something about this woman that Sabina took notice of in a way that was beyond appreciation. Her thoughts drifted back to her conversation with Crystal. Was she wrong? Was she into women after all because she felt something stir inside of her? She didn't *want* to take her eyes off her.

"Zoellll." Her tongue stuck to the roof of her mouth. "You have plenty of playmates but no Queen. Do you not recognize a QUEEN when you see one?" She walked around him, her finger rubbing him as she passed.

She placed herself in between Zoel and Sabina. She wrapped her arms around his shoulders and a confident smirk appeared on Zoel's face. She had his complete attention. Sabina actually looked at her butt which was sticking out as she arched into her hug with Zoel. Sabina was shocked to see Fabia's underwear. She looked over to Flann who was looking at her. She straightened automatically like she had been caught cheating on a test.

Flann watched Fabia prowl around Zoel in her exotic fashion. He had spent plenty of time around Fabia and he was used to her toying with men's desires. Although she was entertaining to watch, he knew her well enough to know she would crush the balls of any man who tried to do anything with her that she did not permit. He liked her. He liked her confidence in herself. She was interesting and blunt, but not his type.

Instead, he turned his attention to Sabina. Her cheeks flushed and her eyes grew big. Her discomfort was clear to see, but she was too curious not to look away. He was amused watching her, but he smiled when she discovered she had been caught looking at Fabia's butt.

"No, my enchantress. My eyes are sore from my long travels." Zoel reached his arms around her back to hold her but she let go of his neck. She playfully slapped him on the face, hard enough that it probably stung but nothing more.

"Don't feed me excuses. You know I like a man who owns his mistakes." Her hands raked down his chest, and she lightly shoved him.

Turning to Sabina, she stepped uncomfortably close to her, grabbing strands of her hair on each side of her face, playing with them.

"You are a baby Queen, but a Queen no less." She leaned in and audibly smelled Sabina. "Mmmm, you smell *wonderful*." She turned and rubbed her back along the front of Sabina's body until she was squatting low to the ground, like she was a cat rubbing against a leg. "Yes. I will help you. You want to do something *fun* tonight. I like the way you"—She stood back up slowly—"think."

~

Sabina felt frozen and terrified. She had never been . . . rubbed or touched that way. She didn't know what to think or do. She looked at Flann, who was holding back laughter and Zoel, who had his tongue rubbing the corner of his lips. *How did she know what I was thinking*??? Sabina thought aghast.

Laughter in his voice, Flann answered Sabina's unsaid question. "She is a Truth-sayer."

With her arms out to the side and feeling out of place, Sabina asked, "What's a Truth-sayer?"

"You don't have Truth-sayers here?" Flann asked while Sabina shock her head 'no'.

"She is mine," the Prince said, grabbing a fist of her hair and pulling her toward him.

Fabia didn't make a sound of protest, but followed his pull and quickly stepped toward him, and shoved her palm into his nose. Sabina's mouth dropped open at Fabia's assault, and the fact she laughed and danced as carefree as a delighted child, making a full circle around him. She had never seen such behavior.

"Evil tyrant," the Prince angrily shouted as he pinched his nose, blood running quickly down his face. "I don't know why I put up with you. VIGGO!!! My clothes are getting dirty," he said. He spat as the blood ran over his lips.

Viggo was already up and moseying over. His dopey eyes

looked sad, tired, and defeated. He cupped his hand over the bridge of the Prince's nose and closed his eyes. Meanwhile, Fabia walked up to him, serious once more, and said, "I BELONG TO NO ONE." She spoke with conviction as she pulled his ear toward her. Releasing it, she said, "And now you have set my brother free, you are free of me." She stood in front of him, with her hands on her hips, feet wide. "And don't pull my hair. You know it turns me on." She pouted.

Flann leaned in and whispered, "Fabia is a special Truth-sayer. You might say one of a kind."

The Prince remained still as Viggo worked. He stared at Fabia as if he had something to say but said nothing. He looked hungry and Sabina didn't understand what was going on.

"Leave the rest of his healing to time, brother. He needs a little pain to remember who he is playing with."

Viggo dropped his hand and walked back to his resting spot on the wall.

"All better," purred Fabia as she walked up to the Prince and stroked his hair and his face. "No, no, no," she taunted. "*I would devour you*," she said lightly.

She turned to Sabina. "Come show me your village and home. I have a gift for you that I am most excited to give to you." She was already walking toward her brother, slightly skipping. The Prince turned and followed. "Viggo, my stuff."

Sabina stood frozen. Her mouth was dry and her head was pounding. She questioned the safety of bringing this mad woman into her home.

"Come on," Flann said. "You will like her once you get to know her. Just remember, she touches you. You don't touch her unless she gives you permission first."

"But, but she is *crazy*," Sabina said in a low voice, through light lips.

"No. Her pain and pleasure sensors work differently. That's all. And she can read energy, which is how she knows so much truth about people."

Flann walked off, leaving Sabina the last one standing there. Viggo had picked up three bags and had thrown them over his shoulder in silence. He followed Fabia who had thrown her arm around Flann's shoulder. The Prince stalked after them, annoyed and not the least bit interested in Sabina.

Sabina swallowed as she watched them walk up the ramp to leave Ceremony Hall. *Well, you wanted to do something fun on your last day of childhood, didn't you?*

The Tut Is Full

The walk to Sabina's tut was uneventful. Very few people were out, and if you ignored the gawking looks they received, everything was fine. Sabina barely noticed any of her surroundings, though. She looked down and occasionally glanced up at Flann and Fabia as they led the way through the village. They were engrossed in conversation while the Prince continued to touch his nose and wipe at the blood on his shirt. Viggo could have been nonexistent, going by his blank face and steady pace. It was odd he didn't bother looking around.

Sabina couldn't explain why, but it bothered her that Flann seemed to be so 'jolly' with Fabia. When he was with her, he was serious, foul, rude, and sarcastic. Although on rare occasions, he was thoughtful and kind. But he was never jolly. Plus, Fabia and Flann walked together with such ease. She wondered if she would ever have that kind of relationship with someone. The truth is that she didn't want their relationship to bother her, but it did. The walk may have been ten minutes, but she already knew that she didn't want to be around them with their familiarity and obvious delight in one another. And so, she looked down and ignored them, ignored the world at large.

Finally at Sabina's tut, Flann opened the door and allowed

Fabia to enter first before he quickly stepped in front of the Prince who scoffed at the rude treatment. Viggo followed, silent and resigned as it seemed was his normal.

All had entered, but none of them had taken off their shoes. Sabina sighed. She was not in the mood to explain to her guests the house rules. She sat down on the edge of the porch and took off her boots. She closed her eyes and let the sun warm her face. She tried to ignore the conversation inside but it was clear the Prince was repulsed by the 'living quarters' and that Fabia was ready to decorate. *I could just stay out here and start my day of silence early. Or go for a walk. Flann will take care of the guests. He seems happy to,* she thought begrudgingly.

"Sabina, are you coming in?" Flann called from somewhere in the tut.

She ignored him. She moved her attention back to the warmth of the sun. She heard someone silently approach. Sabina would not have heard them if it wasn't for the board creaking. She felt two fingers lightly rest against the inside of her wrist.

"That should help," said a low gruff voice, a voice that didn't get used much.

Her eyes popped open at the surprise that someone other than Flann was sitting next to her. She had assumed immediately that Flann was the one who had approached. Odd that she had gotten comfortable enough with the thought of Flann sitting there, but the reality that it was Viggo bothered her. It was diffi-cult to combat that feeling of discomfort with Viggo's soothing energy work. She felt a sense of calm travel up her arm into her chest, and she knew she should thank him. He performed energy work, and it was custom to show gratitude. However, no emotions surfaced, and she lacked the motivation to do so. There was a stillness within her, one that made her feel so content and at peace that she didn't want to move for fear it would dissipate. It was such a welcomed feeling that she could not muster the willpower to thank him despite being consciously aware of etiquette and the future self-judgment that would come for failing to do the right thing. Instead of being perfect, she stared at him while he looked across the pathway, silent and still.

"Who a-r-e you?" she questioned.

"Nobody," he said without fluctuation in his voice.

She continued to stare at him while the Prince came out, agitated.

"I NEEEEED other accommodations. You don't even have running water. It's an insult that you think I would stay here."

Looking up at him, Sabina didn't know what to say. "How did you travel here with running water?" she asked simply.

"Ugh. Water is brought to me like everything else," he said, shifting his weight and looking dismantled.

"I don't have other arrangements for you. I didn't even know you were coming."

The Prince appeared to fume at the impossibility that his presence wasn't anticipated and planned for; Sabina blocked most of this out. She leaned back slightly to see past the Healer's back and saw that Flann was standing in the dark shadows of the doorway, leaning against the wall with his legs and arms crossed, watching. He had a smile on his face, but it was a knowing smile. She squinted to see him better. Their eyes locked before he turned and walked away.

"Are you paying attention to me? **The insolence.** You people are uncivilized. It's going to take me months to train you on how to behave. I don't know why I even try." He stormed down the stairs, past Viggo and Sabina.

"Viggo, get my stuff. We are speaking to the council about better arrangements."

Wordless, Viggo got to his feet, slowly as if he were waiting to see if the Prince would change his mind. Viggo spoke soft and gentle to Sabina. "You get used to him. I'll be back."

She watched him go into the house and grab his bag, then walk past her to follow after the Prince. She looked at her shoes, trying to get the motivation to put them on and escort her guests to the council, but she reasoned they would understand that she was powerless to stop the Prince. Besides, she had other guests she was responsible for and no one should be responsible for this many at once. Where was her help, anyway?

She stayed outside, watching them walk off. She felt calm for the first time today.

"Good, he is gone. Come in and meet Fabia," Flann said with excitement in his voice.

"I already did."

"No. She was buffering the Prince for you. Come in and really meet her."

She turned to look at him standing in the doorway, arms crossed, in a pleasant mood despite more bruises showing up on his muscular forearms. Reluctantly, she got up and walked through the door.

"She is decorating your sister's room."

Irritated, she stared at him with some feeling of disbelief that Fabia could walk into a home in which she was a visitor and could decide to decorate. *She is already making herself at home, I guess.* Sabina tossed her hands up in the air. She felt a lack of control or normalcy in her life, but didn't see another choice. So she walked up the wrapped stairs and down the hallway, listening to Fabia sing horribly to herself.

"Aye, it's about time," she said, her hands reaching up to hang black spider-web material from the walls. "Beautiful, isn't it? It is a veil for lancing. Have you ever seen a lancing before? No. Well, that's too bad. You are missing out. They are EXCITING," she said, bringing her teeth together.

Standing there, feeling like this was going to be a one-way conversation, Sabina didn't comment. She watched Fabia work without any desire to help and come any closer.

Sighing dramatically, she stopped what she was doing. "FINNNNNE, this can wait." She walked over to Sabina's sister's bed and threw herself down and rolled over so that she was lying on her back and her head was slightly dangling off the side of the bed.

"Come sit next to me."

Not moving, Sabina felt much more comfortable with this distance.

"People are *too* serious. Don't you remember how to have fun? No. You don't, do you? *I know you want to have fun.* I read your energy." She flipped over and sat up quickly, moving onto her hands and knees. "I'm a lot of fun. Of course, my fun may be different than your fun."

Not moving but watching Fabia intentionally, Sabina asked the question that was starting to bother her the more time she spent with this wild person. "Why are you here?"

"Oh, that's easy. I go wherever my brother goes. We are a packaged deal. He is great, isn't he?" She spoke affectionately.

"He doesn't talk much" was all Sabina could say.

"He doesn't need to. Most people don't hear, anyway. They only hear and see what they want to. He is wise and conserves his energy. Not like me. I give my energy away, but it always returns to me." She threw her hands out wide and pulled them in as if to hug herself.

The motion shifted something in Sabina. Fabia reminded her of the Ducklings and she relaxed. Of course, none of her Ducklings were provocative, but maybe it was different where she was from.

"No. You got it wrong. I'm responding to your energy and aligning my energy to yours so you are more comfortable. I'm a chameleon like that." She got up and went back over to the wall. "I tried. You can go now. I thought we could be friends, but you are too closed-minded." She went back to hanging up her item.

Cheeks burning, Sabina felt bewildered by this person. Was she really closed-minded? That statement caused her to feel ashamed, as she knew what it was like for no one to understand her or allow her into their inner circle. She took a hard look at herself. She wasn't trying to get to know her. When she reflected on it, she was being judgmental.

"You are unpredictable—" she started to say when Fabia turned with a bright smile, cutting her off.

"Thank you."

Fabia stared at her. Sabina guessed her defenses were up because this was as calm as she had seen her. Sabina continued meekly. "And you act in ways I have never seen before. I'm uncomfortable, but I don't know why. You have-not-done-anything to me. Besides . . . *rubbing* against me, which was different."

"Yes, that was nice, wasn't it? Go ahead," Fabia encouraged.

There really wasn't anything more Sabina wanted to say, but then she doubted herself with Fabia's prompt to say more. Fabia was a Truth-sayer after all, and she seemed to be able to read her without any issues. *What else was there to say?*

Fabia dramatically sighed and sat back on the bed, causing Sabina's Birth Challenge attire to fall to the floor. Sabina's eyes followed it. She watched it hit the floor. She immediately took a step forward as if to catch it and then immediately stopped. That took her a step closer to Fabia, which she really didn't want. Fabia noticed the dilemma and smiled.

"What is this to you? Your energy says you don't care for it, but your body betrayed you and showed me you do care." Fabia looked at the fabric, almost petting it in admiration. This irritated Sabina who didn't want her touching it.

Inquisitively, she said, "This bothers you."

"No." Sabina crossed her arms, determined to relax her stance.

Fabia laughed. "This looks like something I should wear. Maybe it is a gift for me. After all, this is the room I'm staying in and it lay where I'd sleep."

That made Sabina move. She stomped up to Fabia and held out her hand. "That is the outfit **my** sister made for me. I'm wearing it in my Birth Challenge tomorrow, so if you don't mind . . . I'd like it back."

"Ohhhh, but I *do* mind," she purred, head down and looking up.

Sabina felt like ripping her outfit out of her hands but didn't dare as it might tear it. *Fine. I'll tear it and I'll rip it out of her claw nails. I didn't want to wear the stupid thing, anyway.*

"Oh yes. *Fight* me for it! I'd like that." She smiled mischievously.

You know what, she can have it. Why should I fight her for it? Taking a large step backward, not breaking eye contact, and feeling her cheeks heat in anger, she turned to walk out the room.

"Don't you want to play?" Fabia purred.

"**No. No** I DON'T," Sabina yelled. "I want you to get your hands off my garb and leave me alone."

"**T-h-e-r-e** is the truth. *FINALLY.* Now we can be friends." She stood up and did a slight bow. "I am Fabia of Morten, Truth-sayer, strong Influencer, insignificant Healer, and Queen of my life. Some might say I'm a *MISTRESS*." She emphasized the *s's* and shrugged as if they were harmless assumptions. "Others say what they want to be but few are my friend." As she said this, she handed Sabina her Birth Challenge outfit.

"Ahhhhh, what just happened?" Sabina asked, confused but taking the dress.

"To be my friend, you have to be willing to tell me the truth. Speak to me from your heart and not tell me lies or the sickly illusions you feed yourself."

Sabina felt too sheepish to be confronted with this truth. Of course, a Truth-sayer must get fed up listening to everyone's delusions.

"Yes, I knew you were a baby Queen, getting your feet under you. I'll be happy to slap you with the truth anytime. There is nothing like a good slapping. Wakes you UP!" she said, closing her eyes in pleasure.

Feeling out of place in the slipping familiarity of her sister's room, Sabina fumbled with what to say. "I'm Sabina Rockdin of . . ."

"Yes, yes, yes. I know who you are. I have known you since birth. Your life force is tied to my brother, after all. You are like a sister I have never known." She tilted her head and frowned. "I thought you'd be more powerful, though. You are a weak being. Why?" she demanded with her hands on her hips.

"I, I, don . . ."

"Brom suppressed her powers with a magical amulet." Flann strode into the room. He smiled in a way that lit up his face. He placed his hands on Fabia's shoulder and let the touch slide down to her hands, bringing her full attention to him.

"What do you have for ME?" She batted her eyes playfully. "You are sooo good at hiding it from me. I LOVE it."

Sabina watched them and felt like throwing up.

"You have a Gues**t**." He beamed.

"WHAT? WAIT, is it TEVIN?" She pushed Flann out of the way, squealing in delight, and running down the hallway.

"Who?" Sabina asked the empty room as Flann followed Fabia. *Who the tullom is Tevin?*

She followed them at a much slower pace until the house became eerily quiet. Then she stood and listened. Nothing. She went down the stairs more quickly and looked around at the empty house. No one was in the kitchen or gathering room. She glanced into her empty room and opened the door. No one and no sounds. She pinched her eyebrows together in confusion. *How could I be all alone? Where did they go?*

She walked out her front door, closing it behind her, and walked into the pathways. She looked up and down the path. She heard a sound behind her and turned quickly to see Flann standing on the porch.

"Where did you come from?" she said, annoyed.

"Nowhere," he said innocently.

"Oooookkkkkkaaaayyy. Where is Fabia then?"

"She is visiting a friend. She will be back later."

"It's **MY JOB** to watch out for my guests, Flann. They cannot just take off."

He stared at her, seemingly reading her body language before calmly saying, "And yet they all did, except me. I'm still here."

She tucked her hair behind her ears and gave up. "Whatever," she muttered. She was nobody's fool.

She hurried toward the tut and bustled around him as he didn't move for her. She quickly wiped down her feet before entering and ignored the feeling that he was watching her. She went straight into her room, tossing her garb on the dresser. Then she launched into a full argument in her head. Her hair was sticking to her as her anger brought heat and sweat to her face. She could hear the rocking chair creaking and she imagined Flann patiently waiting for her tantrum to be over. Well, it wasn't.

It had been a doozy of a day. Tullom; it had been two days of uncomfortable oddities that had left her drained. Starting with Flann showing up with his it-can't-be-helped attitude. She knew she was making all of this up and getting into self-pity. At the moment, she didn't care. She was alone in her room for the first time in the most bizarre day and a half. She had every right to fume and complain to herself. To the universe, she sassed in her head: *If I am where I am supposed to be and everything happens for my benefit, what am I supposed to learn from my best friend asking me the gender I'd like to date? Markus implying he would date me? The Prince insinuating that he would settle for me being his bed mate? A crazy Truth-sayer demanding I say what I really think? Finding out I share life forces with random men? And my Birth Challenge hours away when I feel disconnected to who I really am! What's the lesson, Infinite Spirit? Huh? That I'm broken? Reallll-llll great lesson.*

Feeling down and depressed, she quietly whispered to the universe. *I am like an orange and people are squeezing out the best part of me. All that is left is the peel and some dried-up pulp. There is nothing left of me. I don't know who I am or what I am supposed to be doing. Where did I go?*

She lay down on the bed and closed her eyes. Her mind quieted as her sulking leaked out of her body, leaving her feeling limp. Feeling her belly rise and fall with each breath, she could have sworn that she was as tired as if she had run from the Loaded

Hurricane to her tut. In that silence and peace, words surfaced for her.

You are not broken. You are finally being born and rising out of the ashes in order to walk the path that was yours. Put your energy toward remembering who you have always been. Acknowledge the cosmic super-being that you are.

HOW?

Overcome your fears. Walk through the darkness and discomfort, embracing the pain, to see the light.

~

Finally being born? The amulet? The AMULET. Curse that thing. She sat up with the realization. Hadn't she been asking herself earlier who she would have been if something wasn't blocking her from her feelings and gifts? *Well watch me now, world. I'm going to kick the doors down and show you who I am!*

Standing with her hands in a fist and her feet grounded, she felt more passion than she ever remembered but . . . *What do I stand for? Kick the door down for what? What am I showing people? That I am a martial arts expert? That I'm stronger than anyone thought? What is my purpose? . . . Didn't the Mistress say that we should find what brings us joy and give it all away? So I need to figure out what brings me joy?*

At that question, the vow she made to herself after leaving Nana Honey popped into her mind. She wanted to do something fun before she became an adult. She could start there, which meant she needed to find that tall Performer. Yes, she was decidedly determined that she needed to take action and do something.

Not knowing what time it was and determined to eat a meal before her silence, she walked outside and looked at the position of the sun. She felt Flann's eyes on her. She didn't turn to look at him. She didn't feel like seeing him, even if she couldn't avoid him.

"Are you hungry?" she asked in a monotone voice.

~

He waited for her to glance back. While she was in the tut, he had been sitting in the chair and his body was getting stiff from lack of movement. He had allowed himself to indulge in whatever thoughts and feelings came up for him as he thought about this 'crossroads'. His mind had been on her the whole time, minus all the interpretations from the council's Messenger complaining about the Prince. He was a piranha, and full of attitude. He bit hard and relentlessly. Flann was happy to say that Zoel was getting kicked out of Silvedome for the night, although he had permission to attend Sabina's Birth Challenge Ritual and was expected for his union interview immediately afterward. The council was anxious to meet their obligations to him and Brom so they could be free of him. *I bet she won't like hearing that her date with him is tomorrow. She didn't seem to like his attention. Cannot blame her there.*

The time apart had given him perspective on what he was resisting. He wanted her. He wanted her attention, the warmth of her body, her sassy attitude, and her wild heart. He wanted to consume her. When he thought about her or looked at her, he felt energy vibrate along his skin. Life now seemed dull without her.

~

Those green eyes squinting at her gave her the shivers. She tried to hide it, but she couldn't. She grabbed her elbow and felt electricity along her skin and her hair rise with static. Confusion set in as a different energy settled over her, quite different from the electric feeling Flann gave her. She could just sense that red ribbon of angry energy reaching out toward her, calling to her, making her gut clench. She turned her body to see him better and watched the ribbon slowly withdraw into him. Her eyes danced over Flann but as she focused on the ribbon. She was about to ask him a question when he finally spoke.

"Sure." He shrugged as he appeared to ignore a message from Brom.

With his boots already on, he started walking forward, preventing her from asking him about her father. She hustled to get her boots on, her nail scraping off some skin on the inside of her ankle. She winced at the minor pain, but took off in a jog up to him.

Before she could say anything, he spoke. His voice sounded full of regret. She'd expected something different.

"Nora will be here tomorrow. Nana Honey convinced the council that she was a family friend and therefore, she has permission to attend your Birth Challenge. She only gets to stay for the day but"—he rubbed at the back of his neck, looking down—"there's a possibility that she could stay."

"Oh," Sabina said quietly, thinking that must be what the conversation was about with her father. He must have told her father his feelings for Nora and Brom probably told him that he was dishonorable to go back on his word. *Yeah, that sounds like my father. No wonder he seems down.*

"After we eat, we need to pick up Viggo. The Prince has been escorted outside the dome. Don't worry, he has a little army to protect him. Viggo says thank you."

She smiled at the thought. "Why? I didn't do anything."

"This will be his first time living as a free man and not under the Prince's thumb."

She raised her eyebrows in shock. "But Fabia is not under his thumb and she is his sister."

He laughed. "NO ONE would be willing to try to tame Fabia. Besides, she can read your intentions through your energy, so nothing happens to her that she doesn't want to happen. She is like a coyote. She slips in and out of situations while tricking you into doing exactly what she wants. But that is NOT the same for Viggo. Because of his rare gift as a Healer, he is the property of the Morten kingdom and belongs to the Prince."

Distracted by the conversation and completely intrigued, she asked, "Fabia said something at the Ceremony yesterday that they would be free of the Prince though."

He looked over at her, licking his dry lips. Sabina realized he didn't have his canteen. "You caught that? You are right. Viggo is Brom's godson. Viggo's dad and Brom were childhood best friends, which is why Viggo was given your life force."

"So . . . I'm the reason he is in bondage. My life force caused him to develop the rare talent," she said, her voice pinched.

"No, it's Brom's fault if anyone's, but no one could have predicted this was going to happen." He shook his head in disbelief. "Brom is a tullom of a strategist and had foreseen a way to help Viggo get out of bondage with your union interviews."

She looked at the dirt on her boots. "I don't understand." She tucked her hair behind her ear as their arms bumped into each other and another shiver of energy ran across her body. She barely moved her head to look over at him, wishing she was shorter so she could see his face as he looked down.

"Your father should have told you all of this. It really isn't my place to tell your father's stories."

Agitated, she sassed back. "No, it's just your place to show up in my life and turn me all around, telling me that the world I've always known has been an illusion. Did I get it right?"

⁓

He hid a smile. He loved that sassy temper. He probably should have been irritated, but it only made him want to pull her into his arms for a dance, a square-off of wills, and battle each other out in a tango.

Smirking, he responded. "I like it when you look for my approval."

"I AM NOT LOOKING FOR YOUR APPROVAL."

⁓'

She felt the angry tentacles reaching for her and she stopped short. Flann ignored her and kept walking. The ribbon shot back into him and Sabina stood looking questioningly at Flann. *What is that red ribbon? It looks like bloody-colored smoke.*

"Your father isn't my favorite person right now. I used to look up to him and have great respect for him." He squeezed his hands into fists. "Now, I am struggling to see his perspective as anything but controlling."

Walking fast to keep up with Flann's sudden, larger steps, she said, "My father is a **good** man."

"IS HE?" He turned to her. His left hand was inches from her hip, his green eyes fierce, eyebrows pinched, and his jaw clenched.

Flann thought it was ridiculous that she was idolizing a man that stole her freedom, but she didn't even question his actions. Why didn't Brom see her strength? She could have handled the truth. She was handling it now. Instead, he ran away like a coward and left him to break her heart and shatter her dreams, not that she had any.

"Does a *'GOOD'* man prevent you from thinking for yourself and discovering who you are? Does a **good** man leave his daughter hidden away like some buried treasure that isn't meant for anyone else but him?"

"I DON'T know what you are talking about." She yelled back at him.

They stood inches away from each other, Sabina's hair lifting in the light breeze, making her look angelic. Flann's hands were on his hips and he was straining to pull his emotions back in when Brom tried calling again.

Sabina gasped at the immediate circling of the red angry ribbon. It stole her breath and then she was yanked back into the present. Flann looked up from the dirt, his eyes full of sorrow, and his voice scratchy. "Your father never accepted your destiny, and in my opinion, that shows me he never accepted you for who you are."

"He was *concerned* for me. He did what he thought was best for me out of love."

"You mean out of fear?" Flann shot back, not backing down.

Ye, y, yes," she said, looking to the side. A lump in her throat restricted her ability to speak. Her eyes burned, but her emotions were already going in lockdown. Quietly, she said, "It's hard to let go of the picture of him being perfect. I don't want to see him as a man who makes mistakes, but I know he *loves* me."

Flann wanted to reach out and tuck her hair behind her ear as it had already fallen forward. Guilt was hitting him. He didn't want her to feel this way. He should not have pushed so hard for her to see his perspective. Plus, he felt anxious about Nora coming tomorrow when his feelings were so raw and intense about Sabina. He knew Nora would see right through him. And he still didn't know if what he felt for Sabina was a side effect from their bond or if any of it was real.

With gaining conviction in her voice, Sabina added, "He went to GREAT lengths to keep me safe. I HAVE to believe that he knew this day would come when I would be free to choose my path and he gave me the ability to be invincible. He trained me in every form of martial arts so that I would be able to protect myself. He sent me you," she said, looking at him, her light red eyes certain, "to stand by my side as a friend, not an authority figure."

Tullom, he was no better than Brom. "I'm sorry. Of course he loves you. I didn't mean to imply he doesn't. I don't know what I mean. I don't want to talk about him, okay?"

She looked back to him and nodded. They stood staring at each other wordlessly until Sabina finally said, "Before we stop talking about him, why does he keep calling?"

"How do you know he is calling?"

"I, I can feel him," she sheepishly said.

"He probably wants to talk about the Prince. I'll talk to him later. He can wait. You know, I'm not that hungry anymore. Where is the temple? I want to pray and clear my head."

Sabina responded. "Wwwweeee don't have temples. God is everywhere. In Silvedome, we believe that God, or Divine Mind, or Universe, whatever you call it, is within us."

"Where do you go to worship then?" he asked, perplexed.

"You can worship from anywhere. You don't need a special place because source is within you."

"Don't you have priests, pastors, ministers, monks, anything?"

"Noooo," she responded. "Like I said, YOU have a direct connection with the creator. Why would you need a pastor or whatever you call them?"

"BECAUSE they REMIND you of God's word," he said defensively.

"What you are telling me is you need SOMEONE else's interpretation of God's word in order to worship?" she sassed. "That doesn't make any sense. The Infinite Spirit speaks to each of us, not a few chosen ones. I mean, how are you to live a life that serves the universe if you are borrowing other people's interpretation?"

"You don't get it. It's not your way, but can you respect that it is MY way?"

"I don't understand. I'm curious. Do you believe everyone is responsible for their own relationship with the creator and if so, why do you put so much trust in the words of another being who is learning their lessons like you? You know, since we are all here to accomplish something that serves the universe."

"We all learn from each other, okay! Pastors devote their life toward living a righteous life and they are like role models that mentor us."

"Okay, sure. But if you ask me, my opinion is you still have to put in the work and have the relationship because he speaks divinely to you in a way that only you can hear and understand."

He looked at her. Maybe she had a point, but so did he. He was willing to leave it at that. Or at least he thought he was.

"What if you don't understand what God's will is for you?"

"It is simple. You talk to the Infinite Spirit and you tell the universe what your heart's desire is and if it is meant to be, it will be. For instance: Infinite Spirit, there is a person who has come into my life that really annoys me and everywhere I go, he is there. I'd really love it if you saw to it that we didn't spend time with each other, but if that is not your will, I will accept that I must spend time with him. Thank you for always providing for my highest good and ultimate healing."

He looked at her, unamused, and said in a dry voice, "Is that about me?"

Her smile lit up her face, but she caved in. "You could talk to the Master who teaches about ancient wisdom. He could be a mentor. I'll walk you over there after I eat. Remember, I'm supposed to stay with you. You are my responsibility," she said, amused.

He really wanted to be alone and as luck would have it, Pretty-Boy Performer was in the village square with Master Clingy Locks. He hated to ask Pretty Boy for his help but he would be doing him a favor by the looks of Locks's claws wrapping around him. That poor man looked suffocated. *But how do I convince Sabina to stay with Pretty Boy so I can find . . . Who am I finding?*

~

Sabina noticed Master Tulk as well and her heart started beating furiously at the realization she was going to be bold and ask him for a kiss. She could do it. Everyone else did it. She had nothing to fear, or at least this is the mantra she started to repeat in her head. Her mouth had gone dry and she couldn't speak. She didn't know how she should approach him. She would have to ask to speak to him privately.

"Ah, do you mind if I talk to Master Tulk for a minute? I have a question I wanted to ask him about—" In her head, she added: *performing a kiss on me*. "Well, I should really apologize for not seeing his show and ask him how it went. That is the polite thing to do. Would you grab us a seat while I talk to him?" *Please don't follow me. Please don't follow me. Please don't follow me.*

"Wait. Is one of those robed people the Master who teaches . . . ancient wisdom?" Flann pointed at the crowd of robed Masters standing in a long line near the river. "What are they *doing*?"

Sabina looked where he was pointing; she hadn't even noticed the Masters. Relieved at her good fortune, her shoulders relaxed. "Yes. Master Walkin is the one with short, dark hair, third on the left. And they are blessing the water. It looks like someone tried to poison it again." She shook her head. "When will the fools figure out that even the water under the dome is protected?"

"What?" he said, alarmed.

"Don't worry. It happens all the time when our kingdom is under attack. They cannot get in so they try to poison the water to break our defenses."

He looked at her, shocked.

"The water is *fine*. It never works. I cannot explain it but a bunch of Masters line the river all along the dome and they pull on energy from above and below to purify the water."

"Your water is violated regularly, and that is no cause for concern? You do know that you cannot live without water?"

She shook her head, bemused.

"How often is the dome attacked?"

She shrugged. "Frequently. More now that the Selectors are confident the Agni is here." Her smile dropped as several images flooded her mind: Markus, or Wolverine, needed at the front line;

men in hospital getting healed; and her father's note expressing his fear that it was she the Selectors were looking for and killing for. Suddenly, she wanted the security of the amulet and went to grab the missing necklace.

~

Noticing her movement and the sudden change in her disposition, Flann put his hand on her shoulder. "You-are-safe. Like you said, your father put a ton of effort into keeping you safe. For instance, Master Tulk is not only a Master Performer but he can shapeshift," he said, whispering.

Flann knew he should not speak someone else's truth. He had no right to, but desperate times call for desperate measures. He had Brom constantly calling his mind; so much so that he had to turn off that awareness, which left him unbalanced and disoriented. He had to find out what was going on with all these attacks on the dome and how much it would affect them in tomorrow's Birth Challenge, and he wanted to get some type of resolution about his emotions with Nora coming into town. He accepted this meant he would owe Benford Tulk something he was probably unwilling to give, but it was done.

~

Sabina's toes started tingling at this information. Shapeshifting was either an extinct gift or super rare. There was very little information on shapeshifters and she had always been fascinated by them. Her heart felt like it was about to explode with joy. She had always wanted to see how someone shapeshifted—and to think that she was bonded to him! Didn't that imply he wouldn't mind showing her? Then the thought occurred to her that this might not be his true form. *No wonder he is so gorgeous. He can change his features to anything. Heaven Above! That is SOOO COOL!*

Like a child, Sabina started to hustle over to him, her one-track mind short-lived when reality caught up with her. She stopped and faced Flann. "Whoops," she said, her face bright red. "If you have not noticed, I'm going to talk to Master Tulk for a moment. Will you be alright talking with Master Walkin?" She managed to sound calm and collected but she was anything but.

~

Flann was smiling on the inside but composed on the outside. This is exactly what he wanted—privacy—which meant Sabina needed to be distracted. "Go. But keep what I said to yourself or it will be my life at risk. I'll meet up with you after I talk to your teacher."

~

Sabina didn't wait for him to complete his last sentence; she was already headed in that direction, using her hand to wave at Flann to show she understood. She weaved through, past the round table and chairs, and slowed herself down, noticing she was drawing attention to herself. She took a calming breath, and then took intentional steps at a casual pace, stopping to look at a plant along the way to hear the conversation between Master Lockin and Master Tulk.

Master Lockin was clearly upset, and that gave Sabina enough sense not to barge in on their conversation. She had intended to politely interrupt and talk to him in private. Now she felt like she should sit down and wait this out as she heard Master Lockin's grievances.

"I DON'T understand. Everything was going perfectly. WHY WOULD YOU GO BEHIND MY BACK"—she looked around, seeming to pull in self-control, and continued more quietly— "and see the council?"

Looking immovable, Master Tulk stood tall with his hands held behind his back. A clear sign that indicated he did not want

294

to be touched. He was offering nothing. His voice remained patient but firm. "I have explained my reasons to you and hearing it a third time isn't going to change anything. I apologize that this is not what you want to hear."

"But," Master Lockin whined. "We were so *good* together. Didn't we have a lot of fun together? We made the perfect couple."

"We were never a couple. I WAS a guest in your home."

"What are people going to say? How will we work together now?" she said, flopping into a chair and letting her head rest on her fist.

Remaining where he was, Master Tulk continued with his same tone. "I would like to continue to work with you in the performing arts as a PROFESSIONAL but will not tolerate any further touching outside of that."

"Tuk-Tuk, I know you are moving out but we can still date. We both enjoy doing a lot of the same hobbies. It doesn't make sense to give up on a good thing—"

"We were never dating," he clarified.

"HOW CAN YOU SAY THAT? WHY WOULD YOU DENY THE TRUTH?" Master Lockin said with her hands spread wide on the table, clearly insulted.

"Let me ask you a question?"

She seemed taken aback and she blinked a few times.

"Were we intimate?"

"No, but that comes later. We were growing into that," she said defensively.

"Did I ask you to date?"

"You didn't have to. It was clear you wanted to." She folded her arms in defense.

Tulk looked exhausted with this conversation. He continued. "Master Lockin, you did me a great honor by welcoming me into your home but as I mentioned before, I am ONLY interested in dating men. I had hoped that we could be friends but I'm sorry to say that I cannot be friends with someone who doesn't respect me."

He turned to walk toward The Mox when Master Lockin took two running steps up to him and attempted to wrap her arm through his.

He stopped. "What are you doing?"

"I can respect you liking men but why not date me too?" she said, trying to cling on to him.

Sabina watched in fascination, taking a few steps closer to hear more. She couldn't believe she had almost asked him to kiss her. "Starlight, thank you for saving me from embarrassment," she whispered. She comforted herself by justifying that she was never going to ask him to kiss her after she found out he was a shapeshifter. That would be too weird, not knowing who she was really kissing.

Forced to stay where she was when Master Lockin took after Master Tulk, she stopped, undecided about what to do. She had nothing to look at that would explain why she was standing in the middle of the tables. She didn't know what to do. She didn't want to be a part of their conversation and she needed him to stay in the food court in order to talk with him. She bit her lip and watched Master Lockin try to pull him back to her. She was surprised by what she saw and it gave her the motivation and courage she needed to take charge.

Master Tulk's face softened as he looked down at Master Lockin. His voice was full of compassion when he said, "Master Lockin, you deserve someone who *loves* you, not tolerates you." He rubbed her jaw bone as he said it and looked into her eyes. Master Lockin dropped her arms to her side; a defeated look came across her face. Before she could say anything, Sabina took her chance.

"Master Tulk, Master Tulk," she said, calling his attention. She started to walk toward them once she caught his awareness. "May I speak to you?"

Master Tulk looked down at Master Lockin who appeared to

be in shock. He dropped his hand from her chin, and said, "Excuse me." Then he headed toward Sabina.

His demeanor had changed, from compassion, to happiness, to curiosity, to concern. He looked like he had a question for her. "Sabina Rockdin." He flashed a smile. "By yourself this morning?"

Now she was in front of him, her mind went blank. She didn't know what to say. It seemed silly to ask someone to divulge their biggest secret to someone they barely knew. Then she realized he had asked a question. *What does he mean? I'm always by myself. Oh, Flann. He has only seen me with Flann.*

"Oh, Flann is talking with the Masters over by the river."

Master Tulk looked over to Flann and frowned.

"I am sorry for missing your performance. I started to feel unwell and stayed in for the night. I'd love to catch your next one but I have my Birth Challenge tomorrow morning. How long do you plan to stay?"

"It just so happens that I became a citizen of Silvedome this morning. We completed the ritual about ten minutes ago. I'm waiting to hear what tut I will be assigned as we speak." A light smile touched his face.

Shocked, Sabina flicked her eyes to Master Lockin who still stood steps away; she was looking down and inching her way back to The Mox.

He glanced back and then looked at Sabina. "She is taking the news a bit rough but to answer your question, you will be able to see my performance at your convenience." They stood in silence for a moment but then Master Tulk continued. "Are you nervous about tomorrow?"

She had been nervous . . . before her world erupted with chaos. Yes, she had been terrified of this day for far too long but the last two days had left her numb and with little time to reflect on it. Seeming to take her silence as an indication that she was nervous, Master Tulk offered, "I know what I did today was nothing compared to what you will experience tomorrow . . ." He looked down shyly. "Well, I should not say."

"What?" she immediately asked, observing his healthy state. She had known lots of outsiders who became citizens and their experiences were more startling due to lack of mind, body, and spirit preparation that all Silvedome were mandated to follow.

"Well, it was intensely pleasurable. This warm light running up and down your body with energy roaming over you like a feather delicately touching the skin. Then there is this mind-blowing self-realization that comes from it. I never felt more alive."

"Huh, that's odd. Most outsiders either don't feel anything because they don't have any Moowin or what they feel makes them sick with raging headaches, nausea, vomiting, muscle aches, and a temperature in direct proportion to the strength of their Moowin."

He was looking at her now with a relaxed stance and his arms hanging by his side. "To be honest, I did prepare in my own way. I fasted, meditated, and did visualization."

"Visualization? What is that?" She liked that she didn't have to look down to talk to him and he was so easy to talk to. He had a presence about him that made her feel like she had known him her whole life.

He smiled. "I cannot believe you never heard of visualization. Are you joking with me?"

"No, please go on. Anything to help me with tomorrow would be great."

He tilted his head, apparently judging whether she was serious, and then launched into the subject in great detail. She learned he performed visualization exercises before every performance—he did this before anything he wanted to feel prepared for—as a way of telling his mind what he wanted to happen. Sabina loved the idea that you could imagine how you wanted things to go and that most often, they played out the way you imagined. It seemed too easy, too good to be true but despite those beliefs, she planned to try it during her preparation time.

Losing all track of time and enjoying her conversation with Master Tulk, she was surprised when Flann came up, stating that they needed to go get Viggo. She realized she had probably spent forty-five minutes talking at ease and smiling. Smiling.

"I need to return to The Mox too. I didn't realize the time. I'll see you around, Sabina." He grabbed her hand and held it in both of his before facing Flann with an expressionless look. "I suppose I will see you too."

Flann folded his arms and responded flatly. "You know you will."

They stared for a few seconds before Master Tulk stepped away.

Distracted by the two men's odd behavior around each other, Sabina realized she hadn't said goodbye to Master Tulk. She decided to be bold. "I'll see you another day for lunch, Master Tulk." She smiled to herself, proud of her forwardness in asking for what she wanted.

Master Tulk turned and walked backward. "Call me Bard. It's my Silvedome name." He turned forward and continued walking away.

"I wonder why he chose Bard? That is a profession not an element of nature."

Flann snorted. "Because he thinks he can sing."

Walking over to the grab bag station and nodding to the Messenger as she took her bag, Sabina burst out with her question without the delicacy she had intended. "Do you *know* him, because you pretended you didn't yesterday but it REALLY seems like you two have history?"

Deciding it was pointless to keep pretending, Flann answered truthfully. "Yes, I know him. He trained with your father the year before me but before he went off on his own, we had some overlap where your father was training us together. He tried to play big brother to me but it came across as a know-it-all. I was not stupid or incompetent; I was just coming into my powers. He'd had his powers for a while and had a year of training over me."

"That does not explain his reservation toward you."

Flann did a one-shoulder shrug. "He wanted to be the bodyguard. He had a lot of good reasons for it too. I agreed with him actually, but I was the only one who could handle the life force exchange."

"What were some of the reasons?" she asked, taking a bite of a sandwich.

"For one thing, he is likable. A team player, as you say. He knows how to get along with everyone. I actually tried to act like him yesterday. It was exhausting."

That made Sabina smile. "And????"

"He can shapeshift into anyone or any animal; he can play any role believably; he has strong Protector skills; and he likes you."

"He likes me? He doesn't know me."

"We all know you. We have your life force in us so we feel some type of connection to you. Don't you feel that?"

"I don't know. Maybe. More so with him. I feel like I've known him my whole life but I don't feel that way with you."

"I don't let people know me. I'm standoffish, but maybe 'BARD' has something right. When I acted like him yesterday, people were eager to make me happy. I could get used to that. I should rethink that. I could build up my stamina for playing nice."

"Okay, what does that have to do with anything? You are saying that your personality trumps a genetic condition?"

"Energy does. That's physics for you. My energy repels people, even you."

She ignored him. "What about Fabia? You like her."

"I do. She is cool. I like Viggo too."

"Where is Fabia anyway? I'll probably get in trouble with the council when we pick up Viggo and someone sees that Fabia isn't with us."

He sighed. "WHY do you ask SOOOO MANY QUESTIONS? Can you not accept anything for what it is?" he said, irritated.

She bristled. "I can ask as many questions as I want. WHY DO YOU RESIST ANSWERING MY QUESTIONS?"

"Touché," he said after a moment's silence. Softly, he said it again.

The sun was indicating the noon hour. The time when silence would fall upon Sabina was almost here. "So, where is Fabia? I think I have a right to know. I AM responsible for her," she pressed, looking at the sun.

He shook his hand and was quiet for a long time, looking at the sun too, wondering how much time he had left before there would be the welcome relief of silence. "You think you are living this straightforward life and that things are what they seem. You believe the system you are in and you don't question it because it is all you know. You think it is normal. You think this is the way it is supposed to be even as you resist it. But then the course of your life changes forever by one small decision. A decision you didn't even make. A decision that's consequences didn't come into play until years later." A gust of wind blew through his hair and he squinted, looking around.

"Then that consequence, which was hidden asleep within you, waiting for the perfect timing, awakens. You are suddenly a different person, living a different life. *Everything* is the same and everything is different at the same time because you are living from a different perspective. Your point of view changes dramatically from a slave who looks down to a free man who has the power of a Moowin. I have so much personal power now that no one can take away from me or deny me. I mean, without this shift in perspective, I would have never hoped for this possibility." He snorted. "I didn't know *to think* it was possible, which is the whole point I'm making. *But, was it worth everything you sacri-*

ficed to get here? You get to the destination you clung to and thought would bring you everything you wanted, only to ask yourself: *Is it what you really wanted?*"

He looked at her and saw her confusion.

"What do you mean? How could you not want your freedom? Are you saying you want to take it all back?" She watched him rub his thumb against his other finger as he spoke. He wasn't answering her question, which annoyed her at first, but then she really listened. Whether or not he knew it, he was sharing a key to understanding him. She listened with a deep feeling of wanting to know more.

"Before this life I am living now, all I hoped for was to earn my freedom, have a good paying job, and marry a woman who adored me. Maybe have some kids and a nice home. Travel somewhere exciting. Have good health. Simple things, ordinary things. But when I wanted those things, they were all out of reach. I wasn't content with being a slave. I wanted more." He let out a long breath. "But it's all the same scarcity I had before, dressed in a pretty package. I'm still a slave," he said matter-of-factly. Taking a deep breath, he explained more. "Instead of being a slave with no rights, I'm a slave to this job and I still want things out of reach. It's like I'm always chasing. I'm always hungry for more but never satisfied. It's like I said,"—he shrugged—"the only difference is I have more awareness and a finer cage now . . . Don't listen to me. I'm annoyed that my life turned out to be a polished turd, that's all," he said.

"WHAT?" she barked out. "If it is a polished turd, it's because you are choosing to view it as a polished turd."

"Hey now, before you judge me, don't you feel the same? Two days ago, you had a life you wanted to improve, but it was comfortable in the sense that you knew what to expect. You knew what would make it better. You probably had a plan for how to make it better too. Then, your world changed faster than you could keep up with and you look back at your old life. What made you happy then ... doesn't satisfy you today, right? The way you are going to contribute to the village is different, your friends have . . . expanded, your routines are different, but are you happy with this new lifestyle?"

"That is not a fair question. I haven't even lived it. I'm only aware that everything is changing but I'm *grateful* to have the truth."

"I'm not saying I'm not grateful. There is so much I wouldn't change about this life. Having my freedom, traveling the world, making friends, having money but . . . I am on a path that is unfolding before me where I feel like I have little say in what is happening to me. This world is beyond what I am comfortable with discovering, at times. That's not the point," he said quickly as if he didn't want to have that discussion. "The point is, some external circumstances used to control me, and now some internal forces are. You know what, I don't know what I'm saying. Forget about it."

Sabina could feel his mood and it felt like sandpaper, rough and ready to peel off her smooth skin. So she remained silent. Whatever he was experiencing was not her responsibility to fix. She busied her mind with thoughts of Bard and how genuine he was. She was telling herself a story that, out of all the life force partners, she liked him best, when Flann interrupted the silence.

"You know the saying of old: Ignorance is bliss?"

"YEEEAAAAHHHH."

"There is another saying. Knowledge is power." He looked at her for confirmation she was aware of that saying as well. "Which would you want, bliss or power?"

"I don't know. Why do you have to choose? Can't I have bliss in power?"

Flann snorted.

"Are you okay? What did Master Walkin say to you?" she asked in concern.

He kicked a rock as they walked. "That I am attached to the past and I cannot live from the past to make decisions based on today. He spouted nonsense about how I cannot fit into the skin of someone I have outgrown. Basically, I am not the same person and as such, I cannot force myself to keep the same agreements from a past life I was living."

"Is this about N—" Air sucked out of her throat, disabling her speech and her words fell silent despite her lips moving. Noon was upon her. She was in preparation and an energy swept over her filling her with heightened senses. The sun was too bright, the wind too loud, her stomach too full, and the smell of the dirt too potent. They had stopped walking and her hand had stopped mid-motion as it reached for the door to the bases of the warriors' offices.

Curd, she felt like she was having an out-of-body experience while being in her body. Tears stung her eyes from the pain she saw in his face with the vulnerability he'd shared. She longed to comfort someone who didn't want comfort and yet she was in no place to comfort anyone. She felt a moment of paralysis from the overstimulation of her heightened senses and couldn't make out anything he was saying.

In The Silence

Flann, at that moment, hated how insightful Sabina was. He cursed himself. It wasn't safe to talk around her. It was like she could make connections between apples and boards when no one else saw any connection. He was about to deny that his conversation had anything to do with Nora but stopped short when he finally noticed Sabina wasn't moving.

He raised his eyebrow. Her muscles looked rigid and he couldn't tell if her chest was moving. Was this her silence? Would she be frozen like that all day? How was he going to get her home?

"Sa-bin-a," he said slowly.

"Brother, she is fine," said a warrior coming from across the field, laughing at Flann.

Flann looked at the person speaking and felt judged. How was he supposed to know? *I'm not from here.* The warrior jogged up and by the time he did, Sabina relaxed.

"See. That first minute can be intense. You shouldn't be here though for two reasons," he said, coming to a stop in front of them and not bothering with niceties. "One, the obvious is that *you* are in preparation for your Birth Challenge and the other, the dome has been under a lot of external pressure lately. Which makes me ask: What are you doing here?"

"Are you in charge?" Flann asked with annoyance. The young man had free-flowing, long black hair and a toned body. But Flann observed he wore nothing on him to indicate that he was a decorated or official leader.

"You could say that." He folded his arms across his chest as if he sensed Flann's disbelief. "And why are you here?"

Sabina wanted to speak, tried to speak, but her throat tickled at the very thought of trying. She didn't recognize the warrior, and she didn't need to. All she wanted was to get out of the bright, burning sun. She couldn't wait for Flann and this warrior to put away their egos. She grabbed the door and felt her whole hand explode with hundreds of static shocks. She drew her hand back to her chest.

"Whoa, you cannot go around touching things in your silence. You need to go sit in silence, by yourself, immediately. Everything you touch that doesn't contribute to your highest good's alignment is going to cause that pain. Trust me. I was terrified to go to the bathroom when I had that experience doing something I wasn't supposed to. But it is safe to go to the bathroom."

The warrior, not wasting any more time, entered the building. He left them behind, most likely expecting them to leave. Sabina stood, panting, holding her hand. She heard Flann curse and follow the warrior. Too scared to move, Sabina stood still. She never wanted to experience that pain again.

Flann opened the closing door and felt his arm scrape on the rough metal as he brushed against the doorframe. The warrior whirled, his hair swinging with the movement. He was clearly in a hurry as he made a good distance down the hallway before Flann was through the door.

"State your purpose, brother. I don't know you and I've made it clear you should not be here."

It was weird that the man managed to come across as friendly and intimidating at the same time. Like he was prepared to launch into a fight at a moment's notice, but confident enough in his skill that he didn't have to flaunt it. Flann could respect that.

"I'm looking for Sabina Rockdin's guest, Viggo. He is a Healer. We were told to come here."

"No, you weren't. You are in the wrong place. All guests are brought to the Ceremony. You know where that is as I can see you are not a local. Move on out, brother." He walked away.

Flann scratched his head. He was told to come here. He had some sense that Viggo was here just from the batch of interrupted calls that Brom kept putting through. Flann tried again. "Ah, your . . . team escorted the Prince out of Silvedome, but not Viggo?"

The warrior turned slower this time with a large smile on his face and his arms open like he was accepting a hug. "That fellow. My friend, you are in the right place, but we need him. He has offered to stay here and assist our warriors."

"Right . . . I'm confused. The council instructed me to get him. He is still under guest policy and must remain with Sabina."

The warrior started to walk toward him. "You are correct. You are Tan, right?"

Correcting the warrior, Flann said, "Flann."

"You are the new citizen of Silvedome who has some Protector skills, correct?"

"Whatever skills I have, I'm serving as a Messenger," Flann said like he was warding off evil. "I'd like to speak with Viggo."

"Huh, that is too bad. We could use every citizen we have with Protector and Healing skills right now. If you were to help out, you'd be able to talk to your friend."

Warning bells went off in Flann's mind. He quickly opened his channel to Brom, who had repeatedly called him. He preferred to speak out loud when communicating as it was easier for him, but he wasn't about to share this conversation with the man before him.

Brom's voice was loud, frustrated, and urgent. He shouted through the link. "We are in crisis-mode, Flann. Why did you reject my calls?"

Feeling calm despite Brom's tone, Flann responded. "I figured you were contacting me about the Prince and about the fighting at the dome wall."

"Tullom. Yes. Okay, I need to figure out how to get the Prince back in for tomorrow. Everyone is here and in place but the Selectors recognized the large energy source coming from Silvedome. More groups are showing up. It's a slaughter fest out here. I've never seen anything like this. Groups killing groups. Each group has claimed a spot along the dome, spreading our warriors thin across such a large area. Our warriors have initiated the ultimate defense strategy and are hacking as many thumbs and big toes off as possible to discourage fighting. I need that amulet back on Sabina. How is she, anyway?"

"Deathly sick when you put the amulet on her, like it is eating her soul away, but otherwise great. Her silence has started. And the Prince gets entrance for the Birth Challenge tomorrow, but nothing more."

"Okay. I hadn't heard that. We need to be prepared for tomorrow. Meet me at the Loaded Hurricane before sunrise. The amulet is a problem. I was counting on that. Don't leave Sabina and keep the line of communication open."

Brom hung up without giving Flann a chance to ask his question. Reconnecting to Brom, Flann noticed the warrior standing idly by, watching with curiosity, but not interrupting. Good.

"Starlight, what is it?" Brom huffed, out of breath.

Keeping it short and to the point, Flann blurted out, "Your warriors have Viggo. They said he volunteered to help heal. Can I trust them? Do I need to find him?"

Worry strained Brom's voice. "No. I don't think so." He

huffed as if he put something heavy down. "They need him. They need as much help as possible. More groups keep showing up. My only concern is they will exhaust him and we need him for tomorrow. Can you see what you can do about that?"

Then Brom was gone. Flann put in place his pleasant smile as he lifted his head and apologized.

"I'm sorry about that. Brom was calling to check on Sabina and her silence. Now, we were talking about Viggo helping you out. When do we need to come back for him?"

"No need. We will walk him back. I know Brom's place."

Tension gathered in Flann's shoulders and he rolled them slack. "When can we expect him? We have an important day tomorrow with Sabina's Birth Challenge, and I would hate for him to be too exhausted to attend."

Cracking his knuckles as his arms rested by his side, the warrior perched his lips. "We will respect that and escort him back in a timely manner. If you will excuse me, I was about to do something before our paths crossed, but please do return if you change your mind and wish to help us. Safety of our people requires the skills of a Protector, no matter the strength of the talent."

Flann ground his teeth. It would do no good to say any more so he pushed his way through the door and returned to Sabina's side. She looked pale and her eyes were squinting. A gust of wind ripped through the back of the dome. Even though they were a good distance from the wall, Flann felt the energy and strength of it as his short, curly locks frizzed in the wind. The wind made him smile, bringing with it a childhood memory of playing in storms with his sister. He looked at Sabina to share that smile, but his smile was replaced by curiosity as he noticed that her long hair didn't stir in the wind.

~

Feeling small pangs as debris and sand hit her skin, Sabina was ready to go home. She saw Flann's smile, and it only made her want to leave more. At least she didn't have to feel guilty, she thought, as she started walking home, wondering where Viggo was. Not that she could ask.

~

Flann followed, looking back at the dome, wondering about the surge in the wind. He didn't know if it was the Mistress named Fog who was responsible, or if it was someone else who possessed influence over the air element that was causing these changes. Either way, he thought that was a cool talent to have.

Having decided he would participate in the silence with Sabina, Flann debated whether he should say anything about the dome being under attack, or explain where Viggo was, BEFORE he started his silence. He had already spoken to the warrior, so what was the harm in updating her? But he felt like no matter what answer he gave, it was a justification. Besides, Sabina was walking with purpose and her actions clearly communicated that she wanted to be alone. He remained silent and did his best to keep up with her hurried pace.

When they were back at the tut, Sabina pulled her boots off and let them fall to the ground. She stopped and looked at the door questioningly before Flann caught on. He was cautious not to touch her, but he opened the door for her. She walked in and went straight to her room while he closed the door.

He stood looking at the empty room, wishing he had his hat in his hand to fidget with. Everything was quiet, so quiet he could hear the dirt blow onto the porch. Flann didn't know what to do now. He was accustomed to being alone in silence, but he was always *doing* in the silence. He was training, cleaning the horse stalls, checking the ledgers, or pulling plants from the garden. He didn't have anything to do here. He decided to sit on the porch in the rocking chair.

~

Sabina pulled her window and door drapes closed to block out as much light as possible. She was relieved she was able to touch these items without pain. After the electrifying shock of the door, she was cautious about touching anything. Gingerly, she sat on the bed, shooting all the way back once she felt safe. She rested her head on the wall and closed her eyes.

She had heard the conversation at the warriors' offices. Though her ears were ringing from the shock of the pain, she had still managed to sense the angry red and black distorted smoke that crept around her force shield. She held her breath and clenched her muscles in anticipation of pain as the smoke touched the shield. Nothing happened. The smoke could not penetrate it and it darted around furiously, seeking her. Her force field was wrapped in ribbon and without the fear of pain or attachment to the ribbon, she was able to examine it.

She had wanted to lean in to examine it closer, but as she leaned, the force field followed so that distance remained the same. Still, she was able to feel it, like it was saying something to her. The harder she tried to hear, the less she heard. She relaxed and closed her eyes. When she did, she experienced a sensation like being turned on. Her body felt warm and tingly, like her nerves were dancing. She felt rich and powerful. And it was intoxicating. Then she opened her eyes and those pleasant sensations fled her body, entangled in an angry energy. It was baffling.

She had been about to close her eyes again when the red ribbon was pulled back toward Flann, then it started to drift to her, then it was pulled back, not to return. Flann finished his conversation and Sabina knew everything she needed to know. People were dying and Viggo was needed. Flann was needed, but he wasn't going to leave her. He wasn't going to help her people.

Although she had read and comprehended her father's words in his letter, she couldn't believe them. Therefore, it wasn't real except that, as time passed, the fear crept in that it was real. How was it possible she was the victim they were searching for—the Agni? She felt like a storm of misfortune, with a past of wishing to belong, and a future of wishing to be hidden. Whatever she was, the overheard conversation made it viscerally clear that her energy brought death and destruction when she wanted to be someone who brought love and light to the world.

Sabina sat on her bed in silence, feeling like a caged animal. Her thoughts were insistent and judgmental. The judgments were a deeper, isolating pain that made being electrocuted the preferred option. She didn't want to sit with herself in silence. She wanted to run away and disappear. She wanted to bury herself in work, beat her mannequin in the Loaded Hurricane, climb a tower and free fall, or cut her hair off and scream until she lost her voice. She wanted to do anything but sit with her feelings of being responsible for the death of her people. What would happen if the Selectors got her, weighed just as heavily as the fear of if the Selectors didn't find her.

An unknown amount of time passed and Sabina thought and thought. She analyzed and asked hundreds of unanswerable questions. *How is this possible? Where could I escape to? What is going to happen tomorrow when I go through my Birth Challenge? Who knows my secret? Would the amulet work to keep me safe? Would it be better if I ended my life so my energy could not be used to hurt people? What are they going to make me do if I'm taken? Will I ever see Crystal again? What happens to all the people bonded to me if I die?*

The questions flowed and the knots and tension in Sabina's body mounted until she forced herself to think of something else. There weren't a lot of options, though. Sit alone in silence in the bedroom or another room. But she remembered her father's letter and pulled it from her drawer.

Biny, I know I was not a perfect father, but I did my best. My heart was in the right place and I fulfilled my purpose with the universe by keeping you safe until you were of age. Tomorrow, you face your Birth Challenge and this is the time that you will reflect on who you are and what your purpose is.

Every person is born with a purpose that serves the universe. My purpose is to be your guardian. It's not being a husband or a father, but a guardian to you, and you alone. I'm not a guardian to the village, although the village would say otherwise.

The world gets confused when identifying someone's purpose. They look at each person and identify how that person best serves the village or what they can take advantage of. But someone's talent is not someone's purpose nor their worth, for that matter. For anyone born with a Moowin, the world will see that gift as that person's only purpose, their only value. They will stop looking for what the universe has truly called them to do. They are blind and forget the universe works in mysterious ways. Nothing so obvious as a talent or a Moowin is someone's purpose or true calling. However, it can lead to their dharma.

The world will be confused about your purpose. They will think your purpose has been revealed on your Birth Challenge when your gifts come to bloom. I don't know what your purpose in this life will be, but I promise you, it's not your Moowin. Your gift is a blessing as much as it is a curse. Do not worry about finding your purpose. It will hound you and will not settle until you discover it. Then it will latch onto you and will be a driving force in your life. It will fill you with a passion that is irresistible.

Many learn their dharma from the pain of overcoming a great trial in their life. They use their pain to serve others so that others are not alone in their struggle. This is not always the case. Your dharma could come from being aware of what lifts you up. Whatever your dharma is, you will know it because it will bring you joy.

Heed my warning though, not everyone's purpose is of good deeds. Some are called to have cold hearts and bring destruction and suffering. I do not wish that purpose for you, my Biny, and if that becomes your purpose, know now—before the world becomes confusing and demanding—that you have free will to direct your life. You can choose to lay down that purpose and open yourself up to a new purpose. Reflect on who you want to be and reflect often, as people and obstacles will try to deter you. Remember you ALWAYS have a choice, so choose wisely. Your father.

A hysterical part of her attempted a desperate laugh, but all she could do was shake her shoulders. Her throat burned with acid. Who she was, what her purpose was . . . was this a joke? Was this a spiritual test by the universe? She was a nobody with insecurities and fears that pulled her down to a deeper and deeper ditch. She was practically buried alive. That was her current existence. She barely got to live thanks to her father and the amulet. And what of the future she had wanted?

Maybe Wolverine was right. Maybe all she had dreamed of was being noticed, being loved, and having a job that contributed to the whole of her people. Flann's words came back to her. What he wanted was ordinary, but it was still a dream out of reach.

She hugged her pillow to her chest. Part of the Birth Challenge was an energy ritual where it was said that one's truest desires manifested based on who you decided to be. Her father's letter reminded her she had a choice. A choice like a direction but not an escape from her destiny, she thought with pain. But one did not waste one's gifts. Feeling sorry for a past that could not be changed was not serving her. She pulled herself together and decided it was time to take what control of her life she could.

When she thought about it, she had everything she needed. She had partners who were connected to her and were naturally inclined to keep her safe. With her partners, she had each of the eight Moowins, all of which were of rare status. It was like having a mini army to support you. She had a father who had planned for several outcomes. Thanks to him, she knew how to fight, how to survive in the wild, how to track, how to be still, how to slow her heartbeat down, how to garden, how to use plants to heal.

For the first time that night, she smiled, for she had realized that she not only knew how to depend on herself, she knew how to survive. She rose from the bed and packed a bag, thanking the universe that though she was born a female, she was raised as if she was a male. She packed her clothes and weapons in a green canvas bag she used for overnight hikes with her father. It only took her a few minutes to finish packing. Looking around, it dawned on her there was nothing she was attached to in her room, in her tut, or even in Silvedome, except Crystal. She rested her bag along her dresser and looked at her room, feeling energized.

Tomorrow she would complete her Birth Challenge and move into the Loaded Hurricane. The Loaded Hurricane was a dome inside of a dome and it seemed the safest place for her. It had clean water, animals to hunt, places to hide, and the gardens where her father taught her how to tend to the land. It would also hide the energy she gave off, and it was protected with a ward so that people didn't find it. Her next objective was to meet all her partners that shared her life force and convince them to stay there. She had minor carpenter skills and felt reasonably confident that she could build small tuts for them to stay in. She reasoned that if her father trained Bard and Flann, he would have trained the rest as well.

It seemed the safest plan for her and for Silvedome that she remain in the Loaded Hurricane. The Mistress came into her mind and she felt a pang of self-doubt in this plan. If she was an amplifier, she could be helping Silvedome's army fight off all the Selectors attacking the dome wall. *But what if I were captured?*

She stood alone in her room, charged with energy, with a plan in her soul like a heartbeat. A plan she was ready to enact. The sooner the better. With all the energy coursing through her and nothing to do, she became aware of Flann, who had been more silent in his movements than she had. She would have wondered if he was still here, except she felt him the same way she felt rain while indoors; she felt him in her bones.

She threw herself into her yoga practice, doing one pose after the next. She focused on her breathing and let the world melt away until her body glistened with sweat and her throat was dry. After lying on the floor for a few minutes, thanking her body for the work it performed, she decided to clean up. She walked out of her bedroom and noticed the light of the day was gone. She could see the back of Flann's head as he sat in the rocking chair. She smiled. She was impressed. He sat out there without movement or sound for hours as if he was a ghost and didn't exist.

She opened the door and stepped outside, feeling the energy between them tightening. Though he didn't move, she knew he was aware of her presence. She walked up to the water basin and wet a towel, slowly wringing out the water over the edge of the porch. She wiped her face, chest, and arms before taking the pitcher of water and pouring a little into her mouth. She set the pitcher down, Flann still motionless. She went to sit down on the step and jumped immediately at the electric shock that sizzled her butt. She spun and saw Flann standing. He moved fast and soundless, Sabina thought as the pain in her rear end calmed down. Flann's attention made the effects of the electric sting wear off.

Flann had sat so long he was sure his joints had locked into that position permanently and yet he still sat motionless, barely breathing. He was sure that if the Healers had checked his heartbeat, they would have pronounced him as dead or in desperate need of healing. Brom had taught him the ancient wisdom of meditation and slowing his heartbeat down. He liked to do it, especially when he felt out of control or powerless to the circumstances around him. It was a time of peace where he separated from the world and went into the void within him. Today was a day he needed the self-care of meditation, as he felt like he was standing between Sabina and the Selectors. Like he was playing a game of Russian roulette where he was sure to be hit, either by being a Shield to Sabina or by getting too attached to her.

Sabina's energy was a beacon to the Selectors, giving away her location and her identity. It was growing more and more powerful with the freedom from the amulet and the fast-approaching Birth Challenge. He had no idea what to expect tomorrow except mayhem. He couldn't help but wonder how long he would live if the Selectors were able to get through the dome wall. He knew that was catastrophic thinking. No one had ever gotten through the dome walls, which was the main reason why anyone with a Moowin longed to live here. Silvedome was a place of safety from the Selectors, of freedom from being a slave, and of acceptance to be who and what you were.

Even knowing the protection Silvedome offered, talking with Brom had given Flann a reality check. Sabina's Birth Challenge was dangerous. And Viggo hadn't returned, which meant there were hundreds of injured men to heal. Plus, he was 99.9 percent certain Brom had been fighting the Selectors on that last call. He was the type of person who would fight next to Silvedome warriors.

As Sabina was in silence preparing for her Birth Challenge, Flann had decided that sitting in a zen state seemed like his best option. Even with the meditation, Sabina made enough noise that his concentration broke several times. Her rhythmic breathing had built a fire in his belly as if he was the one doing the movements. His connection to her seemed to be growing stronger for him and he was pulled more and more into her. Without this meditation, he wasn't sure what he would be doing, but he had a feeling it would either be sneaking off to fight the Selectors or watching every move Sabina made. Neither of those options would benefit Sabina's wellbeing. His job was to protect her, not leave her defenseless without the full strength of her Moowins, or be the one she needed protection from.

He had heard a subtle buzzing in his ears as she approached and his mind flashed with a picture of her bare feet walking across the plank floorboards. He mentally pushed it away and re-centered himself as the door opened. He had ignored her movements as she attended the water pail and was feeling peaceful until that small buzzing in his ears sounded like a loud trumpet. It startled him into standing. He looked at her, noticing her hair frizzing out in a wide, circular shape and a pained expression on her face. He realized she must have been shocked again, which meant that it did not serve her highest good to be sitting out here . . . with him. There was a need within him to ask how she was feeling or if she was okay. But his jaw was locked shut as if it no longer worked. He stood foolishly looking at her with nothing to say, but consoled himself with the truth that she couldn't answer anyway. Instead, they looked at each other.

In that look there was an exchange of emotions, but he wasn't sure what. He only knew that they both saw each other. They were both present; there were no other distractions, no other thoughts. Only an acknowledgment of seeing each other with a deep connection. It didn't matter that there were no words spoken.

His barely beating heart thumped hard against his chest. His heart almost hurt as if someone was wrapping floss around its tender tissue. With each heartbeat, the heart expanded into the floss which cut into him. He was sure he didn't blink for a solid minute as he took her all in. Her skin shone in the moonlight. Her hair was wild and unkempt. Her eyes were enlarged, which made the whites visible. He could see the red in her eyes. The red stood out more than he had ever seen. Her tank top clung to her curvy chest, with her wide shoulders and long torso. Her skintight leggings revealed toned muscles and a perky butt with plenty to grab on to.

He had to look away. That was the only thing he could do. Break the eye contact and break the tension, he thought. Flann pulled his gaze away from her, regrettably, but as a way of honoring her.

～

She never understood that look he gave her, but she felt a sense of shame when he looked away. Maybe she wasn't much to look at compared to her peers. She didn't fit the Silvedome look. She was taller than most, her hair was often in her face, she had a huge bottom lip that was disproportionate to her other features, red irises that made her look freakish, olive skin, and a curvy body. All her peers were slender and small-framed, with bone-white skin, slick, straight black hair, and straight bodies.

That's why she preferred foreigners who came to Silvedome. They were of all different shapes, sizes, and colors, and had different accents. They made her feel normal in a world where there was so much sameness. Especially when she was the tall one. The one who stuttered when she was nervous. The one who hesitated and faltered when called upon in class. The one who stood out for all the wrong reasons and was camouflaged for all the special things about her. She now understood it was no coincidence but instead was the effect of the amulet necklace and the spell upon it. It was what kept her safe. But knowing that didn't help her now. Her mind had a habit of thinking she was what was wrong and that's why Flann had looked away.

The pain still stung her behind, but the stinging of her emotions felt more intense. Sabina stood up straighter and reconfirmed a decision she made long ago. She wasn't going to be a person who catered to an audience. She wasn't going to be like the rest who conformed. She'd lived with disapproval and resistance, and this was no different. Flann didn't matter to her, anyway. He was practically married and he shouldn't be looking.

She gathered herself and walked soundlessly to the door. Flann was still standing, looking over his shoulder out into the dark night. She decided she wasn't going to let his rejection bother her. She was tired of chasing after the attention of a boy she might be interested in. She deserved more. She wanted more. She got to the door and walked in the tut. She turned to softly close the door when she noticed Flann's hands clenched and his chest heavy as if he was breathing hard. As if he had just lost a fight.

She froze and took him in. He was tense and his energy felt like a bull ready to charge. How curious, she thought. It was as if he wanted to look, but knew he shouldn't. Similar to how she felt when she saw Fabia strut across the Ceremony in her attention-grabbing way. Sabina's stomach tingled at this thought. How wonderful that Flann was fighting to NOT look at her.

Then he flipped his head in her direction. He caught her staring at him. The energy between them heated her body as he looked searingly into her eyes. Her stomach dropped and she bit her lip. As inconspicuous as possible, she finished closing the door. She pressed herself into the door and slowed her breathing down. The charge of his look was dangerous and called to a part of her that loved the challenge of a fight.

Her hand rested near her face on the door, and she felt the wood grain to calm her beating heart. Her curiosity encouraged her to edge to the window and look out at him. Whereas her logic reminded her that he wasn't worth any of her attention. But . . . if he didn't know he was getting her attention, what was the harm?

She walked light-footed and as close to the wall as she could, keeping her chest against it for a better view outside. When she reached the window, she saw him with his hands in his hair, pulling at it, and then bringing his hands down to rub his face. He was still standing, glancing at the door, and then burying his face in his hands again. Sabina softened as she looked at him. His demeanor reminded her of a man in a desperate plea with God.

Flann ruffled his hair and strode to the door with determination. Sabina noticed too late and pressed her back into the wall from the immediate fear of being caught spying. Then logic caught up to her that he was coming through the door and she took off running as quickly as she could for her room, all stealth left behind. She could hear the thud of her feet hitting the plank floor as she darted into her heavy, red drapes, flinging her arms to move them out of the way. The pins and needles of adrenaline spiked through her body. She ran, knowing she wasn't going to make it to the safety of her room before Flann walked in the door. But she did.

She spun around and closed the drapes. Then she shook out her arms and legs in an attempt to relieve the buildup of adrenaline flowing through her veins. She hopped around like a boxer preparing for a fight, grateful for the noise it made, as if it would explain away the sounds of her running across the room. After a while, she placed her hands one on top of the other and paced back and forth in her room, slowing her breath and listening as intently as possible for any sound. *What stopped him? My running? Did he see me and decide to stay outside? He must have heard me.*

Flann didn't know what to do as Sabina had walked away from him and back inside the tut. He sensed she was mad at him, but he didn't know why. He also knew he couldn't look at her. He was better than this, he scolded himself. He wasn't some animal with no control over his feelings. He was a man of discipline and control, and that was exactly what he was going to practice right now. Except she lingered, like she had something to say. Her presence toyed with his willpower to remain separate and distant.

Through their connection, he felt a ripple of pleasure go through Sabina as if she stepped into the sunlight and beckoned him to follow. Acting on impulse and giving in to the beckoning, he snapped his head in her direction without analyzing or judging himself for it. He was a man fighting for integrity and feeling torn apart between two realities—his promise to Nora and his desire for Sabina. Like the power of the sunset disappearing behind the ocean, Sabina closed the door, sealing him in darkness once more.

What am I doing? Nora will be here tomorrow. She is to be my wife. It is what I always wanted . . . He pulled his hands through his hair, trying to get some perspective. *Sabina is preparing for her Birth Challenge. She hasn't even given more than one signal that she likes me that way. This life force connection is getting to me. But there was that look. That look of need.* He rubbed his face. *What if Master Walkin and Nana Honey are right? What if Nora isn't the right person for me anymore? What if I have outgrown who I was?*

Flann felt certain he had outgrown who he was. He had sat in silence for hours, clearing his thoughts, and he felt like he could think more clearly now than ever before. He knew in that moment that his soul longed for Sabina in a way that it had never longed for Nora. He was tired of resisting it. A part of him begged to put down the weight of desire, regret, and expectation. He didn't know what he was going to do, but he strode to the door with the intention of facing Sabina.

When he got to the door, he paused at the sound of footsteps thudding fast and heavy across the floor. His gut twisted. It felt like cold water had been thrown over his head. She had known he was coming, and she ran away. She was running away from him. He put his hands on the doorframe and bent over, feeling like he was going to throw up. He felt like he was going crazy. Like he had no direction of what was real and what was fantasy. It was real that Sabina was running away from him and it was a fantasy, a story in his head, that she wanted to be with him. He had made it all up. The pain of that thought rolled his stomach. He felt like he was no better than the sleazy Prince, claiming what he wanted with no regard for how Sabina felt.

As he leaned into the door, bent over in emotional pain, Bard silently approached. He stood there a moment, questioning what Flann was doing. This was not like him. As someone who was trained with Brom and who was a Protector Moowin, he should have been aware of his surroundings. He should have heard him approach, but he didn't. He didn't even sense his presence.

Bard cleared his throat, standing casual and unassuming in front of the porch a good distance for any reaction Flann might have. One of his Protector skills was speed. He could also leap a good distance.

The buzzing in his ears connected with Sabina's Birth Challenge preparation—and the swelling of emotional turmoil—caused Flann to be unable to hear Bard's approach, or even the clearing of his throat. It wasn't until Bard had spoken that Flann was shocked out of his despondent state. He whipped around to face him, recognizing his voice but instinctively raising his arms to block the attack. He immediately dropped his arms as if the weight of them was too heavy a burden and partially straightened up. He was slightly hunched over but no longer bending his knees to spring into battle.

Pursing his lips, Bard stood motionless and examined Flann's ghost-white appearance. He looked like he had been hit in the stomach until he had thrown up. Like the time Bard had the pleasure of doing just that when he'd first shown Flann he was a better fighter than him.

With calm assurance, Bard took a step back. "My mistake. I could sense some weird emotions coming from Sabina but it must have been you I was sensing."

Flann's mouth hung slightly open as if Bard's words were too complex to understand. He stared at him with his arms limp by his side. Bard felt uncomfortable looking at him in this state. This was a man wearing his emotions on his sleeve and Flann was the type of person who kept himself under tight control.

Had Sabina locked him out? No, that couldn't be it. Silvedomeies didn't have locks on their door. Poor man. He looks like a man starving only to find out his food is contaminated.

Bard sent his energy into the ground and counted internally to three, opening his inner knowing. He sensed Sabina a few feet away, her heart hammering. He sensed a feeling of curiosity and delight from her. She seemed more alive, more solid than before. He knew from that assessment that she was fine. He moved his attention to Flann and sensed an emotional wound that was bubbling with regret, desire, confusion, and self-judgment. It was nasty energy and Bard withdrew quickly. *Whatever is going on here, it's none of my business.*

"Right . . . I'll just be going then. Take it easy, Flann. Tomorrow is a big day." Bard stood for a moment debating if he should say more as he stared at the lost look in Flann's eyes. He could tell Sabina was waiting for him to come inside the tut and it seemed like Flann was battling that desire. He and Flann were like brothers who didn't get along, but seeing him like this moved Bard to want to help. However, he learned long ago that helping was hurting. He turned and walked away, disappearing quickly in the darkness of the night.

Bard had always had a gift of night vision and walked surefooted down the path until he disappeared like an illusion in Flann's memory. Flann didn't care what he was doing or why. He didn't even care that Bard snuck up on him and saw him at his weak point. He didn't care because he said something valuable. Bard had admitted he could sense Sabina's emotions. Which meant he wasn't the only one feeling this connection.

He had lived with Bard for a year and Flann knew he loved to play the role of a suave gentleman. However, he preferred his partners to be men. Therefore, he wasn't a good testament as to whether an exchange of life force was what was pulling Flann into Sabina's web of desire. His mind flashed to images of Bard kissing her hand. Was there more going on there? Or was Bard playing a part? He knew one thing for sure: Sabina liked Bard's attention. Whereas she often seemed annoyed by him.

He stood up, feeling sick to his stomach and opened the door slowly. He closed it behind him and dragged his feet across the floor along the back way. He flopped onto the firm couch. He was upset with himself and reeling from Sabina's lack of interest.

He let numbness wash over him at the possibility his attraction to Sabina was nothing more than the sharing of life force—what he had feared deep down since the beginning. There was nothing else to say. He needed to accept this wasn't something special or unique. This was a byproduct of sharing life force with her. It didn't matter how much Sabina had been on his mind or how much he longed to touch her. He wasn't going to get to do that. He was going to be a man of his word, regardless of how much he had changed over the last two years. He was going to be with Nora.

Sabina had worked hard since she was a little girl to get attention and suddenly, she had someone's attention and she didn't know what to do with it. Her behavior was foolish and wild and even as she judged herself for it, she felt alive. She felt free as her heartbeat drummed inside of her. As she worked on collecting herself, her curiosity built as to why Flann wasn't coming inside. She was anxious in an excited way to see what was going to happen next, but then she had heard someone speaking outside.

Focusing her attention on the voice, she heard Bard. She was delighted he had come to visit her and hoped that he would come in. She knew that was silly because she couldn't talk to him and her preparation time was meant to be a time of solitude, not social hour. Her body felt like it swayed into another dimension when she heard him say he sensed her. It felt too personal. It scared her and it felt true. It was so subtle, but there was a connection. She was focusing so intently on it that she was startled when she heard Flann open the door. She lifted her head and her heart fluttered.

Through the small opening in her drapes, Sabina watched Flann shut down. She could feel his gloom. It felt like a part of him was dying and it pulled on her heart strings to see him this way. His behavior calmed her down and made her focus when moments ago, her emotions were scattered. She tried but she could not recall what Bard had said after he mentioned he could sense her. She was so focused that she missed what caused Flann's shift.

She walked over to her bed and sat down. She rested on her side and watched him through the slit in her drapes. The connection between them felt like it was untwining and the lack of its presence made her feel an emptiness that she wasn't aware of before. A creeping coldness drifted her way; a physical confirmation of the distance being rapidly created between them. She didn't like it.

She rolled over to her other side, putting her back to Flann, and curled into a ball to protect herself from the sadness she sensed and to warm herself up. She thought of her Birth Challenge that was hours away and wondered where Viggo was. He had made her feel better this morning. Maybe he could help Flann.

As if her thoughts conjured him, she heard light steps up the porch and then the door opening. She rolled back over to her side to see what was happening.

Viggo was a quiet soul from what Sabina could tell. He seemed resigned to serve without receiving or caring for himself. Those were her first impressions of him but she didn't know him well enough to interpret his sigh as he walked into the door. She couldn't see him and she needed to see his facial expression to understand more. She quickly got up and went to her drapes.

Viggo stood in the doorway, quietly putting his large duffle down as if his muscles were sore. He shut the door. When Sabina could see his face, she noticed he looked drained.

"What's wrong?" he asked Flann. "Your energy is all wrong."

Flann flicked his eyes up and cast them back down, unwilling to answer.

Visibly exasperated, he pleaded with Flann. "It's been a long day. My energy is exhausted. Don't make me work harder than I need to right now . . . please."

He walked over to Flann, his light-green cargo pants barely staying on his hips. The bottom of his gray T-shirt was ripped, showing the line of hair on his belly. He was a tall, lengthy man with no muscle tone or meat on his bones. He sat sideways next to Flann. His knees knocked together and pointed in Flann's direction so that Sabina could not see his face. Flann batted Viggo's hand away when he attempted to lay his hands on him.

"Fine, then I won't help you," Viggo said firmly, clearly having no patience for Flann's insolence. He went to stand up and shift his weight forward, placing his hand on Flann's shoulder for support. It may have been an innocent gesture, seeing how Viggo was struggling to move, but it also seemed to allow him to read Flann.

"Curd, man. You could have warned me," Viggo said, shaking his hand. "I spent the entire day healing men with the physical wounds that your emotional wounds are causing."

Viggo walked over to his bag and dug into it as Flann sulked on the couch. He found a small, clear bag and unwound it, taking a pinch of a twig. He sealed the bag up and stuffed it back into his duffle. He walked over to Flann and held out the twig. "Sorry, man. Not much I can do to help you but chew on this twig for a couple of minutes and you will feel more at peace." Flann looked at the twig and looked away, crossing his arms in defiance.

"Suit yourself. I'm going to bed." He rested the twig on the end table at the arm of the couch and started to head toward the kitchen. He stopped, apparently unwilling to walk away without doing more. "Hey, man. Do me a favor and feel your feelings so they can be released. Otherwise, those emotions will stay trapped inside and poison your spirit like a physical poison will destroy your body." He stretched his arms over his head and bent both elbows as his hands rested on the back of his head. "I may not be able to heal the spoils of your heart, but loving yourself will. And in case you forgot, we are all tied to one another so we are sensitive to your energy. Soooooo when you are ready to stop harming yourself with your emotions, will you check on my sister? I *don't* want to see what she is doing."

He dropped his arms down, placing one hand on the doorframe as he waited for Flann to answer. Sabina saw no acknowledgment from Flann but Viggo thanked him and walked off without any further discussion. Sabina heard his light footsteps going up the stairs.

She walked over to her bed, feeling like she was learning a new language and they were speaking faster than her translation could keep up with. She lay on her bed, looking at the ceiling, feeling the loudness of the silence and the draft of coldness on her skin, before realizing she was burning up. All the excitement must have gotten to her.

She took a deep breath and watched her chest expand, before releasing her held breath. She repeated Viggo's words in her head: 'The spoils of your heart.' Spoils??? *Spoils, like in your food rots? Does Viggo mean Flann's heart is rotting? Ugh, that's a gross picture. How can your heart rot? Poison.* He said something about poison . . . his emotions were poison. She wondered if her emotions had ever poisoned her. She immediately thought of her jealousy over her sister and how perfect she was. *Is that poison trapped in my body?*

Time drifted as Sabina reflected on her emotions, the darker ones that 'poisoned' her heart. The emotions that made her feel like she was a disease, like leprosy in the Bible. Viggo had said to feel those emotions to release them. She wasn't one to cry, and it seemed the only way to do that. She assumed tears were evidence of their release but people didn't cry in Silvedome. They valued joy, not tears.

She wasn't sure if she knew how to feel her emotions in a way that released them, but she allowed them to surface. She felt the hurt, one bomb going off in her after the next, and she forgot about being hot. Though the tears wanted to come, they didn't. She rolled into a ball and tucked her chin to her chest and held on to her knees. Normally she would push these emotions away but tonight, she prayed silently in her head for them to be released. She internally prayed to God that he took them back to the earth or to the void or wherever they belonged, until she fell asleep.

Sometime later, Sabina woke with an irresistible tingling sensation on her nose. In her sleep, she had started to rub her nose, and the action woke her. The presence came into her mind. She didn't know what time it was as the dark was misleading but she figured Viggo must be asleep as there was no movement to be heard upstairs.

She rolled over to her side and squinted in the dim candlelight. She could make out Flann's head resting on the side of the couch, his arms still folded as he slept. Since the candles had not burned out, she knew she had not been asleep long. She also knew she needed to blow out the candles. She decided to change into her nightgown while she was up too.

Going to her wooden chest, she opened the doors and pulled out her white cotton dress. She quickly changed as the cool air made her wish she was under the covers. She tiptoed out of her room and quietly as possible. She walked slowly, hand resting on the wall to ensure she didn't wake anyone.

She came into the living room and looked over at Flann as she walked past him. She blew the candle out on the wall, noticing the twig still sitting on the end table, untouched. Seeing the twig and thinking of Flann's stubbornness made some part of her expand. She looked at his face, longing to place her hand along the stubble of his chin. He looked strong, even in his sleep, she thought, as if there was no place for tenderness. And that was what she felt for him in that moment.

She bent over the end table and blew out the last candle in the room. She stood up and watched the gray smoke dance to the ceiling. Darkness filled her vision and she felt Flann's eyes on her. Her glance moved to his eyes, and he slowly lifted his head off the couch. His eyes adjusted to the light, to her.

It was near impossible to see anything from the remaining light flickering behind her drapes and yet they both stared at each other, the connection between them blooming back into full force. That connection pulled so tight that Sabina found herself sinking into the couch as if her body didn't belong to her. Her hand rested on his chin as she had imagined moments ago. Flann had shifted his body to be angled toward her.

Sabina's pulse was in her throat. She had lost seconds and didn't consciously know how she had gotten into this position, touching him. It was as if warning bells were going off in her head and her mind was paralyzed in fear, yet her body moved of its own will. She felt a powerful current of energy tying her to the ground as if she was locked into this space. This wasn't possible. *This is a dream,* her mind said in panic. *This isn't real.* Yet, she could feel her face moving closer to his. The candlelight cast a sliver of light across his face. She saw his focus on her as if his life was in her hand. She felt his energy around her as if his arms were holding her, though his fingertips were lightly spread across her jaw and neck, like he wasn't sure exactly where she was.

Her body paused and her mind stilled and the spirit within her spoke to her. "Choose. We have carried you here but you must choose your next step." She felt aware of her body again. She could feel the prick of his stubble, the heat of his breath on her face, the warmth of his fingertips on her cool skin. She could feel his pain, his fear, and his desire, and it sent warm, thick energy like glue through her veins. She remembered thinking *Yes* as she closed the distance between them. She wanted this like the crops wanted rain after a long drought and her body thundered as her lips touched his, light and delicate.

At the touch of their lips, the thick glue in her veins turned to liquid lava that pulled down the length of her body. Sabina startled as she felt a wetness in her underwear and pulled away, thinking she was having her monthly. She was surprised to find her hand on his chest as if she had permission to touch him there. She said nothing, not that she could, but she felt torn. A few more moments indulging this feeling could mean embarrassing herself with a mess on the couch. Slowly she registered his reaction as she shifted her focus from herself to him. She realized he had practically jumped out of his skin at her forward movements.

She sprang up, noticing the darkness of the room, when

seconds ago she felt like a bright light was shining on them. She didn't wait for another sign and quickly hurried into her room. She pulled her drapes completely closed for privacy and hustled to her chest, searching for her feminine products, grabbing a pad from the back of her shelf. She shimmied her underwear off and saw there was no blood. Where was the blood? Confused, she stepped into a new pair of underwear and tossed her old ones into the small woven basket by her chest.

Her heartbeat slowed down and no longer thundered in her ears. She felt the cool air once more and anxiously got into her bed, wrapping herself in her sheets. She pulled the blankets all the way up to her chin and listened. All was quiet. Lying on her side with no opening to see Flann, the consequences of her actions hit her. *What have I done? What possessed me to kiss him? What was I thinking? He is going to marry Nora and now I am the woman who tore them apart. Ugh, I got so carried away in my emotions and in receiving his attention that I failed to do the right thing. How will I face him tomorrow? What will I say? How can I excuse my behavior? There is no excuse.* She felt sick to her stomach and put the blanket over her face. Her thoughts tormented her until she eventually fell into a fitful sleep. As she drifted off, her mind reminded her how odd it was that touching Flann didn't cause her to be shocked. This felt important to her, and she asked herself to remember this detail so that she could analyze it later. That night, she dreamed of Flann holding her as they slept on the couch, intertwined and peaceful.

Flann had felt the soft breeze across his skin and opened his eyes to see Sabina leaning over him as smoke surrounded her face, giving a misty, dreamy appearance as if she was not real. She looked beautiful and strong and he held his breath as he locked eyes with her. His body immediately awakened and was on full alert. He had sensations of his arms reaching up and grabbing her upper arms to move her into a seated position next to him on the couch, even though he didn't recall moving. He only knew that he was looking into her eyes as the room went into complete darkness. Then she was sitting next to him. Her ice-cold hand on his chin, soft and real.

As the candlelight strengthened and he could see once more, he realized that he was touching her. His hands were spread out wide as if he wanted to touch as much of her skin as possible. He could not believe he was touching the delicate, soft skin of her neck and she wasn't running from him. She wasn't looking away either. Her lips were slightly parted and though her face was shadowed, his need was mirrored across her face.

His imagination was already devouring her in his mind. As she looked at him, his mind raced to fisting her hair as he kissed her, pulling her into him as much as physically possible. He saw himself moving the elastic, white cotton strip that was holding her nightgown on her shoulder off to the side and licking the soft tissue of her skin between the crevice of her neck and shoulder.

Although his body expanded and his energy stretched outside his body as his imagination went wild, he remained still. His emotional pain was quickly replaced with the fear that she would pull away. That she didn't want this as badly as he did. That she wasn't ready for this type of action. Brom had kept her sheltered. He wasn't sure what she was comfortable with when it came to the intimacy between a man and a woman. He watched her, waiting to find out what she would do as his body told him exactly what he wanted to do.

He saw her eyes flash with alarm and he felt concern rush through him. He was in the corner of the couch and had no room to scoot back to give her space. He had no intention of pushing her to do more but he couldn't bring himself to stand up to create the space that she probably needed. It was as if his hands didn't belong to him and he couldn't will them back from her face. He looked into her eyes, questioning, and held his breath.

Her face drew closer to his, and she paused. Flann didn't

move, but he longed to wrap his arms around her, to embrace her. He let out his breath as controlled as possible. The seconds waiting for her decision felt weighted. His imagination no longer ran wild. He was captivated and presently aware of every subtle movement.

Then she closed her eyes and closed the distance, drawing her hand from his chin down to his chest. Heat soared through Flann and he used all his willpower not to act on all those images of desire fresh in his mind. Their lips had barely touched when he felt his body physically shift into alignment as if he had seen a Healer to adjust his spine. He was taken aback by this shift and before he realized it, she pulled away, startled.

Oh no, he thought. *She isn't experienced. She isn't ready for this. Tullom.* If he were an honorable man, he would have talked to her first. He would have asked her permission to kiss her. He would have prevented this shock on her face.

He was not surprised when she stood up and hustled to her room, closing the drapes in a way where he had no way of seeing what was going on. He rubbed his face and let his face rest in his hands. He should have known better. He should have had more discipline and self-control. He should have shown her more respect.

The room was pitch dark, much like his mood. He stood up and walked up the stairs to his room, shutting the door quietly and lying on the bed. *What does Sabina think of me now? How do I explain this to Nora? What is Brom going to do to me once he finds out I kissed his daughter?*

Not bothering to change clothes or cover himself with a blanket, he let the cold air provide the numbing sensation his body and mind needed. Eventually, he fell asleep, wishing he hadn't been on that couch when Sabina went to blow out the candles.

Preparation For The Birth Challenge

Nana Honey moaned in her sleep, startling Crystal awake. Crystal had one of those dreams where she could hear Nana Honey groaning in agony before her conscious mind was fully awake. She stumbled down the stairs to the chair in which Nana Honey had fallen asleep the night before. Crystal made several attempts before she successfully woke Nana from her deep sleep. It took several moments before Nana Honey's presence returned to her body. Crystal considered this odd as it was not a full moon or a ceremony. She was unsure what was happening to Nana Honey to cause her to have what appeared to be a powerful dream. What was more alarming was that Nana was unable to recall anything about her experience. This was not right, and it scared Crystal. She could see Nana was scared too. Confident, all-knowing Nana Honey was upset and that made Crystal upset too. She suspected Nana Honey did remember something, even if it was on an unconscious level.

With soothing rubs to bring warmth back to Nana's skin, Crystal listened as she repeated to herself that her guides would not allow her to see. Crystal knew this rarely happened and asked her what it meant. Nana Honey told her the omen she had prophesied about Sabina being an amplifier was indeed true, but she sensed it was an omen of a much greater scale than she'd originally thought.

Deprived of a memorable vision, Nana Honey prepared for the worst. She ordered Crystal to find every Healer she could and ask them to attend Sabina's Birth Challenge. She also gave her instructions to lay down protection wards around the Ceremony audience and to send for Master Fis.

~

Returning to the house two hours later, Crystal saw Nana Honey decorating Viggo's face with gems, while Fabia lay on the couch, kicking one of her legs.

"Fabia," Crystal said, walking in and kneeling next to her.

"*CRYSTAL*," Fabia mocked back.

"You look *green*."

"Nice of you to finally notice," she said in a bored tone.

Not taking her sour mood, Crystal disregarded Fabia. In a motherly tone, she asked, "*What did you do?*"

It seemed Fabia saw she wasn't going to get out of this conversation. She answered. "Ugh, I do feel green. I partied with Tevin all night until Nana called me so many times I had to come shut her up." Her eyes flicked in annoyance at Nana and she crossed her arms. "I could have slept for three more hours."

Taking charge, Nana Honey called out orders. "Master Fis, could you clear her aura? Crystal, can you get two of my charged spheres?"

Crystal nodded and started to go upstairs.

"Quartz, Crystal. I need quartz. Vait???? Vhere are the other Healers? I NEED Healers."

"No can do, Nana Honey," said old Master Fis.

"I'm sorry," said Crystal, knowing she had disappointed Nana Honey. She was grateful for the support from Master Fis who normally never spoke. "All the Healers have been contained to heal our warriors."

Visibly alarmed, Nana Honey asked, "Do ve have that many varriors injured?"

"Yes. The entire hospital was full, and the staff was drained. They have Influencers pumping out healing vibes to help the Healers. I've never seen anything like it."

"Aug-MENT-SH-FAB," shouted Fabia as Master Fis waved her hands over her aura, humming. "THAT FREAKING HURTS"—she fussed as she sat up holding her wrist—"in a nail-scratching-down-the-chalkboard way."

Nana Honey turned back to Crystal. "I couldn't see it," she said with deep sadness. "I'm not allowed to in-ter-ferrre vith this. This must happen, but I vill do what I can to help. Bring me a bucket of sand." She waved Crystal away and continued to work on Viggo.

~

"Hmm, but I do feel better," Fabia said, smiling and petting Master Fis. "I like you." She blew her a kiss.

"FABIA," Viggo called without looking. "Behave!"

"Ohhhh. Brother, I was showing respect to the wise Healer."

Nana Honey could not help herself. She smiled at Fabia's willful play.

"I' need you as vell, Fabia. Vatch the skies for me. Call your birds and have them rrready. There, that should be enough pro-tec-tion for you. I need your entire forearms covered in crystals. How many bracelets do you have?"

"I have PLENTY"—Fabia smiled—"to share with my brother."

"Fine. The day has finally come when you get to dress me, sister," Viggo answered.

Fabia squealed in delight, bringing her hands together and bending her knees.

"May I go? Brom needs me," Viggo said without any sign of the impatience he clearly felt.

"Not until ve move Sabina's life force to the sphere."

"What?" everyone said together, looking at her as if she had lost her mind.

Crystal walked over and gently rolled the spheres onto the couch.

"You cannot do that. That is too dangerous."

"I may not be able to heal others without Sabina's life force." Viggo voiced his worry.

"And I may not be able to perform such complicated magic, Nana," Fis warned.

"Shhh. All vill be fine. Trrrrust me."

"THIS ISN'T ABOUT TRUST! Ahhh, I see. Fine." Fabia wiped her hands like she was done with this conversation. "Brother, you will be fine. I'll get your bracelets. Don't you worry about that," she said, her eyes squinting at him. "Now, I must leave. Thank you for the cocktail, Grammy Fis. Let's do it again," she whispered as she walked by her. When she got to the door, she called, "Toodles, witches! I've got to get dressed."

"That girl - such a difficult time staying out of trrrrou-ble. She has one foot in the past, one foot in the pre-sent, and her head is diving into the fu-ture." Nana Honey shook her head as she watched Fabia go. "Ah, but she is gifted."

"Nana, please reconsider. I don't know that your heart can take the loss of life force, even if it is not your life force."

"Don't be afrrrraid. Fear serves no one. It on-ly holds you back."

"I'm being rational."

"Ah, but magic does not flow to closed doors. I taught you that."

Closing her eyes and dropping her head to look up at the ceiling, Crystal could feel nervous energy fidgeting within her body. She knew Nana Honey was right, but she was in her head. She needed to get out of her head. "Okay, give me a task because my monkey brain is blocking my sight."

Nana Honey nodded. "Brrraid crystals into Viggo's hair vhile ve vork on moving Sabina's life force to the sphere."

"I—" complained Master Fis.

"Shh. Open your channels, close your eyes, and ask for help trans-ferring some of the resonance to the sphere. That is all you need to do. Ve vill not move the life force but create a mock-up of its energy to represent it."

"Hmmm. This is more of your magic than mine."

"Yes, and I vill help you. Crystal, vatch vhat I do with your third eye so you can help Master Fis vith mine. Viggo, vhen we are done, you are free to go, but you MUST vear that sphere on your body. I also rec-o-mmend the crystal bracelets and sand in your shoes."

It seemed Viggo was used to taking orders, and he did not question them. He did nothing more than blink.

"Are you ready?" Nana Honey asked them. With a nod, they began to work on storing Sabina's life force resonance in the sphere. Viggo then left to see Brom, and the others worked on Nana Honey. Within the hour, all three ladies were ready for the Birth Challenge ritual: clothed in energy-repelling attire, with their hair covered in crystals and wrapped in turbans, their skin decorated with crystals, and their shoes filled with sand. Then they sat in meditation to prepare until it was time to meet Nora at the Ceremony.

On the outskirts of the village, Viggo met Brom and the other life force partners in the Loaded Hurricane. Flann remained in silence, Tevin was hungover and dehydrated, Kean simmered in anger as usual, Zoel complained of his treatment, Bard was alert and ready, Pond sized up his competition to win Sabina over, and Felix chilled out, resting his back against a log.

"It's about time. Today is an important day. But, if Nana Honey wanted to see you"—he sighed and rubbed the back of his neck—"well, that was probably important too. Alright. Let's move forward. Warriors, gather around."

They all slowly shuffled forward in a circle around Brom.

"Today, Sabina has her Birth Challenge, and I don't need to stress the importance of keeping her energy levels as low as possible. As you can see from outside the dome, her identity has been discovered, or at least they know someone with a lot of energy is inside. They *will* know her identity today if we fail. Understood?"

They nodded in understanding.

"Battles to break our shield and get inside the dome have been non-stop since her real birthdate. She doesn't have the protection of the amulet. Her energy will be shiny to those with the gift to see. We cannot hide her that way anymore. All she has to help her is her life force in you and your Moowins. Therefore, **you must** be next to the stage upon the engagement of the crystals. Your job is to interfere and confuse the crystals. They will not pull directly down to her if they are being pulled by a competing energy source, which means you HAVE to be inside that twelve-feet radius of her. Pond, I need you to stay in the back of the stage and hold the shield without eyes on you. Keep the others shielded so no one notices them. Kean, you need to be in the back by me so I can help you with your other issue. Zoel, you are also in back because you've managed to insult Silvedome. I cannot afford for you to be kicked out again if something goes wrong with the shields."

"Tff, that was NOT my fault," whined Zoel.

"Save it. We don't have time. Viggo and Felix, I want you close to the stage. Felix, work on sending out soothing vibes. That will buy everyone time. Bard and Flann, you two will be next in the circle and Tevin, you will be at the six o'clock position on the stage. GET TO HER. That is all that matters."

He looked around the circle, his stare communicating his seriousness. "We don't know what is going to happen. At best, we will block some of the crystals from being pulled to Sabina's chakra centers. That is our mission. If you have to intercede the crystal to accomplish that, do it. At worst, she will be discovered as the Agni. God help us all if that happens."

"Seriously, she is not the Agni, Brom. You are being a little paranoid, don't you think? I mean, I don't see anything special about her," Zoel challenged.

"She saved your life, didn't she?" retorted Brom.

"Correction. Your wife did," he smarted.

"As soon as this is over, I want you to disappear permanently from our lives," Brom announced.

"That won't be a problem," Zoel responded from gritted teeth. "I don't want to be disgraced by an uncivilized . . . OUCH," screamed Zoel.

Fabia had silently walked behind Zoel and had flicked some oils onto the side of his face, which started to burn his skin. "Looks like I got some oils on you. You better go to the river and wash that off or that burning is only going to get worse."

"YOU DID THAT ON PURPOSE," he accused.

"Yes, I did," she said unapologetically. "What?" She pretended to be innocent. "Your energy needed to be cleaned. Now, you can be upset with me for helping you or you can help yourself by allowing the water to sooth you."

He looked at her. Bouncing on the tips of his toes, Zoel had clearly had it with Fabia. "Grrrr, one day you will be served the justice you deserve." He stormed off to the river.

Fabia turned her focus onto the other boys, crossing her arms. "Were you all going to allow him to talk about Sabina that way?"

Before any of them could respond to her, Brom cut in. "Thank you, Fabia, for your help with our misguided friend. We are all grateful to you, and I believe we can all agree that we are here to focus on Sabina's safety as our primary mission. We have wasted enough time waiting for Viggo to show up. Why did Nana Honey put those crystals in your hair?" he asked, waving his hand, seeming like he didn't want to look at him properly.

Viggo was emotionless about Brom's assessment but answered his question with polite respect. "I didn't ask, and she didn't say."

"Great. Well, she is worried about something." He rubbed the back of his neck in thought. "Fabia, do you know anything?"

"Maybe," she answered playfully.

"Facts, Fabia. I have no time for your games."

"Fine." She pouted. "You know life is too short to be all work and no play. That is the true meaning of death, when you stop playing, stop having fun, stop experiencing joy. It's the death of your spirit that is far more dangerous than the death of your physical body."

"Please," Brom prompted.

She sighed and unenthusiastically complied to Brom's request. "She is concerned about a dream vision she had last night that she cannot see. She believes it is about the Birth Challenge. Her fear is that Sabina will be filtering in too much energy for anyone who shares her life force. She is taking precautions. Viggo is important because he needs to be able to heal others if the energy hurts them."

"Tullom, I hadn't thought about that. Crystals will help?"

"Some crystals can store or transport your energy," she said indifferently. "Look, what is going to happen is going to happen. All this worry and fear is like an invitation for it to find you. You would do better focusing your attention on what you want to happen. Let the energy find that."

"Fabia, we have no time for your woo-woo stuff. Sabina's life is in danger and if her life is in danger, all our lives are in danger."

"Speak for yourself," Fabia said under her breath.

Looking up at the sun, Brom commented. "We don't have time to get crystals. Is there anything else she did?"

Fabia refused to answer, but Viggo responded dryly. "She had me put sand in my boots."

"Great. Everyone go to the river and get some sand in your boots. Wait." He called everyone back. "Everyone knows what to do?" He looked around. His face was serious. His entire appearance was dirty from fighting. He was running purely on stress, which made his energy wired, while at the same time he looked drained with dark circles under his eyes.

"Okay, NO holding back. If we can get through today and deflect Sabina's energy, we all live another day. If we can block her from receiving all her gifts, then the Selectors will see that she is not the Agni. Eventually, they will stop attacking the village. Your fate, Sabina's fate, and Silvedome's fate rest on how successful you are today. This is what we trained for."

Brom stopped talking as Tevin started throwing up. "Sky Above, Viggo, detox him." Viggo moved over to Tevin and cleared his energy field as Brom continued. "Get some protein. You will need your energy but nothing else and only small bite sizes. The energy within the circle is going to flush you out. Remember, the power will push you back."

Felix interrupted, "Boss, we GOT to go. She will be alright."

Brom stretched his arm out and placed his hands on Felix's shoulder. He dropped his head and nodded, avoiding eye contact. With gruffness in his voice, he said, "I'm proud of all of you. Now get out of my face and earn your pride today."

Flann and the others shifted, uncomfortable with Brom's emotional display, and they slowly scattered, walking over to the river. No one talked, but the tension between them all was thick like humid air. Felix stayed next to Brom. He was the oldest of the men in the union interviews and was also an Influencer. Flann knew he often covered for Brom when he was traveling, and they had a good relationship with each other. Felix was a man who rolled with the punches and never took anything seriously. Looking at his bare feet, locked hair, and glassy eyes, Flann wasn't sure if anything could affect his state of peace.

Flann joined the Prince and the others to scoop wet sand into their boots. Tevin followed him, coming down on all fours and throwing water on his face, wiping his mouth. He looked over at Flann with his small eyes. "My friend, next time don't let me party with Fabia the night before a death challenge." He said it with a slight smile on his face, his sharp, high cheekbones shining as if he didn't regret it too much.

Flann liked Tevin. He was humble and easygoing. He was hardworking and had a body made of perfect muscle mass, whereas Flann always felt too toned. Tevin was a rare Seer who worked with metal. He often saw his vision in the flames of the metal he forged. Flann wasn't sure if he could see like Nana Honey, but Tevin seemed to be three steps ahead of everyone all the time. He doubted that Tevin didn't see this coming.

"Fabia is good for you. You work too hard," he said, looking behind him as she approached.

"I see that someone has been good to you." Tevin's smile spread across his face in full humor.

Curd, all these Seers are going to be the death of my pride.

"I heard my name and I know what you are saying," Fabia said, her arms swinging gently with her steps as she came down the small slope to the river bed.

"Want some rocks?" Tevin said, lifting a glob of wet sand and flopping it down.

"I already got mine and my sand was dry," she said, teasing.

"How do you look so good? You drank twice as much as me."

"Tete," Fabia toyed, calling him by a nickname. "I always look good, and don't forget it. But . . . I also got this wonderful energy cocktail from a hummer Healer. You must feel her energy. Soothing and painful at the same time. Delightful."

Tevin got to his feet. "I'm going to light a fire and dry off."

"No time," Flann informed him, looking up at the sun as he sat on a log putting his shoes on.

"Then, I'll change. Walk me to the *party* when you are done?" Tevin asked as he started walking up the hill.

Flann nodded. Fabia sat on the bench next to him, stretching out her legs, her boots going up to her calves. As the rest of the group started to head back, Felix was making his way down the hill to put sand in his borrowed shoes, seemingly calm and unconcerned about the day's events. Fabia watched him. Flann finished putting his shoes on and rested his elbows on his knees.

The two watched Felix fumble with the shoes, walking awkwardly when he put them on. "Come on. Let's get this over with so I can get out of these contraptions. Feet aren't meant to be in shoes."

"Take them off then," Fabia announced. "You obviously have calluses to be able to handle anything. Besides, you have a connection to the earth through your feet. That is all you need."

"I knew you thought my feet were sexy," Felix responded. He was already kicking his shoes off and picking them up. "Here." He tossed the shoes at Flann. "Take these to Brom. Tell him they didn't fit."

The sand flung everywhere and landed a step away from Flann. He wiped the sand from his pants as Felix jumped the river and walked into the thick of the forest where no path existed.

Flann and Fabia were finally alone. As he got up to get the shoes, she said, "Do you want to talk about it?" Her voice was soft and compassionate.

"No," he said reluctantly, keeping his back to Fabia and looking out over the river.

"You know I love your brooding energy. I can bask in it *all* day."

He ignored her.

"What are you going to tell Nora?" Her voice returned to a quiet, sincere tone.

"The truth," he said firmly.

"Which one?" she asked.

He turned to face her. He knew it was safe to be angry with her; she wouldn't make it all about her. "This isn't right. None of this is right. I gave my word to Nora—"

Fabia interjected. "But not your heart."

"I thought I did." He pulled his fingers through his hair, as the other hand held the dripping shoes. "I wanted to. I *still* do." There was quietness for a moment before he continued. "I feel tenderness toward her and more affection than I have ever felt with anyone else. I want to take care of her and I want to provide for her. How is that not love?" he asked, confused.

"She is not a pet lamb that you love and take care of, Flann," Fabia said lightly.

Raising his voice, he retaliated. "I never said she was. I respect her and I've treated her otherwise."

Fabia stood to face Flann. "You *treated* her like a PET. She was someone who validated you and made you feel worthy."

Flann started to speak, but she held up her hand to silence him, her temper clearly engaged. "DO NOT GO THERE WITH ME. You asked me for the truth, and I am going to give it to you. Yes, it may not be easy to hear, but it will save you suffering in the long run." Tugging her shirt down and diffusing her anger, she looked him directly in the eyes, this time with compassion. "Are you ready to listen?"

Flann swallowed, feeling like he had been punched in the stomach and sat in the corner for a time-out. Except his time-out was violet eyes that were vibrant and focused, giving him no room to escape. He closed his eyes for a moment, reminding himself that he was willing to hear the truth. When he was ready to listen, he opened his eyes. He could see Tevin at the top of the hill, waiting.

As soon as he made eye contact with Fabia, she spoke. "I want to consider your relationship with Nora. Does she challenge you? Does she get under your skin and make you want to pull your hair out? Does she nurture your spirit? Does she fill your cup?"

She waited for an answer, and it took Flann a moment to catch on. He thought about his relationship with Nora. It was an easy relationship, and he liked that. He liked that she saw him and not his station in life. They were comfortable with each other, and he felt relaxed and at ease around her. He felt proud to be with someone who was beautiful and kindhearted. If he was honest with himself, he did feel important that a worthless slave could be with someone so valued, so out of his reach. He quickly dismissed this, reasoning it was a thought that only belonged at the start of their relationship. As if to prove it to himself, he thought about how he adored her shy mannerisms and sweet nature. He felt like being with her was too good to be true. Yet they had never had a fight. There was no conflict between them, only the circumstances of his previous station in life and now the distance between them. She didn't get under his skin. She was so forgiving and understanding all the time. And his spirit? He didn't know what Fabia was talking about.

"What are you saying? That Nora is a safe choice?"

"What I am saying is that the universe doesn't give you the partner you want, it gives you the partner you need that will cause you to grow and evolve to your highest potential. It is your choice which path you choose. The easy and safe path or the discomfort and growth path. Neither path is good or bad, right or wrong. That's our human brain's interpretation. It just is. Rest assured, there are no mistakes."

She lightly kissed the side of his cheek as her words sank in. Then she headed up the hill. Flann called to her. "Then why does it feel like there is a right answer?"

She kept walking up the hill but shouted an answer back to him. "When you are ready, you will follow the path that was yours before you incarnated in this body. Until then, you will get lots of lessons to guide you to your path." At the top of the hill, she wrapped her arm in Tevin's. "Come on, boyfriend, I'll escort you to the party."

Flann stood motionless, feeling the discomfort of the wet sand in his shoes. He heard Tevin joke back that he may be a taken man soon. The two walked off, bantering back and forth. Flann turned to the side so he could see Felix walking on the unbeaten path, barefoot, alone, and happy, while the rest of the group unconsciously walked the path of ease to the Ceremony. He wondered which path was right for him. Then, he slowly turned to the path of ease and followed Fabia and Tevin, feeling like a million pounds were on him.

He was about to be in the same place at the same time with two women who were pivotal in his life. *This is a bloody nightmare.* In his mind, he had violated two women that mattered to him. Nora, by kissing another woman when in a closed relationship with her. Sabina, by kissing her when he was in a closed relationship with Nora. He didn't deserve either of them. An honorable man would have done the right thing, and if he had, he would not be in this predicament. Or would he?

He was at the top of the small incline. He believed he was the last in the Loaded Hurricane. He wanted to be alone, so he was disappointed to see Brom, the Prince, and Kean at the entry point to Silvedome. Flann heard Brom saying "That's enough" repeatedly to the Prince. Kean stood in salute, like a warrior waiting for an order. Most of the men that shared part of Sabina's life force were people that Flann liked. The Prince wasn't one of those people and Kean . . . Kean was more like an animal than a human being. He rarely spoke and when he did, it was one or two words, maybe a short sentence. He had this eerily angry energy that was palpable. He had a facial expression that said: I DON'T CARE, or STOP TALKING TO ME. He had bulkier muscles than Flann, yet moved like a snake, fluid, powerful, and surprisingly flexible. He had jet-black, stringy hair that was always pulled back in a ponytail or bun. When he wore some of it down, Flann had noticed that the ends were naturally curly. He had a ghost beard and mustache.

If Kean didn't look like he hated everyone with that energy to match, he would have gotten a lot of solicitation for dates. Instead, everyone avoided him except for Brom. Oddly, Brom was hired by Kean's parents. Someone had cursed Kean when he was an infant, which was why he had this tangible angry energy about him. Kean's parents were wealthy and had sought every solution possible. Including hiring Brom to influence his energy. Brom agreed, in exchange for his life force for Sabina. Flann never understood why Brom would have attached his kid's life to a curse, but he suspected he did so at the direction of Nana Honey.

For years, Brom was able to minimally reduce Kean's energy. Not enough to keep him out of trouble, but enough to keep him alive. However, ever since Brom shared some of his life force with Kean, he lost much of his ability to influence his energy. Now all the group had to suffer the effects of his toxicity.

It was no coincidence that Kean, with his anger, was the group's rare Protector. Though he and Bard were both strong Protectors, Kean was a killer. He didn't seem to be able to control his anger when he fought, as if something was unleashed inside of him. Hence Flann thought of him as an animal.

Out of all the Moowins, the Protector Moowin showed up the most among all of Sabina's shared life force partners. It was as if Brom had manifested several people who shared Sabina's life force to have this defensive ability. Even peaceful Viggo had a mild Protector Moowin, but Kean was special in that he was also a rare Shield. No one knew that except for Kean, Brom, and him. Pond's ego wouldn't have been able to handle another rare Shielder in the group and so anytime Brom talked about shielding, he addressed Pond only. However, Kean understood that he was to subtly assist in a way where Pond didn't suspect it.

Kean was the only one in the group to possess two rare Moowins. Flann felt pretty good that he was a rare Messenger, significant Protector, and mild Persuader. Viggo was the only other with three Moowins, but his other two were mild at best. Flann was practically a rare Protector, and he had wondered if Sabina did amplify him into being a rare Protector. But, then, if she did that for him, she probably was an amplifier for the rest of the group too.

Brom called out, "What are you brooding about?"

The Prince said something under his breath that Flann couldn't hear.

Brom snapped, "That's enough."

Kean had his arms locked in front of him. Flann saw him squeeze his fist and heard his knuckles pop as he ground his teeth. He was looking toward Flann, but speaking to the Prince. Growling, he said, "I vote for knocking him unconscious."

Brom looked over at Kean. Flann wasn't sure if he was annoyed or considering Kean's plan, but he actually liked the idea. The Prince had a way of making every minute with him feel like twenty.

"I'd have my servants cut out your tongue while I watched, you worthless dog, if we were in my country."

"That's enough," Brom firmly said.

Kean chomped his teeth together, trying to provoke the Prince with his straight face and dead stare. Brom, seeing the Prince about to spit on Kean, pulled him to the other side of him causing the spit to miss its target.

"Where is Felix? I could use some help?" Brom said. "Are those my shoes? Did he at least try them on?"

"He is wandering through the trees, barefoot," Flann commented as he handed over the shoes.

"Carry them. I need to keep these two separated," he ordered. "Come on, let's walk and talk."

Brom did a mock bow to the Prince, indicating for him to lead the way. The Prince did a fancy step turn, a step he probably did when he led his people, but it irritated Flann that the Prince got satisfaction out of others following him. Flann fell in step with Brom, and Kean followed. Brom's palpable anger worked up a sweat on the back of Flann's neck.

Flann wasn't about to confess that he had kissed his daughter; luckily, Brom wasn't a Truth-sayer. However, he did have a secret. One that Flann wasn't supposed to know. A secret no one was supposed to know, Flann gathered, since no one talked about it. However, he had figured it out, or at least he thought he had.

Brom was either a significant or a rare Persuader. Flann was observant, and he had noticed people changing their minds easily when dealing with Brom. Also, Flann swore a few times that a few of his thoughts were not his thoughts. There was something off about those thoughts. Almost as if they were a mirage. This was another reason that Flann respected Brom, but didn't fall for his charisma. Although these days, he was all drill sergeant and his charisma was saved for people he wanted to influence.

Images of Sabina immediately came into Flann's mind.

"Are we going to have any problems? You're acting like your favorite horse was shot." Brom said this discreetly, but Flann knew Kean would have heard.

"Why would there be a problem?" Flann answered.

"Don't be sarcastic with me."

"In other words, don't be myself with you. Got it." Flann would rather talk to a toad right now and he didn't talk to reptiles.

"You need to be better than yourself. YOU ARE MY DAUGHTER'S BODYGUARD. You are not some boy mooning over some girl."

Flann flipped his head to Brom, heart in his throat, his temples pulsating with every heartbeat.

"No distractions, Flann. Nora shouldn't be here . . ."

Flann immediately relaxed, blocking out what Brom was saying until he grabbed his arm and turned to face him.

"This is why I specifically said no partners until after Sabina was safe from the Selectors. You cannot focus on what I'm saying, you're brooding, and . . ."

Flann yanked his arm away from Brom, feeling the burning sensation of energy pouring into his forearm muscle. He poured it on thick. Like an elixir of adrenaline.

"Don't touch me," Flann spat, refusing to massage the discomfort in his arm.

"You have a job to do, Flann, and right now, I'm not sure you are up to it. I did what was needed. The energy will settle in a few minutes. Walk it off and be at the Ceremony prepared for blocking those crystals. We will talk later about what to do with Nora."

Agitated, Flann responded. "Nora is none of your concern."

"But your ability to do your job *is*. I cannot have you moping around or running off to be with her when you should be focused on your job."

"I **AM** FOCUSED on my job."

"Prove it." Brom left Flann, walking with large strides to catch up to the Prince, who didn't notice anything going on behind him.

Kean walked up and stopped to stare down at Flann. The two stared at each other for three heartbeats before Kean talked. "Be present," Kean said through one side of his mouth as he chewed on a thin piece of bark. Then he walked calm and sure toward the town.

Finally, Flann was alone, but adrenaline was making his heart race and his breaths feel short. It was an odd way to feel. His emotions felt dread, but his body felt a surge of excited energy. The two contradicted each other in Flann's mind and one had to win. He walked to the Ceremony, letting the adrenaline build and eventually settle in his body, pushing out any feelings of self-doubt.

Without his recognition, a subtle focus settled into his body. One of pure determination to see that Sabina was safe. One that came with a one-second flash: an image of Sabina in the Loaded Hurricane, safe and training with the full strength of her Protector Moowin in place.

~

Brom walked confidently to the Ceremony, knowing he'd personally prepared all the men who shared a bond with Sabina both mentally and emotionally. Even the Prince was focused and blessedly quiet. Then there was Fabia, with her hair pulled in a high ponytail, eyeing him from a distance as the men got into place around the Ceremony. She wasn't bonded to Sabina. She was too wild to control, influence, or reason.

They had a strange relationship as Brom was like an adopted uncle when he became her godparent. If something were ever to happen to his best friend, he would be her and Viggo's benefactor. He had known her since she was an infant and even then, he was unable to influence her, much to her parents' delight and dismay. Her energy was too erratic to sync to, but he was able to persuade her with images. Maybe because it wasn't his initial energy or Moowin but a benefit from a shared life force of a long-past relative. During his cousin's life, the shared life force extended him a hint of the Persuader Moowin but upon his passing, the universe miraculously gifted him with the full strength of it. This was an unheard-of experience and one that Brom had never discovered the reasons to. But there were a lot of things he stopped questioning and just accepted.

He could tell by the way Fabia looked at him, she wanted to know something but wasn't going to ask without first studying his energy. She was a Truth-sayer after all. They trusted the inward expression more than the outward expression. He wished he could give her a job so she would stop focusing on him.

"What is it?" he finally said, giving himself space from the Prince.

"Nothing I want to share," she said.

"Since when did you not want to share something with me?" he asked.

Staring hard at him, she said, "You may be my godparent, but do not fool yourself into believing I tell you everything."

Brom got the impression she was mad at him. He automatically took a step back; Fabia worked best when she had space. Fabia was unpredictable, and he needed today to be as controlled as possible. "Have I offended you? I assure you it was unintended. Come, what can I do to make amends?" He was as relaxed as he could manage.

She was quiet for a moment. The first sound of the beats indicated the ritual was starting. She continued to examine him. "This day has consumed you so much it has changed your identity, even as far as the very way your energy vibrates. Are you so out of alignment that you cannot feel it or do you not care anymore?"

He rubbed the back of his neck. He needed to get into formation with the others. Resigned, he took a deep breath in through his nose and focused on Fabia. She would sense if he was rushing her. "I care. This is very important—"

Cutting him off, she spoke with conviction. "No, you don't."

Brom shut his mouth, his lips firmly closed. He wasn't talking to Fabia, the little girl he helped raise. He was talking to Fabia and the mystic spirit inside of her.

"Up until recently, you have helped others out of service to them. But now you help yourself."

He retorted. "What is wrong with helping myself? We all help ourselves."

"You have deceived yourself. Your willpower is for your fate, not others. It causes harm to control the fate of others." Sabina tilted her head, appearing to read his aura with a "Tsk, tsk, tsk."

"All this when you only needed to allow it," she continued.

"What was I supposed to do?" Brom protested.

"Trust that everyone, including Sabina, would have the journey they are meant to have."

The beats of the drums picked up faster. Brom looked over his shoulder, seeing the two others press forward.

Rushing, he said, "I did what I must, and I played my part. That is my level of trust."

She was not one to back down. He had no authority over her and she knew it. Taking a step forward, and firmly addressing him, she stated, "You fell to your fear and exhausted your willpower."

The truth of those words hit him hard. It was as if a meteorite blew a hole through his chest. Dropping the tension in his shoulders in surrender, he looked down and pinched his nose. Looking up, he saw a beautiful, young woman before him. He felt proud of her courage, integrity, and competencies, but she didn't understand what it was like to have a kid.

Slowing down, he said with compassion in his voice, "Fabia, I would have done the same thing for you. *It's who I am.*"

"And I would have rebelled against it despite my love for you."

He gave a half smile, knowing she would have made it difficult to protect her. "I need to go. Thank you for your concern," he said, taking a step toward the ritual.

Raising her voice to talk over the haunting melody, she pleaded. "You do not understand the consequences of your actions as they come late. You have sacrificed your health, peace, and relationships. What else will you sacrifice?"

The drum's beat was announcing he was out of time. Distracted, he bellowed, "**Everything**."

Her hair whipped everywhere despite being pulled back. The wind picked up speed. Cupping her hands around her lips, Fabia shouted louder. "It's not too late to take responsibility for what you have done and mend this."

He looked at her warily and then took off running to his point in the circle, his blue coat flapping in the wind. He pressed forward and fought the resistance of the ritual's power.

∾

Fabia watched him and felt a deep sadness. She knew he saw his actions as an act of unconditional love. From his perspective, his interference was protecting and helping Sabina from a fate he didn't want her to have, but it was really a selfish act on his part to avoid feeling his feelings. "So be it," she whispered, understanding he had his own journey to experience, and she had done all she could by informing him. Whatever he chose was not her concern.

She walked far enough from the ritual to feel a place of calm energy and sat under a large tree. Closing her eyes, she quieted her mind and called to her birds.

The Day Of The Birth Challenge

S abina's body woke up. Her body was pulled into a sitting position as if she were a puppet and the master deemed her to be up against her own will. She looked around and saw darkness through her little window. *Is this how it is supposed to be? Why does no one talk about their experiences of the Birth Challenge before they show up to the ritual? Ugh, I have no references to go by.*

Sabina stretched, feeling the sleep leave her body. Her hair was in her peripheral vision, which meant it was a mess. She dared to clear her throat and check to see if she could make any sound. Though she made the action, there wasn't any sound despite the forced breath work.

The silence. The silence was like an alarm going off inside her body. The silence was so thick she knew to her core she was alone, something she had always been, or at least always felt, until Flann. There was no electrical pull to him as there had been last night. Without the pull, she felt disoriented.

She swung her bare feet to the cold wood floor and cringed at the chill against her warm skin. She got up and hustled upstairs. She was standing outside his door without remembering walking up the stairs. The silence was there as she stood outside his door, hoping to find him, and knowing she wouldn't. It felt like something was sitting, weighing heavy on her heart. Her heartbeat was slow with effort. She raised her fist to the door and held it there. *What if I wake him? Maybe I should just open the door in case he is sleeping. Don't be stupid, you know he isn't there. You could knock the door down and it would not change anything.*

With her internal dialogue loud in her head, the silence had finally been pushed out to make room for her thoughts. Deciding, she pressed one hand to the door and the other on the doorknob, slowly turning it. She held her breath and felt the loud thrums of her heart. The door silently opened, to her relief. She peered into the desolate room with an undisturbed bed. In fact, it looked as if no one lived there, much like her room.

Her arms dropped by her side and she gloomily walked over to the bed, sitting on it. He was gone just like she assumed. Just like she felt. She laid her head down on the pillow and allowed the sadness to wash over her. Why did it matter if he was gone? What is all this sadness about, she asked herself. She had been abandoned countless times before by her father. Rejection was so familiar to her that it could have been an invisible lover. The kind that always stayed in the shadows, waiting and taking but never giving. And she gave plenty to this invisible force in her life.

She rolled to her side and could smell the smoke fire scent of him and her heart lurched. What was he to her, anyway? He wasn't a lover. She had never had one of those, and she wasn't going to fool herself into believing a kiss made them anything more than they had been before it. That kiss was an experiment, she reminded herself. It was a final moment, capturing her youth and taking action without the pressure of consequences. It was a lesson, and what she learned was more than she had expected. She learned that the kiss said everything about what she longed to be: a person who asked for what she wanted and knew she could have it one day. A person who let go of fear and judgment, and took action to go after her desires. That aspect made her feel incredible . . . powerful. But, on the flip side of the coin, the kiss spoke of what she could not have . . . with him anyway. There was a dark truth in that kiss that taught her that there were internal consequences, even if there were no external ones. That wanting was toxic and led to suffering. It was far better to be grateful for what she had than to suffer over what she did not have.

For a moment, she allowed herself to think of the kiss as that of a woman who recognized she had a need, a need to be wild and free in spirit. A need to be touched and held. A need to be loved and seen. The only reference to those needs she had experienced was a kiss with a man whose bodily reaction told her he did not belong to her. Yet the kiss woke something within her and for that, she was grateful.

The softest touch of lips caused a vibration that rattled her bones and melted her at the same time. No words were spoken after the kiss. No closure was given, yet they held a tension between them. The reality was she wasn't able to speak with him due to the Birth Challenge preparation, and she would not have known what to say anyway. Because she ran away, she would never know what he would have said if she'd stayed. Although a part of her sensed he chose not to speak when he could have. The evidence was clear. He didn't go after her or stop her last night . . . or say goodbye this morning.

Though her heart wanted to focus on the power of that moment as something special, her logical brain could not deny there was an outcry within her that said 'I'm sorry' every time she recalled the jerky reaction of his body. There was the dilemma. Her mind and her heart battling inside of her on what the truth of this moment was. Even as the lack of his presence confirmed one truth, the flush of her body—remembering his lips lingering on hers despite the rest of his body saying no—confirmed the other. Both realities seemed to exist to her, and that made no sense. She distracted herself with other questions.

So, what is he to me now? She knew he was not a partner or a boyfriend. It was obvious he didn't want to become one either, even if his lips had lingered on hers. His actions this morning proved that. Gone without a word, without a note, and without a care to what she needed. What did she need? . . . Closure. A friend to witness her monumental moment, or perhaps a partner who would stand by her side even when she made a mistake. Not to say that she needed him. She didn't need anyone, and the steel within her solidified at that thought. That was a hard-won lesson that she learned in her youth and she wasn't going to forget it now. She was alone in her circumstances. Not alone altogether, for she understood that she was never truly alone.

She belonged to herself and the universe who always took care of her. When she remembered she belonged to the universe, she remembered that was all that really mattered. Her affirmation that everything would be all right came to mind. It was time to let go of the little girl's yearning to belong and instead step into who she was: a woman who was capable of many things.

She sat up and looked around the room, feeling the silence once more. Maybe she had hoped for a friendship with Flann, but he was moody and often withdrawn. Honestly, she didn't know if she liked him. Hadn't she discounted him as a possible match for her from the beginning? If it wasn't for that burning desire to be bold, daring . . . reckless in her last moments as a 'child', she would not have kissed him, she consoled herself.

Then she would not have looked into his intense green eyes before she leaned in to kiss him. Had she not leaned in, she would not have seen his eyelids become heavy and the intensity of his green eyes go soft. And she would not be feeling these feelings and she would not be asking herself these questions. For what did they have between them to make her want any more?

This is what I get for being a foolish girl, she said to herself as she got up, determined to push him out of her mind. She was strong. She was stronger than anyone realized and she was going to show everyone that today. She walked out of his room, feeling renewed with purpose.

However, there was nothing to do but wait for her Birth Challenge as it was early still. She took her time getting ready. She braided her hair, put on red lipstick she found in her sister's closet, and decorated her nails, which was something that she had never ever bothered to do. She had the dress her sister made for her ready for the testing after the ritual.

Despite taking her time to primp, there was still more time to waste. She lit a candle in her barren room and sat to meditate. She watched the glow of the fire and let all thoughts clear from her mind. She sat and sat and wondered if she would ever experience the guidance that was supposed to come from meditation. After a long time, she felt a stirring to trust herself and seek Fabia. Followed by the realization that she needed to have more fun. Well, that wasn't going to happen, she told herself. She gave up and blew the candle out.

She busied herself immediately, grabbing her things to leave and not thinking about that thought any further until she left the house. With the sun starting to rise, her internal dialogue kicked in, as it usually did when she walked. She thought to herself, *There is no way I am spending time with Fabia, the girl who disappeared into thin air and is most likely crazy.* And just like that, there was Fabia gliding out from a space between two houses, making her own path instead of following the path all the villagers walked.

Conflicted, Sabina stood there. Part of her wanted to drill her like a mother and ask where she had been, and the other part wanted to put an invisibility cloak on to avoid any conversation. Neither mattered. She had no voice, and interactions with people caused her discomfort in this state of ritual preparation. That triggered something she wanted to remember, but no matter how she tried to focus, nothing came to mind. Letting the thought go, Sabina reasoned that Fabia was fine. No one from the Ori had been seeking her. *Count your blessings, Sabina.*

~

During this whole internal dialogue, Fabia read Sabina's emotions and discarded her importance and self-pity. It was not her place to teach Sabina, though she really, really wanted to . . . for her sake.

"Beautiful Sabina. You needed a little color on you." Her chaotic hair and black paint smeared on her face might have given the impression she'd slept in a tornado, but she owned her space with confidence. Fabia did a one shoulder shrug. "I would have chosen black."

Fabia walked closer, a tiger stalking her prey, watching Sabina with those violet eyes. "I *hear* your vibrations. Don't worry so. Everything is fine. Viggo is at Nana's and Flann is . . ."

Sabina's head snapped up. She hadn't been thinking of Flann, or had she not stopped thinking about him? *How could Fabia tell? Did she make this stuff up?* Regardless of what Sabina thought or wanted to think, Fabia had her attention immediately, and she desperately wanted to know the truth, as Fabia saw it. She scolded herself. Fabia was not someone she wanted to believe.

". . . he has work to do this morning but I see that you did PRACTICE a little bit of fun." Fabia's eyebrows were raised.

Sabina flushed. *How does she know this? She is not a Seer.*

"Tsk, tsk. I would have had a whole lot more fun." She stood in front of Sabina with her hands on her hips, cocking her head from side to side, looking at Sabina from different angles. "You only tasted fun when you could have devoured it, but . . . I do not know this strange spell they have put on you. **And,**" she said with a tone of disapproval, "you chose a man sealed in self-control and discipline. I am surprised that you got that far with him."

Sabina didn't know if she should feel embarrassed or impressed by Fabia's opinion. The woman confused her and left her feeling uncertain about far too many things. She wondered if she could take a large step to the side and walk around her. If possible, try to forget that this conversation happened and not think about what her words meant.

Fabia reached her hands up as if to touch the invisible shield around Sabina, but hesitated. Looking into Sabina's eyes, Fabia asked, "May I?"

Huh. *Is she asking permission to touch whatever is around me? I did not expect her to be considerate of how that would make me feel.* Sabina shook her head 'no' and watched Fabia drop her hands in clear disappointment. *I don't get her. Why did she ask? Why did she respect what I said?*

"W.h.y are you leaving so early?" Fabia questioned with a puzzled expression. "You have plenty of time."

Sabina pointed to her throat to indicate she couldn't talk, but Fabia waved her off. "Think it and I will sense it."

How was she supposed to answer Fabia when she didn't know herself? That she was bored sitting at the tut? That she didn't know what to do with herself, so she might as well get there earlier? That she felt anxious? That she would rather face her challenge than hide from it? Although Sabina did not allow herself to think about it, she needed to stay busy so she didn't think of him.

"Do you like him that much?" she said, pulling on her bottom lip in thought. "It's not my place to condone your actions or desires, but it's never wise to go after a man whose integrity is stronger than his heart. His word has already been given." She smiled and shifted her weight. "Although, my little Queen, I am loving how much you are tempting him. BRAVO!"

She looked toward the village, "She is here, not that her presence will matter. Nora won't fight you for him and you don't have it in you to fight for what you want, not yet—my little Queen. You are getting there." She turned her attention back to Sabina. "You will grow fast and when you do, I will ride on your waves of power." She seemed distracted as she stepped away from her like she was hearing something that was more entertaining than Sabina.

Sabina stood with her mouth open in shock. She didn't

understand Fabia or where she got her information. Whatever she thought, it was nothing more than an opinion, a story she had made up. Sabina knew she DID NOT like him. She wasn't thinking about him either. And it didn't matter that Nora was here, but at that thought, her stomach twisted in guilt that she had in fact kissed a man who was in a relationship. What did that say about her? The guilt she felt turned into anger at Fabia for pressing her to be something she wasn't.

Fabia, who had been walking away, stopped. Her back was to Sabina. Her shoulders raised to her ear and her arm shot up. She snapped her finger in a downward motion and turned in irritation.

She hissed. "This is what I see."

Sabina's world changed. Everything that once was in focus was still there but a blur. She saw grid lines of different colors. Blue and red were the most predominant, but there was a spectrum of colors interlocking and crossing. She looked down and saw the lines did not cross whatever shield was around her. She could see a thick, white bubble around her that foamed or sizzled at the edges. She looked up and saw that certain lines vibrated as Fabia continued speaking.

"YOU can lie to yourself all you want, but you cannot lie to me." She spread her arms out wide. "Every line represents an emotion, and it vibrates with thoughts. I am able to read that vibration. That is not something I can show you," she said, walking with intentional, dramatic footsteps toward Sabina, not breaking eye contact.

Fabia walked through the lines like they didn't exist and Sabina wondered if any of the lines belonged to her. *Is that how it works?*

"You will have to take my word for it that a part of you loves Flann."

Horror like she'd never felt before oozed from every pore in her body. She felt her hands and armpits wet with sweat and her vision seemed to tunnel. Denial lashed Sabina's mind, as if it was an anchor on a drifting ship. *How can I love someone I don't even like?* she shouted in her mind.

"Oh, that's cute. Nice try, but it doesn't work that way." Fabia kept walking up to her.

"Love, like, hate, dislike . . . they are all connected to the same emotion you feel with varying degrees of intensity, like temperature. That emotion moves through you with each experience. But you do not own any of them, even if you hold on to them for an indefinite period of time. They are meant to be felt and released, making room for the next emotion. You believe you can rationalize your emotions but *you cannot*," she lectured, pointing at Sabina. "You can only think a thought and, in response, feel an emotion. You think you don't feel something because you are not allowing yourself to feel your emotions. That's foolish. You are only trapping that feeling inside of you, pretending your thoughts can control it." She shook her head. "Those emotions will only cloud your thoughts so you cannot think clearly."

Fabia must have seen a confused look on her face. She rolled her eyes. "Do you love yourself?" Fabia asked. She snapped her fingers, and the lines disappeared. The blur of the world came back into focus. But before they disappeared, Sabina noticed a few blue lines jumping with activity that would have gone straight through her solar plexus if she didn't have this shield around her.

Taking her eyes off her abdomen, Sabina felt defiance running warm down her spine. She crossed her arms and leaned on her back leg. She thought, *Of course I do.*

Fabia smiled a vicious smile, like she had captured her prey and there was nowhere to escape. "Yes, but do you like yourself?"

Sabina faltered. *What a stupid question, of course I do.* But then her mind flooded with self-judgment and past criticism. All the times she had told herself to do better, be more, and try harder. How many times had she told herself *That's not good enough,* or asked herself why she couldn't be like her sister or her peers? All the comparison and the ranking of where she fell in the barometer of being likable, being special, being important. The realization was crushing. She thought she would have been on her knees from the weight of it all but she was standing. She lifted her head slowly.

Her eyes glistened with unshed tears as she looked at Fabia, feeling more vulnerable by the second. If she had these thoughts about herself, did she love herself? Did she think she was worthy of love?

"Now we are getting somewhere." Fabia nodded her head in approval. "That's why I like you, even if you are a scared mouse hiding in the weeds right now. I know there is a fierce beast within you desperate to be released, little Queen."

A single tear slid down Sabina's cheek. She was surprised by the tear. Surprised to feel anything outside the normal self-deprecation and longing to belong, to be special. It occurred to her that she wished that what Fabia said was true. She wished she did have 'something'. Maybe not a beast, but something that gave her a purpose. Something that made others recognize her as special. An epiphany hit her. The way Flann looked at her made her feel special, like she could walk through fire without the flames touching her.

"I will help you today. Consider it a gift." At that, Fabia thrust her hand through the invisible shield and locked her hand in Sabina's, holding on firmly. Sabina was racked with wave after wave of pain. A pain radiated through her whole body, like when someone's funny bone was hit in just the right way. It was that same radiating pain that was both tolerable and intolerable. Fabia laughed and threw her head up to the sky, delighting in the sensation.

Sabina attempted to pull her hand away, but Fabia's nails curled into her skin as a reminder that she held the power. Sabina was tired of feeling powerless. The thought slammed into her like it was the most important thought she could have for her survival. Sabina pushed the pain away and fought to find the calm knowing she felt when fighting.

"WAIT," Fabia shouted, as if they were both in a windstorm.

She brought her head level with Sabina's. "First, what do you FEEL right now?"

PAIN, screamed Sabina's thoughts as her ears roared with the sound of white noise.

"Yes, and now?" Fabia asked as she let go and took a large step backward. Her arms were held out wide to the side, her chin was dipped, and her teeth were gritted together. She was breathing hard.

Sabina felt like her eyes were fluttering in her head, but she took breaths and thought words of gratitude. She bent over with her hands on her knees, her Birth Challenge dress barely in her grasp.

Urgently, Fabia shouted, "WHAT DO YOU FEEL NOW?"

Pain, you crazy . . .

"**No**, try again. Do you feel pain or do you remember pain? What do you *feel now*?"

Do I remember pain or feel pain? As Sabina asked herself that question, the fog started to clear. She. Remembered. The. Pain. Awe spread through her at this realization. She was not in pain right now, but she was focused on the pain she felt moments ago.

Standing up taller than she ever remembered, Sabina scanned her body for how she felt now. *I'm fine. I feel . . . solid and grounded, actually.*

"Yesssss, my little Queen. It's time you stopped holding on to past emotions and letting them keep you down. The past is nothing more than smoke that you are grasping to hold on to with a death grip, but the only thing you can hold on to is the present moment." She smiled and winked slowly. "Let go of the phantom pains of the past that are intangible wisps of smoke and choose your thoughts based on the now, for that is all you have. The past is gone."

She snapped her fingers and showed Sabina the energy grid again. All the lines were calmer, steadier than they had been before. Perhaps the lines were thicker. She couldn't say for sure. She noticed her shield took up less space. She heard the snap of

Fabia's fingers and looked up to see her walking away, swinging her hips.

Sabina smiled and thought to herself that Fabia might be crazy, but she was also brilliant. She turned and walked the opposite direction as Fabia, feeling lighter than she had ever felt. She wondered if this was what it meant to be light and love. She had always assumed light meant that she should be a source of light in the darkness, but now she thought maybe it meant to be as light as a feather. To be able to fly over your troubles and burdens because you managed your mind in a way that lightened the load. All you had to do was let go of the pain. Then you would be physically lighter, as well as light from the perspective of modeling a different way to live.

The lightness Sabina felt was short-lived as overthinking kicked in and she thought of love on her walk to the Ceremony. She questioned how it was possible to love herself when she treated herself so cruelly. If she loved herself truly and deeply, would she judge herself without understanding and compassion? Would she try to become like her peers and deny her gifts, or her thoughts? She supposed she must love herself to some degree because she took care of her body and her mind, just not her spirit.

She arrived at the outdoor area with its cement seats, stairs, and stage and looked at the empty theater. She had waited sixteen years for this day and here she was, standing in front of this inevitable destiny to find out what talents she had, if any. Whatever the ritual revealed would ultimately affect her fate, and she had no control over any of it. She clutched the dress her sister had made for her closer to her body, sending a silent plea to help her be that fierce beast that Fabia saw within her.

The stage looked larger and darker than she remembered. The spotlight was already on the stone table that she would lie upon to receive her declared blessing . . . or curse. She knew someone was here, even though she didn't hear or see anyone. All she knew in that moment was she felt a pressing need to pray. The sun was peeking over the land and she knew her ritual would be starting soon. If anyone was going to come, they would be showing up in moments. But it didn't matter if they saw her praying and thought she was crazy or unprepared. She needed the calm she felt when she called out to the Great Spirit. She stood with her eyes closed and her body trembling in fear. She closed her eyes and had a personal conversation with God.

Infinite Spirit, creator of all,

Today I come before you to receive whatever gifts are tied to my purpose in this life. I am aware and understand that how I serve will become illuminated, and I will become responsible for my actions. I accept this fate and the responsibilities associated with it.

I do not wish to downplay the importance of this ritual, but I would like to make a vow to myself as I transition into adulthood. That vow is to love myself completely. I vow today, the day of my Birth Challenge, to care for myself and give myself love, forgiveness, and compassion as I grow and evolve. I vow to treat myself like a Queen who is worthy of love, respect, honor, and an exceptional life. I vow to love who I am and value what I bring to this world. I vow to trust myself and the way I feel. I vow to let go of self-judgment and fear as well as my past and my ego that prevent me from embodying love for myself and thus others. This is my declaration to the universe to serve and be someone willing to make a difference in this world. This is my intention and I ask that you lift my spirit and protect this vow. In gratitude, it is done.

She opened her eyes and saw the small figure of the Mistress standing halfway between her and the stage, looking pensively at her.

Blushing, Sabina realized her face was wet with tears. She wiped them as discreetly as possible.

"We must hurry. I am needed at the border." The Mistress turned and walked down the stairs to the stage, obviously used to everyone falling in line behind her. She continued talking as she hurried toward the stage. "I would have canceled this ritual even though it would have hurt my pride to not keep our commitment. You would have been the first ritual canceled in our recorded history," she said as she walked up the stairs. She held onto the railing and turned to look at Sabina with a serious eye. "The truth is we need your ability to amplify immediately."

Sabina had been following, feeling like an animal led to the slaughter house. *This is a spiritual death,* said an alarming voice within her. She felt jittery. Like every pump of her heart released spikes into her bloodstream.

Her mind raced. *But I don't know how to amplify. That's why I'm getting trained in it. How am I supposed to do this?*

Not bothering to coddle her, the Mistress surged up the rest of the steps and around the corner. "I hate to say this to you, but death is the best teacher. It's sink or swim time, girl. You either face your fear and walk through it or . . . Let's not focus on an alternative option. I have complete confidence that you will find a way to access your gift and hone it before the day is over."

She pulled a curtain back from a small wooden box that represented a changing room. "Your robe is in there. Change into that. You can leave your Birth Challenge attire in there. You won't need it. With the attacks on the dome, there are few available hands to do the rest of your Birth Challenge," she said, slightly out of breath. "We are making an announcement after your ceremony that we need every person of age to help, even your guests. There are more attacks than we have ever encountered," she said, looking grim.

It was as if unsaid words—'This is war'—floated between them before the Mistress left Sabina standing outside the changing room, trembling. Unable to ask questions, Sabina felt burning in her stomach, recalling the professors at the water. Flann hadn't said what he learned, and she had been focusing on herself.

She thought of her father's letter. This was her fault if she was in fact the Agni. Sabina was aware she was the problem. Her spike in energy was drawing the Selectors to Silvedome. Thinking it might be safer for the village, she asked herself if there was any way of avoiding this ritual? No. Not really. She would have to leave Silvedome if she chose not to do the Birth Challenge based on their custom. Plus, she needed to enact her gifts to be safe. Plus, the Mistress said they needed her. Her plan to go to the Loaded Hurricane seemed cowardly now she knew her people needed her to help keep them safe.

She went into the small box to change into the dress that bore no resemblance to a robe. It was soft against her skin and light enough to make her feel like she was not wearing anything at all. She could hear noises outside her changing room and she pulled back the curtain to find Wolverine sitting on a box outside, looking at his hands in silence. He looked up at her with deep purple bruises along his face and a cut lip. A section of his black hair looked charred.

Automatically, Sabina went to ask what he was doing, but her voice locked. All that was heard was the straining sound of air being sucked down a tube.

"I came to see you fail," he said without any bite behind it, as if he was too tired to fight.

Feeling even more naked, Sabina wanted to wrap the changing room curtain around her, but she didn't. She looked at him, feeling a sympathetic pain as she watched him stand slowly. She knew the pains of fighting and he looked like he should be in an ice bath, not mincing words with her.

Standing, Wolverine felt like he was swaying. The day and night of fighting had left him drained and without aptitude for caring about keeping up his 'old' persona. He was here because she was always a mystery to him, with flares of brilliance and strength for someone who couldn't get anything together. He was here because, for the last two days, he couldn't stop thinking about her. He was here because he thought no one else would be. He was here because he hated that Sabina had easily struck him down in those rare moments of sparring and he had to know if she was a Protector. But the real reason he told himself he was here was because Nana Honey asked him to be here and you did not cross her. He was also here because in the thousands of seconds since his Birth Challenge, he had lost something he could never get back. Something called to him to know more.

"I'm surprised your boyfriend isn't here. Not the Prince. I was happy to see him go. The other one with the hard stares and fake smile. Doesn't he know this is an honored tradition for our people?"

He started to fall and Sabina automatically reached out to catch him, feeling waves of pain at the physical contact. He quickly pushed off her arm and stood up. Sabina felt like a bucket of ice water had been dumped on her at that brief but unsettling touch.

"You don't have what it takes to do what I did. I am not saying that to be cruel. I am saying that so you don't follow in my footsteps."

Sabina looked away. His normal 'better than' attitude was gone. He spoke with a tired sadness she didn't understand. Despite the mental and physical pain he was obviously in, his words still hurt. His judgment affected her. She didn't want him to see that effect on her face, but it was too late.

"What? I'm the bad guy here," he said, putting more energy behind his voice than he had shown in the whole conversation so far. He pointed in her face but it lacked aggression. "I see the hunger in your eyes when you watch me fighting." His voice became smaller and Sabina looked at his lips as he spoke. "This isn't what you want. There is no glory in it." And his parting words were "Trust me."

Anger swept over her. How dare he presume what she

wanted? He didn't know her. He only knew how to upset her. As quickly as the anger came, it fled. It was replaced with concern at watching him move like an aged man with arthritis.

He stumbled down the stairs, managing not to fall thanks to the grip on the handrail. He walked slowly but with his head up. Sabina watched him, feeling like her feet were glued to the floor in fear. *What happened to him? Why is he here? Why hasn't he seen the Healers? Why isn't he with the Healers now? With his ashen skin, he . . . he looks like one of the sick ones that don't make it through the night. There was no warmth in his touch either.*

"Wolverine, you did well," the Mistress said with respect in her tone but with worry on her face. Her hand was on his shoulder, and she gently guided him toward her. "Have you seen the Healer?"

He shook his head 'no' and it looked like tears were brimming in his eyes.

"Go home and get some rest. **Then** *see* the Healers."

He nodded and walked on.

What happened to him? Agh, I hate having no voice. I have tullom questions and it's so frustrating to be silent.

The Mistress faced her, walking up the stairs. "It is time. Everything is prepared. MOVE, Sabina. We must proceed."

Managing to move her heavy feet, she walked over to the edge of the stage. Her heart was fluttering and her body felt like a hurricane. Taking steadying breaths, Sabina looked at the stone table with the light-blue pad resting on top of it. It had a hole cut out for the face to rest in comfortably as she lay facedown. She glanced up at the metal contraption holding the special magnets attached to smoothed crystals representing each of the chakras. These crystals would be magnetized to the individual's charkas along the spine based on the strength of that person's gift. She had seen it a thousand times before from the audience but never from this angle. The attached crystals looked to be five arm's lengths away from the table.

Looking out and realizing she had an audience caused a

butterfly sensation in her gut. She had anticipated being alone with the Mistress until Flann showed up in her life. Then she assumed he would be there but, as she looked through the crowd, she couldn't find him. She felt his presence though like a warm hand on her back.

It was her nerves she told herself. She noticed her Duckling friends sitting well-behaved between Master Frock and Bee. She smiled with love at their presence; they took up the entire row. She saw Scholar Sandalwood on the other side of Master Frock, cross-legged and sitting up tall, beaming with positive energy. Several of the hospital staff were there but not her mother and not her sister.

At least she had Crystal. She could always count on her. Crystal, Nana Honey, and Master Fis sat together with a slender, frail redhead with hollow cheeks, high cheekbones, and a peaceful glow. That must be Nora, thought Sabina gazing at her with appreciation. She was beautiful even as she sat there looking uncomfortable and glancing around. Probably looking for Flann. *Where is he?*

Sabina scanned the crowd again. There were a few villagers who enjoyed witnessing the rituals and a professor from school. She wasn't quite sure, but it looked like Wolverine sat in the back of the stage by himself. She focused on him. He rocked slightly, looking at his interlocked hands. Where was his confidence? It was unnerving to see him not gloating over this victorious battle to save Silvedome. A wave ran down Sabina's spine.

Mistress had finished walking the stage, tossing out salt and chanting vowels. She stood at the table, looking at the audience as someone behind the stage beat a beautiful rhythm on drums. The deep, quick vibrations seeped through Sabina and helped her heart know what beat to follow. When the drum stopped, and silence was in its place, the Mistress called out in a surprisingly deep voice for her tiny, frail body.

"We gather today to witness Sabina Rockdin's Birth Challenge Ritual where she will shed the skin of her adolescence and step into her role as an adult, a servant of our people, and an honored citizen of Silvedome. This ritual will awaken any talents within her that may have been hidden or not ready to embark. The divinity within her will answer the call of the Infinite Spirit and she will become who she was always meant to be. Today starts the first day of her life. Her parents and loved ones release their hold on her and her identity so that she may accept the truth of her purpose. Today she honors the universe and accepts her path. May all who are gathered here today respect and surrender to Sabina Rockdin's ascension. SABINA ROCKDIN, you are called forth to meet and align to your higher self."

The Mistress swept her hand over the table and faced her. Sabina swallowed. She thought to herself, *Today is a good day to die but, if possible, let me live.* Taking deliberate steps, Sabina walked onto the stage with the crowd watching. She looked down at her white, thin silk gown, seeing her bare feet with each step over the rise of her chest. She ignored the display of the shape of her nipples. She reminded herself that everyone went through this ceremony. There was nothing to fear or be modest about.

She could feel a light breeze touching her bare skin along the spinal column opening of her dress. The dress was designed for the entire spine to be accessible to the magnetized contraption. This allowed the crystals to have open access to the chakra energy centers within the body. Even the men wore shorts with a V-shape cut out to expose their spine.

It was tradition to braid, knot, or wrap your hair, but the crown and back of head had to be open for the crown and third eye chakra. Sabina had her hair pulled into a side braid and the braid naturally rested over her right shoulder. She turned to face the table and looked at the audience. Her heartbeat was in her throat and her fingertips tingled. She felt as if she was in a story of old where a sinner faced ten lashings for their wrongdoing. She could almost feel the presence of someone behind her holding the whip in their hand, smiling at the future pain they were going to inflict.

She was grateful that she was still fasting. Otherwise, her stomach would have been churning and she would be running for the bathroom. She saw black spots in her vision as she looked out over the crowd, still searching for Flann. He wasn't there! *Why isn't he here?* She breathed quicker, still feeling the restriction on her throat.

A light drumbeat started, soft and slow. She scanned the crowd again, frantic for his presence. She swore she could feel him but her eyesight gave her self-doubt. She closed her eyes and felt for him. *There, to my left, the outer edge of the stage.* She looked up and saw a person's shadow. *Why is he standing at the edge of the arena?*

The drumbeat suddenly became fast with a final thunderous boom and Sabina felt her chest pull forward, gasping in a large breath. She coughed at the rush of fresh air against the back of her dormant vocal cords.

"SABINA ROCKDIN, DURING YOUR BIRTH RITUAL, YOU WILL BE TESTED FOR EACH MOOWIN AS IS OUR CUSTOM. MAY I PRESENT TO YOU THE EIGHT MOOWINS REPRESENTED BY THEIR ASSOCI-ATED CHAKRA CRYSTAL AND PLACED IN ACCOR-DANCE WITH THE CHAKRA CENTER." The Mistress pointed to each crystal and named its purpose.

"HEMATITE, ROOT CHAKRA, *PROTECTOR.*
"ORANGE CALCITE, SACRAL CHAKRA, *PERFORMER.*
"CITRINE, SOLAR PLEXUS CHAKRA, *INFLUENCER.*
"ROSE QUARTZ, HEART CHAKRA, *HEALER.*
"BLUE APATITE, THROAT CHAKRA, *MESSENGER.*
"SODALITE, THIRD EYE CHAKRA, *SEER.*
"AMETHYST, MIND CHAKRA, *PERSUADER.*
"CELESTITE, AURA CHAKRA THAT RESEMBLES THE ENTITY OF MIND, BODY, AND SPIRIT, *SHIELDER.*"

• • •

The Mistress continued. "The stronger your Moowin, the stronger the pull of the representing chakra crystal to your chakra center. For those with a mild Moowin, the crystal will vibrate but remain attached to the magnet. If you have a medium Moowin, the crystal will detach from the magnet and show your strength in that Moowin by closing the distance to your chakra center. If you have a strong Moowin, the crystal will attach to your chakra center. But be forewarned, for those with an extremely strong Moowin, the crystal will slap fast and hard against your chakra center. And in the event of a rare Moowin capability, the crystal will melt into the chakra center which is known to be painful but brief. Be at peace as this is a rare occurrence, hence the title, and an honor to receive.

"SABINA ROCKDIN, DO YOU UNDERSTAND and AGREE TO THIS RITUAL AND ALL IT CONTAINS?"

Moving her jaw around to create saliva in her mouth, Sabina let out a weak "I understand and accept the terms of this ritual."

"AND WHAT IS THE CHOSEN NAME YOU WISHED TO BE CALLED HENCEFORTH?"

"Roots."

"MAY THE RITUAL BEGIN." The Mistress held her hand out to help Sabina take the steps and crawl onto the table. Sabina had her knees up and slowly lowered her body to the table. With arms supporting her, she looked up to see if she could find him. She saw Crystal's effort to smile as she looked beyond her. Flann. Though she could not see his eyes, she knew he was watching her with his heart beating just as fast as hers. She lowered herself on the table, resting her forehead on the pad and feeling her breath bounce off the stone and back into her face. She heard the movements of the Mistress and knew she was bowing to the table.

Despite feeling like she was facing her nightmare, she was able to manage a smile at the sight of Crystal and Nana Honey decked out in their finest attire, with their hair wrapped and crystals beaded along their faces. *It was really thoughtful of them to treat this as a wedding. I guess it is a wedding of sorts. I am marrying the Great Spirit and devoting myself to serve the Infinite Spirit through my ascension of my higher self. I wonder if anyone else ever thought these thoughts as they waited for their chakras to open and for divinity to speak to them?*

Sabina lay facedown, feeling the weight of her body settle into the padding and listening to the silence and her inner dialogue. Nothing would happen until the Mistress was twelve-feet clear of her. This was custom to prevent any interference with the energy of another person's Moowin. Sabina slowed her breathing and listened. As she quieted, she felt it. The angry ribbon of energy reaching toward her feet. It was so alarming she almost shot up and looked around. She relaxed her arms back down. She was supposed to remain still, and she did not know what would happen to her if she moved. Her mind raced. This meant her father was here. OR, calming down, she thought it was more likely he was messaging Flann. *CALM DOWN, Sabina. I mean Roots.*

In the audience, Nora whispered, "Roots? What type of name is that?"

"A good one," answered Nana Honey with pride, her voice shaking a little, overwhelmed with emotions. "She is showing the world she is strong and root-ed in self-acceptance. She is communicating to Silvedome that she vill grow into something that provides for the universe. Provides shade for the traveler, a home for the animals, firewood for the cold, oxygen for the earth. She is telling all of us she is vise beyond her years."

"It's an ugly name," Nora said, sounding appalled.

"Our names are chosen to represent us in our adulthood," Crystal whispered across the others to Nora. "I named myself

Crystal to represent my vibrating energy, healing powers, and sharp beauty."

"I am named Honey to rep-rrresent my healing powers. Honey explains my ability to find the trrrruth in a sticky mess of life, and the sweet rrrrelief of providing answers to those who are searching. I can be sweet and delight your senses, or I can cause an allergic reac-tion or increase blood sugar levels. Both light and shadow are needed for my vork to exist."

Nora looked at Master Fis expectantly but she said nothing. Crystal answered for her.

"Her chosen name is Songbird, and she heals through humming as she works."

"And what did Flann choose," she asked with curiosity.

Nana Honey answered with thick disappointment. "He hasn't. He has twwwooo weeks to choose name and brrreak free from his old identity."

There was silence until the Mistress sat behind the Ducklings. Before the ritual could begin, there was a loud shout from one of them. Sabina heard Master Frock quiet them before the beats of the drum started, slow and steady at first like a trickle of water. As the beats picked up, a warble came from a flute and tied into the beats of the drum. Sage burned and wafted along the stage.

It was all about to begin. The time had come for Flann and the others who were tied to Sabina's life force, and were a part of the union interview, to edge their way closer to her. They were all positioned to surround the Ceremony and were waiting idly by for this moment. They didn't have much time to creep forward unnoticed before the energy would gather in the salt circle and the crystals would be engaged.

Flann looked to his left and saw Felix, the Influencer and to his right, Tevin, the Seer. Beyond Tevin was Bard, then Viggo who uncharacteristically had decorated his face in reflective stones, and behind the stage were Brom, Kean, Pond, and Zoel. They were all walking swiftly forward with sheer determination. Flann and Tevin were the furthest back. Flann couldn't feel the energy prickling his skin until he got closer. All he sensed was his heart beating in sync with hers. He immediately located Nora with regret, hoping he could find the man he was for her. The flash of Sabina arching under him came into his mind, the feel of her body as he looked at her chin. Last night's kiss. A kiss that sent a jolt through his body even though their lips had barely touched. Her soft, plump lower lip that begged to be kissed.

As if his thoughts were being broadcast, Nana Honey looked at him with contempt as her eyes flicked to Nora and back to him. 'Crossroads' slammed into his mind like the reverberations of a powerful hit. He hated what he had done to Nora. He should be with her now. He should be confessing his weakness to her and asking for forgiveness. Instead, he walked past her as if she meant nothing to him. She sat with Nana Honey, unaware of his presence. They didn't have the pull toward each other like he felt with Sabina. Despite the pull toward Sabina, he felt he owed Nora. She was friendless in this new town and here because of him. She was probably confused why he didn't come to her. After all, it had been two years since he last saw her. She looked as docile and delicate as ever. Long-lost feelings stirred.

Flann's attention was pulled back to Sabina as the music increased speed. With the increase in tempo, Flann noticed he and the others slowed as a resistance like walking in water hit them. He looked over and saw a small blue child had started to unwind a wheel that brought the crystals closer to Sabina. The flute started to play a haunting melody that didn't match the speed of the drums. The contrasts stirred emotions in him and made him feel like a trapped animal about to face his death. He looked at Tevin and saw alarm in his eyes. He wasn't the only one feeling this tension.

With the dropping of the crystals, it was time to be at the outer edge of the stage. They needed to be closer. To his surprise, Flann was closest to where he needed to be compared to the others. He thanked God he had fasted and sat in silence. Tevin had spent the night with Fabia drinking and menacing the night away and it showed now as he was not making ground. Flann watched as Tevin closed his eyes and gritted his teeth. He circled his arms like he was swimming in a pool of energy. Despite looking odd, he was getting closer. Flann copied his movements and saw the others do the same thing.

The heat pressed Sabina into the pad and the weight in the air felt like a wet sauna. She felt beads of sweat along her forehead but was grateful that the sweat streamed along the padding and not into her eyes. She knew she wasn't supposed to move but a sense of being trapped settled over her. She couldn't move if she wanted to. The weight against her was heavy. She couldn't hear anything except the music and the music seemed to swirl along her skin. She had a vision pop into her mind of standing on a hill, holding a ball of energy. She was directing that energy toward an army. *Does this mean I am a Shield after all?* she thought.

The vision switched. A beautiful man with darker skin than hers whose face changed, flickering back and forth between his own face and that of a brown bear. This man was tied to another who lay on the floor, a metal collar around his neck. This second man's face changed between his own face and a dog's. This man was haunting to look at, full of rage and beaten down. His eyes stared at her like a hungry dog willing to attack anything for survival. She heard a voice within her. *"Set him free."*

The vision changed. A woman was inches from her face. A woman who looked like her, with bangs, and thicker brown short hair who reached out and held her cheekbones. "This was never supposed to happen. I'm sorry. I cannot stop it. Know that I love you and I will guide you through this." She melted into the light.

~

Nana Honey, watching through her third eye, saw it all before it was about to happen. She didn't have much time to act or explain.

"Master Fis, make me unconscious NOW and give Sabina back her life force i-mmed-iately. Take some of my life force and give it to Crystal before it's gone."

Master Fis's eyes enlarged at Nana Honey's suggestion, and she shook her head, worried—no, frantic. "I cannot do it and this will kill Crystal. She cannot take on more life force than complete."

"You don't have a choice, my friend. Now be quick. Ve don't have time. You vill have to dirrrect Crystal's ex-tra life force to Sabina. She vill need it. Crystal, my vill and intention is for you to receive vhatever gifts of mine the Infinite Spirit vill allow you to have and that vill serve your highest good."

~

Master Fis and Crystal moved toward Nana Honey but were too late. She arched her back in pain and slid to the ground, convulsing as foam gathered in her mouth.

Master Fis, in pure fear and panic, called out to the source within her. Adrenaline pumped violently through her at seeing her best friend's energy slip out of her body. She didn't even have time to hum for her magic to surface. It was all rushed. A desperate internal cry of need deep within her.

The sphere that Nana Honey held tied to her body shattered with a popping sound. A white light drifted up and zoomed with lightning speed to Sabina. Crystal, who had managed to get around her, was holding Nana Honey's head and chanting with her eyes closed, but the spell was cast. Crystal's words were stolen by the magic in the air.

Master Fis reached out with shaking arms to grab Crystal. Crystal groaned in pain as her chest expanded and her head was thrown back. Light slithered out of her throat and drifted in the air, pulsing like a confused child not sure where to go. Then Nana Honey stopped convulsing and her body went still and heavy. Her last breath let out a puff of energy that floated up and into Crystal's chest. Crystal's life force shot toward Sabina and then stopped. Master Fis watched all this in horror at what she had done. She should not have been able to do this. This wasn't even possible. Master Fis felt the growing pressure of fear over what she had unintentionally done. She watched as Crystal's life force changed directions and started backtracking. To Master Fis's horror, Crystal's life force flew into Wolverine's chest, and he was knocked backward off the seat.

Shaking, Master Fis looked down at her beloved friend while she still gripped Crystal, realizing that she could not sense her friend's life force anymore. Crystal was sobbing; her tears fell down, splattering Nana Honey's face. Nora sat on the bench with her knees drawn up into her chest, shaking as if she had seen a ghost. Master Fis, still consumed with failure, looked down at her lifelong friend in shock. She pulled both hands to her face, gasping. There was no life to her friend. She had transitioned. Master Fis's body trembled harder.

All of this happened during the time that Sabina got her last vision. She was holding both hands of a golden creature made of tiny circular, moving lights that came together in different shades. The light shaped a tiny girl with Sabina's facial features. She had wings, all made of this circular, moving light that flapped, as the light circles moved back and forth to keep with the action. Although there were no words, Sabina understood this was her higher self. She felt delighted and privileged to know and see this beautiful moving entity of golden light that shone brighter at the edges of her body. The edges looked like white light. It dawned on her this was an important moment and she quickly thought of what she could ask. But before she could, the entity jerked her head to the side. She heard something. The golden entity shrieked, revealing sharp jagged teeth, then flew away.

Sabina panicked. If that was her higher self, it scared her, and she didn't know if she trusted being with that entity again. Yet Sabina didn't want her to go either. She formed the thought to call her back but before she was able to, she was engrossed by burning, raging pain. Her entire body jolted off the table and slammed back down. She could hear her voice screaming but had no conscious control of it. Her entire spine was on fire and her vision swam with fiery pictures until there was nothing but white light in her vision. Her heart was being squeezed. She imagined someone holding her heart in their fist and squeezing it shut as her heart was torn into shreds from the pressure. She could no longer hear the external world because of the rushing sound of water in her ears.

She felt that red ribbon of angry energy wrap itself around her until it reached her throat and then she tasted smoke in her lungs. Sabina didn't understand what was happening but part of her trusted that red energy, knowing deep down that it had not hurt her in the past. She clung to the lesson from Fabia that this was an illusion of pain. Conceptually, she understood that she might experience pain if she had a rare Moowin but never anything like this.

She was paralyzed by the pain and fear spiked within her. She couldn't take it anymore. She attempted to move her limbs and push herself upright but all she felt was her body being burned alive. That was the last thought she had before she was swallowed by darkness.

In The Fog

The Ceremony erupted in screams and chaos. They watched Sabina's body violently convulsing to the point that it briefly lifted from the pad and slammed back down. The Mistress stood up immediately in alarm and fear. In all her years, this had never happened. Wind and energy coursed outside the salt circle making it difficult for her to see what was happening. And then she noticed the crystals. All eight glowed as if their center was melted. They vibrated against the base and looked ready to explode. *This must be a sign Roots is an amplifier for all eight Moowins.*

"S.K.Y A.B.O.V.E," the Mistress whispered as she brought a hand to her lips. She needed a Messenger and she needed one now. The council needed to know about this immediately.

A cry from behind the Mistress sounded, and she turned to see Nana Honey's lifeless body and Crystal rebounding as if something had hit her. The Mistress climbed over the cement seat to get to the cleared row behind her. She needed to get to Nana Honey. However, by the time she had yanked up her long black dress and straddled the seat, the Ducklings had started shouting. Frantic cries over the roar of the wind picking up speed.

The Mistress glanced over her shoulder to see blood splattered along the invisible walls of the salt circle as a crystal landed with so much force it tore savagely through the tissue of Roots's skin. The Mistress automatically flinched at the blood spray that looked as if it was going to land on her. She felt a moment of fierce pride to see Roots claim the status of strong Shield—possibly even rare Shield, by the intensity of the crystal's landing. She sent an arrow prayer to Roots. She knew when it made contact with the skull, the Shield Moowin was one of the most painful to experience.

Pulling her attention away from the ritual, the Mistress could feel her body in reaction-mode. She was aware she needed to slow down. She paused in the middle of chaos to be the observer and to take in the scene. She could feel wisps of hair being blown out of her tight bun and she was still straddling the seat as she looked all around her.

The Ducklings were flapping their hands and screaming, standing and ready to bolt. Scholar Sandalwood and the others were standing up in front of them with their arms outstretched wide, as if to catch the Ducklings from spreading out and crossing the salt barrier. That's when the Mistress noticed men within the salt circle, on their knees or facedown, some with blood coming out of their noses, convulsing in harmony with Sabina.

She recognized Master Alf. He was lying on the ground. His face was fortunately turned to the side as drool ran out of his mouth and his eyes rolled up into the back of his head so that only the whites could be seen. She didn't recognize any of the others except for Master Tulk, who was kneeling, one arm reaching out as if to grab something. He had a slow drip of blood coming out of his nose. He looked to be shuffling forward with determination on his face. Before she turned away, she saw a strange shirtless man with dark hair and a muscular physique who was standing, taking one small step at a time, approaching Roots. He looked to be using all his strength to fight the power of the salt circle. His neck muscles strained and his mouth opened in a scream, or perhaps a growl. He looked close enough to reach her.

The Mistress quickly turned around and saw Scholar Crystal

and Master Fis sobbing over Nana Honey's body. A movement caught her eye and she looked toward it. She was shocked and unnerved to see Wolverine place one foot on the seat, then the other as he moved into a standing position. He stood completely rejuvenated and whole, minus the burned hair. As far as she was concerned, it was like his body had risen from death. He stood full of energy and power like he was possessed by some spirit and he looked at Crystal, ready to charge.

"Bloody hell," the Mistress said quietly. There was no mistake that he had looked ashen and close to death before the Ceremony and no magic was permanent in a ritual. But magic must have taken place as he now radiated with energy that was different from his own. A chill ran down her spine and concern pumped through her veins at a pace that made her feel like she couldn't breathe. She didn't know if this young man was in fact Wolverine or a creature wearing his skin.

What is going on? How many things can go wrong? She felt like she was needed everywhere all at once. There were too many problems to solve.

NO, she told herself firmly. *I AM NOT a victim of circumstances. It is a simple choice of what serves Silvedome best at this moment, so choose your best choice, Fog.*

Decisively, she weeded out the lost causes. Those young men were most likely going to die in the salt circle and there was nothing she could do about that. She couldn't help Roots or Nana Honey either. All their fates were outside of her ability. The Ducklings were in good hands. She could trust the hospital staff to take care of their charges.

That only left Scholar Crystal who was in imminent danger of this unnatural presence. With that quick assessment, the Mistress decided she could help her now. She assured herself she would get a Messenger to communicate to the Ori the oddity of the crystals and what it could mean as soon as possible.

She raised her hand, a signal to stop Wolverine from jumping over the seats, but he had tunnel vision for Crystal and it seemed she was not in his view. He hurdled over the seats like an animal with unlimited energy and agility to get to Crystal. Seeing him move unnaturally over the seating sent another wave of panic through the Mistress. They could not lose Nana Honey and her backup in one day, especially now with Silvedome in great danger.

Despite the ancient wisdom and warning to never use magic at the same time as a ritual, the Mistress counted on the forgiveness of necessity and threw a shield around Crystal and Master Fis as best as she could. She ran breathless toward them. As she hustled to the aisle and feebly ran toward them with her arthritic joints, she noticed a redhead sitting huddled in a ball, but she couldn't identify her. This woman had not gone through the approval process that all visitors were required to do. How did she get in? Who was she?

It didn't matter now, the Mistress told herself. She was clearly no threat as she buried her face in her knees and clung to her shins. Whereas Wolverine was a threat and it was clear he was going to make it to Crystal before she could. In a state of shock or grief, neither Scholar Crystal nor Master Fis were aware of what was happening or what was approaching them. Desperate, the Mistress called out their names—"Scholar Crystal, Master Fis, CRYSTALLLLLLL"—breaking yet another rule for the audience to be silent during a ritual. Ancient wisdom warned them to never draw unwanted energy or spirits to themselves during a ritual. However, the Mistress would rather be cursed with spirits and save her people over keeping herself safe. She knew in her heart there was only the now and the future was not a guarantee. Her efforts were wasted as the wind carried her voice away.

A boom sounded, causing the Mistress's ears to pop from the air pressure. The earth trembled. She bent her knees and squatted down to the earth for balance. She was looking at Wolverine who was over Crystal, snarling at her. She was confident Wolverine had snarled "What have you done" before the minor earthquake.

While the Mistress was distracted with forming and executing her plan, Kean fought his way to Roots as one crystal after the next overcame the pull of forces from the other Moowins within the circle. Each crystal came down, thwacking hard against Roots's exposed back. Bard, who was still a distance away, exposed his secret and used his shapeshifting to lengthen his arm and catch the performing crystal that hit with such focus and potency that it appeared to burn a whole into his palm. Screaming in pain, he shocked the crystal out of his hand, which landed with a thud on the floor. It started to vibrate with energy. It was only a matter of time before it was pulled back into Roots. He had only delayed the inevitable.

Kean saw Bard had stopped moving toward Roots and was slowly sidestepping on his knees toward the fallen crystal, presumably to attract it to his energy. But its vibrations were getting strong enough to bounce it off the floor. It gained momentum. Once Kean reached Roots, he saw the Shield crystal had already embedded and melted into her skull. He wouldn't go for the Protector crystal for several reasons. One, it was in too intimate of a place to touch, and two, Brom wanted her to have the full strength of Protector power. The crystal didn't change the fact Roots would be a rare Protector even if he had blocked it, but the crystal did stabilize that energy, which was a benefit.

Not wasting time, Kean used his non-dominant hand—which had shreds of his shirt wrapped protectively around it—to plunge into Roots's skull and pull out the crystal. The crystal was melting into her skin and the heat of the crystal was melting the skin off his fingers. He roared in pain. His shirt singed at the edges and blood oozed over it, mixing with Roots's. Despite her hair being pulled in a side braid, it was matted with blood and melted crystal—white crystal with chunks of charred black spots contained within it.

Kean gagged at the sight. He squeezed his eyes closed and

begged his body to pull out whatever remains of the crystal he could. He could feel his nails scrape against the crystal despite his fingers losing nerve sensation. He demanded that his hand pinch his fingers together. He pulled his shirt-wrapped hand back as the crystal clung to it, already cooling off. His hand shook uncontrollably, and his fingers felt permanently curled as the skin charred, black and weathered. As he looked at his hand in disbelief, a popping noise sounded and the wind disappeared like the shutting of a door.

He had all his weight leaning into the wind and with its absence, he fell hard into Roots's lifeless, bloody body. His charred hand smeared blood and black grit on the side of her ribs where the silky white had somehow remained clean. He slid down hard on his knees, feeling his kneecap crack against the cement. He fell over to the side, passing out in pain.

Bard, lying with his head rattling on the stage, saw what happened to Kean. During Kean's fall, he had managed to loosen the crystal from his wrapped hand. It rested on the table next to Roots's body. Bard himself had fallen with the dissipation of the energy circle and had rolled partly on his side, cupping his burned hand. His body was rigid as he felt Roots's crystal hitting his heart. He would have moaned in pain if his tongue had the ability to move. He fought to remain conscious as the earth shook.

But it wasn't only the trembling of the earth that had changed everyone's attention. The shimmering energy around the salt circle was gone, along with the wind. The ritual was completed and with it came the tremors from the earth which the Mistress had instantly thought was an earthquake. Now she knew it was the sound of hundreds of horse hooves hitting the earth. The dome that had shielded Silvedome for hundreds of years without fail was gone. The once bright, beautiful sunny skies disappeared and in its place were dark clouds and smoke-filled skies. She could tell it was dark and cool outside, something the people of Silvedome had never experienced.

The war was visible and the people of Silvedome would see and know the truth: They were not as safe as they thought they were. They were unprepared for this day or for anything like it. What would they do with the dome walls down? There was no protection to the people of Silvedome. The Ceremony was close to the dome borders. They would be among the first civilians attacked.

"BLOODY HELL," the Mistress whispered.

Her priority shifted once again. There was no time. The people of Silvedome needed the protection of the shield walls which made the dome. The Mistress crawled into the row of seats and lay down, giving herself some shelter. Using all her strength, she attempted to pull the shield back up. It didn't flicker despite her will and effort. She needed the team. What had happened to them to cause the walls to fall? Though she hated to admit it, she needed Pond. He may be arrogant, but he was indisputably the most gifted of them all at keeping the shield reinforced. He alone could save them. Her stomach clenched to think what must have happened to cause him to lose his ability to hold the wall.

As she lay looking at the grayed sky, asking herself what she should do now, a trumpet sounded in the near distance. She pulled herself up using the seats and stood. Bringing the dome wall back up may not be possible on her own, but the weather was. That is what she could do.

She stretched out her arms, fingers spread wide, and called to the skies for their protection. As she looked up, she saw the sky fill with hundreds of black crows, circling over the Ceremony. Not knowing if the birds were her doing or whether they'd always been there—having never seen the real sky before—the Mistress claimed her gift and pulled fog down upon Silvedome. And as simply as using her intention and authority over her gift, a thick fog crept in out of nowhere. The grounds disappeared under it and the fog slowly rose to cover everyone's heads. She felt immediate relief and a sense of victory, feeling the trembling of the earth slow.

She could hear Wolverine's voice. "You have to leave her. It's not safe here. We gotta go. I'm telling you the Selectors are here. Did you forget they want to collect everyone with a Moowin?" he said, clearly frustrated.

"DON'T TOUCH ME," Crystal yelled. "Go if you must. I'm not leaving her."

The Mistress felt for each row of seats and closed the distance between them. She could hear Master Frock commanding the Ducklings and feel the drunk cocktail of calmness sweep over her. *Smart woman,* the Mistress thought.

Worrying over the precious Ducklings, the Mistress started to go into problem-solving-mode, thinking the hospital wasn't far. But neither were the Selectors. *Where is she taking them?* The Mistress's stomach burned with fear. Her strength was low from creating the fog, but she stopped and sat on a seat, closing her eyes, visualizing the Ducklings, putting a thin shield of sound around them. They would still be seen, but at least not heard. That was the best she could do for them.

"Crystal, you are smarter than this. *Why* risk your life for someone who is dead?" Wolverine said, flapping his arms by his side in frustration.

"Don't talk about her like that. Why are you even here? Why do you care? Just GO," Crystal commanded.

"Tullom. Trust me, I want to leave you but for some reason I CANNOT. Grieve later. You have to leave her body. We don't have much time."

Gathering her strength, the Mistress stood. She could feel more hair coming out of her bun and falling forward in her face. She swooned slightly forward and stumbled painfully into the next row. Crystal noticed through the thick fog.

"Mistress, are you okay?" Crystal asked in a calm, uncertain voice.

Looking at Wolverine in front of Crystal, the Mistress saw the change in him but sensed no danger. Something was different about him though. She turned her attention to Crystal, and she saw something shimmer in her aura. *Is it the fog or has something happened? Why is she dressed for a wedding?*

Cotton-mouthed but authoritative, she responded. "No. I'm not okay and neither are you. When we get through this, I'd like an explanation. You are now the council representative in place of Nana Honey. I know you are grieving and rightly so, but YOU have responsibilities for our people and I suggest you do them **right now**. What do we need to know to keep our people safe while the dome is down?" Though she felt disheveled, the Mistress said this in her most commanding voice.

Crystal looked at her with a blank face, blinking. A dried path of tears marked both cheeks and the crystals alongside her face sparkled despite the fog. She blinked slowly, and the Mistress saw a woman go from shock to control in that slow blink. Wolverine sat down and then immediately stood back up, looking prepared for action.

"They are almost here," he whispered.

Crystal kissed her two fingers and placed it on Nana Honey's forehead. She gently laid her head down. She got to her feet with a glazed look and talked without making eye contact with anyone. Her voice was mild, almost monotone.

"Pond is able to re-secure the dome wall once he is healed. He will trap the Selectors on horses inside the dome walls but will block the rest. The warriors need to be pulled into the dome wall to fight. The other Selectors will leave soon after."

This was not how Nana Honey guided the council, but the Mistress didn't have time to question the vision. Thinking out loud, she asked with concern, "But where is Pond?" To her surprise, Crystal lifted her arm toward the stage with her eyes still out of focus.

Following where Crystal was pointing, the Mistress was unable to make out anything through the fog. "Wolverine, help Scholar Crystal to the stage. Master Fis, you are coming too." With abrupt directions given, the Mistress hustled toward the stage as she listened for the Selectors. She could no longer hear anything outside the sound of a horse nickering.

Nora, who had been sitting huddled in a ball, terrified of looking at the lifeless face of the woman who had brought her to this strange place, asked, "What about me?" in her soft, high-pitched voice as the group followed the Mistress. She watched as Wolverine guided Crystal by the shoulders in her zombie-like state and as Master Fis wrung her hands, mumbling "This is all my fault" so low that only Nora heard it when she walked by.

No one paid any attention to Nora. The group disappeared too quickly into the fog, leaving her defenseless and alone. She jumped up and nervously followed the group, taking tiny steps, reaching her foot out timidly, patting the ground to make sure each step was safe. She extended her arms out in front of her. Unaware of what was happening, Nora's thoughts were on the fog, thinking this was worse than being in a steam bath. She was totally uncomfortable and out of her element. She felt small and uncertain about what was happening and what she should do about losing the group. She couldn't remember any of their names to call them to her, so she settled for a cry for help.

Her plea of "Wait for me" was high-pitched and weak. As she walked, an older man with soft, wrinkled skin and several large, dark aging spots grabbed her wrist and pulled her toward him. He was wearing a long robe and was bald with a few missing teeth. Nora cringed.

"You don't belong here. Who are you?" he hissed from his crouched hiding place between the rows of seats.

Nora's mouth gaped open. She had never been treated this

way in all her safe, privileged life. She was too taken aback to do anything but suck in a large breath. After her eyes adjusted and her heart came back into her chest, she realized the man wasn't hurting her, despite his strong grip. He had only alarmed her. She was not used to dealing with peasants of his age. He should be in bed being cared for by his family, Nora thought, taking pity on him.

"Never mind. Get out of here, girl. You have no business being here and you certainly have no business up on that stage. There is enough magic on that stage to turn you into a fried egg."

"Where am I to go? I was only brought here this morning by a crazy woman who is now deceased. She was supposed to bring me to Flann Alf," Nora said, looking around, seeing nothing through the fog and feeling anxious for Flann to come find her. "Do you know him?" she asked softly.

"Get your head on straight, girl. This is the eye of the storm and you best be getting out of here with or without this elf mister," he urged, trying to pull her to the side of the Ceremony.

At that moment, the fog shifted with a light breeze. Cool air rushed over Nora's thin, bare arms as more of the air from outside the dome settled over the land. With the stirring of that breeze, Nora was able to see a young man lying lifeless on the ground with short reddish-brown curls and a wide chin. Even though she only saw him for a brief moment, she knew in her heart who she had seen before the fog moved back in. Her heart sank. *Oh Flann, what am I to do now?* She started to hyperventilate and crumbled where she stood. The older man caught her and sank to the ground with her.

~

"Sky Above," he complained, wishing he had never tried to help this girl. He had things to do. He had revenge to seek against the Selectors for killing his only daughter all those years ago and leaving him alone in this befuddled world. Despite his age and the fact that he was no warrior, he planned to take down as many Selectors as possible. He thanked his good fortune that he happened to be close by, cleaning the office floors.

The old man let the girl cry on his shoulder for a few moments as she fisted his robe and blew snot on it, still unable to catch her breath. He was a patient man, but not at a time like this. Not when a quietness was settling over the land, and black birds were circling above like an omen of death to come. He had hoped that giving her a moment to cry would allow her to move on, but this redheaded girl with no weight to her was fragile of body and mind. Tullom his luck.

Even with the fog being as thick as a curtain, the old man had the ability to see through the veil. He had his Birth Challenge some twenty-five years ago when Silvedome took him in after Selectors murdered his wife and daughter for their unwillingness to go peacefully with them. They each had multiple Moowins, though weak on the scale of desirability. But according to his ritual, he only registered for being a mild Protector and Performer. Nothing grand or worthwhile, but still a potential partner to pass along his talents to his unborn future offspring. However, he wasn't interested in starting a family, and he made that abundantly clear. And still Silvedome kept him. He never understood why Silvedome granted him the honor to live in the protected village under the impenetrable dome walls.

The old man was never able to see how his talents contributed to Silvedome. Even now, as he crouched holding an unfamiliar girl in his arms, he was nothing more than someone who cleaned up messes. Most people in the village called him Eagle—they thought he had an uncanny ability to see great distances—but his chosen name was actually Cactus, for his ability to weather the storms life brought him.

He hushed the girl, seeing long-cast shadows approaching from the back of the Ceremony. "What are these hysterics about, girl?" he asked more firmly. He had to get her to calm down.

Using the back of her hand, she wiped her nose and looked at him with big tears gathered in her eyes. "My partner." She broke down in sobs once more. "The person I came here to be with, my partner, is . . ." She pointed in the direction of a young man lying on the ground. Then he turned and squinted to see what was happening on the stage while the girl buried her face in her knees and sobbed quietly.

"Death is natural, girl." He awkwardly patted her head. "It hurts to lose a loved one, but you never truly lose them. They go to the ether, and parts of their energy and love always remain with you if you choose to hold on to it. Trust me, I know," he said as his defenses fell. His memory flooded with the loss of his daughter and wife all those years ago. A pain he didn't want to look at or face. But he could not protect himself from it in the presence of this girl spewing emotions in a way that he had lost touch with in this perfect, harmonious village.

On the stage, there appeared to be a disagreement occurring around Roots's body, which had been picked up and carried to the floor. She was surrounded by Master Fis, Bee, a long gangly young man with thick shoulder-length hair, a shirtless Protector who looked to be angry at the world, the Mistress, Scholar Crystal, the young pup of a boy now called Wolverine, a dark-skinned man with sharp cheekbones, and his old friend Brom, wearing a ripped shirt.

Roots lay unconscious on the hard, gray cement floor with seemingly little life force to sustain her. Her upper body had been propped against Bee's chest who'd done some quick healing of her wounds along her spine to stop the bleeding. There seemed to be building pressure among the small group surrounding Roots. It appeared they were keenly aware they needed to escape to safety. But they were faced with too many injuries. Being unable to deal with them all seemed to create friction among them as they decided what to do. The Mistress knew that those who were able to leave felt an obligation to help those who weren't, especially since there were Healers among them. A heated discussion of quiet mutters took place: Who should be healed first? When both Master Fis and Bee had exhausted their healing powers while healing warriors injured in the war outside of the dome walls.

"I **need** Pond to be healed. We are all in agreement that we need to stop more warriors from coming into our borders?" the Mistress asked.

"Yes," they all muttered.

"Then what are we waiting for? I'll take Master Fis and we will begin working on healing Pond. You all can decide who Bee is going to heal." She stood looking down at the others who were kneeling or sitting on the floor around Roots. "Master Fis?" she hissed, waiting for her to slowly stand up. She looked at the rest of the group, knowing they needed a leader, but knowing she had to delegate this task. "There is no wrong answer *except to hesitate*. We will adjust to whatever unfolds. Brom, make the call and don't overthink."

∽

The quiet and humble Viggo cut in before Brom could speak his orders. "If you heal me, I can heal the others."

I don't care about the others. I care about my daughter, Brom thought, but he bit his tongue.

Tevin spoke up. "If you heal me, I can portal at least three of us and Roots to safety. We can find a Healer there to help us."

Fabia approached—apparently unbothered by the entire scene—and squatted next to the group, putting her elbow casually on Brom's shoulder. "Sabina needs you all to be healed. You all carry her life force. Let me be clear. Are you all paying attention? Good. Your life force is the only thing keeping her alive. Flann needs to be healed. He has given the most life force to Sabina." She stood up, looking like she was in a pleasant mood. "Oh, and the Selectors have us surrounded." She beamed with a gleeful smile as she started dancing on the stage.

Looking annoyed with Fabia, Bee said, "It's Roots now." She was clearly unhappy that Roots wasn't getting healed immediately. "I can feel her life force slipping away," she said urgently. Brom looked at Bee and saw her holding his daughter like she was her own.

Brom wanted his daughter to be healed and his fear had him agreeing with Bee; however, he knew Fabia had insight that was undisputable. "Crystal, you have been quiet. Do you have any sights you can share with us?"

Crystal, in a checked-out state, kneeled at Sabina's feet. "I have her life force now and she is dying," she said quietly.

"She is **not** dying," Brom denied in anger. "We are going to help her. *WHAT* can you tell me that will help me?"

She lifted her gaze to Brom, the whites of her eyes no longer white. "Take her to the Loaded Hurricane. Heal her there. He," she said, pointing at Tevin, "Flann, Bard and Fabia will be there."

Brom nodded. "Bee, heal Viggo then Tevin, if you have any juice left over. Viggo, heal Flann and then Bard. After that, take off."

"Who shares a life force with Sabina . . . I mean Roots?" Bee asked, angrily looking around at everyone but getting no answer. Brom diverted his eyes. She continued. "If what Fabia says is true, then Viggo needs to heal all of them. Is that everyone?"

"BEE, just start healing. That is all I am asking you to do. Let me worry about the rest," Brom said.

"Fine. I will IGNORE the fact you are choosing not to be honest with me as I risk my life to help YOUR daughter. I really thought more highly of you than that," she complained under her breath as she gently settled Roots onto the floor.

Brom shifted quickly to support Roots's head and ignored the twisting of his gut as he listened to Bee. He knew he could trust her, but it was a habit not to trust anyone.

Bee asked Viggo to lie down, and he obediently complied. She sat back on her heels, her palms resting on her thighs as she gathered what was left of her chi. She took slow rhythmic breaths until she felt her chi gather in her heart center, and then she placed her hands above Viggo's body. Her astral vision saw the problem. Part of his life force was contained outside his body.

Confusion and apprehension hit her. She had never experienced this issue before. Her logical brain wanted to lash out at Brom for doing something so corrupt to the soul, but she could taste Nana Honey's energy around this sphere. Nana Honey would have had good reasons for doing this and so she dug deeper into the energy. She worked for several minutes in silence, pulling, enticing, shifting, and eventually moving the energy back into Viggo's astral body. She could hear him wheeze in the background of her consciousness, but she kept scanning his body to find dark spots on his brain. Blood. She moved the blood into his veins to return to his heart and circulation.

As she worked, she could feel her body slowly losing the strength to hold herself up. She was shifting forward and then Crystal's hands were on her shoulders, holding her up. Crystal's energy singed down her arms, shocking Bee out of her work. Her eyes fluttered slowly, too weak to untangle herself from the burning energy that Crystal put out. Her finger was to her lips, indicating she shouldn't speak. She couldn't speak if she wanted to.

Viggo sat up slowly, looking around. The fog was still thick, but he could see it parting far off in the distance. He silently got up and squatted next to Flann, placing his hands on the sides of Flann's neck to pour healing vibes into him. He reached into his pocket and put a thin dried leaf into the side of his cheek and then rolled him onto his back. He placed his hands above his heart and stilled. He gathered Flann's chi to his heart center and then lifted his stacked hands high in the air. He shoved his energy hard and fast into Flann's gathered chi. Even though Viggo didn't touch Flann, his body jolted. Flann's eyes opened and then he rolled back to sleep. Viggo did that two more times. Finally, Flann croaked. "Stop that. I'm not dead, I'm just tired." Viggo patted him on the shoulder and leaned in close. "Shhhhh, we have visitors. Do you remember the Selectors?" he said quietly.

Flann pushed Viggo away and then sat up slowly. He had his knees bent and placed his elbows on them so he could hold up his head. His head ached and every muscle in his body was sore. His mouth tasted of soured orange juice, which made him realize something was in his mouth. He pulled out a crumbling leaf from his cheek.

Obsessively, he started trying to get the rest out as he watched Viggo apply a sap onto both Kean and Bard's hands. He was closing his eyes and chanting something softer than a whisper over them. As he chanted, the thick sap moved like liquid over their injuries, disappearing into their skin. The blood pulled back from their skin into their injury. He watched in fascination as Kean's charred hand flaked black debris until smooth skin formed.

With a fire suddenly blazing in his heart, Flann jerked both hands to his chest, feeling the loss of the connection to Roots. His eyes scanned the fog, unable to see anyone except Kean, Bard, and Viggo, who were next to him. He called forth his Protector eyesight and the fog became nothing more than a watery speck of dust. With his eyesight unblocked, it took him a second to locate Roots on the floor, pale and covered in dried blood. Her hair was still perfectly contained in her braid. Her face was positioned away from him so she wasn't lying on the freshly healed skin over her shield chakra. Her hands were folded in her stomach like in burial, which unnerved him.

He didn't understand or remember what had happened. He made it through the salt circle and onto the stage. Then he felt like a million pounds of red fire ants hit him at once. That was the last he remembered, and looking at Roots now, he felt his throat constrict. He had to assume she was alive or Viggo would be attending her first. After all, his life was tied to hers in a way that motivated him to care for her as he would care for his own body. On second thoughts, that wasn't comforting. Viggo had a serving heart and put his needs low on the importance totem. However, to the side of Roots was Crystal, who was aiding Bee. Bee had all the indications of someone who used too much magic. Weak, pale, dark circles around her eyes, dried lips, harsh red patches on her skin, and a loss of consciousness. She must have helped Roots.

Trusting that Roots at least had internally healed, he looked around. He saw the Mistress behind him with Master Fis, over Pond's body. Master Fis was humming with her eyes closed. Her hands were floating above his body in fast, lengthy circles. It appeared she was getting faster and faster with her humming and her movements. Next, he saw Brom and that boy . . . Wolverine. They were both searching the back of the stage for objects, probably weapons. He followed Brom's movements and noticed Fabia sitting on a prop box, looking bored. She looked over at him, smiling and waving her finger, indicating she wanted him to come to her. He shook his head 'no', and he watched her pout playfully at him. As he shook his head, he noticed white pants with knee-high boots. He squinted and saw the Prince propped against a pole, his arms behind it and his mouth gagged. He was unconscious. *No wonder Fabia is happy. The Prince is her prisoner.*

Bringing his focus to Tevin, it took him a moment to figure out what he was doing. He was unsuccessfully attempting to create a portal near Roots and was getting more flustered by the moment. That was a lost cause, Flann mused, knowing that Silvedome was heavily protected from portals. The only one that existed was in Brom's home.

Who am I missing? Flann asked himself. He ticked off the partners on his fingers. He didn't see Felix. He got to his feet to look but didn't see him anywhere. The man was such a nomad. *He is probably taking a peaceful walk in the woods enjoying the sounds of birds singing, ignoring the fact we are here for Roots.*

He looked up at the sky and shivered with the cool air. He was poorly dressed for this weather, only now becoming aware that the perfect scenery was gone. Fabia's birds were circling the sky, waiting for her command. She only brought her birds when she was stepping into her full power. Flann recalled the past year of knowing Fabia, and he knew those birds symbolized that someone was going to be sorry for messing with her. He shivered again, not from the cold but from the gruesome memories of the last time she called those birds down on her prey.

This helped him to get his bearings. The severity of the situation was calling urgently to him. Adrenaline pumped through his veins, helping him to move easier. He walked over to Brom and reported with certainty: "We have to leave now. It's not safe."

Instead, the cocky young man answered. "Can't." He nodded to the back of the Ceremony. Looking in the direction, Flann felt his nerves fire from his toes all the way up to the crown of his head. He was expecting Borax who was notorious for his raids. He led the strongest group of all the Selectors, taking over all the lands. But this was not Borax. He saw the fog parting for a woman, indicating that she was at least a rare Shield. She was in a lacy hooded robe lined with cream silk. He could see her perfectly-defined wavy hair framing her face. She had light-brown skin with splattered, large, dark-brown freckles. It appeared that her face had an animal tusk as part of it, while her followers wore masks of antlered animals. The girl's mask only continued with the same pattern of brown freckles.

The army following her appeared to be all shirtless men with stark, white skin and short, white hair. They all wore masks that were bright white, as if the animal bone was bleached. Each mask was marked with colorful painted symbols, like it was a signature for the wearer's name. Their mouths were sewn shut and black. All their ribs could be seen to such an extent that Flann questioned how they were even alive. The similarity between all of them was beyond unnatural and made Flann feel uncomfortably unsafe.

The Selectors were riding beastly horses that were unnaturally tall with massive, long legs. As they approached, the horses stammered and walked backward. The girl kicked her horse forward, one hand holding the reins in front of her. But the horse circled and shook his head. The others were having similar problems. None of the horses were willing to enter the Ceremony. It bought them time.

"WE HAVE TO GO!" Flann said, his eyes enlarged at the sight of all the Selectors covered by the fog. With his extra vision, he could see the entire army encircling them, but most of the group would only see the leader and a few of her followers. The leader cleared out the fog around her.

"Go, I'm staying here," Wolverine answered bitterly, not making eye contact as he busied himself with sharpening the legs of chairs.

Flann looked frantically around for options, seeing dark shadows approaching. Viggo was finishing healing Tevin, who stood with his eyes closed looking in perfect serenity. He could see Viggo getting thinner and paler with each healing. To Flann, it felt like the door to possibility was closing with each step the Selectors took toward them.

He looked down at Roots, feeling regret for not protecting her, for not reaching her in time, for being helpless right now, and for not telling her he gets lost in emotion when he is around her. He supposed he should be gathering weapons to fight, like Wolverine and Brom, now that he was feeling more of himself and alert, but he couldn't help looking at Roots. This couldn't be the end. He wasn't willing to give up and throw his life away like Wolverine.

A low male voice with vibrato sounded across the Ceremony. "I have come for the one who is releasing energy. I wish to see if this person is the Agni. Show yourself. There is no place you can hide."

Lifting his gaze to the voice, Flann saw the woman lower the hood of her robe. She was walking down the hill toward the stage, her army a good ten paces behind her, reminding him of the salt circle that Roots had around her.

He studied her as she walked to meet them, looking for signs of weakness and observing her behavior. What he saw gave him the impression she was not merely human. She was other than human, with a bony forehead containing cream-colored tusks sawed off into short stubs. Her nose was flat and wide and she moved slowly and intentionally. Her lower arms were thick masses that seemed to lack bone. Her hand was webbed with fat sausage-like stems for fingers. She had a long, free-flowing gown of simple fabric. The design appeared to show overlapping silver stars outlined in a gold circle. An earthy smell of dirt became stronger as she closed the distance between them.

Fabia silently jumped off the box she was sitting on when the woman spoke and shook out her arms. Her eyes were closed and he could see heat radiating from her body as she prepared to attack. Flann knew it was now or never. He bent down and picked up Roots's limp body, staggering under her weight. Fortunately, Bard was there to stabilize him.

"Your magic is no test for me. Do as I say and you will experience the blissful peace of death. Fail to cooperate and I will convert you . . ."

Fabia opened her violet, spinning eyes and stood facing her with the confidence of a goddess. Her sheer determination was a magic of its own. She came to Flann, Bard, Roots, Tevin, and Viggo, and spoke with an authority that could be felt in one's soul. Flann's whole body felt the power of her words when she said, "It's time to go." She slapped Tevin's forehead with a white light while Viggo was still healing him. He was still standing, eyes closed and in a land of serenity, completely unaware that Fabia used his body as a portal. Before the portal closed and they disappeared, Flann saw Fabia reach out her arm to the sky, her fingers spread wide. Her fingers curled and twisted as she brought her birds down from the sky. His vision vanished, and he was rushed into a dark tunnel. Hot air flooded the tunnel. His brain felt the crushing pressure of moving from one destination to another as his hair whipped all around him. He lost the sensation of his body as he was dumped into the hard, dried earth. Unable to feel his body, he was terrified that he had dropped Roots and left her behind as he was shoved into the freefall of the portal.

However, when the world stopped spinning, he saw he had fallen on his knees and to the ground still holding Roots. He jumped off her and patted her body to see if she was okay.

"She hit her head. She is too unconscious to feel it. Come on. It's time to go," said Fabia, helping Tevin off the ground.

"Go where?" asked Bard, holding the side of his head.

"It's time to see for once and all who is the best warrior among us," she said, starting to smile ruefully.

"You cannot be serious," Flann said, looking around at the empty Loaded Hurricane.

"Not here, silly. Silvedome's dome is down and the warriors cannot keep the Selectors out. We are going to help them."

Viggo started to get up, looking weak and gaunt.

"Not you, brother. You will stay here with Roots, but DO NOT DO ANY HEALING ON HER until you have healed yourself."

Viggo slumped back down to the ground, clearly relieved.

"What about Roots? I thought we were going to heal her? I assumed you needed us here to protect her."

"And you will protect her after we slay a bunch of pesky Selectors. She will be fine. There is nothing we can do for her right now. No one is available to heal her until Viggo heals himself. We have got nothing but time on our hands. I don't know about you, but I crave a little ass whooping," she said, picking out a weapon from Roots's training gear.

"Well, I won't bet you but I can at least take down fifteen Selectors before Flann figures out how to use that brain of his," Tevin said, adventure in his eyes.

"You were just unconsciously portalling us through time and space, Tevin. Do you really think you should be fighting?" Flann asked.

"No time for thinking. Only action," said Bard as he practiced twirling a weapon and making sure his healed hand was able to perform.

"I feel GREAT," Tevin said, answering Flann's question. "Better than ever." The lights of his eyes were shining bright, and he seemed to be glowing with energy. Not waiting for the rest, he took off running. Bard followed, betting that he would take down three before Tevin took down one.

Flann was still reluctant to leave and looked at Roots and then at Fabia.

"Look, I was able to tap into his unconscious gifts while he was in a state of healing and peace. Now he has had a taste of what he can do if his conscious brain realizes it . . ." She looked down at Flann. "Are you coming? Tevin could use your help, and you know Bard thinks he is better than you?"

Flann pulled his hand through his hair, deliberating.

"You know what your problem is?" she said, tossing her stick in the air and catching it.

"What?" he asked, curious.

"You are a hider. You hide your feelings, your gifts, your desires . . . If you keep hiding, your life is worth nothing at all." She squatted down next to him and took out a container of black paint. He sat still and watched her as she swiped a thick stripe of black paint under each eye, along the sides of his face, chin, and forehead. "There, now you can hide and do your job. Or have you decided you are no longer a bodyguard?"

She wiped her finger off in the grass and stood up as Flann defensively answered. "I am doing my job."

"Then stop those Selectors from getting into her village. Viggo, berries."

"Yes, boss," he said, waving her away. "Get out of here. I got her," he said, sounding sincere.

Flann rubbed her cheek and then took off after the rest of the group, forgetting to grab a weapon. He watched Fabia practically fly over falling trees. She ran through the forest like it was her playground and her giggling laughs matched Flann's bouncy thoughts.

As they approached the wall of the Loaded Hurricane, he could see several Selectors making it past Silvedome's warriors and running full speed through the open field to the town. But Tevin and Bard flattened the numbers as they cut down one person after the next.

Fabia put her fingers into her mouth and gave a loud whistle. Snakes came out of the pond and the tall grass struck runners in the thigh and Achilles' heels. Flann faltered. He hated snakes, but he knew Fabia wouldn't allow one of her animals to hurt him. He took off running once more and watched as she threw her stick right through the armor of one of the soldiers. She swung around and dodged a hit, swinging them both around and coming up with his weapons. Her foot went powerfully into his chest and she swung his axe down on him. Already letting go of the axe, thrusting a small knife to cut through the soldier's throat, she rolled to the ground and came up jumping into the man running in her path. She wrapped her arms and legs around him and sunk her teeth into his neck, pulling back.

Flann could not watch any more as he was faced weaponless with an axe-throwing soldier. He moved, dodged, dunked, and jumped two feet back. The soldier was fast but Flann was unnaturally gifted with speed and timing. Flann managed to get behind him and grab the handle of the axe. He jumped his feet to the man's shoulder blades and kicked off his back, holding the axe handle in both hands, allowing the axe handle to crush the man's throat. Flann managed to get out of the way as the man tumbled backward. The handle broke, and Flann used the broken handle to jab the splinted end forcefully into the soldier's throat.

Flann was on his feet and taking down the next charging warrior. He bellowed a warrior cry as he stopped holding himself back and allowed his true Protector skills to be unleashed. In this bloodlust, there was no fear. Only movement and trust.

The World Burns

The woman-creature shrieked as she watched Roots be portalled into safety. She called out to her army. "Kill them," she demanded, pointing to the old man and redheaded girl. "Capture them." She pointed to the stage.

Wolverine looked down at Crystal and he knew he was doing the right thing by staying. His life was only as valuable as protecting those he cared about. It took death to realize how much he cared for certain people. Two particular people. One that he lied to himself about and the other he could not explain.

"I'll protect you," he shouted over the black birds' screeching cries as thousands dove with speed, piercing into the painted-white skeleton bodies.

Crystal had drawn a salt circle around herself and the passed-out Bee. She quickly chalked a star on the ground with other symbols inside the circle.

"Don't be a fool. I don't NEED your protection. NO ONE OR NOTHING can get into my circle. Go protect the Mistress and Master Fis," she said defiantly.

He paused, then said, "Why cannot the rest of us go in your circle?"

She rolled her eyes. "BECAUSE, I cannot manage your energy. Bee is passed out. Now GO!"

He looked behind him and saw the Mistress was on the ground, her back to the army, helping Master Fis and Pond. They needed Pond. He yelled at Brom, "I've got them. Help Kean."

Brom didn't listen. He was already running toward the army, launching sticks with such power that his white buttoned-up shirt became unbuttoned, revealing his lightly-silvered chest hair. Kean stood with his feet apart, bare-chested with black parachute pants, watching the horned woman make her way to the stage. It seemed like there was a universal agreement that this was their match and no one was allowed to interfere. *Fine by me,* thought Wolverine.

Kean remained untouched by the zombie-like men painted in white. These men reminded Wolverine of animated skeletons. Three skeleton men got on their hands and knees, creating a step for the horned woman to continue walking from the walkway straight onto the stage. She said nothing to the skeletons, yet the skeletons seemed to know exactly what she wanted. Two skeletons came to each side of her and provided their hands to stabilize her as she stepped on the backs of those on the ground.

Wolverine had positioned himself in front of the Mistress and glanced at Crystal. She was chanting as she looked toward the sky. Her circle seemed to entice the skeletons, which took the pressure off him. He was grateful to see she was safe behind her circle and a part of him relaxed. He did not understand how her powers worked, but he witnessed light shoot up to the sky each time a skeleton hit the salt circle. Then the skeleton bones turned to white, powdery ash. The remains of the skeletons fell to the ground in a white puddle of liquid that eventually turned to white powder and disappeared.

Wolverine had two long, black chair legs in his hands that had been sharpened into weapons. He had fought these creatures before. Bullets, axes, or any other metal didn't affect them. Their bodies welded back together, but wood splintered them. The good news was it didn't matter where you stabbed them or that the wood was withdrawn. The skeletons were simple to fight. If wood pierced their skin, they were paralyzed and would start to shrink in on themselves until they disappeared into powder. The bad news was if they got hold of someone, they would crush their bones into dust. The trick was to keep moving.

The skeletons surrounded him and his party. He started to fight, bracing one leg in front of the other and stabbing one after the other skeleton. They moved slowly and were clumsy, which was an advantage to Wolverine. He easily leaped from side to side, stabbing them with his impressive speed and maneuvering. He spun, kicking one skeleton to the ground. He reached out and stabbed another as he arched his back over Pond, launching himself forward to stab another.

He was a rare Protector. He had speed and foresight that was no match for the skeletons. However, the pure quantity of them and the fact that he was protecting the Mistress, Master Fis, and Pond, all of whom were immovable, was a disadvantage. Sweat fell into his eyes as he flipped, twirled, and jumped over Pond. He was doing his best not to disturb them or hit them as he fought. He used as many kicks and punches as possible to knock some of the skeletons down and buy himself time. Time to get to the other side of his party, to stab one in his reach, or to block more from coming. He wished for help as he moved and dodged.

His energy jumped when the knocked-down skeletons started to crawl through the mass of melting skeletons to get to the people he was trying to protect. One almost got hold of Pond's ankles. His mind felt overwhelmed, and he started thinking he was outmatched. Distraction seeped in and he spared a glance around.

He saw all the birds seemed to be focused on the skeletons attacking Eagle and that redhead. The old man was using his body to shield the girl as the birds dove and attacked the skeleton. It seemed their beaks were also able to penetrate and destroy the skeletons. None of that was useful to him right now.

He placed one hand on the ground to anchor himself, then he

split-kicked out over Pond and the Mistress's body. His kick landed on two skeletons, one on each side. As he kicked, he lifted his head to see Crystal doing healing work on Bee, safe but inattentive to the help he needed. He could feel her magic, like ants crawling on his skin. In the past, he despised her and her magic. Now a part of him called to her and wished to reach out to her. *Why doesn't she feel or sense what I do?*

Kean fought the woman and seemed to find it difficult to land a hit. She predicted his move, but he was faster. Wolverine had his own fight and did a cartwheel as he stabbed more skeletons. He stabbed and stabbed each skeleton until his cheeks felt hot. As he fought, his mind drifted, and he recalled what Kean had said before they started fighting. He had said she wasn't a rare Protector. She had responded that it didn't matter, she was close enough. Who was she? What was she? He had never before seen someone who was part animal, part woman. She was clearly gifted, and he reasoned that she could have really hurt him by now. Why was she toying with him?

Lost in thought, Wolverine smacked his weapon into a skeleton instead of stabbing them, and the stick fractured. What was left was too short to do much with. He tossed it to the ground, feeling desperate. He heard the Mistress and Master Fis's conversation as he did his best to knock the skeletons down and blindly stab with the other hand.

"You have to hurry. We-don't-have-time," the Mistress pressured.

Master Fis firmly responded. "*Don't* you rush me. I cannot work under pressure."

"What's taking so long?"

Master Fis sat back on her heels, wiping her forehead with the back of her hand. "Every time I try to reach the next level of healing, his shield blocks me. He seems to have some type of protective shield in place to prevent anyone from messing with his energy. I think I was only able to get this far because his life was in danger. I've attempted to impress his mind with the danger of our circumstance, but it's not working. His mind doesn't sense enough danger to let me do any more." She sighed. "I have done enough healing; he needs to give his permission."

"No. Try again. I'll help. I will work on disabling his shield as you heal him. Can you avoid my energy and still heal him?"

"Why not? I've done other impossible tasks today," she said, sounding worn down.

The Mistress asked, "How is your energy?"

"Almost out."

"Let's get it right on the first try then."

Kean had been fighting with unfailing confidence in his ability until the woman touched him on his forearm. That touch sent a message from his muscle to his nervous system that he was getting weak. He registered the effect immediately. He threw an invisible energy shield around himself so she could not affect him that way again, but he couldn't expel the energy she spewed into him. It was a black, gritty energy that hit his muscles and made them burn with inflammation.

While he fought, he attempted to energy floss his system. Moving his energy up and down and sending the unwanted energy into the earth. He asked the energy to leak out of his feet and go to the earth, but it lingered. She touched him again in his distraction and raised both eyebrows.

"It seems you too are more than what you appear to be," she said with cool interest. "Your shield tastes like hot peppermint," she said as she licked her lips and whipped both arms in a circle as she spun.

Kean saw her move and thought of a tornado. She didn't fight with any martial arts that he knew. She used the elements and mostly anticipated his moves. Her style was more of grappling. He sensed she wanted to take this fight to the floor, though he couldn't say why he thought that. What he knew for certain was that her hand strength was unnatural and that her forearms felt like steel, so he avoided hitting them. His body was taking a beating just by punching and kicking hers. She seemed unfazed by his hits. She didn't wince or react in any way. It was as if the hit never occurred.

He could feel himself getting weaker by the moment, like she was toying with him, waiting for him to resign to some fate she had decided for him. He was not a man of resignation, though. He was a warrior with a caged spirit inside of him. Though he hated to lose control over that spirit, he was becoming too tired to fight her and his brother. His energy was wasting away with the added effort of dispelling the energy she leaked into him. The more time that passed, the more he could feel his brother's presence taking over.

Kean had been cursed as an infant because of his father, who had dishonored some black arts witch named Dras. According to Brom, this witch was said to be older than any human was physically capable of being. It was rumored he lived before the nuclear war, before this world contained Moowins. He was searching for a woman who would willingly agree to marriage and would bear his children. However, he only seemed interested in women who had multiple Moowins of strong or rare capabilities.

No one knew why he appeared to some and not others. There were theories, of course. Was it a person born under a certain star? Did they have to be of a certain bloodline? The fact was, he was a mystery. All who searched for him failed, for he only revealed himself when he chose to. Little was known about him, and those who encountered him often died within months of receiving their curse. Except for Kean and Kano. They were still here and Brom was still trying to find a way to undo their curse.

What Kean learned was that his father had denied Dras his older sister in marriage, and in retaliation, the witch cursed his father's most valuable possession, his twin sons.

Kean had lived his whole life with the curse that caused him to be destructive and angry, not because that was his identity, but because it was his twin brother's. He was linked to his brother permanently. His spiritual essence was inside of him and vice versa. The witch had cursed the twins to switch their spiritual essence anytime they were near another person. His brother was born a psychopath, unable to feel his own pain and delighting in the pain of others. He desired murder, rape, and torture, and anger fueled him like gasoline. He felt alive and vibrant in his anger.

Kean could not be cured of this curse. For anytime he was around someone, he could not control his brother's spirit from emerging and embodying him. All anyone saw of Kean was that he was a bad kid, and a criminal. He was an unworthy, spoiled rich kid. For the longest time, Kean believed them. However, when he was alone or alone with his brother, their true identities came out. Kean observed that when he was by himself, he was a gentle soul, a man who loved reading and baking, not hurting others. The more Kean realized that he was not his brother's identity, the more he fought his brother's spirit. This pleased Kano, and he found joy in Kean's suffering. Especially since his brother still managed to find a way of bringing out his true identity when he was alone with someone else. He couldn't do it for crowds, but he was capable of being his evil self when one-on-one.

Brom was brought to Kean when he was a child to help soothe the 'beast' inside of him with his Influencing talent. He had been the only successful Influencer to soothe the spirit inside of him, but that was only possible because he unknowingly implanted him with Roots's life force. No one knew that Brom was using that small amount of Roots's life force to control Kean. From Kean's family standpoint, Brom had been successful in keeping him from destroying property and hurting others. What was evident was that when Brom was around, Kean appeared civilized. Therefore, Brom was requested often. The Dagston family was royalty and they couldn't have a disobedient child.

Brom became family. He was encouraged to visit often and was richly rewarded at each visit. Kean knew Brom didn't care about the money. He cared about preparing him for this day. The day of Roots's Birth Challenge. With this agenda in mind, Brom had come often, and he had spent a great deal of time with him.

On those visits, Brom trained Kean in every form of martial arts. He showed him how to meditate and use breath work to calm the festering energy inside of him. They hiked together, and he learned how to track, hunt, and survive the wilderness with nothing more than a knife, boots, and a cloth to wrap in. Over time, Kean saw Brom as a father. One that was proud of him and encouraged him to use the anger he felt to move faster and smarter when fighting. It seemed Kean's training became the template Brom used for all of Roots's life force partners.

But they never practiced fighting when Kano had full control over Kean. As the weakness spread in his body, Kean couldn't keep his brother suppressed. He could feel his brother's sadistic smile move across his face as the anger spread out wide in his body, like a bird shaking out their feathers. It felt like his lungs expanded and his chest became proud as the brother became more present. Ashamed, Kean hated how powerful and magnificent he felt when his brother took over.

The woman crouched, coming in to hit his ribs with her steel-like forearms, which would have broken a rib or two had she completed the move. But apparently sensing the energy shift, she leaped backward.

Words came out of Kean's mouth that he had no control over. *"Hello, you, pretty little thing. Aren't you interesting?"* he said, stalking closer to her with arrogant manners.

The horned woman stayed crouched and examined him for a moment. She straightened up and smelled the air, lifting her nose upward.

"I know that smell," she commented breathlessly. She squinted at him, as if she saw through him.

"You will know nothing but how it feels to have my nails scraping your raw flesh as I tear off that mask. YOU can expect to feel the rope pinching your skin as you jerk in response to my touch."

"You." She snorted in a half laugh. "You are a child playing with things you do not understand. You don't see what you have done."

Shrugging both shoulders with his hands out as if in invitation, he said confidently, "Let's play then."

He taunted her to come closer, and she did so without reservations. Though Kean's body knew how to move, Kean's brother Kano did not. She hit him several times. Kean took the hits without a care, unable to register the pain. He wrapped his arms around her in a hug and squeezed her while he headbutted her. He let go at a precise time and she flew back three steps. She immediately came forward, undeterred. He plowed into her, his head into her abdomen, and picked up one of her knees, tripping her to the ground. Moving quickly, he jumped on top of her, placing one knee over her arm, pinning it down, with his opposite elbow over the other shoulder. His forearm was pressing hard against her throat.

Kean could feel delight well up inside, knowing he had her pinned. With his free hand, he started to dig his fingers into her flesh, just under the mask. He was struggling to get enough purchase to really pull it off. Her skin was clearly welded into the mask, but the challenge only excited Kean more. It was too late for him by the time he realized she wasn't fighting back or struggling to breathe. She was completely relaxed, lying on the ground, waiting for him to collapse.

His body touched hers. He ignored any pain or burning he felt until he noticed he couldn't move his fingers anymore. He started to speak, but his lips and tongue weren't responding.

"VHA HAV U DUN T ME?" He became too heavy to move his muscles. He collapsed all his weight onto her.

She pushed him to the side and stood up. Kean could feel Kano retreat, and his body deflated slightly as he left. Kean was able to open his eyes and look at her. He was determined to face his opponent and show no fear of death, though he probably only looked like a bag of muscles heaped on the floor. She looked down at him curiously. She had wide eyes with clumpy eyelashes. Her eyes glimmered with water and were reptilian; she had an iris and pupil but no white sclera. She answered. "Short version, I drained your energy. You and your brother don't have aligned energy, so you were not able to use your shielding power to protect yourself. I'm sorry for what Dras has done to you."

As Fortress was bending over to talk to him, the dome's shield started to flicker halfway up. She stopped and looked around. There in the audience were hundreds, if not thousands, of dead black birds and the powdery remains of her army. The two humans were gone, with barely a trace of their blood on the ground.

She glanced to the left side of the stage and saw the girl in her protection circle staring at her coldly. Anger was in her eyes and a sleeping woman was curled around her. She turned behind her and saw two men fighting the remains of her army over a boy lying on the ground. Two old women hunched over him, working magic. Her anger flashed. She sensed her entrapment as the shield flickered into place, too weak to stay but getting stronger with each attempt.

Retaliating, she lifted her arms out to the side, stretching her power as far and wide as it would go. Low fire started to burn across all the areas her magic could reach. The cement would take a moment, but soon it would heat, crack, and become brittle. She felt satisfied knowing they would feel the cement's heat and be afraid.

She asked herself what could be salvaged from a plan that had gone wrong. She had come with the intention of taking the Agni. She expected it to be the one who was in the ritual and when she had disappeared, she had made a new plan to take these people as hostages until she could trade them for the Agni. Fear was mounting in her that she would be trapped in Silvedome, but she trusted the universe to provide.

She paid attention to what she noticed, and she noticed that the older man was different. There was something about him that was unusual. She read his aura as he fought and was surprised to find that he had all Moowins. That was not necessarily unusual, but they were all of rare abilities and practically invisible. They were of small quantity and of dim glow, as if he never explored his power to let them grow. They appeared to be as weak as a mild Moowin.

She was baffled. He was old too. Much older than the prophesied Agni who was meant to be young. Plus, the vibrations of his Moowins were almost nonexistent.

She flashed back to the memory of when Dras kidnapped her from Borax, who had kidnapped her from her family when she was a child. She had come into her Moowins at a young age and Borax had taken her from her family thinking she was the Agni. She thought she was for years too as she had all seven rare Moowins and a strong Protector Moowin. Plus, she had other gifts. Gifts that would label her as a witch. She was exactly what Dras wanted.

It was both a blessing and a curse that her Protector Moowin didn't come into rare status on her Birth Challenge. Moowins could grow stronger, but they rarely did. Although she had no desire to be the Agni, she assumed that if she had been, she could have prevented everything that had happened with Dras. Was she to repeat the same mistake that Borax made with her when he believed his Moowin only needed to grow? Was there someone else whose energy she sought? She could not deny what she saw. He clearly possessed all eight rare Moowins. Had he found a way to disguise them?

～

Kean lay on the ground once more with drool spilling from his open mouth. His heart felt like it was failing him and his body rasped for breath. He wasn't sure he was getting oxygen despite how his body rattled. He couldn't keep his eyes open. His consciousness was coming in and out, but he had one moment of clarity where he saw Pond and the Mistress's energy combine to put the shield up. The shield flickered. He knew they needed more power. His body had become cold and had stopped shivering. He had forgotten that he was cold until he felt the cement under him soothingly warm his skin. He didn't think that was odd. He only knew he faced death and he welcomed it. He also knew he could help.

Kean poured the last of his energy into the cement, which was a conductor, and asked his guides and guardian angels to send his energy into the shield. He could feel his energy traveling down his arm and into his hand, resting on the cement. The woman-creature's burning magic had disguised his energy, and she didn't seem to realize what had happened. Kean fell unconscious.

Fortress planned her escape with the mysterious man. She sent mental pictures to her army to kill the survivors rather than capture them but to leave the one in white alone. She would handle him. She still had plenty of men left to do the task but had lost too many to ask them to preserve these lives. Though her men would not be able to kill the two in the salt circle.

She set her spell for the two in the circle and walked over. She smiled with one side of her cheek. "You are a cheeky one. Smart, no one can get in, but then again, neither of you can get out without risking my attack."

Worry creased Crystal's face as the cement she was sitting on was getting hot. The others noticed too. Pond moaned and Master Fis and the Mistress shifted how they were sitting like it was a game of hot potato. Although she and Bee remained unharmed in the salt circle, they were in fact stuck.

Crystal saw the Mistress slam more of her energy into Pond and stand up, looking woozy but confident. She yanked her arms down, her hands into fists, and rain came falling from the sky. The rain splattered on the cement and sizzled, but the magic continued to burn.

The woman-creature leaned back and laughed. "Silly old woman. You cannot fight elements with this kind of magic."

Wolverine hadn't anticipated the Mistress's bold move and wasn't able to block the skeletons from reaching her. Had she only stayed low to the ground, she would have remained safe. But before they could shift their focus to her, the Mistress lifted her chin and opened her hands. The wet floor turned into ice and the rain turned into snow. "Then at least I can slow the effects of your magic."

The skeleton closest to the Mistress slipped on the icy surface. Instead of grabbing her, it knocked into her, taking her down. The skeleton landed on the Mistress and then kneeled over to keep pushing on her neck, which was covered in a sheet of ice. The skeleton's hands kept slipping off, especially with the Mistress batting at them.

They were getting more vicious and difficult to fight. Wolverine could see his own breath, and he struggled to remain on his feet on this unfamiliar slippery white surface. He stabbed and kicked the skeletons until four gained up on him and took him down. Their bodies crashed onto the hard floor and he scrambled to get up. He was pinned. A skeleton approached him to stab him with the very weapon he had used to take down so many; the four others held him down. Wolverine looked into his eyes as he struggled against the four, drawing on his Protector strength to fight them. The skeletons' eyes were black and empty and their movements clumsy, so it was like watching the grim reaper approaching in slow motion. He could see Master Fis being picked up and her legs kicking in the air, silent but resisting in her way. The skeletons must have registered Pond as dead because they left him lying on the floor untouched. Brom was surrounded and fighting fiercely. Crystal was watching from her safe haven with tears running down her eyes.

There was a pressure in Wolverine's ears and the dome walls sprang to life. The snowy weather continued, but the gray sky turned to a beautiful sunny dawn instead of the gray, angry clouds. The skeletons froze and Brom stabbed furiously, seizing the moment. The horned woman screamed. "YOUUUUUUUU. This is YOUR FAULT," she said, seeming to grind her teeth together. She marched over to Kean and picked his limp body up like he was a four-year-old. Her hands were around his neck and she was screaming.

Wolverine saw all this while he lay on the ground, thrashing, trying to wiggle enough space to get his arms free. Master Fis was held suspended in the air. Wolverine wondered whether her knees were stuck in that bent position because of arthritis. Crystal was on her feet, worry on her face, and one hand on her heart. Brom had deserted the frozen skeletons and was approaching the woman like a spooked animal. He had bent knees and calm movements.

～

Brom, feeling the pang of pain in Kean, looked up to see him dangling from the creature's hand. The sight caused him to have tunnel vision so strong it almost knocked him off his feet. He needed help. He was a practiced man at meditation and immediately went inward in a blink of an eye. He called upon his powers for help. He called upon his guides and he pictured how he wanted this to go. Then he opened his eyes and trusted it would go as he envisioned, despite the pressure he felt building in his shoulders.

His guides shared a vision of the past with him. A girl without reptilian eyes or a horned face. She was shy and loved helping her family. She must have been eight when he had seen her last, and she had no control over the energy that flooded outside of her. He came to help her, but her family thought he was corrupt, a spiritualist on a crusade. She went missing three years later.

"Morgan. Morgan, isn't it?" Brom said, coming a little closer. She looked at him in confusion, like she didn't remember that name. Brom had worked with cursed ones for years now and recognized the struggle between the human and the animal. He needed to make her feel safe to bring out the human side of her.

"Do you remember me? I visited you and your family once. You made me the best mud pie under a large apple tree near a vineyard. You had a tent set up under the tree to sleep under the stars."

"You speak of a past life that has been forgotten. I was reborn," the animal side of her reasoned.

"Tell me, what may I call you?" he gently asked, while internally pleading with his guides to support Kean.

"I AM Fortress," she answered with power in her voice, looking at Kean in fascination.

"Fortress, did you know I asked your parents for permission to bring you here to Silvedome? To come live with me and be safe from the Selectors?"

Kean was turning purple and Brom's gut clenched, though he knew he showed no visible signs of his emotions. Kean was a son to him. His favorite of all Roots's partners. The one he secretly wished Roots would mate with, so he could always have Kean as part of his family.

He continued. "Your parents refused my help, but I ask your permission now that you can speak for yourself. May I help you?"

"THERE ISN'T ANY HELP *available* TO ME," she growled bitterly.

Watching Kean's body involuntarily spasm for lack of oxygen caused Brom to draw upon his power. "Put him down UNHARMED and I will help you **leave**."

Fortress glanced behind her to look toward the back of the Ceremony. All her horses were gone. Her army was frozen and useless to her except as a shield. She asked herself, addressing the threat: *Where would I go in this land of gifted people?* She was alone inside this magic wall that she'd only recently been able to penetrate. What if she couldn't get out? She returned her gaze to the limp body in her hands. She was not happy with the Agni's suggestion but was instead angry to be trapped. She started to tilt the young man's head, ready to snap his neck, but the other part of her fought not to harm him.

"YOU'RE NOT TRAPPED, **but** *it's true* that you cannot leave the dome without my help. *I am the only person who can* and *is willing to help you* . . . You cannot create a portal on these magical lands, either. You will be stuck here, hiding while your curse steals your life. IS THAT WHAT YOU WANT?"

"How do you know I won't kill you like your friend here?"

Brom, being a strategic planner, pulled a quick analysis of her behaviors. He realized her army didn't aggressively fight him and were only trying to capture him, whereas they were clearly attacking Wolverine. He trusted his observation, and he trusted his ability to persuade others to align their thoughts with his.

"You won't kill me and, with my gifts, the chances are you won't be able to, no matter what that ancient black witch did to you. *I'm the one you came here for* . . . Bravo for being the only one to discover what I have hidden all-my-life," he said, flattering her.

Her eyes fluttered and came into focus. "You are the Agni?"

Standing tall and speaking with conviction, Brom declared, "YES, Yes I am."

He wanted to come across as confident and persuasive, but he couldn't stop his chin from wobbling. Without the action of fighting, he was freezing. He managed to stop himself from crossing his arms and rubbing his forearms, at least. The sweat on his shirt was frozen to him, like an ice cube stuck to bare skin. It was becoming difficult for him to think about anything else other than how cold he was and how Kean fared.

She cocked her head, listening. "Prove it," she challenged.

Brom had indeed received talents from Roots's partners that he kept hidden, so much so that he rarely, if ever, practiced with them. But at that moment, all he wanted was warmth, so he sent his intentions out and the ice disappeared, as well as her magical fire that was causing havoc across Silvedome. Brom took a step back, shocked. He hadn't expected that. Maybe he was more tied to Roots and her partners than he realized.

Fabia's words came back to him. Roots's life was preserved because of her life force partners. Brom squinted at Kean, feeling even more pressure building in his chest at the thought of losing both his adopted son and his daughter. *Yeah, but you'll still have one daughter alive.* He pushed that thought away.

"I won't help if you hurt any of them. That's my word and my bargain with you. All of Silvedome and their people are to remain safe and unharmed," he said, standing in his power.

"I can make you do anything I want," the animal side of her threatened.

He shook his head 'no'. "Isn't that what happened to you? Didn't Borax try to make you go against your will? That is not how the Moowins work and you know it. No amount of torture or black arts can change that. Isn't that why you are relying on your magic to help you and not your Moowins? Your Protector

Moowin won't let you kill him. And your magic looks scary, but it's all protection magic. You-don't-want-to-hurt-anyone. Which is why you are choosing to do repairable harm but not real damage." Brom felt the truth of his words only after he spoke them.

She looked at him and seethed.

Brom could feel Kean's life force blinking out inside of him.

"PUT HIM DOWN NOW," he commanded in a low, firm voice. "I am willing to help you, but you must agree to harm **no one** else in Silvedome. Isn't that why you want me? You want my help to undo what was done to you, yes?"

She dropped Kean and he crumbled onto the floor. She faced Brom.

"WHY aren't you trying to kill me?" she asked suspiciously.

Brom didn't have time for this. He wanted Sabina's life force partners to be healed and the longer they stayed, the more their energy attracted the Dark One. He needed to get her out of Silvedome. Although the animal side had almost completely taken over, the human side was strong-willed and fought. He had to put his trust in the human side of her and that part of her didn't come here to conquer, but to get help.

Seeing Kean was alive, Brom was able to feel compassion for Fortress's circumstances and he spoke with love. "The only difference between love and hate is a few degrees. I could choose to hate you, but what would that serve? You'd still be reacting in fear, willing to forsake your identity to save yourself. Fear is the enemy here. Not you."

He walked up to her and got down on his knees, arms hanging by his side. She looked down at him, confused and hesitant.

"You were in danger. Fear drove you to react without using logic and reason. That is normal. That is NOT YOUR FAULT."

"HOW CAN YOU SAY THAT???" Tears came to her human side and her body deflated. As the human side kicked in to being fully present, she seemed unable to hear the words and shook her head 'no'.

"We all have survival skills hardwired into us when we are in fear. Look around you. All of this happened out of fear. You acted out of fear that if you didn't get the Agni, your curse would worsen and you would die. We defend ourselves out of fear of what you would do to us." He paused. "You may not be from Silvedome, but we are not that much different."

She screamed. "CAN'T YOU SEE THAT I AM BAD? I AM WRONG." She waved at herself, indicating the disfiguration she had suffered under Dras.

"NO," Brom said firmly. "You are **not**. There is no good or bad here."

"LOOK AT ME!!!! LOOK WHAT HE DID TO ME BECAUSE I REFUSED TO BE HIS WIFE."

Out on the open field of Silvedome, a war took place between the remaining Selectors, Silvedome warriors, and Roots's life force partners. Flann, Tevin, Fabia, and Bard all fought individually, but near each other. As the fighting progressed, it was moved to the path that led to the village. The people of Silvedome were huddled in their houses without weapons and without a way to lock their doors. They had pushed furniture in front of the doors and windows to keep them as safe as possible. The hospital had released all almost-healed warriors to join the battle. The professors had joined the fight, as they all were gifted in some way. Professor Tiris fought like she was born to be on the battlefield. Her long whip struck down as she flipped through the air to attack a foe near her. It was like she had the peripheral vision of a bee, able to see in all directions.

There was no longer a stream of invaders pouring in. Who was on the battlefield was on the battlefield, but the strategy had changed from mass attack to controlled attack groups. Small groups huddled together, some with shields which blocked the arrows starting to fly, allowing them to gain ground. Thanks to some unbeknownst Shielder, all of Silvedome fighters were shielded. Unfortunately for Tevin, he wasn't, but he was a metal worker. He managed to use scraps of fallen soldier's gear to fashion something to protect himself with, though he stayed far back enough that it didn't much matter.

∼

Fabia seemed to be getting bored now that the battle scene was changing.

"Can we catapult me into their shields? I feel like I'm standing around waiting for a brave soul to come out and play?" She pouted, squatting low to the ground.

"Just keep sending your snakes and critters to attack them," Flann said, looking at the pond, wishing for water. "Does the ground feel hot to you? I'm suddenly feeling hot."

Jumping up to rub his hair, she said, "Oh, you sensitive boy." Her face lit up with excitement. "You are right." Then her face fell. "Wait . . . That rat is hurting my animals," she said in indignation. "Quick, get to a tree. Start climbing. The flames will rise in a moment."

She clapped and did a bird cry, then waved Bard and Tevin over. "Get in the trees NOW. MOVE." Placing her hand on the ground, she whispered, "Find shelter." Her snakes stopped attacking the soldiers, and all ran for the tree line.

Flann didn't waste time. He danced his way through the fighting and found a tree to climb. The open gash in his arm pushed and oozed as he climbed. He got himself on a tree branch and looked out at the field. Tevin and Bard were almost at the tree line, hiking their knees up as they ran across the field of flames that seemed to burn but not catch on fire.

He looked over to the tree next to him and Fabia was lounging on the branch laughing at all the warriors oohing and aahing as they ran for the pond or the trees. The men that reached the water ran into it, throwing themselves into the water, expecting relief, only to find the water like a hot tub. Once they realized it, they ran out of the water, drenched, and seemingly no longer interested in fighting. They paid no attention to who was next to them as they ran for the trees.

A cascade of water poured from the sky but the flames remained. Some men stopped running, looking as if they thought the water solved the problem. They looked miserably at one another. All the fight seemed to have gone out of them. But they were enemies, so they fought half-heartedly, only to start high-stepping as the heat burned their feet. They gave up the fight and headed for the safety of the trees. Flann saw people in their houses dumping water out the window to stop the flames, but the water only made the flames rise higher.

In the distance, he could see where the flames ended, and some men were heading toward the safe grounds. However, before they could make it, the rain turned to ice in an instant. Snow started to fall to the ground. A deep cold hit the land with an intensity that was sure to quench the flames, but the flames kept burning.

"What is this?" Flann asked as he crossed his arms and hunched his shoulders.

"The BEST kind of fight," Fabia said, smiling like she was looking at a lover who had just given her a gift. "The witch is using magic and that old lady is using her talents. The witch must be a light witch who is threatened and scared for her life because this magic is to keep those who would harm her away. It's an illusion but our brains think it is real. Therefore, it is real." She laughed as she watched soldiers do the splits and reach out to each other as they fumbled to the ground.

"If it's an illusion, why was I hot and why did we climb a tree?" he asked, confused.

She sighed. "Stop using your analytical brain. I already told you the answer, you just don't like it. I'm NOT repeating myself."

"I listened," Flann argued. "You are saying I'm cold because I think I am cold. Right?" Flann asked as his muscles spasmed uncontrollably.

"No," she answered sweetly. "You are cold because that's the element the old lady brought into existence. That's real."

"But the magic isn't real?"

She looked annoyed and gave him her full attention. "THEY ARE BOTH REAL. They are just affecting different dimensions. Look at your shoes. Are the soles melted?"

"Noooo." His teeth chattered.

"Exactly. The flames psychologically affected you and your brain responded."

"Your brain can do that?"

"Yep. All day, every day," she said, relaxing against the tree, apparently not cold, unlike Flann.

"Why aren't you cold then?"

The dome walls sprang up around them. They saw several men from the Selectors' armies were caught in the dome, separated from their leader and their comrades. There was an outcry from those men but they quieted quickly as Silvedome warriors spotted their locations.

Fabia looked over at Flann with a satisfied smile. "Magic. I'm choosing my thoughts instead of letting my thoughts have power over me. I'm choosing to believe I am not cold." She nestled herself back into the tree, watching people run for their tents. "What's up with Brom? He is actually telling the truth, and it's throwing me off."

"He said that the Prince pooped his pants and is standing in front of everyone pretending it didn't happen?"

Fabia threw a nut at him. "Ha, that would be something to witness. No, seriously, Brom has the vibes he gets when he wants to save someone from the Dark One."

Flann would have shrugged but he couldn't voluntarily move his shoulders. He stuffed his hands into his armpits and thought warm thoughts. "I don't know. He is not drawing on my powers."

He closed his eyes and waited to feel something from Brom. The door was closed. "I've got nothing from him. How could Brom find another cursed person at a time like this? Isn't he fighting off the Selector?"

She looked over at him..

"Right." He shivered. "Is he fighting her or trying to save her?"

"He *was* fighting her, but then he realized what happened to her. Now he wants to save her," she said with her eyebrows raised but staring off into space.

"Figures," Flann said under his breath. "They all end up dying. I don't know why he tries so hard to help them. Doesn't it matter that she was trying to hurt us? And HIS DAUGHTER for Sky Above."

Addressing his first comment, she pointed out, "Kean hasn't died."

"Only because of Sabina . . . Roots . . . whatever," he mumbled, annoyed at the name change and recalling he only had a few more days left to change his.

"He got super upset when she tried to hurt Kean. She has terrible control over her fear."

"Kean alright?" he asked reluctantly.

"He is alive . . ."

Flann ground his teeth. "Does she know? Is she giving her energy voluntarily or involuntarily?" he asked angrily.

"Viggo was helping her," she said with a calm assertion.

He looked unpleasantly at her and communicated the answer wasn't good enough.

She shrugged. "Right now, the grid is flooded with emotions of overthinking about freezing to death."

There was a quiet silence over the land. The action was over. Everyone appeared to have lost the desire to fight, and those in the trees seemed focused on staying warm. Despite freezing, all Flann wanted to do was go and check on Roots. As he sat in the silence, his thoughts of that kiss kept him warm. Until he remembered he had left Nora without even thinking about her safety.

"I hear your guilt. Finally thinking about her?"

"Don't give me trouble. I had a lot on my mind."

"Whatever excuse you need, buddy."

Flann exhaled loudly through his nose. "Is she alright?" Then he pleaded softly. "I do care about her. You know I do. It's been a confusing last couple of days."

Fabia seemed to let him stew for a few seconds. "I *know*," she agreed. "She is fine now."

The ice and snow disappeared in an instant. Flann closed his eyes and rested the back of his head on the suddenly dry tree, relieved to be warm again. He saw everyone sit for a few minutes in disbelief or waiting to thaw. Slowly, some Silvedome warriors gathered and waited to escort the compliant remaining soldiers outside the dome walls. Tevin and Bard climbed down first and then Fabia. Flann delayed, feeling like he needed to choose between Roots and Nora once more. His desire was to see Roots, but his obligation was to Nora. He took a breath of regret, mentally making the decision to find Nora. His desires would have to wait.

The ground was dry and hard as Flann landed on it. Fabia immediately wrapped her elbow in his and leaned in on him. She spoke to the group. "Let's go to the Loaded Hurricane and wait for the others to return." She looked slyly over at Flann. "Maybe check on Roots and see if she is any better."

Resolved, Flann announced, "I need to go." He looked at her and thought *Find Nora* so the others would not know he had violated Brom's contract.

"Nonsense." Fabia leaned in to kiss his cheek and whispered, "Nora is fine." She pulled away and happily walked with him saying loudly, "I think Roots will heal faster if ALL her life force partners are near her and healed themselves."

He gave her his brooding look, and she gave him her unabashed look right back.

Tevin teased. "You two should be a couple."

At the same time, Fabia and Flann responded. Fabia theatrically said, *"He COULDN'T handle me."* And Flann announced. "And ruin her fun?"

"Oh, you are too right my friend," she purred. "I do love the chase, but I would also love the sweet victory of seeing you lose control."

This is me losing control, he thought. Fabia ignored him.

"Actually, Flann has a love. Isn't that right, Flann?"

Tevin and Bard who had been walking in front of them both turned around.

"Meet someone so soon? You were here, what, three days, you dog!" Tevin teased.

Bard seemed less enthusiastic. "You know what is expected out of you. Aren't you a man of your word?"

Looking cross at Fabia, Flann responded. "Don't give Fabia's matchmaking desires too much attention or you will be the next one to suffer under her skills."

Letting go of Flann's arm, Fabia smiled with joy and pranced on her tiptoes in front of the group. "I do love love. So, what say you, Bard? You have been a bachelor for a long time. I can *help* you . . ." she said alluringly.

"What about me?" Tevin asked with mock offense.

"I already know that you are holding out for Roots but not Bard. Bard is special."

"Alright, enough," Bard said, seeming to let go of the tension he felt toward Flann. "Maybe I will let you play matchmaker with me. I do love adventure."

"How can you NOT want to be with Roots? Did you see how stunning she looked at the ritual? Could you not *feel* how radiant her spirit was?" he said with his palms up, elbows bent, and his forearms shaking with energy. "Man, oh man, she has a gravitational pull that makes you take notice."

Tevin spoke light-heartedly and with a large smile on his face, but a part of Flann's chest felt heavy with grief. This is what he feared. That what he felt for Roots was because of the shared life force and not because they shared something special. This was what he was waiting to find out and now he knew the truth. He felt his mood darken immediately. *He should go find Nora and be grateful for who he has in his life.*

"My sister is a **Queen**. She is *tantalizing* and stepping into her power. *I couldn't be more proud of her.* But she will need a partner who can do more than admire her qualities and her beauty. You find her POWER appealing, but do you find her soul aligned with yours? Think of this when you have your union interview. Brom made certain that each of you had something that you could offer his daughter. He worked with Nana Honey and Roots's gifted mother to make sure of it, b . . . u . . . t . . . Roots is the one who gets to decide what is right for her," Fabia claimed.

"So, she is your sister now?" Bard smirked.

"Unequivocally, yes," Fabia attested, stretching out her arms in delight.

"Then I am your brother for Roots will be unable to deny my charms," Tevin noted.

"Is it not the old way that you marry your best friend? Then consider your chances over for Roots and I are sure to be best friends." Bard bantered with Tevin.

The group cheerfully discussed what they could offer Roots if they were in a relationship with her, including Fabia who apparently didn't see a problem with dating her adopted sister. But Flann was silent. He had no right to see himself with her, but he could feel his teeth grinding at the thought of her being with someone else. He was being ridiculous, jealous, and possessive over someone who rejected his kiss for whatever reason.

Fabia looked over at Flann as she brought the energy down by becoming serious. She announced confidently. "She needs a partner who can allow her to shine and be the creator of her own destiny. Someone who won't stand in her way, who won't make or support any excuses for her not following her heart, and someone who will accept her for her authentic self without any design to change her. This may sound easy, but it takes a partner who is willing to detach from their fears and insecurities. It takes someone with *courage,* inner strength, and the ability to surrender."

As Fabia talked about what type of character Roots needed, doubt filled Flann's head whether he could live up to those qualities. He couldn't deny that everything Fabia said felt true, even if she wasn't a Truth-sayer. He didn't feel that he was that man . . . as he stood today. This was more evidence that he wasn't the one for her. Another brick of grief laid on his chest.

"Now, let's not discuss this further. Roots needs us now."

"What's happened?" Flann asked in alarm, snapping his head up.

"I will update you all when my brother is present," Fabia said solemnly.

The group became silent as they crossed the riverbed and headed toward Viggo.

Crystal had been grief-stricken and overwhelmed by the download of memories that Nana Honey's life force had shared with her. She was hit with the truth of the situation. She stood up and dropped her circle, seeing she was no longer in danger.

"YOU LIED TO US." Self-esteem and the power of knowledge permeated from her body. "This whole time I thought I was protecting Sabina from the Selectors. That she was the Agni, and we needed to hide her. But you were protecting her from **Dras.**" Crystal stood in her anger and contempt for what Brom had brought upon the people of Silvedome.

"I **didn't** have a choice and Nana knew. You have her memories now. Look for yourself. This was a mutual decision," he objected. "AND, I was protecting her from both. How do you think Dras finds so many gifted women?" he challenged.

"There is NO PROTECTION from the Dark One. This

dome, all the talent in the world . . . I'm going to be sick," she confessed, grabbing her stomach, and folding over.

"That's not tru—" Brom started to argue, but the Mistress managed to get onto her feet and interrupted.

"CRYSTAL, I WILL HANDLE THIS. Brom, you need to leave now."

Brom interjected, but she held her hand up to silence him. "Consider yourself **exiled** until further notice." She limped up to the horned woman, clearly displeased. "If you had come to us, *we would have helped you*. We DO have protection from Dras but now your fate is tied to Brom's. Be grateful you did not seriously harm any of our people."

Fortress looked confused and concerned. She did not want to encounter the Dark One again, and she did not think that she could escape him twice. She looked down at her hands, recalling the torment she suffered for refusing to bond to him.

She stood there, unsure what to do. Part of her fought her pride knowing that she did not like to be told what to do. Yet this woman was letting her leave freely after she invaded her land with the intent to kidnap one of her people. She also did not know how long she could hold on to the humane side of her before the animal side took over.

"Be gone," the Mistress declared, dismissing her by turning her back. But she softened enough to look over her shoulder and say, "I wish you well with the curse laid upon you. Please know that despite my quarrel with Brom, he made it his dharma to help people who the Dark One is after or has affected," she confessed, looking down at Kean lying on the floor. "You are in good hands."

"Crystal, you are to come with me and explain what you know. The rest of you, seek the Healers." She lightly kicked Kean to make sure he was still alive. "That includes you, Bee," she demanded. "But it looks like you will have to help this one." Bee was using her arms to walk herself up into a sitting position, holding her head. She squinted at Crystal for help.

Outraged, Wolverine commented, "Aren't you going to have them escorted out?"

Brom took two steps toward the Mistress. "What of Sabina? Will you help her? Is she safe?" he pleaded.

"It's ROOTS, and she is under *MY protection*. **Not yours**. I WILL NOT punish the innocent for YOUR deceit," she spat.

"And mine," said Bee, raising her hand as she sat on the floor still looking drowsy. "I've been more of a mother to her than Marigold ever allowed herself to be."

Visibly relieved, Brom bowed humbly. "Thank you. I will earn my way back into your good grace, Mistress. Talk to Crystal. You will see my intentions . . ." He stopped talking when she looked at him scornfully.

"Brom, you have served Silvedome well but you let your ego get in the way in this matter. Many of our family suffered because you failed to trust us with your information. You abused the power we extended you. WE are all FAMILY here whether by blood or bonds. There is no place for someone who thinks in terms of I instead of WE."

Daring to ask, Brom continued. "And Roots's union interviews? May they stay as planned?" He looked down at Kean, indicating that he was someone who did not go through the Ori and their clearance processes.

The Mistress sighed heavily. "We will KEEP our word. They may stay." She looked up to the sky and spoke the truth of Silvedome's situation. "Sky Above knows we need more men to balance out all the women under our protection."

Brom nodded his understanding and lifted his fingers to say one more thing.

Tiredly, she spoke. "Not another word, Brom. You have pushed your luck enough. If we find favor in you, we will message you, but I do not know what it will take for me to trust you again. This was a hard blow, leaving us in a defenseless position. I guess I should thank you for teaching us a valuable lesson."

Brom looked around, still heavy with the need to wrap up so many details. He needed to make sure all the life force partners were okay, to give Crystal details, and to escort this woman to safety. He bent down and squeezed Kean's hand. "I'll be back," he whispered. He nodded to Wolverine whose eyes pierced through him. He made his way to Fortress who was quickly making her way to the back of the Ceremony, her skeletons already melted into the earth.

As he chased after Fortress, he used his rare Persuader skills to imprint a message into Crystal's mind. He sent thoughts of how important it was for Roots to find a mate as soon as possible. The sooner the better. He warned that they had fifteen days tops before the Dark One was at Silvedome. He sent his solution to Crystal that the Dark One would lose interest if Roots was already mated. That was a sacred bond that even he could not affect.

Normally he was subtle when he used his Persuader skills, but his talent was no longer weak like before. Now he had Roots's power to draw upon and she was an unlimited resource. He did not hold back because he wanted his message to be unforgettable. He used the power of his conviction and urged her to comply with his solution. She was no longer a girl but a woman with a strong opinion of her own. He knew what he asked her to do was against her core beliefs. He knew she would resist, so he showed compassion. Before he left the Ceremony, he looked at Crystal. He placed both hands over his heart and bowed to her.

~

Crystal helped Bee get over to Kean to be healed and the Mistress checked on Pond. As she sat with Bee, Crystal felt a massive headache come over her and then clear ideas pop into her mind, pulsing in sync with the onset of the headache. She placed her palm to her forehead at the weight and pressure of the message she received from Brom, someone she once admired and felt tremendous gratitude toward. She looked up at him, shaking her head. Not only had he violated her privacy by implanting a message, he asked her to do something she couldn't do. She felt beyond betrayed by him. Then she saw him place both hands over his heart, bowing.

Tears came to her eyes because she also loved Roots. Though she wanted to hate this man who claimed to be her father, she understood the role he played and the role he asked her to play. She understood why he asked it of her too and she couldn't deny that a part of her also wanted the safety of that answer. As her headache disappeared just as quickly as it came upon her, the last thing she understood was that as soon as Brom stepped outside the Silvedome walls, his Moowins would doom him. First by the Selectors and then by the Dark One.

He was as good as dead. That meant Roots would suffer further, knowing she lost the grandmother she never knew she had and her father all in one day. Crystal couldn't bear for that to happen to Roots. Nor could she bear to only have fifteen more days with her. There had to be another solution, another way out of this situation besides Brom's plan to bond her to a man that didn't love her or deserve her.

She looked up at Wolverine who was studying her. *What does he want?*

"We need to talk," he admitted.

When Will I See You Again

Needing the help of a Healer, Pond lay on the floor, lacking the ability to dispute the Mistress's rage. He was almost too tired to care but even when he felt like he had been pulled from the void of death, he still felt the need to tell this old woman that she was not his mother and that he didn't need to listen to her. Instead, he lay with his head resting on his arm, drool slowly spilling over his cheek, but he made sure his eyes communicated his anger.

"There will be no more of this nonsense shielding Sabina. She is now Roots. And as an adult, she is the only person who can give you permission to shield her. Brom is no longer the authority over her, nor a citizen of Silvedome. Furthermore, if anyone is to have authority over her, it will be me," the Mistress said, thrusting her thumb at her chest.

Pond wished he had the strength to roll his eyes. He rather liked shielding Sabina. It gave him an excuse to see her weekly, and it gave him the feeling of pleasure knowing that he was hiding treasure that only he had access to. For he had always known Sabina was powerful. He could sense it even before she was displaying any signs of her powers. He had reserved himself for her, believing he deserved to be with someone as powerful as he was. So far, she was the only one that measured up to that feat.

"I *mean* it, POND. Now that I have worked on your shield, I can taste your energy. I will be working with Roots daily. You will not be able to hide it from me."

Rats, he thought. She was right about that. That was going to be a problem, but he was sure he could figure something out. He wasn't going to quit that easily. She was his, as far as he was concerned.

~

"This is useless. I cannot tell if you are understanding anything I say." She turned around. "Bee, come assist him when you have a chance." She eyed Wolverine. He had that determined look on his face. The one that usually meant he was up to no good. *Boys and their hormones.*

Barking out an order—"Wolverine"—she waited for him to take his eyes off Crystal. "You are hereby sworn to serve the Ori and keep all matters today confidential. As such, you have been assigned to escort these foreigners to the hospital and to find that redhead who was sitting with Crystal. She is to be escorted out of Silvedome once it is safe to leave. Bring her to the Ori and we will find someone to house her *until* the Selectors have moved on," she said, pointing her finger to make a clear distinction.

~

Wolverine hesitated and looked down at Crystal, feeling torn. This was an important job. An opportunity that someone double his age and experience would have had to fight to earn. Guilt twisted in him and he couldn't understand this physiological response. He knew he was an ambitious man, and this was a dream come true. Why was he hesitating? He closed his eyes in frustration and squeezed his hands into a fist. Because he didn't want to leave Crystal. A hard lump formed in his throat at the thought of leaving her, and he couldn't understand why.

This was absurd, he scolded himself. He stopped liking her years ago when she made it clear she didn't want anything to do with him. Using his anger, he pushed whatever he was feeling toward Crystal away. He was NOT going to let this sudden uncanny connection to her stop him from taking this opportunity.

He nodded in understanding to the Mistress, still looking at Crystal, who was pointedly ignoring him. "Yes, ma'am," he answered, feeling the Mistress's eyes on him. He looked at her and she looked at him, apparently studying him.

She crossed her arms. "What is going on here?" she asked calmly.

He said nothing. He was not obligated to answer. Keeping his mouth shut, he shifted his weight and stared through her.

"I see. Why aren't you moving then?" she asked curiously. "It appears to me that you seem very fond of guarding Crystal, who is completely capable of defending herself."

Relieved that someone recognized her abilities and the oddity of Wolverine's behavior, Crystal mouthed "THANK YOU" to the Mistress. She looked up at Wolverine with an expression that said, 'Get lost.'

"I wanted a quick word with Crystal. Besides, none of the men are ready to go to the Healers. I think the redhead is with Eagle . . ."

Interrupting, the Mistress said sternly, "Then see to it that Brom and Fortress have indeed left Silvedome, or should I find someone who is more willing to assist the Ori? Perhaps"—she paused, delaying—"Flann?"

Habitual thoughts pulled up quickly. Who did Flann think he was and how dare he be considered for this privileged position? He pictured punching Roots's shadow in the face.

Pulling his pants up a little, he ground his teeth and nodded. He started to take off in the direction that Brom left.

"Wait," Bee shouted, holding her finger up with a chip on her index.

"Ahh, thank you, Bee," the Mistress said, walking over to a box and sitting down.

Crystal helped Bee up as Kean moaned from the abrupt stop in healing. Wolverine ran back and lifted his nose, indicating he would prefer the secrecy chip to enter his nostril. Bee placed the chip into his nose and Wolverine kept his eyes on Crystal, who folded her arms in annoyance and looked away. He stared unapologetically, thinking she wasn't going to be able to avoid him forever.

Patting Wolverine's shoulder that he was fine to go, Bee bent over Kean with a pleasant smile. "You will feel better in a few minutes. Go put your hands in some dirt and rest."

Kean had rolled onto his side and looked over his shoulder, feeling miserable at the smiling woman with the sun framing her face like a halo. He wasn't sure if she was an illusion or if he was dreaming. Sometimes he struggled to awaken in the right reality. However, the fiery woman with dark skin and short curly hair who formed the salt circle grabbed the pleasant woman's shoulders and guided her away.

He could hear the happy one whisper. "He is cuuuuuttttteee. How old do you think he is, twenty-two?" Kean smiled to himself as the other woman silenced her.

"Shhhh . . . You are just saying that because he is shirtless and you're drunk. Come on, let's get Pond fixed up and put you to bed," she whispered into the happy one's ear. She merrily followed with no objections.

~

"Oh, darling Master Fis. You are *exhausted*. Here, let me help." Bee smiled and fell forward as she reached out her hand to Master Fis. Crystal grabbed her and pulled her back. But Bee managed to make enough contact that Master Fis smiled with relief.

"Hmmmmm." Master Fis closed her eyes, appearing to feel warmth spread down her skin. "I needed that. Thank you, but you best not extend your energy much more. Besides, Pond has blocked healing."

"I'm coming." The Mistress got up from resting on her box. With her hair pinned back into place, she slowly kneeled to help Bee heal Pond. They worked on him until he could walk. Afterwards, they all sat and rested. Activity could be heard around the village, but no one came to check on them. The Mistress demanded that Crystal go with her to the Ori and explain what had happened, while the others went to the hospital. As they walked out of the side of the stage, they saw the Prince tied up and passed out with a pool of dried blood soaked into the ground.

The Mistress, annoyed, looked at Crystal. "What is he doing here? Never mind. We will discuss this later. Master Fis, I think you will have to help this one."

Outside the Ceremony, the Mistress felt relieved to see Silvedome in much the same order as before. Putting her fingers in her mouth, she whistled loud and waved her arms to flag the people across the river. A few men came over, and she directed them to get Pond, the Prince, Kean, and the two Healers to the hospital. The Mistress could see Wolverine in the distance as she and Crystal made their way to the Ori's building. They waited for him outside.

Fresh blood dripped down the side of his head; he was walking, keeping one knee bent. His eyebrows were drawn together and his mouth sealed shut. The Mistress noticed the dome walls had restored the beautiful, perfect weather. The sunshine was bright and a harsh contrast to Wolverine's mood.

~

He ignored Crystal and had a hard stare toward the Mistress.

"They have him," he fumed as he stood in a warrior stance, as if he was reporting to his commanding officer.

The Mistress nodded sadly but seemed unfazed, whereas Crystal felt her eyes tear. She looked away, resting her hand around her neck, and took a few breaths as her emotions wrestled with her decision not to interfere with his doomed fate. Her mind went to Roots. She could not help thinking Roots may not forgive her for standing by as her father was sentenced to a fate he worked his whole life to protect others from. But she affirmed that he deserved his fate. He had betrayed them all and put everyone in danger.

"I tried to stop them. Fortress got away, but Brom was recognized as the Agni by the Selectors. He was swarmed. Borax's people took him. At first, our warriors tried to protect Brom and came to his defense but, I—" Wolverine swallowed and took a moment to gather himself. Louder, he continued. "But I announced his exile. Our warriors retreated just in time. Borax was creating a portal to take Brom through when a tree in the field lost its illusion and became the Dark One. I saw it. I saw the whole thing." He paled, looking down in shock.

"He was . . . He was upside down, balancing on his hair. Like above-ground roots. The tree roots became his hair. His arms were crossed and tucked in. He was covered in mud. When he opened his eyes, all you could see was glowing white. HE WALKED ON HIS HAIR and his clothes defied gravity by staying in place. I've never seen anything like it. He reached out with stretched arms and pulled the whole portal into his stomach. He devoured light and substance into his being and they all disappeared. The Dark One, Borax, his men, and Brom. He is gone. Now the Dark One has the Agni."

Wolverine looked over his shoulder and sucked his lips into his mouth as he moved his jaw back and forth. After several moments, he spoke again. "Our warriors have retreated into the dome. The fighting that remains is among various groups of Selectors, but it's squabbles."

Softly, the Mistress told Wolverine he had done well and ordered him to the hospital. She reminded him of his order to watch over Roots's visitors and asked him to escort the Prince from Silvedome after his union interview with Sabina tomorrow. They watched him leave, Crystal feeling more uncertain than she had ever before felt. She felt like a child playing adult games. She refrained from saying anything until she was unable to hold her tongue any longer.

Staring coldly at the Mistress, she said, "You knew he would be taken."

Not bothering to make eye contact, the Mistress walked the few steps to the secret opening, pushing the button. As she opened the door, she met Crystal's eyes steadily and in a weathered and tired voice said, "As did you." She walked through the door while Crystal marched in and continued. "As did Brom."

Crystal wanted to blame someone. There was a burning need for her to have someone she could be angry at, to expel this energy that built within her, but she knew she was being childish. She did not want to take any responsibility for Brom's fate. This was his doing, not hers, but she also made a choice to do nothing to safeguard him when she could have helped. She could have done something.

Still marching with anger, Crystal realized she was angry at herself for doing nothing to help the person who had once protected her from the Selectors, but she had been too self-righteous, thinking only of what his mistake cost everyone. That did not sit well with her.

Before entering the council room, the Mistress faced Crystal.

Crystal could see the haggard look on all the faces of the Ori and their attention on them. She wondered if she would have to tell them about Nana and she closed her eyes, looking for inner strength.

"I'm not going to pretend this will be easy. We may be asking a lot of you, but you are capable. You are strong and no matter what happens, everything will be fine."

"Fine . . . Did everything work out fine for Brom?"

The Mistress looked at Crystal, raising her chin so her eyes were narrower than usual. "I see. You are feeling sorry for yourself now?"

"NO," Crystal spat. "He wasn't a bad person. He was a father blinded by love and fear. Was he wrong, yes? But isn't our mission to protect people from the Selectors and especially from the Dark One?"

"Brom is one of the most strategic men I know. He knows when to hide his talents and he knows when to reveal them. What he did today, he did on purpose. Most likely to draw attention to him and away from Silvedome and Sabina. Excuse me, Roots. HONOR his choice and do not make it about you. The same goes for Nana Honey. Now, this will be the LAST conversation we have about this. It is a waste of energy to wish to change the past."

The Mistress rolled her head and shook herself loose, as if washing herself from the past. She focused her eyes back on Crystal and continued. "We must move forward. Let's work together to come up with a plan, starting with securing Silvedome. You will need to find Roots and those who disappeared with her. Then, we will need to figure out how they created a portal inside the dome walls and disable that ability immediately."

Crystal remained quiet, taking it all in. The old bat wasn't one of the people she cared for, but her words did give her a chance to see a different perspective. Despite the fact that neither of them liked each other or were nurturing individuals, the Mistress's words did sooth the harsh emotions Crystal was feeling.

"Ready or not, let's go." The Mistress walked through the invisible tunnel that led to the entrance of the council.

The invisible tunnel was dark and filled with shadows before the light of the council room. Crystal followed, familiar with where she was going. She thought of what the Mistress asked of her and whispered to herself, "I don't know all that." As soon as the words left her mouth, Crystal felt a sense of foreboding.

The Mistress had stopped before the entrance, waiting. Crystal looked up to find the Mistress staring at her and she answered her whisper. Her voice was certain and ominous when she spoke. "Of course you do. You only need to trust the intelligence inside of you." Then she walked into the bright room with her arms open, asking for their attention.

Crystal looked down, toeing the invisible line that separated her from this new fate. She was to fill the role Nana Honey had fulfilled and had prepared her for. Now, she was reluctant to step over the threshold into the council room despite doing so thousands of times before. Was this her mistrust or Nana's? Crystal's entire being was different, sharing a small piece of Nana Honey's life force. She hadn't adjusted and she couldn't separate what was hers from what was Nana's energy. All she knew was it felt like an alarm going off inside of her.

She placed her hand on her neck and commanded that her voice would only speak the words that would serve the universe. She wasn't going to feel bad that she wasn't here to serve Silvedome or even the Ori. Then she rolled her shoulders back and walked through.

With her head throbbing and her vision wavering in and out with a red tint to everything, Sabina lay packed into the cold, hard dirt. She couldn't move her head; her lips were chapped and her skin felt blistered. She tried to speak. Her voice made some pitiful scratching sound. She wanted to moan, but even that took too much effort. She closed her eyes, drifting in and out of sleep.

"That bad?" said the unenthusiastic Healer. "Give me a minute. I'll get you unburied."

Taking a gardening tool he'd found, Viggo carefully scraped the mud back from her body. As he worked, the group returned. He continued to work quietly. By the time the others reached him, he had her propped up, her back resting on a tree.

Flann hung back from the group as they approached, not sure he was ready to see Roots. He didn't know what state she would be in, and he wasn't sure she was alive. He felt no connection between them. Then again, he felt no connection to Brom, either.

Fabia ran up and tackled her brother, happy to see him. The others gathered around Roots, who was so weak her head lolled from side to side. She looked at him.

Flann stopped walking. He could see his chest taking large breaths, but his ears rang too loudly to hear his own breathing. Like an arrow shot into his chest, an energetic line between them flared to life once more and anchored deep into his heart. Every cell in his body felt like it reverberated from the force of the arrow, slowly scattering outside of his body toward Roots. Only to be slammed back into place. He was almost knocked to his knees. He was in trouble.

With her arms still around her brother and a smile on her face, Fabia looked intentionally at Flann as he was hit with the force of his feelings. She cared for him but he was as stubborn as they came. She knew he would not take this realization well. "Viggo." She nodded her head in Flann's direction, drawing his attention to Flann's symptoms of shock.

"On it," he replied, unwrapping his arm from his sister, and heading over to Flann.

～

Not able to catch his breath, Flann sat on the ground, turning to the side to avoid seeing Roots covered in mud, in a bloody tattered dress that was too revealing for the onlookers. Resting his head in his hands with his elbows propped on his knees, he concentrated on one sense at a time. Feeling the cold underneath him, the smell of moss. Still nauseous and clammy, he could finally hear the group's conversation drift to him.

Viggo placed his hand on the open gash on Flann's forearm. "Done. What else . . . yes. Geez, brother. You are killing me."

Flann looked up, putting his hand into his hair and pulling it through. He felt a million times better, minus the arrow lodged in his heart. "What?"

"You better change your name to Goner or Pine," Viggo concluded, wiping his hands on his pant legs.

Confused, Flann inquired. "Am I that bad?" He thought Viggo meant he wasn't able to heal him.

"I told you, man. I cannot fix lovesick."

"Oh."

Before Viggo left Flann, he assured him. "Healer's oath. I won't tell a soul. Not even my nosy sister, but she will know nonetheless."

Distracted, Flann answered, "Yeah." He risked a look over to Roots. Her color was already better, so he dusted himself off and walked pensively over.

～

Sabina tried to focus on everyone, but no matter where she looked, her focus was on Flann. The connection between them had suddenly bloomed back into life, providing her with the energy and the support she needed to be able to function. She promised herself, *A quick look,* and then back to focusing on the others recounting what had happened while she was unconscious.

She glanced casually over and full-on stopped. He had black paint smeared and worn down on his face, his eyes blazed with intensity, his gait was confident, his shirt ripped open, revealing his toned chest muscle and side abs, and the pull between them was tantalizing. *Was he this sexy before my near-death experience?* Butterflies sparked in her belly as he approached and she suddenly felt warm all over. She wanted to fan herself, but wasn't going to give herself away. She suddenly felt antsy and squirmed on the ground. She wished she was standing. Looking down, she was horrified to see her dress was ripped at her breasts. *Oh, Sky Above, my breasts are so noticeable.* Her nipples were pressing firmly against her thin, dirty gown. She knew her mouth was hanging open as she looked around for something to cover herself with.

Fabia leaned on a tree and giggled, enjoying the entertainment as she watched the lines of emotional energy. Tevin talked merrily with his eyes glued to Roots's chest. Bard wished he had somewhere to sit. Viggo was misreading Roots's squirming. Flann, not able to take his eyes off Roots, wished he didn't have feelings for her and was resisting them with all his willpower. Fabia sighed dreamily. She loved her life.

"Alright, it's time for Roots to get cleaned up and fed. We need to get her back to the house where all my medicines are, now it's safe to do so. Fabia?" Viggo requested.

Flann's mouth was dry as he watched the two help her up and over to the bathhouse. His stomach rolled in sympathetic pain as he watched them. He wanted to step in and he was afraid to touch her too. He was afraid his self-control would crumble and he would behave worse than he had the other night. Last night.

With Roots stepping into the bathhouse, Flann faced the direction to leave. He had seen her, now he needed to go find Nora. And what? Break her heart? Tell her to go home? Confess that he kissed another woman? He pulled his hand through his hair.

Bard stepped in front of him. Flann was tempted to scuff dirt on his boots. He looked up at him. He was standing close, composed as usual. Flann took him in, looking up at him. His broad-shouldered, with his buzzed hair, shaded eyes, and perfect narrow nose.

"What?" Flann said in a flat tone.

He stared for a long moment, his eyes scanning back and forth as if he was debating what to say. "I watched Nora leave with Eagle Eyes. He lives on Obsidian, toward the back of the village."

Surprised, Flann faltered for a moment. "Thhhhhhank you. That is actually . . . helpful."

He stepped a space back, giving Flann room to leave. His face was expressionless. "Don't thank me. I am doing this for me." He looked over to Tevin who was watching intentionally, his smile gone from his face.

Tevin was friends with both of them and he was a Seer, which made it difficult to hide anything from him. He got up from lounging on the ground and walked up casually. "What Bard is saying without saying is that he may not like you, but at least he had respect for you. Now he wants to see you fall on your face and suffer."

Confused for a moment, Flann put his hands on his hips, thinking.

Tevin squinted his eyes at Flann. "You should not have kissed her last night. It was wrong. We are all here to win her over, and this puts you on unequal grounds." Then he smiled. "But I see no harm in it if I am next to kiss her."

Flann looked over at Bard, anger starting to build. "You spied," he spat out.

Bard shrugged. "So what if I did?"

Flann gave him a shove. "Shunk's breath! Have you heard of privacy?"

Bard stepped up closer to Flann, anger clear on his face, snarling. "I should have been her bodyguard. I am the only life force partner who isn't going to try to sleep with her. **I** can have her best interest at heart. CAN YOU?"

"Get a life," Flann said, squaring up to Bard, ready to challenge him.

"BROTHERS, please. Walk it off. Trust Brom. Besides, you will see soon enough what we are up against."

They both turned and looked at his mischievous smile. He pretended to zip his lips and twisted his wrist to 'lock' his mouth shut.

"I hate it when you do that," Flann criticized. He pulled his hands through his hair. "I'm going to go find someone. I'll be back later." He walked out of the village, determined to find Nora, and determined to fight for what he wanted.

"Bard," Tevin called. "Let's go kill something and cook it up. I'm beyond hungry and Roots is bound to be too."

Bard flashed an annoyed look at Tevin, but took a breath and let his anger at the injustice melt from him. Composed once more, he transformed into an owl and flew past Tevin's face.

"CHEATER," Tevin accused, taking off at a run after Bard.

In the bathhouse, Viggo continued to heal Roots as she floated in the water. At first, she had thought she would be uncomfortable being naked in front of him, but it seemed he was clueless to noticing 'her' body. He was seeing with his third eye like Nana Honey used to.

She closed her eyes and felt the weight of her heart, thinking of losing a woman who had been a comfort to her. Someone who didn't make her feel like an outcast. It was hard to imagine her gone. Especially when she felt like she could be in the room with them now.

Staying out of the water, Fabia looked lost in thought but would occasionally say random bits of information as if she was spreading out the news in bite-size pieces. Until she got to her father. Then she paused. Roots stopped floating on her back, lightly splashing Viggo, barely noticing his sadness had deepened.

Roots could see Fabia was talking, but she couldn't hear anything. She looked at Viggo and directed him to fix her hearing. She was pointing to her ears, but he kept his eyes downcast. Feeling charged with energy, she swam to the edge and got out, throwing a towel around her, and sitting in front of Fabia. Water was still spilling over her skin as she looked at Fabia with large eyes.

Fabia reached out her hand and put it on top of her arm, no longer speaking. Roots's heart was beating fast, and she felt like the room was spinning. She couldn't think straight and was over-stimulated in this dimly lit, quiet space.

Getting out of the water, Viggo came behind Roots. Sitting next to her, he put his bare chest to her back. He encouraged her to lean back, and he wrapped his arms around her. Roots didn't understand the tears that came. She didn't hear anything, but her soul knew. She leaned back into Viggo, the warmth of his skin soothing the abandonment feelings ripping her heart apart, and she cried so hard she could feel her ab muscles tiring. Snot spilled out of her nose and she cried more. Gasping for air as a realization hit her. She faced years of wishing her father was around, and now she knew the future guaranteed he wouldn't be.

Fabia occasionally wiped her face with a towel and when the tears slowed, she put both of her hands on the side of Roots's face, looking into her eyes, seeing her. Viggo got up to rinse off in the water while Fabia repeated over and over, "We got you. You are loved. This too shall pass." Roots heard this and her head fell into Fabia's arms. Fabia held her like her sister would all those times she had felt shunned by her peers. This time, she cried for her father. That he was gone. That she never made him proud. That they never got to know each other between the hidden truth and his travels.

By the time they came out of the bathhouse, a snake and a few birds were smoking over the embers of a fire, with Tevin and Bard joking around. Roots walked over, appearing calm and serene, full of power and grace. "Where are the rest?" Her smoky voice broke up their conversation.

They both turned to face her. Bard started coughing and Tevin catcalled.

"My girl cleans UP!" He made small hops like he was walking over a fire.

Roots flashed a small smile but returned to her stoic look. "Thank you."

Shaking his head back and forth and blowing on his fingers, Tevin answered. "Just crossing into Loaded Hurricane. I'm Tevin by the way, the Seer."

Fabia stepped over a large log and sat down. "Flann will be along later, but we can start without him."

Bard and Tevin took the food from the fire and let it cool as the others approached. Crystal and Wolverine joined them and were looking around. Wolverine looked suspicious, but Crystal had Nana Honey's memories guiding her. The group all sat along the fire, all staring at Roots as the night settled into darkness.

Fabia stood. "This may surprise you, but I don't care to be the center of attention or make speeches despite all *my wild behavior*." She made a coy smile appear on her face as she tucked a lock of hair behind her ears. She cleared her throat, rubbing her fingers together as she spoke. "Let me get to the point. Roots is in danger of Dras. For those of you who don't know, he is a sorcerer from before the nuclear war who has been searching for the Agni to bear his children. What you may NOT know is that the Agni is supposed to be his twin flame reborn. That is why Dras KNOWS that Brom is not the Agni. Even if the rest of the world cannot tell that Brom's powers are shared, Dras will know and he will be able to find the source pretty easily. While two of the crystals were not fully absorbed into Roots chakras"—she nodded her approval at Bard and Kean—"there is no way to hide that Roots isn't the Agni anymore. Her powers are growing."

"So, what are our options?" Bard cut in.

Bitterly, Crystal interjected. "Brom wants Roots to bond with one of you." Her hands were clasped one over the other. She huffed out air as if it pained her to say that. "She has fifteen days at most before he is back for her."

"How do you know that?" Wolverine scolded.

"What is it to you? This isn't your fight," Pond challenged.

Defensive, Wolverine leaned forward. "IT IS if I am to protect Silvedome."

"That is MY JOB," Pond said.

"Excuse me, but what does this mean to me?" Roots interrupted. "What is the worst that can happen to me if I DON'T bond with one of these . . . men—" she questioned Fabia, looking around with respect at the group, "—but refuse Dras. Will he turn me into a creature? Is that possible when I am the"—she choked on the word—"Agni?"

Crystal shifted and sat up taller. "Nana Honey was unclear on what would happen to you if you met Dras."

Grasping her hands in front of her, Fabia sat. "No one knows really, but I suspect the risk is that Roots will not be able to resist him IF he is her twin flame, no matter how bad he is for her. No matter how dangerous their combined forces are for the world."

~

Words were shouted over the fire, everyone having an opinion but no one person noticing her eyes glass over, or the whites of her eyes turn a pink-red as a truth surfaced within her. Roots clenched her belly at a past life memory of her feeling a baby move in her stomach and a very different man with kind eyes holding her shoulder, with one hand on her back as she crouched in pain. How is that possible? He is a monster? Isn't he?

Roots could feel the ancestor energy still trapped in her solar plexus like a hard, round ball and nausea faintly crept up into her sinuses. Through the dark remembrances of her thoughts, she heard Kean speak of her father and at the mention of his name, her heart fluttered. Her tunnel vision of that past life faded. She blinked several times until she was focusing on Kean's face, which was full of personal strength at a time when she felt small and confused. She felt the warmth of his red energy wrap around her like a protective blanket. It was always seeking her, and she had grown accustomed to it. In his energy, all she could think about was him. Her connection to Flann that burned so bright felt subtle, like a soft caress. Then his words sunk in through the cocoon that she found herself in.

"I'm going after him. Brom is the answer," Kean remarked. He stood up with determination on his face. Though the others begged him to reconsider with statements that he would be dead by the time he found him, or that he would never find him, Roots clung to the hope that her father lived.

Standing slowly, ignoring the agreements, Roots felt her energy stretch out over the group, fused in Kean's. With his energy, she felt UNSTOPPABLE. "I'm going with you," she said, unblinking.

Everyone stopped talking and looked at her, apparently having forgotten about her desires in this discussion. However, for just a brief moment, it was Roots and Kean looking at each other over a flaming fire in the dark of the night with a red energy that tied them together.

~

That was what Flann saw as he came into the clearing of the Loaded Hurricane. The moment was like a picture that froze in his mind and though he wasn't able to see the red energy, he could feel it. He could feel it blocking his connection to Roots. Flann found himself taking steps backward until he hit a tree. He slid down the tree, feeling like he couldn't stand.

He watched the group surround Roots, pulling on her arms, making demands of her, but she remained locked eyes with Kean like he was her savior. Flann felt like the air was knocked out of him. Fixating on the connection he witnessed between them made him feel despondent. Coldness deep inside of him took over and the fire inside his heart went out. Although he was not shivering, he felt like a world of dreams vanished before his eyes, stealing the warmth from his heart. He couldn't watch what was happening. He managed to get up and stumble back into the village, his intent set on Roots's tut.

~

Fabia called out Flann's name and Roots snapped out of her trance. The light within her flared with a desire to see him. She could feel heat hit her cheeks as she thought of what Flann must have seen. She took a double look at Kean, confused by the attention he demanded on some deep level she wasn't familiar with but couldn't deny. She had to work to pull her attention away. His swirling energy propelled her toward him like a magnet, while her heart screamed 'no'.

She gritted her teeth and pulled her attention away from him with an inner strength that wasn't going to tolerate someone taking away her will . . . again. She looked at Fabia and followed her gaze. Flann had rushed to get away, stumbling when she knew his Protector skills made it almost impossible for him to retreat in such distress. Outrage filled her as everyone pulled on her arms and fought to keep her alive.

Thoughts struck her with a vengeance. She had already sacrificed so much of her life playing small and safe. She had fifteen days left before Dras cursed her or brainwashed her into a marriage. Or the alternative, she was forced to marry when she hadn't even lived without the heavy hand of her father dictating who and what she was.

She wasn't going to stand around and let others dictate her life one more minute. One way or another, she faced some type of death, whether that was physical or the death of a life she had dreamed of having. As far as she was concerned, today was the first day that she lived—for her.

ENOUGH. ENOUGH, her thoughts screamed as she thought of her grandmother's necklace that blocked any empowering emotions or thoughts.

Pushing everyone away, she stepped over the tree stump and took after Flann. Fear attacked her of what might happen, but she listened to her inner voice that said living was taking chances and fighting for what you want. She felt alive as she raced after what she wanted. As she ran, she allowed the power of her new skills to take over, ignoring the cries of the others who chased after her.

Although Viggo walked lazily after Roots, Fabia was the only one to remain behind. She gave a celebratory dance and pumped her fist into the air, feeling victorious. The power of Dras's energy leaking out of Kean and into Roots had unnerved her. For a moment, Fabia worried they were all doomed to be ruled by Dras who would have significantly more influence over Roots than this small remanence of his energy.

But Sky Above, Roots ran after Flann. It pleased her that

Roots saw something in Flann for Flann was special to her. She marveled at how well Brom and Nana had chosen which individuals would become Roots's life force partners for they had many obstacles to work around. The chosen life force partners had to be able to handle her energy, be of age, have some connection that allowed them to be able to exchange life forces, and then have some matching qualities for Roots to want to be bonded too.

Most of the life force partners were well suited for Roots. She detested the Prince, and Pond wasn't far behind. Obviously, she had her favorite but then again, so did Brom, Nana, and Roots's mother, Opal. All four of them had picked a different suitor for Roots for different reasons. But in the end, it didn't matter who Roots picked as long as she didn't choose Dras. With Roots's unpredictable energy and emotions, and the past connection she had to Dras, anything was possible.

Fabia brought her fingers to her mouth and kissed them in gratitude to the universe. She knew the fight wasn't over, but at least she knew they still had a fighting chance.

When Flann got to Roots's tut, he found her mother and sister waiting. Both of his hands were on the doorframe. He leaned into the doorway, catching his breath from running, taking in the scene. Her sister sat on the couch; worry creased her face. Roots's Birth Challenge dress draped across her lap looking as delicate as she was. Brom's wife was standing, burning with anger and ready to attack. His eyes flicked to her shadow on the wall, distorted from the flickering candlelight. He saw the shape of a bear.

He looked at her fisted hands, and like a true bodyguard, his Protector skills blasted into his energy field. His broken heart pushed to the side and his desire to protect Roots from this woman became his only focus. He had never wanted to be Roots's bodyguard. He had resisted it. He begrudged the fact this was the only way to help his family. However, there was no denying who he was and what his purpose was when it mattered.

He walked into the room, tall, proud, and filled with an unstoppable energy that made him feel like he made a difference. That he mattered.

The tiny woman stood at least three inches taller than her physical frame could project. The black, sharp cut of her hair fell right at her jawline. Her bangs fell at the top of her eyebrows, accentuating the fierce look in her eyes. "WHERE IS SHE?" she growled.

The human race's extinction was expected. Most assumed it would be caused by an act of God, the climate crisis, disease, or illness. Even pollution, lack of clean water, and overpopulation were considered to be potential catalysts. No one thought to pay attention to the heart of man, and the loss of peace, as the hunger for power grew. Mankind's emotions finally reached a breaking point when the collective lost their awareness to do no harm.

No one thought much of another war, another battle for dominance and control. Each country acted as they had been taught. They minded their business and allowed the strongest to survive. It was, after all, inevitable that the country with the most resources and power would win. War was common, so common it was no longer news. Each country fought and defended itself against others. Except, one country decided to do what no one else had the courage or the foolishness to do. They released a nuclear bomb on the country threatening invasion. An idle threat was finally realized. It was no longer a tactic to scare and intimidate. A line had been crossed; an irreparable boundary that changed the world forever.

It was in the year 2060 that the world experienced a man-made near-extinction through nuclear war. It wasn't meant to have universal ramifications. It was meant to be an isolated attack from one country to another. However, grave errors changed the future in a way no one could have expected. Despite research and testing on the terrestrial impact of a nuclear bomb, the expected radius was significantly underrated. No one factored in that each country had zealously made, collected, and strategically hidden nuclear bombs. One isolated attack led to a domino effect. Nuclear bombs detonated all over the world. Within seconds, the end of the world was complete.

Years of structure and progress—destroyed. Vast populations —gone in an instant. The insects, the plant life, the animals on the ground—ravaged. Air and water, vital for sustaining life— poisoned. Less than one percent of the entire population survived. With no food, no untainted soil, no animals to sustain them, no shelter or clean water, their deaths seemed inevitable. To say it was a bleak and uncertain time for the survivors would be an understatement. And they would have died too, if it were not for an unlikely phenomenon. A few select individuals inherited supernatural abilities.

No one knows why there were any survivors at all after such a massacre. It was said that those of pure heart were spared, but it remains a mystery. Why did some survivors develop supernatural abilities, later known as Moowins? And why did others remain as they always had been—limited in their human capabilities? No one knows. However, one truth is certain: It was because of these supernatural aptitudes that the world began all over again.

A number of abilities developed in the exact adaptation the world needed to be able to grow and thrive once more. If it were not for the immediate ability to shield the survivors from the toxic waste and particulars floating in the air, no one would have survived. Those individuals became known as Shielders. They concealed survivors and saw to it that they could not be penetrated by things that would bring them harm.

Some developed the ability to heal the land, the people, the animals, the reptilians, and so on. They were the Healers, and they healed the survivors so they could function once again. They brought the soil back to health and purified the water.

Others developed super strength and speed. They foraged scrap from far-off places, which they brought to the people. They had the strength of many and helped rebuild homes and bridges. They also had the ability to defend the new territories against any attempt at hostile takeovers. They were known as Protectors.

Then there were the Messengers. They could communicate telepathically, and they brought people across lands and seas to form communities. They could also be called on to find Healers when they were required, or locate any necessary resource a community might need.

Communities could thrive only with a shared direction and purpose. This was assisted by people who developed the ability to influence others. They shaped emotions, which created harmony and uplifted the people's spirits. They became known as Influencers.

As time passed, some developed the ability to memorize facts and store unlimited amounts of instantly retrievable information. They were named Persuaders. They were the best scholars and often traveled from territory to territory, bringing back new ways for communities to overcome obstacles. They possessed the ability to give people different perspectives that often aligned with their leader's agenda.

Later, some people developed foresight, which helped communities decide whether to move to different locations, or set up border controls. These predictions helped communities become more aware of what needed to be done to support a brighter, easier, and healthier future. The individuals with this skill were called Seers.

The last Moowin to develop was that of people with the ability to entertain. Their gift was so incredible and outstanding that it was recognized as a supernatural ability. They brought joy and wonder with their singing, dancing, acting, drawing, writing, and fashion designing. They gave the people something to look forward to. They were known as Performers.

Without Moowins, the world would have ceased to exist.

Ashley Pitzer is the author of her debut novel, The Birth Challenge. She pursued many endeavors, including starting a business called Practicing Life, before fully investing in her lifelong dream of writing a novel. Ashley graduated from Stephens College with a Business Administration degree. She is a certified Success Coach, NGH Hypnotist, and Yoga Teacher. In her spare time, you'll find her hiking, reading, and going to Broadway musicals. She is married and has two children. Her website is www.ashleypitzer.com. Follow her on linktr.ee/ashleypitzer.

www.ingramcontent.com/pod-product-compliance
Lightning Source LLC
Chambersburg PA
CBHW050845210726
48290CB00004B/1084